# The Creosote Bush

C A Legorreta

Published by C A Legorreta, 2022.

.

THE CREOSOTE BUSH
**First edition 2022**

.

Excerpt from Wildwood comic by Dan Wright

.

Please direct all inquiries regarding this publication to
calegorreta@protonmail.com

For my Light, my Dove, and my inspiring Dawn.

And for you, my Sun.

# Part 1

I beg you ... to have patience with everything unresolved in your heart and try to love the questions themselves as if they were locked rooms or books written in a very foreign language. Don't search for the answers, which could not be given you now, because you would not be able to live them. And the point is, to live everything. Live the questions now. Perhaps then, someday far in the future, you will gradually, without ever noticing it, live your way into the answer ...

–rainer maria rilke

# Chapter 1

I was twenty-three, full of wide-eyed optimism, when I arrived in Seattle to study photography and test my limits. I had no idea that everything I took for granted, about everything, was about to change.

That was, incidentally, the day I met Kurt. I walked into his office, and my internal axis shifted. Just like that. North would never quite be north again, and it would be years before I fully recovered my equilibrium.

His smile was warm as he held out his hand. It was a smile that said, I see you and I'm glad you're here. He was the Resident Director of my dorm and looked to be in his early thirties. With close-cropped brown hair and deep warm-brown eyes, he looked big –but big by contrast, with arms perfectly snug in the sleeves of his red plaid shirt and a chest and neck that seemed huge over his trim waist. But he wasn't so big as to be unapproachable. He wasn't so huge that I couldn't imagine what it must feel like to put my ear to his chest and listen to the rhythm of his heart –the way I did when hugging my brothers, who all three towered over me. I was absorbing the way he moved and reacted to the space about him when, after a long moment, I was reminded of my reason for knocking on his office door. My room. A room. Demo room? Kurt's voice and the question in it snapped me back to reality.

"Yes," I said. "I'd love to see the demo room."

TWO DAYS LATER, I WAS bouncing on my toes like a kid at a carnival as I waited for the elevator in the lobby of my apartment building. I was conscious of looking and feeling like a child, but I was just so happy to be there, in that city, moving into what I thought was *the* most amazing corner dorm room with its huge windows looking out north and east over the city, that I didn't care.

When the elevator arrived, Jim, the Resident Assistant who had offered to help me carry up my belongings, leaned all his weight into the sliding iron gate. The metal squealed in protest. "This thing only gets stuck about once a week," he said, shooting me a half-grin as we stepped inside. "If it happens to you, give up all hope of a quick rescue because the alarm button doesn't work." I smiled back and wondered how many times and to how many people he'd said those words, but I played along and said, "But it's glowing red." "Just for show," he whispered.

As we rose, I watched the parking lot grow smaller through the wire grating at the back of the elevator. A bullet hole scarred the thick glass between the fourth and fifth floors. Gum and graffiti colored the ceiling and each of the shiny silver walls, and my shoes made little sucking noises every time I moved. I couldn't stop staring at everything. It was all so different, so ... *city-like*.

I glanced up at Jim. He was looking at the pickle jar in my arms. Inside, my two goldfish swam lazily about.

"You know those aren't allowed, right?"

"What? Pickles?"

"Pickles, yeah. Pets, no. Where did you even find a pickle jar that big?"

"Costco." I held up my pickle jar and stared at my fish. Maybe I could hide them. Under the bed or in a kitchen cabinet. Or in the bathroom. I could give them foamy toothpaste smiles as I brushed my teeth or draw smiley faces on the steamy sides of their jar after a hot shower. Of course, I knew this wouldn't do for either my fish or my conscience.

"Where you from?" he asked, interrupting my thoughts.

"Arizona. I guess."

"You guess?"

"I mean, yes, I'm from Arizona, but I moved around a lot."

"Same here. My dad was in the Marines. I joined too, right after I graduated." He ran his hand reflexively through his crewcut as he pointed his chin at me and asked, "What about you? Why'd you move so much?"

"My parents' work."

"They in the military?"

"No."

I was an "MK," but not a military kid. In my case, the "M" stood for missionary. This made for a fun childhood, with lots of travelling and meeting new people. But in my experience, the word "missionary" projected many different connotations, not all of them positive. Even some of the people back home treated me as though I were somehow different, on religion's inside track and therefore out of touch. They were sometimes startled by my questions about God and consciousness and meaning until I felt as though my thoughts were spilling out of an inner breach –from a dark place filled with doubt and daring and defiance. Surely that darkness inside me didn't belong and was something that could be expelled. I was afraid of my own mind, of the wild ferocity barely contained within, even if people still treated me as though I were calm and sweet and innocent. It was as if, behind my pale, high cheekbones and dark hazel eyes, an untamed creature lurked, wanting out. If I tossed my orange-red hair, would someone see the flash of fur? The reflective eyes? The hungry teeth?

At fourteen, I thought I must be possessed. After several serious conversations with my parents and a trip to pray with my pastor, I was told gently, as though I were fragile, "No, no. You have nothing to worry about. This is just ... adolescence." I hoped this was true, wanting to be reassured. But I had my doubts.

Back then my thoughts kept me awake for hours each night. I had entered that beautiful, terrifying part of growing up when the mind becomes consumed with wondering what it all means. From the state of the planet to the passing glance of a classmate in the hall –there was so much I didn't understand. Lying prone on my bed, I would let my mind go, feeling delirious and dizzy as my thoughts raced outward. I tried desperately to catch a glimpse of what came before the existence of humans, before the existence of time, but a cold terror overtook me whenever my thoughts ventured out too far. Reluctantly, I would reign them back in, afraid of them becoming untethered, only to have them race out in the opposite direction as my attention shifted to what lay beyond. Beyond our galaxy, beyond civilization and religion and my own safe walls.

Later, after high school, I headed off to study history at a conservative university in the South. There, my questions were met with rebukes. I decided I needed a new environment in which to grow and learn, somewhere I could discover for myself what life and the world were all about. Art school in Seattle seemed like a good place to start, so here I was.

I looked up to see Jim was watching me.

"What'd they do?" he asked, referring to my parents.

Just as I opened my mouth to reply, the elevator stopped on the ninth floor with a cheerful ding. Previous question forgotten, Jim opened the gate, hoisted a duffel bag in each hand, and with a glance at my pickle jar, he winked and mouthed, "I won't tell," before heading out into the hall.

# THE CREOSOTE BUSH

I WAS IN FOURTH GRADE when my family first arrived at the Field Training Camp, or FTC, in Uvalde, Texas. Over two thousand languages throughout the world possess no written form, and as relocating to a remote village in order to learn and transcribe the language can require certain, how shall we say, *lifestyle* adjustments, FTC was designed to teach future missionaries how to avoid, or at least lessen, the culture shock they might one day face. My parents spent six weeks learning how to build mud stoves, pluck chickens, treat snakebites, and purify their water while living the joys of cold bucket showers, one-room cabins, and outhouses. During this extended camping holiday, my two older brothers practiced the many ways they could look charming while collecting firewood and pitching tents, and my younger brother and I took this as our opportunity to run about like the wild creatures we were. The minute I finished my schoolwork, I was out catching hornytoads (otherwise known as "horned lizards"), studying scorpions, and going on adventures with my very first true love, Bobby.

Saying goodbye to Bobby on the last day of training just about broke my heart. Everything was congratulations and chaos with everyone leaving for different parts of the world. Bobby's family was headed to the Philippines. After that day, I never saw him again. At least not in person.

Instead, I watched him grow up in the yearly newsletters his parents sent out. Each year added to the miles between us. He was a distant acquaintance by the time I read about his daring rescue of a drowning boy during his junior year of high school. And by the time I saw his engagement photo many years later, I no longer knew him.

But my only thought as I waved goodbye to him in Texas was how lucky he was to be going to a new country. He would soon be enmeshed in the exotic, tasting freedom, and living an adventure while I'd be mired in the mundane. My family was returning to Florida to raise financial support, which was still too low for an overseas assignment, and somehow this felt like being turned away from the best roller coaster ride ever because I was half an inch too short.

A year later my family returned to FTC, this time as staffers. My dad taught people how to start a fire with little more than rocks and twigs, and he led them on four-day-long hikes during which they set up huge tents using tarps, ropes, and whatever they could find. My mother, who was a nurse, trained people to give shots using tomatoes, and she showed them how to treat burns, breaks, and scrapes. That, and she taught Spanish. She was an "MK" too, born and raised in South America. "You guys better learn Spanish before I'm old and senile," she was always telling my brothers and me, "because they say you revert back to your first language."

We never fully mastered it though. We learned bits and phrases, and one brother even spoke it in his sleep, but that was all. However, we could build a fire better than anyone else we ever met. Which is to say, we learned as we met people that our background was different –that *we* were different. Part of us was proud –look what I can do, look where I have been. Another part did our very best to adapt. Not to ignore our backgrounds so much. We wouldn't have changed them for the world. But we learned that sometimes people didn't want to know, that sometimes it was good, necessary even, to sit back, listen, and blend in. We were chameleons, trying on new skins and occasionally misplacing our own.

LATE THAT FIRST SATURDAY afternoon I paused a moment in the lobby of my building to scan my list of "helpful places." Thanks to the "Surviving Seattle" orientation I'd just come from, I had a good start on where to go for milk and TP, food and art supplies, entertainment and emergencies. I leaned over and picked up a copy of *The Stranger*, Seattle's event guide and alternative newspaper, and tucked it under my arm. Now all I needed was a church because, after all, I'd heard the stories, read the novels, and rolled my eyes at all the movies of the good religious girl who tastes freedom and chucks her childhood convictions out the window, winding up a pregnant addict, or at least a scandalous tale of caution. Even in those instances where she pulls through older and wiser, she is still scarred somehow and transformed into a newly-minted religious cynic. I didn't want that for myself. I wanted to taste life, faith intact. I wanted to stave off stagnation, hopefully within a warm and welcoming community fed by hearty sermons, humor and, if it wasn't too much to ask, the occasional free Sunday homemade meal.

I was pouring over phone listings when Kurt startled me with a loud, "How's it going?" He gave the elevator button a loud thwack, before stepping closer and asking, "What are you looking at?"

"Churches, but I'm not sure where any of these are." I showed him the addresses and wondered what he would think, even as I soaked in his closeness and the texture of his chin and the way his warm brown eyes moved over the page before meeting my own.

"This one on Virginia must be close," I said. "I'm thinking I could walk there."

"Possibly," he said, looking back down at the list.

A minute later the elevator dinged, making us both jump, and he stepped inside. As I followed him in, he asked, "You want a ride tomorrow?"

"That'd be awesome!" I said, feeling a happy warmth spread through me.

"Which floor?" he asked as he thumbed the ninth.

"The same."

"What's your name again?"

"Ani, with an 'i.'" I tapped my fingertips against the side of my leg.

"That's right –from Tucson, Arizona. What made you chose this school?"

"The city, the activity —I heard there's a little of everything here."

"The University of Arizona's a good school."

"It is. And Arizona's a great place —to be *from*. But here everything's so green! And the air is so much cooler. And there are *seasons*!!" I scrunched up my shoulders and did an excited little butt-wiggle before remembering myself and adding nonchalantly, "which, you know, is nice."

"I'm guessing cactus spines don't change color."

"Yeah, not exactly. But they bloom in springtime! The cactus, I mean, not the spines. It doesn't compare to the trees and leaves here, though. Look!"

I produced a large, green leaf from my bag.

"It hasn't even changed yet," he said.

"I know!" I whispered, like this was the most marvelous secret. "And it's still so beautiful. Look at its texture!"

"I can see our trees are no longer safe."

"I don't need *that* many. Just enough to wallpaper my room and send to all my friends back home."

Matching his grin, I put the leaf away and added, "Plus there's so much to see here all within walking distance. In Arizona you have to drive twenty minutes just to get anywhere. Everything's so spread out. But what about you? You from here?"

"No, I'm from back east. Been here a year now."

"You like it? The students and all that?"

"Little responsibility, so, yeah, I like it." He smiled, which crinkled the skin at the corners of his eyes —good-natured and knowing and shining with humor.

The elevator doors opened then.

"My church starts at 10:30, so we have until then to find yours."

"You go to church?" I asked.

"A small, Baptist church –I'm one of the few white men and I'm learning how to 'Amen' this and 'Preach it, Brother' that. It takes some getting used to. I'll be half asleep and someone right behind my head will 'Halleluiah' the shit right out of me. What time does yours start?"

I checked my notes. "10:00."

"All right, let's leave around 9:30 –no 9:00– that should give us enough time."

"9:00 then."

He waved before stepping through his door at the far end of the hall.

In less than a year, I had gone from a school where the strongest exclamation was "Oh my gravy!" to a school smelling of weed and incense and where the expletives I heard in the hallways made me marvel at their crass creativity. I was surprised to find that I loved the contrast. Even so, swear words still occasionally startled me. I was so fervent back then. And on the alert for insincerity and hypocrisy. A pervasive mentality gripped many at my previous school –one where the music you listened to or the questions you asked could work like an infection within you until hell was an inevitability. Unless you embraced full and complete abstinence of … pretty much everything. That was one of the reasons I had left. Faith should be a deeply personal relationship with God, I thought, not a ritual or a shunning of everything considered by someone, somewhere to be evil.

The next morning the cool, autumn air felt electric. I breathed it in as I waited just outside the lobby. I tilted my face up and closed my eyes as sunlight dripped from the leaves and splashed at my feet.

"Good morning!"

His voice was like a clap on the shoulder, and I jumped, heart pounding.

"Good morning," I said, squinting against the reflected glare of the windows behind him. "How are you?"

"Horrible!" But he was smiling. "The car's this way."

As we pulled out from the parking garage in his blue SS Camaro, he cheerfully began describing Seattle's layout. We followed Pike Street east, over the interstate, as he pointed out Capital Hill's limits. I had just stretched my legs and leaned back when we turned left and came immediately to Virginia Street. And there was the church. It had taken all of three minutes. Kurt parked as I stared up at the very tall, very square, very grey brick building, disappointed at the remarkable speed with which we had reached our destination. My hand slid to the silver door handle.

"You have an hour," he said, his words stopping my hand. He leaned back a little, seat creaking, and looked over at me. "Now that we know where it is, you want to see more of the city?"

I glanced at the clock, at him. "Yes!" I said, nodding too enthusiastically, but unable to stop myself. "Yes, I'd love that!"

Releasing the breath I didn't know I'd been holding, I leaned down to set my purse next to my feet. His eyes followed my hand and ... was he looking at my legs? He couldn't be attracted to me, I thought, as I turned to look out the window. Not really. I felt so much like a child, chased by the feeling that pretty much everyone else was smarter than me, funnier, wittier, more interesting. I'd been told how young and sweet I looked, but I remembered being teased, as all kids are, for looking, sounding, *being* different; for my red hair, ill-fitting clothes, and the big, plastic glasses I wore until my sixteenth birthday, when my parents got me contacts. I wore my resulting shyness like a heavy coat that I sometimes found uncomfortable and burdensome, but occasionally retreated into while pulling the hood down low so I could peer out from the safety of obscurity.

We drove everywhere –circled Greenlake, shot through the University district, wound in and out of parks. Kurt's whirlwind way of giving a tour made me laugh out loud. He seemed to have been waiting to share this information with someone, anyone –information about the city, about things to do and where to eat. The words poured out, and I soaked them in –tasting them and a hint of something else. Coloring the good-natured jokes and tour-guide-like enthusiasm was a loneliness so minute, so distant, that it almost didn't exist. But there it was, and I surveyed it with surprised wonder. Kurt didn't seem the type to need other people.

"So what'd you do before this, before Seattle?" he asked.

"I worked the graveyard shift in an ER."

"What was that like?"

"Wild. And humbling. It left me hating the smell of beer and made me appreciate life in a whole new way."

"Not squeamish then?"

"Not around blood. I mean, there was this time it was spurting from the head of a little old lady who'd just fallen, and that was a bit much. But she was just so cute and cheerful and making jokes as though nothing had happened that everything seemed fine. Like it would be fine. Even the guys who'd been fighting or had just crashed their ATVs weren't so bad. What really got to me was the family members. Put me in front of a sobbing relative and I was done for.

"But what about you?" I asked. "What did you do before this?"

"I studied interpersonal relationships in a tiny village in Africa. Then I spent a year touring Australia."

"Wow!" I said, and I pressed him for details. Why and how and where and what was that like? He laughed, and as he answered I felt so captivated that I had no idea anymore where we were or what street we were on.

"Do you miss it? Traveling, I mean?" I asked.

"No, not really."

"But Africa! That must've been so exciting!"

"I liked it, that's why I did it. But then you realize people are the same wherever you go. The women still gossip, and the men still talk about sex. The world lost its mystery."

So many more things to ask him, but how to phrase my questions? Was it too many questions? Did I seem too interested? Feeling suddenly awkward, I leaned back and looked out the window, searching for the right words to say.

Then I took in the beauty flowing past us. Green and purple trees reached for us while bright bursts of color flashed from the giant planters in every entryway. Moss crept up stone stairs as red and gold leaves danced down. I was used to Summer hoarding as many months as possible, but here, Fall seemed to take his time stretching and shaking himself out, sending leaves spinning and hair flying.

I sighed, feeling happy. "Arizona has a beauty all its own with its rocks and sunsets and mountains that change color, but this ... I don't think I could ever grow tired of this."

Kurt looked around before smiling at me.

"And these buildings!" I marveled, staring up at the intricate detail along their topmost edges. "So different from all the pink adobe in Tucson. So many neighborhoods there look like giant anthills."

Becoming suddenly conscious of my nose pressed to the window, I leaned back and wiped the smudge off the glass. I glanced over at Kurt, but he was smiling with a sort of amused softness. I relaxed back into my seat and said, "I never noticed all those figures and designs up along the tops of the buildings."

Kurt leaned forward and nodded. "We so rarely look up," he said. "Too busy going places."

"That's why I like photography –I see things through a lens that I never noticed before. Hey, have you ever read Ayn Rand's, *The Fountainhead*?"

"A while ago. Back in school."

"Do you remember the part where Dominique and ... what *is* his name? Wyland or Wynand, I think. Yeah, I'm pretty sure –anyway, they're talking about buildings and how they make some people feel small. But for Dominique, they remind her of man's ability –his strength and ingenuity. I mean, people have gone to the moon! They've cured diseases and crossed the oceans and found ways to talk with people thousands of miles away! And they've made art and music and poetry. The human mind is beautiful."

"I don't remember that part," Kurt said, "but I like the way you describe it."

"My youngest brother's like Roark, I think."

"He's a genius architect?"

"No," I laughed. "But he's got a strong personality and his own way of seeing things. And he's not afraid to stand up for what he believes in."

"Who are you like?'

"You mean as far as book characters go?"

He nodded.

"Not Dominique, that's for sure. I think perhaps the girl from *Great Expectations*. The one who couldn't get close to people. Estella –is that her name? I know it starts with an E. Goodness, I'm so bad with detail. That's why I stopped studying History. Was it King Louis XIV or King Louis XVI? I have no idea. I loved the stories though. What about you? What did you study?"

"Anthropology."

"Oh. So, uh ... what do you do with that?"

"*Exactly*. I have only to write my thesis to get my Masters, but afterward it'll just be 'now what?'"

"Do you like what you're doing here, at the school?"

"Yeah. For now, anyway. I like to think I'm helping the students."

13

I looked at him. Then I looked past him and recognized the street we were on. With dismay I checked the clock as he parked. We had barely made it back to the church on time. I wouldn't have minded missing the service. I'd have gladly spent all day with him.

I climbed out, my legs feeling heavy and numb, and waved goodbye as I walked clumsily up the steps to the huge, wooden doors. Then I turned and watched him go, my head buzzing with the sort of energy that comes from being stimulated, drawn in, and left wanting more.

A FEW YEARS BEFORE Seattle, on a fine, bright day in South Carolina, I sat across from a professor I'd never met before. I'd merely seen the Science Department sign above his door and taken this as an invitation. He was a welcoming stranger –with thick, salt-and-pepper hair, a mustache, and large, black-rimmed glasses. He had smiled and beckoned to a chair with his outstretched hand when he heard me say I had a quick science question that I was wondering if he could help me with.

The room was windowless and dark, as though we were a hundred feet underground. I could almost imagine that the massive shelves with their massive books were hiding rough-hewn stone walls. That wasn't the case at all, of course. We were in a large university building, two stories up, surrounded by spring-happy birds and exploding daffodils.

"What's on your mind?" the professor had asked, and my eyes stopped their wandering to focus on him.

"Stars," I said.

He leaned back, silent and patient, so I continued. "The Bible says to stay away from people and beliefs that try to predict the future. So then why did God use a star to lead the wise men to the baby Jesus? Isn't that essentially astrology?"

The man studied me a moment, as though wondering who this too-young-looking red-haired girl was. I was nobody. A child. An unfamiliar face coming from an unknown state of mind.

"To me," he said finally, "that just goes to show God's great ability to use any means to bring people to himself. He used the methods those men were familiar with in order to bring them to a better way –the way by which they could be saved."

"Oh," I said, looking down at my hands. "But would you say it's blasphemous to think that maybe the God who designed the heavens might have done so in such a way that the stars and planets with their accompanying forces could affect life on earth?"

"Blasphemous, no. However, there isn't really any evidence suggesting this is the case. The distances are too great, and no one has been able to create double-blind studies yielding repeatable results."

"Repeatable results," I echoed softly. I felt like a speck floating in an academic universe. We were sitting just a few feet apart, but he suddenly felt miles away, as though I were looking at him through the wrong end of a telescope.

I thought of him as I sat in Kurt's office a few days later.

I had entered the dorm lobby as he was unlocking his office door.

He called to me and asked, "How was church?"

"Disappointing," I said, walking over. "Yours?"

"Rousing!" he said. "What didn't you like?"

He held the door open for me, and I followed him in and sat down on one of the worn couches facing his large desk. Pulling my legs up under me, I saw the professor's face, his desk, his books. Sharp at first, and then the image grew indistinct, replaced by Kurt's smiling form. I sighed, surprised by how natural it felt to be sitting there with him.

"It felt empty," I said, referring to the church on Virginia Street. "I couldn't help wondering, if we really possess an eternity-altering gift, a relationship with *the* God of the universe, shouldn't something

15

like that show through a little more? Do you know what I mean? The God who made heaven and earth inside us?! Inside me? How is that not more visible? I wanted to go around asking everyone, how do you know he's there? How do *I* know he's there?"

"Why didn't you?"

"At the school I went to back East they told me I don't read my Bible like I ought, or pray like I ought, or meditate like I ought. I ought. I ought. In fact, my dorm supe there told me that maybe I didn't really *know* the love of God. But if so, it wasn't for lack of desire. Or effort. I honestly want to, but ... I don't know. Maybe the problem is me."

He smiled.

"I'm sorry," I said, suddenly self-conscious. "That's probably more information than you wanted."

He waved the words away. "Don't apologize. Especially not when I asked. So that school you went to, is that the really strict one with pink and blue sidewalks and barbed wire to keep all the students in?"

I laughed. "Strict yes, but no barbed wire, or pink and blue sidewalks."

"What was it like?"

"Interesting. Some really good teachers. But I think I learned more about people than anything else."

"The rules didn't bother you?"

"Everybody always asks that, and it's true I got my fair share of demerits for having skirts that were too short and necklines that were too low. And I didn't care much for being told when I could or couldn't leave the school grounds–"

"I didn't realize you were such a rebel!"

"I know, right?! But I knew about the rules when I applied there. What really bothered me was how those rules determined how I was judged ... whether I was a 'good' person or a 'good' Christian. If I didn't take out the trash or get out of bed in the morning at the specified time –was I *really* a rebel? Because that's honestly how they made us feel. Or if someone outside the school listened to secular music –did that mean they were going to hell? It was almost as if they thought a relationship with God was a product of and not the cause of habitual good behavior. I didn't understand how controlling every aspect of our lives was supposed to make us closer to God. It created nothing more than a Christian walk by habit.

"But really, I'm not giving the school enough credit. They had some *amazing* teachers, and the fine arts there were incredible. And the school tried in some ways, other ways, to develop the spiritual lives of its students. It just wasn't for me. I left because I felt evil just for asking questions."

Kurt leaned back and regarded me. "Coming here must be quite a change."

"Oh, my goodness, yes! But it's been good for me. And finding a church will help."

"Let me know how it goes."

"Thanks," I said. "I will."

# Chapter 2

Toucans. Those were what I liked best. Oh, there were the monkeys, the jungle ice-cream, and the endless mysteries of the jungle itself with all its many noises and strangely-growing things, but the toucans were my favorite. Their large, colorful beaks made soft clicking noises as they caught the bits of fruit my friend, Donny, tossed to them. We were at his house, barefoot and with our hair sticking to our foreheads in the humidity. He turned his dimpled face to me and handed me a piece of the mango he had just sliced with his pocketknife. I laughed as I chucked it in, but my aim was off, and the slippery golden wedge landed with a wet splat in the corner of their cage. "I'm sorry," I whispered to the birds, and I stood back then, so my friend could take over. He reached in and picked up a little red ball. With a flick, he sent it up, and one of the birds snatched it out of the air. As the two birds tossed the little ball back and forth and up, I let my focus relax and watched the swirl of yellow, orange, and black as their beaks wove through the air. I was mesmerized. These birds were large, but gentle; exotic, but tame. I loved them.

To be fully honest though, I loved everything about the jungle –that small part I experienced in central Colombia, anyway. It was the summer between my fifth and sixth grades, and my family was staying at a place called *Loma Linda*. Pretty Hill.

Fragrant air flowed through the open windows of our house during the day and the dripping-water sound of chirping geckos filled the rooms at night. *Loma Linda* boasted a small school, a large auditorium for social gatherings, and a *bodega* where all the kids bought chocolate bars and lukewarm sodas –the orange ones being the best– with the money we earned from picking up rotten mangos.

My friends were mostly American –MK's whose parents were working with language helpers to transcribe the native languages they'd been assigned. A few families lived further out in the jungle, but most traveled back and forth between the outlying villages and *Loma Linda* where they had community support and supplies. All the kids spoke Spanish and English, and most of them knew the indigenous language their parents were learning as well. I felt inferior, knowing only English, with a few bits and phrases of Spanish. But it didn't matter, not really, because my two best friends, Mike and Donny, never judged. Each was only too happy to act as guide, protector, and translator for me. Not that I needed protecting, I thought, but I liked the extra attention. When Donny started speaking secrets to Mike in Spanish, I had only to hint that I was remembering everything and would ask my mother to translate as soon as I got home, to watch him blush and beg me not to repeat a word of it. His little sister told me in a hot whisper that tickled my ear that he liked me, and I held this knowledge close, right next to my own ardent feelings for Mike.

We three were inseparable. We shot lizards with Mike's BB gun, so we could feed them to his boa constrictor –wounding, not killing, because the snake wouldn't eat them otherwise. I was a pretty good shot. Although once I missed, and the lizard died anyway. "Heart attack," we concluded decisively. "Maybe if we dangle it on a string?"

Everyone had boa constrictors. I'd have gotten one too, if allowed. I loved snakes. Instead, I had to satisfy myself with the steely feel of Mike's boa wrapping itself around my arm. And then, later, with staring in wide-eyed wonder at the twelve-foot-long one some local men had caught. My father had sent someone down to the river to fetch me. I ran, barefoot and dripping wet, to the clearing. I was still in my swimsuit, with my short hair plastered to the sides of my face and the back of my neck, when I first glimpsed the writhing mass of muscle surrounded by six men. A loud buzzing filled my ears as I approached, but whether it was the shrill chorus of insects or the blood racing in my temples, I couldn't tell. The trees themselves seemed to be leaning in, fronds rustling as they grasped and pushed at each other. I caught the word "pig" as someone pointed to the large bump in the middle, and I felt a swirl of awe and horror. My whole body thrummed with the hammering of my heart as I stepped closer. "Can I touch it?" I asked, my voice so quiet in my intense excitement that I had to repeat my request several times before anyone heard me. The head, disproportionately small compared to the bulk in its belly, lunged at me. I flinched, but large, rough hands held it back. I reached forward again and stroked the cold, tight scales. How had it managed the pig? It seemed impossible. What could this dangerous, beautiful creature do to me?

Everything in the jungle was beautiful. The way the afternoon rainclouds moved over the pulsing treetops, crushing everything below with wonderful, pounding drops. The way the river rippled as the older kids described the caiman, anacondas, and piranhas that swam within. The way the sounds of all those unseen creatures blended to create an enveloping symphony unlike any I'd ever heard –howler monkeys and insects and birds and I knew not what, with the wind lifting and twirling and carrying the combined song in waves that rose and fell.

I was in love! I was in love with the creatures –the large, translucent blue butterflies that floated over our heads during church and the fist-sized snails that slid along in unhurried glory. I was in love with the rain and the river and the waving trees. I was in love with the way the bananas tilted up and with the foot-long green pods that peeled open to reveal white seeds that we all called jungle ice cream because of their sweetness. I was in love with Mike. And with Donny, too. And with being alive in a place where I was so free and happy, where each day unveiled new and exciting experiences.

*Loma Linda* was the place I longed to return to when things didn't go right somewhere else, which, for a long time, was quite often. The next fall, I was dropped into a middle school crowded with American peers whose pop-culture references may as well have been another language.

I loved the excitement of preparing for a new school year. I loved going to the store to buy colorful notebooks and supplies. I loved imagining new friends, maybe even a *boy*friend. I loved the feeling of possibility.

But once school started, I found myself at a loss. I didn't know who or what the other kids were talking about. I didn't know what to say to them or how to relate.

One day after lunch, I sat outside near a group of girls, trying not to be noticed. One of them looked at me and said, "I don't like you."

I couldn't think of anything to say, so I said nothing.

"I don't know why," the girl went on. "I just don't like you. From the moment I saw you, I just didn't like you."

But I knew why. It was because of my plastic glasses and heavy bangs and my clothes with their faded flower prints and ill-fitting seams that my mom had picked up second hand from a place where the women who donated the clothes gushed about their grandchildren together. It was because every mention of current music and movies went right over my head. It was because my heart began pounding in my ears whenever someone talked to me, and I would start to panic as my mind tried in vain to settle on an appropriate response.

I realized then that this girl didn't see me as a person with feelings, or as a person whose feelings mattered anyway. Maybe I would be better without feelings, I thought. It would be better if I didn't care. But even knowing that I shouldn't care, I still did, and I hated that I did.

I cared when our P.E. teacher stepped out of the gym after telling us to pair up for a dance lesson, and all the kids told me to partner up with Dwight, the boy who smiled as everyone made fun of him, who stumbled over his feet the way I stumbled over my words, who always looked like he had just been woken up whenever someone spoke his name.

"Huh?" he said, and he laughed nervously when the kids told him to be my partner.

"C'mom, you guys are perfect," they insisted.

When we protested, they started pushing us towards each other. I pressed my feet down as they slid me forward, and my sneakers squealed against the waxed basketball court. The sound was awful.

Our teacher arrived then, and everyone dispersed, innocently attentive. I faded into the background, my heart aching for the freedom of my life in Texas and the boundless joy of tramping through the jungles of Colombia.

At home, bursting through the door, I shook off the marionette strings of my self-consciousness. If people could only see the real me, I thought, maybe they'd understand. But since they couldn't, I escaped. I escaped into my backyard where I explored the uncharted territory along the creek behind my house as blackberry vines clawed at my legs. I hand-fed lizards in my free time. I stalked frogs, making detailed notes of their physiology and stamping their little feet in black ink so I could document their size and texture. I released them into the crawlspace beneath my house and brought down jars of grasshoppers and crickets that I watched them eat in the spotlight of my flashlight. I diagrammed praying mantises and built forts and considered every scraped knee and scratch on my cheek a royal badge of honor.

But everywhere else, I did not belong. I was an outsider in my own country, and I felt desperately claustrophobic. Already shy, I withdrew into myself even further. I analyzed my clothes, my mannerisms, but felt helpless to alter them. And soon, just the thought of my mascara running in the rain or the sound of my stomach gurgling in the middle of class or the sight of the thin row of hairs on my knee that I had somehow missed when shaving the night before was enough to leave me mortified. My mouth began to betray me, with my words coming out all wrong. Before long, whenever I was spoken to, I began responding with painful blushes and a deer-in-the-headlights stare while my mind ran through fifteen possible replies. By the time I chose one, I either stuttered or resigned myself to silence because the moment had passed. Even a question as mundane as, "what chapter are we supposed to read for history?" could leave me red-faced and mute.

I was acutely conscious of it all –of the stares, whispers, teasing, and laughter, of my own *differentness,* which of course I thought could be nothing other than a vast shortcoming on my part. My intense striving to change, to mold myself into someone passable, or even anonymous, yielded no results. And the idea that it was okay to stand out –good even– never crossed my mind. I had spent my life up to that moment trying to be "all things to all people." Also, though I hated to admit it, I lacked the courage to "just be myself." So, I could neither assimilate with my peers, nor could I ignore them.

At night, unable to escape outside, the noise and violence of my thoughts blackened my vision. No amount of pressing my fists against my temples could ease the pressure, and if I buried myself beneath every one of my heavy blankets, the tempest followed. My only respite came when I searched out my God. Clutching my Bible on my lap, I read and re-read Romans, escaping into the love laid out for me there, from which nothing could separate me. Except maybe myself. But even then, the apostle Paul understood. He described his struggle with doing right and his desire to be rescued from "this body of death." And when he spoke of hope, of acceptance, of Someone who understood and loved anyway, unconditionally, I believed him. It was as though his words opened the door to a cozy room filled with comfortable couches and a blazing fireplace, next to which Jesus himself stood, hand extended, beckoning me inside. I wanted to go in, shut the door, and leave the rest of the world behind. Forever. Only, the door wouldn't close. Night gave way to morning, and morning brought with it more school and more homework and all the many things that melt one hour into another. Thankfully though, words of hope, once internalized, are portable.

At school and at large, I tried to wrap the feeling of God's reassuring presence around me. I talked to him during the day. I reminded myself that he had a plan and purpose that extended beyond the present moment. I looked and I listened, my mind on a quest for echoes of his beauty woven throughout the world. A weathered statue next to someone's door, the tiny blue shard of a robin's egg, the sound of ice tinkling in my glass, the dancing plant shadows on my walls. I treasured each of these as little gateways to wonder.

I added these moments to my collection of memories, and they became a means of escape in and of themselves. On the bus or in the cafeteria, surrounded by the noise and chaos of middle schoolers, I'd lean my head against the window, smelling the cracked and dusty vinyl seats and feeling the rumble of the bus all around, or I'd close my eyes in the cafeteria until the shouts and sounds of clashing silverware faded, and instead I'd smell the marketplace in Mexico or hear the thrilling calls of unseen jungle creatures. I'd see the rippling river water as my fingers sliced through the surface while my brother saw how fast he could row. I'd remember the hooked spines of my pet cactuses in Texas with their twirling grooves and shiny tips, or I'd wave my fingers and feel again the way my ribbon snake used to wind between them, cold and smooth, like a secret. I'd dream of Colombia and running barefoot and swimming in the warm river. I'd remember and relive and feel again that wonderful sense of belonging.

My faith and my memories clothed me, guarded me, until gradually, I began to acclimate. I learned the lingo and developed my own style. I talked to strangers and made new friends. But I did so from a distance. Now, although curious and eager, I was safely detached. This made me feel strong and resilient, with any lingering insecurities mostly obscured by my growing optimism.

ART SCHOOL EMBRACED me with an ease and indifference that made me feel right at home. The halls were filled with people who were all ... *different*, each of us united by our shared desire to capture and create art. Within this environment, my confidence began to grow, and I felt as though I were emerging, wings unfurling, as I stepped from my chrysalis.

Little time was needed to fall into a rhythm. The days grew shorter until soon I was leaving for class in the dark, only to have the afternoon sun slide into darkness again by three thirty. Those of us studying photography were left with the weekends to get most of our shooting done.

That was fine by me. I walked for hours on end, awestruck. My eyes were fully open to the world back then. I saw beauty everywhere –in the play of light upon individual strands of hair and upon bricks and leaves and the geometry of stairs. Even the broken bottles with their gleaming edges and the weathered graffiti and rust-colored leaves half melded into the concrete, the dumpsters with their shadows and the alleys with their blowing fragments of band posters

–all of it called to me. I was fascinated by the histories in hands and the movement of tattoos. And by faces. Every face whispered its secrets. Every expression made my heart swell with love as I ached to know more. I wanted to embrace the city, the world, and everyone within. The simple act of bearing witness gave me purpose and filled my days with meaning. I was a ship on the ocean of my joy, collecting treasures.

On one of those early Saturdays, I spent eight hours with my roommate, Keiko, and a guy named Yoshiko walking the city, from the Space Needle to Pioneer Square. Yoshi, as everyone called the Japanese star of all our shared photography classes, directed his powerful charisma at a select few and withheld it from everyone else. Everything he did, he did emphatically –complete with flying hair and hand gestures. Despite professing how much he adored his far-off German girlfriend, he still freely offered entire commentaries on every girl who walked by –declaring his love for each– before turning back to Keiko and calling her his "pet."

The light was fading by the time the three of us exited the big wooden doors of the Elliott Bay Bookstore that evening in Pioneer Square. The streetlamps glowed, altering the atmosphere of the city. The energy was still there but had changed from playful to seductive.

Yoshi, Keiko, and I absorbed it all with fascination. This was a world with which I was utterly unfamiliar. My curiosity was a small dog yapping at my feet, impossible to ignore. I wanted to investigate, explore, and observe. I wanted to understand.

Passing The Bookstore Bar, I pulled Yoshi and Keiko in with me. Smiling at the doorman, I led the way to a table in the back. The dark and smoky interior was as comforting as it was mysterious. Candlelight reflected off the tall waitress's hoop earrings as she brought over menus and asked what we'd like to drink.

When it was my turn, I looked up and asked, "Do you have any Scotch?"

"Scotch?" The waitress looked at me like I was mental. "We have about a hundred."

Yoshi laughed –a short, staccato laugh– and I felt my cheeks burn in the darkness.

"Oh, okay, umm ... which would you recommend?"

She finally brought out a Highland Park, which I sipped, eyebrows raised, before declaring it syrupy and hot. I handed it to Keiko and looked around as she tasted it. Each bookshelf beckoned, hinting at secrets waiting to be revealed. I wanted to open every one of the cigar boxes embedded among the old books to discover what small treasures they might contain. I wanted to thumb through the dustiest books and look for intimate inscriptions. I wanted to hold each of the knights from the various chess sets scattered here and there to ascertain which felt the heaviest and which had weathered the most use. Two guys sat playing at a table across from us. My fingers itched to play.

As Keiko handed back my glass, I caught the softness in her face, the light in Yoshi's smile. How quietly eager and optimistic we were as we tasted the world in our innocence. So sweet. So unjaded. A sense of happy exploration radiating off us. If happiness were a contagion, I thought, soon everyone –all the people sharing this tiny bar and city and planet– would feel their sorrows lift and their hearts swell with the spread of our joy.

"ISN'T THIS EXCITING?!" I asked each person in the darkroom by turn, fists clenched in front of my chest. Most barely looked up from their trays of chemicals. "Ah ... first quarter enthusiasm." I was undeterred. Within the murky red glow, I'd discovered a source of excitement I'd never known before.

I tried to explain my wonder for the darkroom to a guy named Kellie over a game of chess later that week. As an animation student with absolutely no concept of how other people perceived him, he seemed to see himself as one of his own comic book creations.

I took him to the darkroom once, and he leaned close and whispered, "We should totally make out –it'd be the romantic thing to do."

I laughed and ducked under his skinny arm to get to the tubs of chemicals. I was becoming conscious of my own laughter and thought it beautiful, which was a revelation. The sound was physical somehow –something I could toss up and catch again, like a shining bauble.

Kellie and I had met through chess after Kurt suggested I put up a sign, inviting others to play. The result was a quickly designed printout that I tacked onto the downstairs bulletin board. Kellie was the first to respond. When I opened my door, he was standing there, so tall and thin, and sporting a confidence that didn't seem to come naturally, as he cracked jokes and took me up on my offer for a little competition.

I liked watching him play. His fingers were quick and his eyes animated. We were setting up the board for a second game when we began debating who the real hero was in one of our favorite books, *The Lord of the Flies.*

"Jack was the first to lose touch with reality," I said. "That hardly makes him a hero."

"He's totally the hero!"

Kellie had this way of thrusting out his arm, palm up, as though he were delivering a proclamation. "Jack was the first to hunt for real food –how long could they have lived off fruit? Jack brought in the *meat.*"

"That had nothing to do with food. He wanted blood."

"The boys all followed him because he did what had to be done. He was the true leader."

"Kellie, he was reduced to basic animalistic behavior. He lost all respect for human life. Like Sal, in *The Beach*. That's the whole point of the book. Both of them actually. And *The Heart of Darkness*, for that matter. Each of us is capable of the most monstrous atrocities, and it's only society with its laws and consequences that keeps the majority of us from acting on those impulses."

"Okay, here's a question for you:" –as if the answer to this would solve everything– "does character shape circumstance, or do circumstances shape character?"

"Character or circumstance?" I repeated, mulling it over. "Well, I don't think any of us starts off as a blank slate. We each have our own inherited disposition, which I guess is what you're calling character. But I also think we can all change, to a certain extent."

"Because of circumstance," Kellie cut in.

"Because of our *reaction* to circumstance."

"Which still requires circumstance."

"Does it though? What if you hear about something that happened to someone else and change your behavior because of that, does that still count? And what about the fact that different people respond in different ways?"

"It's because of how they were raised," he insisted.

"But siblings don't all respond the same way."

"Siblings might grow up in the same house, with the same parents, but that doesn't mean their circumstances are the same. My parents treat me way differently than they treat my sister."

Circumstances give character expression, I mused, but do they shape us to the extent that we have no say in the matter? Affect us, yes. There's so much outside our control, like drunk drivers, stray bullets, and cancer. Life leaves its mark. But are we only a product of our environment? Of our circumstances?

In a world populated by pessimists and optimists, it seemed to me that when faced with the same trials, each often becomes their own self-fulfilling prophecy. But why? Because they were born that way? Or shaped that way? And really, wasn't character just another circumstance? I mean, who can help their genetic make-up with its built-in set of predispositions?

Finally, I said, "I don't see how either character or circumstance can be completely independent of the other."

"But if you had to choose?"

"If I had to choose, I'd say character."

"How can you say that?" he almost yelled.

"How can you look so upset?" I laughed.

"Name one instance." He looked defiant as he crossed his arms over his chest.

"Oh, come on. It happens all the time. Bad things –horrible, awful things– happen to people all the time, both young and old. And each person, each *character*, responds in his or her own unique way. Some play the victim, others become the hero. Some turn into monsters, others into well-adjusted members of society."

"Because of circumstance! Because of their parents, their schools, their childhoods."

"But then wouldn't everyone from just the right circumstances be guaranteed to turn out well? And too bad for all the rest? If it were that easy, wouldn't our problems be solved by now?"

"Yeah, but look at the prison population," he said. "The majority of them come from low-income, poorly educated homes."

"I'm not saying circumstance has no affect at all. I'm just saying that not everyone born into those circumstances is destined to end up the same. And anyway, what is it exactly that makes us who we are? What *is* character?"

"What?"

"I mean, are you referring to genes only? Where does our personality come from? What part of you makes your decisions? Is it only so many chemical reactions and electrical synapses inside your brain? Or is it a product of something intangible inside you? A soul, if you will?"

"What does that have to do with anything?"

"Well, if it's only a matter of science—"

"—of course it is."

"Hang on, if it's only a matter of science then I guess the answer would be circumstance because there would be nothing else. Character would be nothing more than the product of our parentage. After all, we can't help what genes we're given. By going all the way back to our beginnings, with only science determining how everything acts and reacts, then even the forming of our DNA is a situation outside our control that shapes us, our physical and psychological make-up and therefore our 'character.' Maybe. I mean, even if we argue outside nature, and say that the nurture of our parents, being unique individuals, shaped those circumstances which then shaped us, we're still saying that we're only the product of so many circumstances —programmed by science. And then the whole question becomes a moot point because there'd be no such thing as free-acting 'character.' I'm starting to confuse myself, but all that aside, I think it's more than just science. I mean, it has to be. Wouldn't you agree there's some immaterial part of us that stays the same throughout the years —a soul, or self-aware consciousness, or some such? I think there's a part of us that stays the same no matter what. A part of our 'character' that remains untouched by 'circumstance' and can act in spite of, and not because of, the circumstances around us."

"No one who lives remains untouched."

"I agree, but maybe we're looking at this all wrong. I mean, there're so many variables. How can we even separate the two? Circumstance influences character, character responds to circumstance and then character creates a new situation. The two are co-mingled in such a way that you could never look at one without the other. They affect each other, yes, but I don't think we can say definitively that one solely determines the other."

"That's a cop-out."

"Maybe. All I know is that if I had to choose, I would say character. Even if there is no free will, of which I'm undecided, we have to live as though there is. And we can only do this by taking responsibility for our actions –regardless of what circumstances come our way. I want to think –*need* to think– that we can each make something beautiful, something meaningful, out of what life throws at us. I admit circumstances affect me, but I don't like the idea of being changed or controlled by them. I want to be the author of my own story."

Kellie laughed, shook his head, and walked out of my room. I stared after him, confused.

I brought it up later that week with Kurt. After our initial conversation, I had begun stopping by his office a couple times a week, drawn in by my insatiable curiosity and by how comfortable I felt around him.

"I don't understand why he reacted so strongly," I said. "Maybe he wasn't looking for a discussion of the self, but I can't stop thinking about it. Did you ever see that movie, *The Three Faces of Eve*?"

"A long time ago."

"So, it's based on a true story about this woman with multiple personalities, right? Each personality was completely different and separate from the other –with their own thoughts and feelings and reactions. Eve and her doctor were able to get rid of –is that even the right way to describe it?– some of the extra personalities. But it made me so, so sad because, even though she couldn't go on that way, when each of the other personalities left it was as though they had died. Even though they all shared the same body, which kept on living, when a personality disappeared, that *person* died. Does that make sense? It makes me wonder what we are. Are we our thoughts and feelings and memories and preferences? Or is it something deeper inside us –something that remains untouched even when our minds and memories and synapses aren't functioning properly? Or are we really nothing more than the chemical reactions inside our brains?"

"They were all her," Kurt said. "Just different aspects of the same person."

"But if I get into a car accident and wake up with no memories and a new personality, is that still me?"

"What do you think?"

"I'd like to think so, but so much of who we are is wrapped up in our memories. Kellie's right in that respect, we are shaped by our circumstances. But there's something intrinsic, right? Something that gives continuity despite everything external?"

"You mean the 'I'? The one doing the experiencing?"

"I guess, but what is that?"

"The question of who we are is an old one."

"Yeah, and I haven't heard an answer I like. There is so much I don't understand! Kellie seemed so sure of himself. He was so emphatic! Do you know he is still giving me the cold shoulder! I asked him about it, and he says he feels so strongly that circumstance is more important than character that he has a hard time even talking to me because I don't agree with him. Why? If we only spend time with people who agree with us, how will we ever grow?"

"And who would there be left to talk to?"

"I know, right? But everyone agrees with *you*. By the sheer force of your personality!"

Kurt laughed and leaned back in his big office chair; one arm draped over the armrest while the other made a slow circle at the wrist.

"I'm just here taking it all in," he said.

I smiled and pulled at a loose thread at the bottom of my shirt. "This school, this city –it's all so perfect for people-watching. I think everyone has a story –something to share, something for me to learn. Even people I've never met, who live a world away. I once saw a photo of an Israeli soldier in a news magazine. His face was so haunted, it made me hurt inside. I wanted to comfort him. Does that sound silly? I almost felt like I knew him. There was this other time I read about a woman who'd been murdered. I was only eight or ten at the time, but I couldn't stop imagining what it must have been like for her. I hated those thoughts because they horrified me, but I felt like I needed to think about it so that then she wasn't alone. So that in her worst moments someone was thinking about her, even if retroactively. That probably doesn't even make sense. I guess what I'm trying to say is that in those moments, I feel so close to people. Connected. The rest of the time I feel like a ghost. Like I'm there but looking in from the outside."

Kurt studied me a moment, then asked, "Why do you think that is?"

I pulled my legs up onto the couch and hugged my knees.

"Because of moving around so much, I guess," I said. "I have friends all over the world, but when we write to each other, it's like talking to a memory, a picture. It makes me feel cold. Detached."

"You seem to have a lot of friends here."

"The same as anybody. But I don't get *close* to them –emotionally close. I could say goodbye to any of them knowing I'd never see them again and be perfectly okay with it."

"Is that surprising?"

"Isn't it?"

"Not really. It's safer for you that way. I'm not saying it's healthy, but it's understandable. It doesn't hurt as much then when they say goodbye."

"Yeah, okay" I said, nodding. "That makes sense, but I don't know how to turn it off. And it feels weird when these people say how close they feel to me. I've been bridesmaids to people who barely knew me. And if they did, if they knew the real me and some of the things that go on in my head–"

"Like what?" he asked, leaning forward and grinning. This was the sort of stuff that interested him the most –the scandalous inner tickings of other people.

"I don't know," I said, evading him, "... things." I blushed and looked away. "But if they knew, I'm sure some of them would never speak to me again."

"That's true of most people."

"You?"

"Me especially."

I smiled. "Maybe," I said. "But I've known some people who were true saints. And others who seemed so sweet and transparent that I just can't imagine anything bad in them at all."

"Many would say the same about you. And here we are."

I laughed. "I guess people aren't so different from each other. Like how we can read books written centuries before in countries far away and still get caught up in feeling what the characters felt. I've even heard people describe ideas I thought were unique to myself. Once my ego recovered, I felt even more connected."

Kurt leaned back and put his boots up on the desk with a slight thump. The room was warm and still.

"Have you ever been in love?" he asked.

"Me?" The bluntness of his question surprised me, and I felt suddenly embarrassed. "No. No, I wish. I mean, I've been attracted to people ... my goodness, have I ever!"

"Anybody I know?" The interest in his voice was no doubt due to the amusement he got from seeing people reveal things they never meant to show. Or maybe it was more.

"What? Ha!" I snorted as if he was being ridiculous. As if I wasn't attracted to *him*. I looked away, thinking about how much of my day I spent collecting moments that I could share with him –just on the mere chance of seeing him smile or eliciting a reaction.

The coarse fabric of the couch tickled my fingertips as I said instead, "Anyway, it doesn't really matter because of my whole emotionally detached thing. I've met a lot of cool guys, but you can't help what you do or don't feel." Even in his case, I thought my attraction was likely more cerebral than anything else. If we said goodbye, I'd likely feel only the bland regret of missing out on getting to know an interesting person.

The muffled sounds of students drifted in from the lobby. Their laughter was lighthearted, unrestrained, distant. I felt as though I were cocooned in Kurt's office a world away from everyone else.

"What about you?" I asked. "Ever been in love?"

He looked away. He seemed to be studying the cabinets on the wall. I became suddenly afraid that I'd broken some unspoken rule. Was my question too personal?

When he looked back at me, a line of separation seemed to materialize between us –one that stretched up and up until we were no longer staring at each other. We were staring at formality.

He sounded almost impatient when he finally replied.

"Sure, I've been in love."

I studied him –I couldn't help it– and then forced myself to look away so as not to make him uncomfortable. Should I let it drop? Should I leave? But my curiosity wouldn't let it rest and although I tried to resist it, a word –that simple, one-word question– popped out:

"Oh?"

"There was a girl," he said after a moment.

"What happened?"

"We wanted different things."

I looked around the office, wanting to ask more but not sure how, or if, I should.

"I'm sorry," I said.

"What are you sorry for? It was a long time ago."

"And now you have girls throwing themselves at you."

He laughed, relaxing.

"Another girl asked me to go to the ballet with her," he said rather casually.

I felt my cheeks grow hot. I had imagined doing the very same thing. He wasn't looking at me though. He was rubbing at a pen mark on his desk.

"What did you say?"

"I made up some excuse," he said, licking his thumb and rubbing again. "Some belly dancing class or other that I had to go to."

"That sounds sexy!" I said.

He looked up for an instant, flashing a smile, before dropping his eyes and sliding a folder over the now-smeared ink stain. "Actually, I thought it'd be easier to meet people here," he said finally, straightening in his chair. There it was again. That loneliness.

"But you get asked out all the time."

"By girls young enough to be my daughters."

Did I fall into that category? How did Kurt see me?

He continued, "I've got all the old ladies at my church trying to hook me up." He smiled at the thought. "One woman they set me up with is an English professor at the U. She offered to write my thesis for me. I almost took her up on it."

"How's that going –your thesis?"

He had told me he was writing about the social evolution of African Pygmies. Secretly though, I sometimes wondered if we students had become his new subject of observation.

"It's not," he said.

"Not motivated?"

"I sit down to write" –he made a face and started typing in the air– "and nothing comes. It's all garbage."

I shook my head. "You're too hard on yourself."

"It doesn't matter. I'll finish it one of these days. Or I won't."

I got up to go. "I hope you find your motivation."

"I will. Perhaps." And he waved goodbye as he put on his reading glasses again.

MOMENTS OUT OF KURT'S office, I wanted to turn around and go back in. To see him, hear him, to just be near him. He was complex, intelligent, and seemed so different from all the other men I'd met. Was this curiosity only? Nothing more than a mental pull toward the challenge he represented? I didn't know. I knew only that I loved being near him. At times I thought I glimpsed a mirrored fascination in his eyes. Even so, I doubted he'd let anything become of it. He was my Resident Director, after all. But that was only part of it. I suspected getting close was as hard for him as it was for me. I remained an idealist though, and so consciously pursued my curiosity.

# Chapter 3

Under a grey, breezy sky one evening a few weeks later, I roamed the streets and alleyways, no destination in mind. I wanted only to be outside. Beautiful, dying leaves caressed my palms as I walked, arms raised.

I craved touch, the language of it. There was power in communication so intimate, so revealing. I was conscious of that power always ... although I feared it in relation to other people. With the natural world, I felt no such restraint and touched everything, feeling alive as I did so.

As I reached out to trees and ran my fingers along brick walls, I looked at the people I passed, wondering what they looked like as children ... before they started talking to themselves, reeking of urine and sleeping in doorways. Was there any foreshadowing hidden in their eyes back when they still wore the freshness of youth?

I felt almost guilty ... as though it was wrong for me to lead what I felt was a charmed life when others were suffering. How could I continue in my sheltered existence when this felt like I was ignoring the pain of others? I sometimes longed to haunt the streets, invulnerable and free from constraints, so I could walk up to people one by one and take their hands, touch their cheeks, embrace them fully. I wanted to share peace. Acceptance. Hope.

But this evening, I shared only a smile.

The sun was setting, making the buildings glow and the windows catch fire. In response, the streetlamps popped into being, lighting up the sparkling flecks in the sidewalk as I walked toward the bay.

At the far end of the concrete canyon, two barely visible sailboats winked at me, causing me to draw in my breath until my chest felt full to bursting with melancholy happiness.

"Ani! What are you doing?"

Startled, I turned around, releasing my breath. Yoshi was smiling in that big, emphatic way of his.

"Just walking," I said, as I watched him pack up his camera and fold his tripod.

"Hey, you hungry?" I asked. "There's this little place on the pier that serves clam chowder for two bucks. Want to go? We could watch the sunset."

His hair fell forward as he dipped his head in a nod and joined me.

The old diner was all lit up and welcoming as we bought our food and carried our trays past the old black and white photos of Seattle to a booth in the back.

"So, kids or career?" Yoshi asked once we were seated, although he wasn't looking at me. He was looking at what he had just speared from his plate of fish and chips. He turned the fork around and around, studying the steaming chunk closely.

"Kids, of course," I said, wondering what on earth he was doing. Best not to speculate. "That's all I've ever wanted –a little boy who looks just like his father and two little twin girls."

"Haha!" The light reflected off his yellow lenses as he laughed.

"I've been saying that since I was in high school." I said, grinning and poking at my food. "It may or may not happen like that, but honestly a family is all I want. I mean, I love photography and I want to do something with it, but even if I don't, I'll still have it –even if it's only a hobby. But without a family ... I don't know. I think I'd feel incomplete somehow. What about you?"

"Career. I'm going to be the best!"

"That's modest of you."

"Of course, I am the most modest."

"And no kids?"

"Kids would tie me down."

"And it's not worth it to you?"

"If I'm going to be the best I have to work hard. There wouldn't be time to be a good father."

"And having only pictures as your legacy –that is enough?"

"That is a lot."

"I want to touch the future through my children."

"Of course, because that is you." He sighed and looked out the window. "Ani," he said, "do you believe in God?"

"Of course."

"Is that why you're so happy?"

"You think I'm happy?"

"Yes –all the time."

"Well, yes, I think I'm happy because of God." My belief in God encapsulated my whole reason for being. He gave point and purpose to my existence. Not only that, but I felt my faith was the only thing keeping my looming darkness at bay.

"Because he makes you happy?"

"Yes. I know he makes me happy."

"Are you sure?"

"What do you mean?"

"I think people are happy because they choose to be happy."

"What, and people who aren't are that way simply because they choose not to be?"

"Yes." Yoshi stretched his long arms out alongside his plate, food forgotten.

I stirred my clam chowder, thinking a moment before asking, "Like rose-colored glasses?"

"What?"

"I mean, you're saying it's like our beliefs take on the shape of glasses –some see the world through rose-colored glasses and others see everything as dark?" My reliance on analogies to clarify ideas too often required further explanation.

"Yes, rose-colored glasses, haha!" He stared at me, his fingers tapping out a rapid beat on the table, and I wondered how his expression could be so good-natured and brooding at the same time. "People's realities are based on their beliefs," he said.

"But then, you have people like the cook in *The Sea Wolf* whose life seemed to be one bad experience after another. 'God must've hated me when he signed me up for this bloody voyage called life,' he said. What of him?"

"Nice voice. It's like you were him," Yoshi said. "But I have no idea what you're talking about."

"You know, *The Sea Wolf,* by Jack London? It's an *incredible* book."

Yoshi shrugged. "Haven't read it, but it doesn't matter. He believed that way. He thought God hated him."

"So, basically, you're saying that I'm happy, not because God makes me happy, but because I'm happy believing in a Being higher than myself?"

"Yes." He nodded, and I wrinkled my forehead. Yoshi had taken all the weight I placed upon God –all my faith, my hope, and my experiences– and transformed it into Dumbo's feather.

"No," I said, more obstinately than I intended. "I disagree."

"Of course you do –because that's how you believe." He picked up a chip, then looked at it in disgust and muttered something unintelligible before dropping it back onto the pile.

His arms were alongside his plate again. "What would you do," he asked, "if you were surrounded by complete darkness? You don't know where you are and cannot see or hear anything. What would you do?"

THE CREOSOTE BUSH

the sheep that went astray, Threw His loving arms around me, Drew me back into His way." When the chorus rang out, with the deeper voices echoing the higher ones, I had felt the sound as much as I heard it, felt hope and happiness fill me as we sang – "He will keep me till the river Rolls its waters at my feet; Then He'll bear me safely over, Where the loved ones I shall meet." I imagined the smiling, happy faces of my loved ones –still alive, but one day living forever. My mother no longer in chronic pain and my father fully satisfied that, at last, he could rest after working so hard. I saw John, grinning and enthusiastic, and my two older brothers. Only ... they didn't believe in God. The story of death, resurrection, and eternal life was nothing more than a fairytale to them.

And that's what did me in. Were my brothers really going to hell? A literal hell? Did it even matter whether it was literal or figurative? The thought of them experiencing any kind of eternal torment twisted my insides.

As soon as the song was over, I had escaped down the aisle and out the door. Blinded by the sun, I ran out into the desert heat with my hands hiding my face, and I didn't stop until I fell to my knees in the shadow of the saguaro. There I sobbed with the anguish of losing my loved ones forever. And ever. Denied peace, denied joy, because they no longer believed. It was more than I could bear.

I felt Neva's hands on my shoulders as she tried to hug me, but I couldn't stop rocking. Instead, she rubbed my shoulders and whispered soothing words as the sorrow poured out of me. Her words and the soft wind caressing my temples had a calming effect, and gradually my turmoil ebbed, and my tears dried, stretching the skin across my cheeks. My breathing still came in small, uneven gasps, but I could at last take the tissue Neva offered. Wiping my nose, I smelled the rain again. I waved my hands to cool my cheeks, and gave Neva a small, sideways smile of appreciation.

By the time Neva's family was ready to go, I had composed myself sufficiently. But even as I found myself laughing at the story her brother related, I knew the pain inside me would remain for as long as I could still picture my brothers in torment. I had to hope. I had to keep trusting that God would work it out. He had a plan. This divine plan gave my parents peace. This plan gave Neva purpose. It was this plan, created by a loving God, on which I resolved to anchor myself so as not to fall into the abyss of doubt and disillusion.

"HOW WAS CHURCH? YOU still going?"

"I am," I told Kurt. I was beginning to love the couch in his office and the desk where he sat. The worn places were all familiar to me, and the sight of them comforting. "The sermon was about godliness. The pastor was saying how having a form of godliness, but denying its power, is wicked. A *form* of godliness that treats religion as a tradition, a habit, rather than a source of power. It got me thinking about the story of Noah's ark. People were considered wicked because they 'did what was right in their own eyes.' It wasn't necessarily that they were doing horrible, awful things. They *thought* they were doing right. Which makes me wonder, what about me? I think I'm doing right. Living right. I'm trying to, anyway. But is it just a form, and I'm denying its power? And the power to do what, exactly? To trust fully or to perform miracles or to see life from a higher perspective, with everything in its proper place? I want the power, I think I even need the power, but it's something so vague I wonder how I'd even know when I had it."

I looked to Kurt for an answer, but he just shrugged and said, "Beats me."

"I once asked my best friend from high school to describe who God was to her. She is one of the most devout people I know. She believes in God whole-heartedly and lives it too. She's got these kind, clear blue eyes and a huge smile, and when you look at her you just think, she's so *good*. And genuine, you know? Her faith is a part of her, very natural and pure. I thought, she's the perfect one to ask to describe God, seeing how she's devoted every aspect of her life to him. So I did, and she said, 'Well, he's good to me.'

"'In what way?' I asked.

"'Well ...' and she thought about it a moment, probably wondering why I was asking, 'he loves me.'

"'Yes, but, *how* do you know?'

"'Because the Bible tells me so.'

"'But *tell* me about him.'

"And she couldn't –not one clear, personal description about him. An intangible aura instead of a Person. A Muslim friend once told me that's what's wrong with Christians –we try to personalize God and *know* him instead of just living morally in the hope of heaven. But Christianity prides itself on the Person and love of God –the God who loved us so much he sent his son to die for us. Do you think it's wrong of me to ask questions instead of just trusting?"

"You have to ask questions if you're ever going to think for yourself," Kurt said. "There's nothing wrong with doubt. It paves the way to greater understanding."

"Do you think I'm evil?"

He laughed. "No. Do you?"

"I mean, not 'evil,' exactly. But do you think I'm a hypocrite?"

"Was Solomon a hypocrite?"

"No."

"Because that's how I see you–"

"–super wise and blessed by God?"

He smiled. "I was going to say, I think you're trying to live life and figure it out. That's a good thing."

I realized I'd been asking the same questions, just worded differently, for a long time –even before going to the school back east. I thought back to the first time a guy I was seeing started to unzip my pants. I'd taken his hand and moved it up and away, and as I quietly withdrew myself from his grasp, I realized I wasn't thinking about God. I was thinking about two things and two things only –getting pregnant and what my family would think. This was a revelation to me. Could it be that I had nothing but a *form* of godliness, an empty set of do's and don'ts? When it came to faith and actions, it seemed to me that people sometimes confused which was the cause and which the effect. I wanted to know God more fully –to talk with him as I would with a friend, a family member, or a teacher ... as a real person. I wanted to talk and know he heard me and to hear him back. If I was sincere about anything it was this.

But my questions were only growing. I talked to everyone whose conviction I admired. I implored them. I listened. But the questions continued. Not that I was without faith. Even while I envied the conviction of others, I believed. But their faith seemed like something beyond my reach. Or, perhaps, like something that was slipping through my fingers –my grip loosened by my need to know the how's and why's of a world in which "good" and "evil" seemed as much a creation of man's intellect as they did part of a divine plan.

I didn't doubt my salvation. Not exactly. I had consciously chosen to surrender my life to God years before. But I wondered sometimes if I had all the facts. And to think how many people I was told were dying in agony for eternity because they didn't have what I supposedly had –what I had and couldn't even feel.

# Chapter 4

A week after I got back from Christmas break, I had my first meeting as an "RA," or Resident Assistant. The title felt funny to me since I didn't see myself as an "authority" figure. I hadn't planned on applying until Kurt said, "You should. We need someone like you. Someone who's kind, fun, and approachable. You've got that nurturing quality that makes people feel welcome and safe."

"Oh, stop," I said. "You had me at 'you should.'"

He stopped by my room after the meeting to ask if I was okay. "You've been quiet," he said, and I stared up at him, wondering what he meant and what to say and thinking, my goodness, he cares, at least a little. Personally, I didn't think I'd been all that quiet at the meeting, and I wondered if he meant I'd been quiet towards him. I told him I was fine.

"Well, if you ever want to talk ..." His eyes were intent, and I wanted more than anything for them to see me, to see everything, because I knew, I *knew*, he would understand. That he already did understand. He understood what it was like to be different, to move around and never quite fit in, to get close, but not that close, to feel restless while craving stability, to have questions you couldn't answer, and for this to be as exciting as it was disturbing.

"Thanks," I said.

"There are some things we need to talk about," he said, and instantly my head raced with the possibilities. I waited, afraid to do anything that might scare him off. He looked timid just then. Or maybe not timid so much as fully absorbed in thoughts that were welling up just beneath the surface –thoughts on the verge of spilling out into the shared open space between us. A minute more and I'd see them –I was sure of it.

Yoshi laughed suddenly from inside the room –a staccato interruption that shattered the fragile stillness surrounding us. He and Keiko were perched on her bed, flipping through Japanese magazines and completely absorbed in each other.

Kurt leaned forward, enough to see around the door. He spied them and in an instant his demeanor changed. All emotion fled, and his confiding air turned into one of rigid formality.

"Well, I'll be seeing you."

"No wait!" I wanted to say. Wanted to, but didn't. "Don't go," I wanted to plead. "What were you going to say? What is it we need to talk about?" But he was already drifting away down the length of the hall and about to disappear into his room. He waved, briefly, and then his door shut behind him.

I closed my door and stood there, feeling like I'd just lost something precious.

My growing feelings for Kurt unnerved me, and when I confided in Keiko later that evening, I hated how awkward and vulnerable I felt. She gazed at me sympathetically. Finally, I took a deep breath, looked around the room, and then, trying to sound neutral, I asked, "Do you think I should I go see him? Or am I being ridiculous?"

When Keiko didn't immediately respond, I began to think I was reading far too much into Kurt's visit. I thought Keiko's silence meant she agreed, but then she made a soft *hmm* sound, and I looked up to see her toying with a little teddy bear.

"I don't know," Keiko said gently, "but maybe sometimes I want to go out with somebody, but since I am shy, I have a hard time asking. I know how hard it is to invite myself to things or to reach out. Maybe Kurt feels this way too?"

"So you think I should go see him?" I asked, feeling instantly hopeful.

"Yes."

That weekend, nerves humming, I walked down the hall to his room and knocked at his door. His face glowed, and I basked in his warmth as I followed him in. Settling onto his couch, we began talking. Not about why he had stopped by my room earlier, or why I had come that evening, but instead about the places we'd been, the people we'd met, and what had fascinated us about each. Soon we were laughing and sharing our thoughts on religion, our families, and all that amused, irritated, and moved us. The hours flowed by until night blackened the windows, emphasizing the bright interior as we leaned toward one another in animated conversation. I soaked in everything about him, feeling captivated, entranced, and entirely comfortable. I felt as though I could discuss anything with him –openly, honestly, and without judgement.

As we were talking, I looked up to find him staring at me. No, not *at* me, but *into* me. And in such a way that I saw him too. My heart began pounding as something deep within me stirred. I forgot what I was talking about. I forgot everything except him. And those eyes. Those deep, warm, brown eyes.

Emotion flooded my chest with such intensity that I should have felt elated. I should have been thrilled at everything contained within that one look. Defenses down, souls bared, here at last was the closeness I'd been craving. And in that instant, the connection slipped as the warmth inside me gave way to an icy terror.

I looked away, first to my hands, then at the black windows. I looked for something to say but was at a loss. I left shortly after that and once I was away and out of his room, the distance that grew with every footstep restored my courage, and I wanted to say, *Please, have patience –I won't always be so afraid.* But whatever he thought, whatever he might have seen in me, was as yet a mystery, and I felt I had little choice but to wait until time revealed all or distanced us completely.

THE SNOW STARTED ON a Saturday. A guy named Alex and I decided to hike up to the greenhouse in Capital Hill's Volunteer Park. Alex's room was across the hall from mine, and we'd hung out a few times before. With his solid build and dimpled grin, he had a good-natured charm that balanced his brooding artistic genius.

As we walked, tiny snowflakes swirled around our heads and cooled my warm face. Soon there was enough accumulation on the tops of cars for the two of us to throw at each other. Our walk up the hill that led over the interstate left my heart pounding and my cheeks flushed. Alex's too were pink and happy. I laughed as I ducked away from another sailing snowball. Enchantment flowed around us, up the street, over ivy-covered stairways and around the cute, little houses. Alex's affection was there too, and I didn't know what to do with it. *Friendship only*, I thought, I begged, I pleaded. But didn't say aloud.

Inside the greenhouse everything was cozy, bright, and humming with vitality. Condensation gathered on the windows as I ran my fingertips over everything –every leaf, flower, and cactus spike. I made Alex touch them too. He didn't need much encouragement, being physical by nature. I watched him, fascinated by his moving hands. I wanted those hands to feel what I felt, to feel more, to feel me. I wanted to stand before him and explore and be explored. But it would have been for sensation only, detached, and devoid of emotion. I couldn't do that to him. So I kept myself just out of reach.

"Why won't you look people in the eye?" he asked. It wasn't the first time a guy had asked me that. "What are you afraid of?"

"I'm not afraid of anything. I just can't."

56

But he wouldn't let it go, so I said, "Maybe I *am* afraid. Not so much of what I'll see, but of giving too much away. That my thoughts'll be read." I was thinking about the time a guy in Arizona had asked me the same question. He was always asking that and "what are you thinking about?" I hated it. I'd turn my head away and say, "Nothing." After all, how could I confess, "The truth is, I find you shallow and temporary, but I'm curious."

This was hard for me to admit even to myself —that I could let somebody hold me and kiss my neck the way that guy did when I cared nothing for him. My skin ached for the touch of his warm hands and the feel of his body casually pressed up against mine while we watched movies sprawled on the couch in his parents' basement. We went to church together, and his parents knew mine. We'd hung out a couple times. I was between schools and lonely, and he was okay company. So, when his hand brushed mine, and he sat close, I let him. When his hand travelled too far, I redirected it to a "safer" area. Nothing sexual. Just sensual. I was like a ghost materializing just long enough to feel something before slipping back away into another world, a world apart.

I once read a comic strip called Wildwood that featured a bear with a fishing pole clutching a catfish who insisted, "All life is **sacred**." To which the bear replied, "Some of it is also **delicious**." I wondered if that's what I was doing —tasting life at the expense of those around me.

I didn't want to do that with Alex. I didn't want to lead him on —using him to feel something physical, and physical only. Alex was sweet and sensitive, and looking for more than what I could offer. I told myself to be careful.

"THAT IS NOT PHOTOGRAPHY!" Yoshi fumed one day after our Product Photography class. Moments before, our teacher had dispassionately described the next assignment in which we were to create a still-life of an old tool placed inside a box. "His examples made me want to vomit!" Yoshi followed this with an angry combination of spitting and swearing that lasted the whole walk back to the dorm.

I loved watching Yoshi when he got worked up. With him there was no middle ground –he was either completely for something or all against it– and there was never any doubt as to where he stood.

"Classes like this make me want to leave," he said, still shaking his head and spitting a little as we neared my room. "There is no *life* in this assignment. If we could use *anything* –a fish, an object, something other than a *tool* for our still-life– then *maybe* I wouldn't mind."

"Something with personality," I said, opening my door and throwing my bag at the foot of my bed.

"Exactly! And you know what I'd shoot? I'd shoot a dildo!" His laugh ricocheted around the room.

His suggestion shocked me, but only momentarily.

"Oh, you should!" I said. "It is a *tool* after all. Oh, Yoshi, you have to –can you imagine his reaction?! *Everyone's* reaction."

"I could give it to you –when I'm finished." He cocked his head to one side, eyes bright.

My cheeks instantly flamed, and I shook my head, saying quickly, "No, thanks."

"Haha! You Americans," Yoshi said, "so shy when it comes to talking about sex."

"What are you talking about? Sex is everywhere."

"Yes, but you act as if it's dirty."

As if it's *sinful*, I thought.

"People are just animals," he said.

"We have a conscience and self-control. We should use them."

"*Use* them," Yoshi echoed, and he laughed again. "Sex is like eating. People need it."

"But even unrestrained eating is unhealthy," I said. "And besides, what about love?"

"Haha! Love! That's just a word we use to elevate our selection methods when we find a mate. Women are looking for strong, attractive men to procreate with and when they find them, they say they're 'in love.' But it's just procreation, which we need to survive as a species."

"I think it's more than that," I said. "I can find someone who I think is attractive, who's smart and would make a good father –but even knowing all this I might feel nothing inside. I've met guys who would've been 'perfect' mates on an evolutionary scale, but nothing inside me responded. I know love exists. I've seen it in others –the way it lights up their faces. The way it makes them laugh and sacrifice their own desires for that of the other person."

"But people change. And so do 'emotions.'" He said the last word as if it meant nothing. "I think you won't always be in love with someone. At first, yes, it's exciting. And then you get used to someone; you get familiar; you get bored. Then you'll want a divorce."

"At times, maybe. But love is a *commitment*, Yoshi, a decision to stay."

"What if he cheats on you?"

"Then ... I'll be crushed, and the trust'll be gone. But I think yes, I'll still love him."

"What if he wants a divorce?"

"I don't know. Depends on the circumstances. But even if we split up, I think I'd still love him. Love is unconditional."

"Society says not."

"That's hardly a valid reference point. People fall in love with love, not always knowing the person they marry."

Yoshi's smile radiated amusement, as though he found my naivety adorable. I smiled back, defiant, and even raised my chin a little as I declared, "I refuse, Yoshi, I refuse to give up my faith in love."

"With one person?"

"Yes. There may be a 'right' person at different points in our lives, but once the commitment is made, it's for life."

Yoshi sighed. "I wish I could live in your ideal world."

"And I wish you weren't so jaded."

"DO YOU EVER FEEL AMORAL?" I asked Kurt one night.

He considered for a moment before responding with a half grin, "All the time."

"It's weird," I said, ignoring his teasing tone, "I don't feel immoral –like I've done anything wrong– but I feel amoral, as if everything that's considered good and bad is somehow arbitrary, with most of us following the prescribed moral code only to secure the outcome we desire. Not that there aren't absolutes when it comes to right and wrong, but I wonder sometimes how much of it is social etiquette, rules meant to keep our behavior nice, safe, and orderly?" I looked up at him, briefly. I'd grown up picturing my choices as doors. Hand on the knob, I'd hesitate before each, considering, while a voice in my head rang out, "Be careful! The consequences could be eternal." It left me terrified of making a mistake. But this voice didn't feel like my conscience. It didn't feel like the voice of God either. It felt like an impulse spawned by fear and guilt. Something in me was beginning to resist, not as an act of rebellion against either God or my conscience, but as a desire to be free from the constant terror of my own inescapable fallibility. Without the anchoring weight of fear and guilt though, I felt breathless and untethered.

"I don't like feeling this way," I said, "–as though I could do *anything,* and it wouldn't matter, not really." I was thinking of things, terrible things –like taking the health and happiness of another into my hands and holding them there with a sort of detached curiosity, maybe even squeezing a little.

He studied me for what felt like a long time.

"What have you done that makes you feel amoral?"

I wanted to say, "*Nothing* –it's just a feeling," since nothing specific came to mind. But then I paused and thought of Alex. Had I been toying with his feelings? Or with the feelings of others? I was trying to be careful. And anyway, this feeling of amorality didn't seem like the result of guilt over something I'd already done. It seemed instead to accompany the freedom that tugged at me, pulling me away from a morally safe place. I was standing on a threshold –inside which every devout believer abides– looking out, and I wasn't afraid. I felt as though I could just ... step out. And it was my incredible nonchalance over what I'd always imagined would be such a huge move that puzzled me. Did it mean I loved God less, or believed in myself more? Or did it mean nothing –was it all just *nothing*?

Kurt kept on, apparently intent on eliciting some sort of confession. He began casually listing immoral activities, slowly narrowing them down, and I watched the whole predictable process with growing impatience. I could see it all over his face –he wanted to talk about Sex.

"So," he asked finally, "are you fooling around with anybody?"

Had it been anyone else I wouldn't have bothered with a reply. Just the words "fooling around" annoyed me, like he was asking if I was doing something stupid and my whole point was that I was thinking about everything, trying to do the smart thing.

"No. Of course not," I said, leaning back and feeling bored at the direction we were headed. "But when I had the opportunity, I knew that if I had done it, I wouldn't have felt guilty. And that's my point —I didn't think about God or heaven or hell. All I thought about was my family, pregnancy, and that it'd be one less thing I could give my husband on my wedding night."

He breathed out softly through his nose, obviously amused, but said nothing.

"Go ahead," I said, smiling, "tell me I'm 'quaint.' It wouldn't be the first time."

He shook his head. "You have your values. I respect that."

"Part of me was curious though. But I had no feelings for the guy."

"An emotional connection is essential. But you know, most of the world sees nothing wrong with sex before marriage," he said. "Physical contact is a good thing. People *need* it."

Within the right bounds, I wanted to say. I knew touch was a good thing. A necessary thing. And I craved it. Kellie told me an anecdote once about two people on a bus. A man gets on first, takes a seat. Then a woman gets on. The bus is crowded, so she sits next to the man. Each has a completely different life. Each will go a completely different direction. But when their arms touch, neither moves, although both are conscious of the contact. A couple stops later, some passengers get off, opening up several seats, but the two stay where they are. They keep on touching. Arm to arm. Finally, the bus comes to the woman's stop, and they part ways. Neither spoke a word, or even glanced at the other, but each *needed* the touch. Unspoken dependency.

So many people are reaching out. Or wanting to. But I didn't tell Kurt this. I didn't say anything. I just smiled back at him. I didn't want to be talking about touch, or sex, exactly. I wanted to talk about how I felt I could do anything, and nothing would change –not heaven or hell or the good that lay within me. I knew being "good" had nothing to do with getting into heaven, but I felt a strange and growing freedom –and the apathy that had replaced the magnitude surrounding this freedom worried me. I was beginning not to care what I did. I wanted to experience life –to taste it and see what it all meant. I wanted to study people and sensations and explore the interactions between them. I wanted to lean forward over the table toward Kurt, so close we could feel the heat of each other on our cheeks, and whisper into his ear, "Of course we *need* it. But is experience how we truly live, or is it how we die? Why don't you come up to my tower, and we'll figure it out together?" But I didn't. I just sat there, and we stared at each other.

ONE SUNDAY LATE IN March, when spring was everywhere and glorious, I accompanied a guy named Terrence to his church in Bremerton. On the ferry ride over, we discussed the photo shoot of him we were planning to do after the service. He was putting together a modeling portfolio, and already I was posing him in my mind, eager to capture the expressive arc of his eyebrows, the curve of his mouth, the warm hues of his skin, the easy grace of his build.

"You'll be back by three," he told me. "And, just so you know, my church can be a little, uh … *overwhelming* for people who aren't used to it. Let me know if it gets to be too much."

I waved him off. I'd been to a *lot* of churches, with each possessing their own unique style. As far as I was concerned, this would be just one more experience.

I was unprepared.

The enthusiasm his church exuded entered through the soles of my feet and set my bones to humming. My red hair and pale skin drew attention, but the faces turned toward me were kind, if curious. I listened as the slow rhythm of handclapping and foot-tapping picked up speed, and I felt the magnificent pulse of the church infuse everything and everyone until even the pen and paper I'd left lying on my seat jumped to the beat. People took turns stepping out into the center aisle, arms raised and faces exultant while everyone smiled their benevolence on them. The choir leader danced her way to the end of the stage and back, then up and down the aisle, clapping her thick hands and beaming as the rich alto of her voice filled the room. I clapped too, and heard my own voice rise and get lost in the cloud of sound swirling above our heads.

Over the next hour, Terry looked over a few times, eyebrows raised, to see how I was doing. I nodded and smiled my reassurance. The tempo was, after all, invigorating –even if everything seemed to be stuck on repeat, as though that moment in time was skipping a little on the great universal record player of life. Still, I felt conspicuous. More than the whiteness of my skin, my inability to clap on time and to move my feet beyond a shuffle made me feel ever the awkward outsider. I tried to surrender to the rhythm pounding its way through my body but became distracted by the little girls mimicking the throes of spiritual ecstasy enveloping most of the women at the front of the room.

Terrence leaned over. "How you doing? You okay?"

"Yeah," I said. "Of course." I smiled again, wanting to put him at ease.

He looked around before leaning over again and whispering, "You know, I'm kinda worried that people are going to think we're dating, or something."

"Oh?" I said, laughing.

"Yeah. A lot of people here would have a really hard time with me dating a white girl."

I looked around. "Well ... we're not."

"I know. But they might *think* it."

The current song seemed like it was winding down and my heart was beginning to beat on its own again so we both focused our attention up front. The pastor came forward and stood before his congregation, smiling and nodding his head as he let the rhythm and mood fade to the point where he could transition from song to sermon. In the brief stillness, I could hear a faint ringing in my ears. The pastor looked around and in a calm and confident manner started laying out what was on his mind. Over the next half hour, he described the power of God and the beauty of knowing the "height, depth, and width" of his divine love. After lingering a while on these verses, he walked to the side of the podium, leaned on it with one arm, and, with a sad shake of his head, informed us all that we each had someone keeping us from fully grasping the power and knowledge of God's love. Who was this enemy? Not to worry –he had a picture. At this, two elders on either side of the room whipped out mirrors, which they held high for all to see.

"*This*!" the pastor said in a booming voice, "... *This* is the enemy within!"

The room erupted as people stood, clapped, and shouted their agreement.

"We are strong. We are loved. We are loving!" he chanted, and everyone shouted it back to him.

"For God so loved us, he gave his life!"

"Gave his life!" we echoed.

"As God's children we conqueror all!"

"Conqueror all!"

As his voice rang out, he moved through the room, occasionally placing his hand on a woman's forehead. At his touch, each woman convulsed violently until two ladies came, carrying a white sheet which they wrapped around her before leading her to a front-row chair. There she'd sit, alongside the others, until calm. They took turns entering this paroxysm of rapture, and one of the little girls I saw earlier –she couldn't have been more than four– was right up there with them, her tiny limbs perfectly matching each spasm with ardent abandon.

Terrence kept asking me if I was okay, despite my insistence that I was fine.

"I may not be able to hold a beat, but I'm loving it," I told him, happily absorbed with what was for me a cultural, if not a spiritual, experience.

Afterwards, I sat waiting on the curb outside while Terrence made the rounds assuring everyone I was only a friend. I considered how culture influences belief and the behavior born from that belief. At the school back east, it was the most natural thing in the world to infuse every conversation with, "I'm praying for you" and "God bless!" and "Praise God!" This was how we showed that we were thinking about the other person –sharing either their concern or excitement. But at art school, and even some churches I'd been to, such phrases would've come off as incongruous or pretentious.

I wondered again just where the line lay between morality and behavior born solely out of what was deemed socially acceptable. Showing one's ankles, wearing a hat, not wearing a hat, eating certain foods –these past indiscretions now go unremarked. Swearing, alcohol, and premarital sex are inconsequential acts to some, but to others, enough to transform the embraced into the excommunicated. Where were the absolutes? Even as I sat there wanting so much to set aside the judgments of myself and others, I wondered if I was only rationalizing.

## THE CREOSOTE BUSH

Terrence returned then, and we proceeded with the photo shoot. By evening I was on a photography high. Nothing more was said of the church, and our ferry ride back to Seattle was relaxed and quiet.

# Chapter 5

I hurt Alex.

   –enough for him to slam the elevator door so hard my entire hall echoed with the sound.

Would it be meaningless to say I didn't mean to?

He'd been calling more, giving me a hard time when I didn't come over or call him for any reason other than to invite him to soccer on Sundays. He'd also been getting more physical. I rather liked the feel of his arms around me. I liked the way his arm would reach slowly up and over my back as we lay on the floor watching movies. He'd slide his arm under my shirt and along the surface of my skin, until his warm hand came to rest on my stomach. I lay there, my back pressed up against his chest and neither of us paying much attention to the movie. Closing my eyes, I felt my skin come alive, and I soaked up his warmth as the light from the television danced on my lids.

Be careful, be careful!– my mind told me. *But it doesn't* mean *anything,* I argued. It does to him. *But he's a guy, and guys like touch. Harmless.* Back then, my curiosity was wrapped up in the naïve delusion that someone like Alex couldn't be hurt. After all, I thought, he wasn't interested in me. Not really. He just wanted sensation too. Somewhere (was it a product of my upbringing –bestowed by my protective brothers, a word of caution given by my parents, something picked up from books or church or TV? I don't know, and it doesn't really matter), somewhere I had picked up the notion that most guys were only interested in sex. I had safe-guarded myself against this. I had sworn to myself that I would never be unconsciously used. It never occurred to me that I might become what I had hoped to avoid in others. We weren't going to sleep together, after all. I felt that so long as I didn't cross that line, we were both safe. And morally intact. Touch, in and of itself, wasn't wrong, I reasoned. And the whisper that I was playing with another's emotions was drowned out by the thought we both wanted the same thing –to connect briefly.

I was careless, but not malicious.

Alex was sweet and fun and cute, but I couldn't talk with him the way I could talk with Kurt. Alex's mind, though deep and dark and beautiful, was preoccupied with things foreign to me. When my mind's eye imagined us together ten years down the road it pictured a life in which he was caught up in sports and beer and thwacking me on the butt, all while kidding me in a way that would make me feel like a child, even when he'd mean it good-naturedly. I'd be expected to provide snacks for him and his buddies during hockey season, and when I'd bring up a book I was reading he'd kiss me like I was adorable, and then blow me off. In short, I felt as though we'd gradually lose everything in common. As though I'd have to lose myself to be with him or sacrifice our relationship to remain myself.

He came over on a Friday night as I was making dinner. I stood in front of the stove while he paced back and forth behind me, a caged animal with power and beauty in the fluid energy of his movements. I liked the sensual heat of him, the surety of his movements. When he started giving me playful jabs, I turned around to face him with both fists up.

"You'll break your thumbs like that," he said with a teasing smile. His hands covered mine as he pried my fists open. I clenched them tighter to make him try harder and watched the points of his mouth pull up unconsciously. His eyes shot to mine, and I quickly looked back down at how his fingers were closing my hands into fists, thumbs on the outside. As soon as he released me, I punched him in the arm, and he stepped back with a surprised laugh.

"Exactly. Just like that. Wait, ow! No, like this," and he grabbed my fist again and moved it back to a different starting position. There was light in his blue eyes. I fought the urge to tackle him in a bear hug –my resistance increasing my desire to touch, to feel, to use, to take and take and take. I turned my back on him abruptly and grabbed a pair of plates.

We ate quickly, before putting in a movie and throwing some pillows on the floor. The palm of his hand was so warm –his fingers strong and deft as they traced the skin along my arms, my hands, my back, and belly. I felt his arm, the muscles beneath, and the outlines of his hand, our fingers intertwining and pulling apart and revolving around and around. Touching. I lay pressed up against him, comfortable, relaxed, feeling the weight of life and flesh and blood and energy in his heat. It felt good. The human body was so beautiful. Capable of feeling so much. The *body*.

But the *heart* ... now that's a different matter.

I felt it coming, again.

"Why won't you look at me?" His voice was soft –a warm whisper in my ear.

"I just can't," I said just as softly, hoping my words would fade away and take his question with them.

"I know I'm not that nice to look at–"

"No, it's not that –not that at all." I gave him a quick sideways smile. His blue eyes were glowing with a deep brilliance.

"Is it because I'm Montanian?"

I laughed. "No."

He tilted his head down, trying to get me to look at him. I took a deep breath and sighed. "I just can't get close to people, that's all."

A heartbeat later, he abruptly straightened. "Well, I've got news for you –you're pretty fucking close!"

My mind raced. "That's not what I meant."

"In every way that matters." His voice was growing more serious, insistent. "So why can't you look at me?"

"I ..." I wanted to change the subject. I wanted to forget about this and just go back to feeling the warmth of his hands, instead of the heat of an interrogation. "... I just can't," I finished lamely. Why couldn't he understand that and let it rest?

"Can't, or won't? What are you afraid of? Are you afraid of being real?"

"No. I'm afraid of being fake."

And there it was.

"*What*?" He pushed back from me suddenly. "Are you being fake –is that what this is?"

"No, no, not at all," I said, backtracking as quickly as I could. "I meant in general –I never want to be fake. I want more than anything to be real."

"So what is this?" He stared with such intense directness that I knew he was seeing right through me. And it hurt.

"I don't know what to say." I was ashamed. "It's always been like this for me."

"You've never been close to anyone –outside your family?"

I thought about it. I really did. "I don't know. I don't think so."

"Not in the last two years?"

"No, definitely not."

"So, there's no emotional involvement?" And still he stared. I wanted to brush his gaze off my shoulder the way I would a dry leaf, or a piece of lent.

"It's not that," I said, feeling sheepish and guilty and not wanting to hurt him while realizing I was doing just that, and worse.

"If you feel nothing then that's exactly what it is." He shook his head, still in disbelief. "And if no one gets close, then you're just using them."

He ignored my protests. "You're treating people like toys, Ani."

"I don't know what to say. What do you want me to say?" I felt a helpless desperation expanding inside my chest, making it difficult to breathe.

"I want to hear what you have to say. I mean, I can't believe you could let me hold you like that when you feel *nothing*."

So it was true: I was a cold, heartless person. But still I argued with myself. Did every touch have to *mean* something? Did I have to be in love with someone to enjoy the way their body felt next to mine? Even as I asked myself these questions, I knew the answer. I should never have let him do as much as he did. I should have let the surface of my skin sleep –safe from outside stimulation. I should have protected him, kept his heart safe from my inner coldness. I had known this would happen. I had told myself to be careful. Instead, I'd been greedy with his affections.

"It's not fair, you know," he said to me, "never letting people in. Not telling them anything about yourself. What kind of life is that going to be?"

"I don't think it will always be like that." I was thinking to myself that I just needed to find the right one, that was all. And Alex was not, and never would be, the right one for me.

"It will be until you let someone in. So why don't you?"

"It doesn't work like that. I can't help it."

"That's the stupidest thing I've ever heard."

How could I explain to him? How could I get him to stop looking at me as though I were some sort of monster?

I offered up an analogy –one where hearts are rivers. Some people wear theirs on their sleeves –easy to get in and out of. Others have theirs just under the surface where the roots of friendship reach it easily. But in my case, I told him, my heart was so far beneath the surface that few ever reached it. "But those that do are there for good and to remove them would be the same as ripping out a part of me."

Alex got up. He walked over to the chair where his jacket was hanging and pulled it on. At the door, he paused and put an arm out. I leaned in and hugged him, with something like a plea, but he didn't respond. He was just making a general gesture.

"If your analogy is true," he said, "then a lot of hearts are going to get hurt in the process."

He would've slammed the door had I not caught it. I jumped a moment later when I heard the resounding bang of the elevator door.

I sank onto the floor. Oh, Alex, I thought. Sweet and sensitive Alex. How could I see the hurt in his deep blue eyes and still feel nothing except sorry for him, and angry with myself? No other stirring in response to his affection. Only a vague empathy –the condescension of which was insulting to us both. It was true –I had knowingly used him. This awareness was the source of my shame, and it resided solely in my head, and no lower.

I wondered what it would be like to feel something inside. I'd had boyfriends, but always managed to keep them at a distance until, finally, I'd start hating that distance and break up just because I didn't know what else to do. One guy asked if I'd been abused, which surprised me, although probably it shouldn't have. No, I'd said, I think it's just because I've said good-bye to everyone I've ever known, except my family, and now I see every relationship as temporary. I told myself later that this would all change once I met *the One* –my "Mr. Right"– and that in the meantime I could still be friends. I could still engage Alex and the others verbally, if not emotionally. The problem then was that all my connections were only surface deep, with me selfishly taking far more than I was giving. The way

Alex had looked at me when he realized this showed me the ugliness of my deception. Had our roles been reversed I'd be just as hurt and pissed off as he was. *What had I done?*

Not only that, but what was I doing to myself? To my faith? My faith was the one thing I thought would never change. And now ... was it diluted or dying? Both were equally bad. Was I drowning out my conscience too? Was it, even now, becoming insensitive? Or was there in truth nothing –or no One– to stimulate it? I felt like the Lady of Shallot –bound by the threat of a curse to busy her fingers with needlework, with her only view of the world being a mere reflection in her mirror. I grew up with the assurance that boundaries were for my own protection –a safe perimeter within which I should live. And, like the Lady of Shallot, venturing beyond this perimeter to interact with the world beyond would mean my death –physical and eternal. So, I was compelled for my own good to stay within my sheltered existence.

But was I so wrong to want to look out my window and see for myself the world below? To want to feel what others felt, to *live* as others lived? Was it so wrong?

*"I'm half-sick of shadows," she said ...*

I was missing the point, of course. My body confessed what my mind preferred to ignore. Nausea rose and spread from deep within my stomach after Alex left. It could be anything, nothing, I thought. But I knew better. My subconscious had been shouting out the message through my dreams –the offense lay in my failure to be straightforward. Touch, in and of itself, was a beautiful thing. But never at the expense of another. I was so hung up on sex and avoiding it to preserve my virtue that I was ignoring my true transgression, dishonesty.

Perhaps I *should* stay in my tower with its sheltered existence, I thought. Or was it too late ... was the curse already upon me? I shuddered when I remembered something Nietzsche once wrote:

"The path to every kind of vice and knavishness is a slow one proceeded along step by step. He who walks it is, by the time he reaches its end, wholly free of the insect swarms of the bad conscience and, although wholly infamous, he nonetheless goes in innocence."

ONCE, YEARS EARLIER, when Neva and I were walking to the university dining hall one day in South Carolina, skirts swishing and shoes click-tapping, I looked over at her.

"What?" she asked.

"It's just, everyone's always asking why suffering exists or how can a good God let bad things happen. And the answer they always give is that suffering exists because of sin, like it's some great sickness. And it is, definitely. But ... sin *had* to exist. It couldn't *not* exist."

"Are you saying that because it gives people freedom of choice –free will?"

"Yeah, but, more than that. Even if Adam and Eve had chosen not to eat the apple, sin would have entered the world another way. It had to."

"Why do you say that?"

"Because we know everything by contrast. Adam and Eve never fully knew or appreciated what they had until they lost it –even though they had perfection. We love our health most when we've been sick. We lose someone we love and we'd give anything for just one more moment with them. And yet we don't even notice the hours, months, days slipping by when we're with them. We never fully appreciate *anything* as much as when we're about to lose it. And it's not enough to hear about it or even to see another person's pain or joy or love or suffering. We understand most fully when we experience it for ourselves. And when we get back what we've lost, we cling to it, rejoice in it. For a while anyway. Light and dark, good and bad –the contrast is how we experience and understand –and *value*– everything. Without shadows we wouldn't be able to see. Without sensation, we wouldn't be able to feel. Without sin and suffering, we'd have no idea how good we have it, even if what we have is perfect."

Neva considered this for a moment before saying, "In one of my classes we were just talking about how the Platonists believed that evil isn't a thing in and of itself, but an absence of good. A corruption of it, kind of like a sickness but more like a separation. Or privation. It makes sense to me that the farther we are from God, who is the Ultimate Good, the worse we'd feel. But still, even if this separation was bound to happen, are you really saying you think God *made* it happen?"

"No. I don't know. I just think we'd never have fully understood or appreciated anything without it. So in that sense evil was necessary."

"Evil is evil. The sooner we're free from it, the better."

"Oh, I agree."

"Although, honestly, I'm surprised there's not more suffering."

"Why's that?"

"This world is corrupt."

"Yeah, it's corrupt. But it's beautiful too. And that's just it: the pain and the beauty, the joy and the suffering –each makes us feel the other so much more."

"So you *want* to suffer?"

"Not really, no. I'm a wimp. But I see its value. You?"

"Ask me after the fact." She leaned into me and smiled.

"I'm just glad for the friends who make it easier," I said.

She wrapped her arm around my shoulders and squeezed.

"Yeah," she said, laughing, "me too."

# Chapter 6

There is nothing quite like springtime in Seattle. Everyone walks around in a state of bliss. You can almost hear the energy racing through the streets and up the trees, across the rooftops and out into the wind where the current catches stray wisps of hair and infuses the mind and body until every heart suddenly starts pounding out a joyful rhythm.

I thought I would explode with the restlessness building up inside me. I wanted *more*.

After a camping trip with Keiko and Yoshi, I rushed to tell Kurt all about it. I described with waving hands what it was like to ride in a car with someone who's only ever driven on the left side of the road and how the three of us had played freeze-tag in the moonlight. I told him about trying to start a fire with wet wood, which was all there was, and how Keiko and I had blown at the tiny, timid flame until we were dizzy and choking on the thick, white smoke while in the background Yoshi kept insisting that we should "just add more lighter fluid."

As my words tumbled out, I watched the light play in Kurt's eyes. In that moment, I could almost believe his was more than a casual interest –that the corners of his mouth were pulled up by invisible strings held by me. Caution quickly stifled my happiness, and I left his office, puzzled by my feelings for him.

He once told me, "To know you is to love you." Despite the offhand way he said it, I didn't hear anything else after that. I was stuck on that phrase –it meant everything ... and nothing.

Every now and then he would say "we" or "us," and my ears always caught on the words. Like the time I mentioned seeing some art I thought he might enjoy, and he said, "You should have picked us up some."

Us. The word represented a place where I longed more and more to be. I felt he was inviting me there, unsure of it himself but toying with the idea, but I didn't know how to cross that threshold and find him ... find the "us."

While talking a few days later, lunchtime rolled around and when I got up to leave, he asked if he could take me out to eat. My heart zigzagged ahead of us like a happy little chickadee the whole way to the Dragonfish, a sparkling restaurant several blocks away from school and the formality of his office. I was prepared not to care, already accepting that it might not mean anything.

Once settled at our table, I studied the menu for a moment before glancing around. Would it matter if someone from school saw us? Beyond that one time with Keiko, I hadn't told anyone at school about my interest in him. Who would I tell? Most of my friends were guys who at one point or another had wanted more from me. Even Katrianna, a girl I discussed nearly everything else with, had confided how she wanted to set Kurt up with her mother. After that, I was too embarrassed to confess my feelings for him. And now, what if someone did recognize me and Kurt? Would they see us as a couple or as a student having lunch with her Resident Director?

Between bites, Kurt and I described our ideal birthdays. At his mention of a future wife, girlfriend, lover –I couldn't help it, I imagined myself in that role. He described his childhood and how a scholarship to study art at a prep school had pulled him out of the projects. "Art," he laughed, anticipating my questioning glance, "–exactly. But at the time I was into it, and it got me out of there."

Watching his eyes dart playfully about, I stared at him with what must have been blatant infatuation. I leaned forward, wanting to soak in every bit of himself that he was willing to share.

That night, while laying on my bed replaying our time together, moment by moment, I realized that I was afraid –terrified, actually– to surrender to my happiness. Here was someone whose opinions mattered to me and with whom I desperately wanted to be close, but a growing self-doubt was beginning to restrict my words and movements. What if I was wrong about him, and we were horrible together? What if I made a mistake? Feelings shouldn't be so complicated. Either you care, or you don't. I had to stop suffocating my emotions with incessant over-analyzing. What I wanted most was to let go and enjoy the moment, for however long it lasted.

LATE ONE NIGHT, I STOOD in the rectangle of light spilling out from the dormitory doors onto the sidewalk. Turning away from the bright lobby, I looked back into the shadowy streets with their glittering lights and loneliness and freedom. The night called and my feet itched to head back out into the cool, clear darkness, even though it was nearly midnight. Everything was so peaceful, and the streets were growing more and more deserted in a way that invited exploration.

Kurt's light shone from the top-floor corner window. Maybe he would walk with me. Two minutes later, I stood before his door, breathless. At my knock, he cracked it open, phone pressed to his ear. "Just a minute," he said, peering out at me, "let me get some clothes on."

Once off the phone he invited me in and showed me two shirts. "This one? Or ... this one?" He held a blue and brown plaid one against his chest before looking at me more closely. "Wait, are you on duty tonight? Does this have to do with work?"

"No, I just came from school, but the night is so gorgeous and eerie that I feel like I need to go walking. I'm so restless. You want to come?"

"My feet are sore," he said with a note of apology. "But here, have a seat."

He led me to the small kitchen table next to the window. Almost instantly he jumped up again and asked what I wanted to drink. He brought over cranberry juice with club soda, crackers, and caviar. I leaned over the little round jar and stared down at the tiny black diamonds with curiosity and delight.

"You've never had caviar?" he asked.

"No."

"Well, here you go then," he said, handing me a cracker.

"Oh, they *pop*!" I said, laughing around my first bite. "And they're so salty!"

He grinned, eyes shining and happy, and I asked him about his day. The minutes stretched and unfolded into a half hour, an hour, and more as we talked.

At one point, we began discussing what we found creepy.

"That guy in your chess club," Kurt said, "*he's* creepy."

"Yeah. And he's really touchy too," I said, grimacing. The guy had practically tackled me in the stairwell. Just when I was about to kick his shins, he finally let go.

"I don't like how he acts around you."

I didn't know what to say, so instead I said, "So can a woman be creepy?"

"Pshh. No."

"What about an old lady, hunched over with yellow teeth and bugged out eyes, who won't stop staring at you on the bus?"

"What's creepy about that?"

"What if half her teeth are missing, and she's drooling a little as she grins at you –unblinking and occasionally waving her long, yellowed fingernails in your direction."

"C'mon, I see that all the time."

I thought for a moment. "Okay, say a woman's kissing you and she starts whispering an incantation. Then she whips out a knife, pricks your neck and starts licking the blood?"

"Hey –if that's what does it for her," he said with a shrug.

"Or –how about this– how about if a woman asked you to make love to her in a graveyard?"

"Okay, yeah, *that* would be creepy."

"What? Just throw a couple blankets down in a mausoleum. Could be cozy."

"If you don't mind an audience."

"You believe in ghosts then?"

He shrugged. Then something outside the window caught his attention. I followed his gaze. High up in the tall, black office building across the street, a dim figure was flipping switches and moving about with a vacuum cleaner and a cart streaming a fountain of trash bags.

"I don't know," Kurt said, shaking his head. "I bet she's up to something." His eyes twinkled. "She has to know things. She's got access to every part of the building."

He leaned forward, and we began devising devious plots on her behalf.

"Quick, look. She's doing something new." Still intent on the window, he motioned for me to lean closer. I did, conscious of the minute details of his face, his lips. "She's walking toward a picture –see it?" I saw the fine lines dance at the corners of his mouth as his lips quirked into a smile. "She's adjusting the frame –no wait! She's lifting it and there's ... there's a safe behind it! I *knew* it! Where're my binoculars?! Quick! We've got to find them! How can I see the

83

combination without my binoculars?" He looked around frantically before throwing his hands up in exasperation. I laughed. He smiled, eyes bright, and watched me for a moment before resuming. As he spun out more and more details, his face animated with intrigue, I laughed harder. Soon I was hiccupping and struggling to catch my breath, but I couldn't take my eyes off of him. I watched him, completely absorbed, occasionally offering tidbits to fuel his fancy.

"So," I said, after he had exhausted every detail explaining the lives of everyone who could possibly exist within the rooms lit up before us, "if you could choose anything, what would you most like to see through someone else's window?"

"You're such a voyeur," he said. "Okay, no wait. Let me think." He leaned back, and I noticed again just how big his arms were, just how strong and beautiful every curve and line of him was. I longed to touch him, to feel the heat of his skin.

"A murder ...?" he started. "Definitely not sex. Maybe a robbery. No, too boring. Oh, I know, how about a man practicing his dance moves before going out on a date?" He looked at me. "I think I'd cry if I saw that."

"Really?" I asked. "You'd cry? Why?"

"Because he's trying so hard to be good enough to impress his date and make it a nice night for her."

Before I could respond, his eyes fell on something just behind my head, and he reached past me in order to pull it down. It was a wooden box, from which he pulled old pictures –driver's licenses and photos from Africa. I spread these treasures out, holding my breath. I was so silently happy, pouring over these pieces of his past and feeling his eyes on me. I'd been granted a small wish –a wish too good and sweet and intimate to last, but I held onto it –onto this moment– like it was something precious. Staring at the birthday printed on each of the licenses, I memorized the date and did the math. He was thirty-six, older than I had thought, putting twelve and a half years between us. It didn't seem like so much really, and he didn't act as though the gap mattered. I flipped through more of the pictures. His hair used to be longer –short in back, long and sun-bleached on top. It suited him –framing happy eyes and an unguarded smile. He kept his hair cut close now –everything, kept so close.

I flashed him a smile. The pictures were invoking memories. I could see them playing out behind his eyes. There was still so much I didn't know about him –I wanted to ask him about everything.

"Kurt." I said his name just for the sound of it.

"What?" His question almost surprised me.

"Oh, um, who are these people here?"

He told me, and I held up more, begging the story of each and laughing out loud when we got to his New Mexico license. He had a bandana strapped around his head and a big mustache, like a biker. Kurt shuffled it to the bottom of the pile.

"This one's my favorite," I said, growing still and staring down at a candid photo of him in the jungle. His perfect profile was laughing and looking so care-free and happy that it filled me with a longing ache. I'd have given anything to see him look that way again. I wondered again why he was here, at this nondescript school, babysitting a bunch of artists, half of whom were stoned most of the time.

I left shortly after that, walking the few steps down the hall to my room. I smiled at Keiko, asleep on her bed with the phone still pressed to her ear. She was so lovely. I climbed up onto my bed and stared out the window, reveling in inexpressible joy.

THE FOLLOWING SUNDAY I went to church with a friend and fellow RA named Jimmy. This guy, a Jamaican with an accent that could make readings from the phone book fascinating, spent the next forty minutes drawing cartoons and writing notes about how boring the pastor was. The sermon cheerfully assured us that Jesus was our guide and the Bible our map, which obviously cleared up a whole lot for everyone.

I longed for substance and depth –something that would teach me how to develop a stronger, more personal relationship with God. I'd seen devout people I'd known my whole life question everything in the face of a tragedy. Everything that stood as their foundation and infallible belief structure came tumbling down –even though they had been so *sure*. Missionaries, grandparents, pastors, and teachers –no one is ever entirely immune. How then could a relationship –with God no less– be so fragile? Or was it the faith of the individual that was fragile? And if this was the case, then how could God let all of eternity rest on something so embedded in human frailty?

As I sat there in my pew, I thought about free will. *It's the choosing that matters*, I'd heard some say, *even if it takes them straight to hell*. Wouldn't this make Christianity a spiritual survival of the fittest where those without the proper levels of faith or personal desire to do right will perish –*forever*? And along with them, those who had the proper levels of faith, but happened to misplace them in the "wrong" religion?

I mentioned none of this to Jimmy as we hopped the bus back downtown. We got lunch and then met up with Kurt at the dorm. We begged him to go bowling with us, and when he finally said yes, we headed off to Ballard in Kurt's blue Camaro.

"Well," Kurt said as we gathered our things together afterward, "it's been fun beating the two of you, but I have to get going."

I didn't want to say goodbye to him just yet, so when Jimmy said he was heading off to meet someone, I turned to Kurt and asked, "Could you give me a ride then, so I don't have to take the bus?"

"Yeah, no problem."

As soon as we were alone in the car, Kurt asked, "So what should we do now?"

Caught off guard, I stared at him.

"How about we stop by Fred Meyer?" he suggested, referring to the local grocery store.

"Fred Meyer it is," I said, laughing and tugging on my seat belt.

And then we were there, strolling down the aisles tossing strange-looking fruits and vegetables at each other while making jokes and trying not to bump into anyone.

"What should we eat tonight?" he asked, bending over the fresh seafood.

"We" –could he know what that one little word meant to me? I pulled it out of the air like it was a butterfly, almost tripping over a barrel of peanuts in the process. It was an assumed togetherness –me with him, him with me– and the way he said it was so casual that he seemed to speak without reference to time, so that it was together now, together later, together here and always. The thought thrilled me.

He picked out eggs and steaks and tortillas.

"Have you had clams before?" He looked at me, and I shook my head. "No? Then we've got to get clams. What about this, have you ever had this before?"

"I don't even know what that is," I said, looking at the bright orange, spiked Kiwano that he was holding up. I took it from him and played with it, feeling its odd weight and texture bounce in my hand as we walked up and down the aisles.

At the check-out, he joked with the cashier. I stood quiet, amused, and watchful as his quips made the people around us laugh out loud in spite of themselves. He seemed waiting, at times almost cuing me, to turn his act into a duo. But when he threw out a lead, I felt the glare of the spotlight and froze up, unable to think of anything. So he'd finish it himself. The need to be witty suddenly felt very burdensome. But my reticence didn't hinder him –he was on a roll that night.

Back at his place he cooked for me. I sat with my feet tucked under me, watching as he cooked the clams.

He suddenly swore.

"What's the matter?" I asked.

"I don't have any white wine."

"I think we'll live," I said, laughing.

He handed me a glass of red wine instead.

"Thank you," I said. "Can I do anything?"

"Marinate the meat!" He pointed to plate of steaks and handed me a skinny bottle. I sloshed what I thought to be the appropriate amount of sauce on both sides of them and turned to him.

"Okay, done! What now?"

He steered me toward the living room and handed me the TV remote. After he retreated into the bright and steamy recesses of his kitchen, I stood still for a moment on the spot where I'd been deposited. His living room felt cool and formal with its modern, geometric furniture and bare, white walls. I walked around. From the edge of the couch, I flipped through the channels rather aimlessly, but the TV didn't interest me. I got up again and stared out the large windows on either side of the room. It was dark outside. I could see my reflection in the window.

"Why are you so self-conscious?" I asked myself. It seemed the closer I got to Kurt, the less sure of myself I became. The fear of doing and saying the wrong thing silenced my tongue and restricted my movements. It was self-defeating, but I couldn't seem to do otherwise.

He brought out the food on a fancy little tray, everything looking and smelling delicious.

Every bite was perfection, and I told him so, but still I felt an insipid quiet spread through me. I cursed it. I called forth my curiosity and creativity. To no avail. I could tell he was growing tired.

"I should go. Thanks so much for the meal. For everything." I smiled and stood.

"You don't have to go, unless you want to."

I didn't want to. I wanted to find a way to bridge the gap between us. I wanted him to throw me a line that I could tie to a tree and step on with his words coaxing me along until I reached the other side.

"I don't," was all I said.

He served ice-cream, and as I savored the creamy coldness, I felt the moment approaching when I would have to walk out his door and away from him. The night was ending. All the energy he'd exhibited before was beginning to wane, and I realized with some embarrassment that I had overstayed.

"I used to be a whole lot more charming," he said as he yawned.

"But you are. You are so very charming." My words made it about halfway to him, and then they fell flat. Why couldn't I express what was going on inside me?

I left then, stepping out into the cold, impersonal blandness of the hallway, with eyes that stared at the floor and thoughts that lingered behind me.

THE NEXT DAY, JIMMY and I were playing chess while eating grilled cheese sandwiches and tomato soup when someone knocked at the door. Terrance had said he was going to stop by, and I figured it was him. I opened the door with a sandwich in one hand and looked up to see Kurt. My mouth dried up at the sight of him. He asked to use my computer since his had been stolen a few days before.

"Hi, Jim," he said lightly. If he was surprised to see him there, he didn't show it.

Jimmy was still sitting at the table. He waved, before turning back to the board and taking my rook with a wicked grin. Even as I slid my bishop and called out "Check!" through a mouthful of sandwich, I inwardly groaned, wishing Kurt had arrived an hour or two earlier, or *any* time when I didn't already have company. Did he want to talk? What did he have to say? Was he really just here for my computer?

Kurt didn't stay long –said he couldn't access his email account. Disappointment crept over me as he left.

The previous Monday I'd shown him pictures I'd just taken of Katrianna. In my favorite one, her hair was all done up in braids that wrapped around her head, and she was standing under a fountain with her palms up and her eyes squeezed shut as she laughed at the cold spray of water.

Kurt's smile had lit up his office, his eyes going from me to the photos and back again as I gesticulated wildly, unable to hold back a stream of happy babble. His eyes were positively shining, and at the sight of his happiness I thought my chest would burst.

I met him in the lobby on my way to the darkroom a few hours after he used my computer.

"You can use my computer again if you need to." I heard the lameness of my words.

"That won't be necessary."

"Thanks again for dinner," I said, my feet pulling me away while my insides tried to stay. How was I supposed to act in this situation?

"Didn't you get that little slip of paper?"

"What paper?" Suddenly hopeful.

"The bill. That'll be twenty dollars."

"Oh." Hope crushed. "Is there interest? Cause as a broke college student it might be a while before I can pay you back. Unless you want me to wash your dishes." I laughed as I spoke, but this kind of joking confused me. I didn't understand his moods –how he could be so sweet one moment and so distant the next. Was that how I appeared to him –by turns absorbed and aloof?

At the RA meeting the next day, he was in the same, sarcastic mood. We were discussing program possibilities for the dorm, and with an air of detachment he told us to do whatever we wanted. Someone suggested a dorm-wide pillow-fight, and a guy named Randy looked at Kurt in that half-gullible manner of his and asked, "Will housing go for that?"

"Hell no! But what does it matter? They'll never know." He laughed, and everyone laughed with him, although a few of us stared.

His flippant manner was funny at first, but when it continued, people began to give each other questioning looks. He didn't say anything serious the entire meeting. Everyone was familiar with his light and teasing manner, but this ... this was different. This time his sarcasm had an edge to it, and a few people shifted uncomfortably. I watched them and him, not saying anything. A voice in my head whispered that his strange mood was related to me and his own unsure feelings of where we stood. After all, I was always spending time with other guys, like Kellie and Jimmy. But the idea felt self-absorbed, so I hushed it. Any one of a thousand factors could have triggered his mood, and I felt disqualified from guessing the whys. That didn't stop me from being mystified –and desperately curious. Notwithstanding, I made every effort to put him out of my thoughts in the days that followed –with only minor success.

# Chapter 7

At the beginning of June, Keiko and I left student housing and signed a six-month lease on a new apartment. She was the perfect roommate, although I rarely saw her. She'd stop by to pick up a few items now and then, or to shower and use her computer, but for the most part she was with Yoshi. Just before the quarter ended, she quietly confided, "Yoshi used to annoy me, but now ... it's confusing."

Were it not for my diminishing savings, I would have told her not to worry about her share of the rent. This was when I first entertained the thought of leaving school early. Several students on the verge of graduating described the second year of the program as little more than practice.

"*Practice!*" I said to my brother, John. "I don't need to spend twenty thousand dollars just to *practice*."

Even so, I wasn't ready to leave just yet.

MY SECOND OLDEST BROTHER, Leo, was something of a cynic. We wrote a lot back then through chess emails, discussing everything from books, movies, and people to sex and relationships. Differing perspectives notwithstanding, I respected him and valued the chance to see things from a new angle, especially when it came to Kurt, because if there was anything I couldn't quite get a handle on, it was him.

"Ani ... thirty freakin seven?? lordy," Leo had replied.

"36 –mind you, and is there really any issue here? I mean, didn't you yourself say that I needed an older man?"

"But hey," I went on, "how long before you knew Rachel was the one you wanted to spend the rest of your life with?"

"2 – 3 years ... before that i thought that it could develop into something long term but i wasn't ready to make that type of commitment even in my head to myself ... there's no timeline ... that is what i was trying to tell you before: that you shouldn't think of every relationship as 'the one' or not the one ... just freakin relax and see where it takes you ... enjoy the ride and try not to constantly overanalyze ... can you do that? Can you???? heh heh heh :)"

As much as I agreed with him, when it came to Kurt, I found it impossible to relax and let go.

A couple of weeks later I knocked on Kurt's office door under the ruse of "getting my mail." We ended up talking, as I had hoped, and when it was time for him to leave for the day, he invited me up to his room for a sandwich. While we ate, I told him all about my new place and how Keiko was never there.

My eyes were drawn to him as we talked –his dark brown eyes, the familiar curve of his mouth, the shadow along his jaw. When he glanced up, I looked away, fascinated once more with the scene beyond his kitchen window –a collage of brick and stone saturated with the warm glow of evening.

"Let's go for drinks," he suggested.

The air outside was lovely –perfect, really. He was in high spirits, full of conversation and easy to talk to as we walked to one of his favorite bars on First Avenue. He greeted the tender by name as we entered, and when the drinks arrived, we clinked them together with matching smiles. Cocooned in a crowd of friendly strangers, we were soon laughing and talking with everyone.

There was Christine –a forty-something, recently engaged woman here on business. Kurt ordered a round, and we loudly toasted her happiness. Her eyes sparkled with pleasure at the attention. When she faded away, Valentina took her place. Valentina, whose Costa Rican accent made her abundant friendliness even more attractive, had large, lovely eyes that danced around the room as she offered us her impression of the city. When she dipped her head and disappeared, we turned again to each other and began inventing stories about the rest. Just a few spinning stools down the bar, a distinguished older woman sat with one hand, heavily laden with many sideways-sliding rings, possessively clutching the arm of a well-dressed man in his twenties. Although her thin red lips moved rapidly in energetic conversation while her gesturing free hand flashed with reflected light, she never released her grip upon the young man's arm. Before long, the tip of his shiny black shoe started tap, tap, tapping, ever so nervously against the foot rail that ran along the length of the bar. The tapping increased until Kurt and I could feel the rhythm racing up our legs and through our elbows.

"Hear that?" Kurt tilted his head down a little as though to better hear the beat. "I think he's trying to tell us something. It's a message!" Pausing, his expression frozen in wide-eyed concentration, he suddenly glanced up at me.

"Yes?" I breathed. "What is it?"

"Wait ... just a moment." He looked down again, listening with furrowed brow, before whispering, "Yes, I'm sure of it now. It's an SOS!" He snuck a peak over his shoulder in the direction of the mad foot-tapper. "Ani, this guy's in distress!"

"We've got to help him!"

"But how? He's barely touched his drink and seems intent on toughing it out. And honestly, she scares me."

"You, scared?"

He raised his eyebrows and nodded.

I burst out laughing, eliciting a sharp look from both the woman and her escort. Kurt smiled down at the table, ignoring them, and then turned back to me. We broke into huge grins. The warmth of the alcohol was spreading all through my body. I could tell it was the same for him. When he lifted his hand to the tender, the dark blue fabric of his shirt stretched across his broad shoulders, and I wanted to drape my arm across his back, to feel his warmth on my skin. He nodded his thanks when the glasses arrived and leaned forward, a half smile playing about his lips as he slowly sipped his drink. The overwhelming happiness I felt in that moment crowded out everything else. What a relief to let the cautious, overactive, analytical part of my mind go to its room and sleep. For once it wasn't marching around like it owned the place.

Kurt glanced at me and smiled. His joy was genuine. He too was relaxed –no traces of work or the thesis he should maybe write or the dissatisfaction that seemed to be following him around with increasing frequency those days. No, he was feeling the moment right along with me.

"Tequila. This is what my brothers and I always have," I told him, raising my glass a little. "We order a round and we toast, 'To family!'"

"Well, then –to family!" he touched his glass to mine. The light shining through them made little leaping patterns on the smooth surface of the bar. It reminded me of Christmas.

"And to friends!" I added cheerily.

"And to the newly engaged and the travelers." He swung his head in a vague attempt to see if any of them were still around.

"And to men in distress –may that never be you."

"Oh, I don't think it'd be all that bad –getting paid to accompany a rich, older woman," and he looked over at the pair again.

"You wouldn't mind being somebody's eye candy?" I asked with a grin.

"Well, what do you think," he said, sitting up taller, "could I be?"

I sat back, regarding him with an appraising eye. "Let's see ... your build, well, your build is exquisite–"

"Exquisite, eh?"

"Oh, yes. It's mighty fine. And your face ... well, you've got wonderful, strong lines along your jaw and forehead. I like what you've done with your hair, although a little longer wouldn't be so bad. Your eyes are intelligent, but a little mischievous. And your mouth ..." I leaned closer. "Hmmm." I sat back again, shaking my head.

"What? My mouth is what?"

"Your mouth ... well, no, I can't go on. Really, what am I doing? I'm objectifying you."

"So? Go on."

"Well, I *suppose* any woman would be proud to have you by her side, though I can't presume to speak for all of them."

He lifted his glass, chuckling a little. His pinky finger stuck out at an awkward angle. I reached over and touched its unnatural bent. My touch caught him by surprise, and he sucked in his breath. He looked down at his hand.

"Can you straighten it?" I asked, still tracing it with my fingers.

"No." He was quiet, still looking at our hands.

"Is it all right that I asked?"

"Yeah. It's just an old sports injury." He sat, thinking for a moment. "That's what I like about you," he said, eyes meeting mine. His expression and voice were soft. "You notice the small things."

I withdrew my hand with a shrug. "I was just curious," I said, embarrassed.

"Kurt, good to see you!"

We looked up to see the bartender from the opposite end approaching with a warm smile. Kurt straightened as he introduced us. Little sweat shadows remained on the counter where his hands had been. Hot hands. They told me what his words did not. *Touch me, Kurt!* I thought. *I want you too.* My imagination brought those hands to my face so that I could almost feel their heat ... their pressure. I imagined them pressed against my belly, my hips. Then sliding along my waist and slowly up my back. So absorbed was I in the sensation that I heard nothing of what was being said as the two continued talking.

Salt crystals collected on my finger as I traced the rim of my glass. They glowed on my fingertip like tiny, fallen stars. I played with their texture before touching them to my tongue. My lips closed around my finger, and I wondered if the skin above Kurt's collarbone would taste the same. Closing my eyes, I caught floating bits of conversation, lifted by laughter and studded with the sounds of silverware. The door behind us swung open and shut, letting in a rushing flow of cool, summer night air that whooshed around my legs like a playful puppy, followed by new and eager voices. High heels tapped, and voices murmured. The salt lingered on my tongue.

My lips made a noise then, soft, nearly imperceptible, but loud enough to make me fully conscious of myself. My hand flew down, and my eyes shot to Kurt, who, although still talking to the tender, was now watching me. His look, undisguised with eyes afire, caught me off guard. The instant heat made my heart hammer and my armpits prickle.

"So goddamn sexy," he said softly, turning fully to me.

Suddenly self-conscious, I raised my glass and half-hid behind my hand.

"Why do people swear when emphasizing something good?" I asked, swirling the amber liquid around.

"You believe me, don't you?" His voice was insistent, as though to show me this wasn't another of his jokes. "Do you know how beautiful you are?"

Pleasure and embarrassment flooded through me, and I felt my cheeks grow hot. I deflected the attention back to him.

I reached out and let my finger slide down the curve of his ear. I studied the path my finger made, unable to look him in the eye. I leaned closer so I could whisper and escape his unrelenting gaze. "If you only knew how sexy I think *you* are, Mr. Eye-Candy Man."

My fingers continued their tracing, exploring the back of his head and the curve of his neck, until my arm was resting lightly across his shoulders. I felt the softness of his shirt, the heat. I felt the door open and close, the rise of mingling voices, and the way everything flowed together in a sea of intoxicated happiness. I was flowing toward him, merging with his pulsing light, wanting to press my lips against that part of his neck where his heart beat so feverishly. It seemed only natural to touch Kurt. I could remain there, just as I was, touching him forever. I felt his heat soak in through my arm, rising through my body, and I watched the goose bumps appear just above his collar. I leaned closer and breathed into that place just behind his ear. He smelled like an old house surrounded by vast woods. Remote, but inviting.

I noticed his face then, from my safe perspective. A big, clumsy smile revealed a Kurt I'd never seen.

"I always knew that about you," he said, eyes closed. "That you'd be ... sensual."

I felt his ear with my lips and despite the heat I shuddered. No longer attempting to redirect his attention, I touched him now so that my skin would go on singing, and my heart would go on beating, and my lungs would go on filling. I touched him because the tickling of his hair along my wrist sent currents racing up my arm and because the air around us seemed to glow brighter the nearer we got to each other so that everything was heat and light and the need to be closer.

"I find you so fascinating, Kurt. I have for a long time." My voice was the shadow of a voice, an echo.

He sat there, quiet, but breathing hard.

"I've made up reasons to talk to you, to see you, to be close to you." And now I'm *touching* you, I thought. I'm breathing into your neck. Your ear is playing on my lips. Your heat is my heat, is our heat.

My fingers continued their travels along the muscles of his neck, his arms, his shoulders. How easily he could pick me up, spin me around, or lay me down beneath him.

He turned a little and reached up his hand, running his fingers into my hair. He cradled my head, and I leaned into his warmth, like a cat leaning into his affection.

"I always wondered what it'd be like to touch you." His soft, thick voice soared through the space between us, a runaway spark that dipped and twirled before lighting upon my ear and setting off a roaring chain reaction.

What perfect bliss!! In its perfect, crystal box, which I clutched lovingly, frightfully to my chest. If only I knew how to set it free!

My heart pounded with the realization that he was feeling what I felt. The attraction was real, mutual, so much more than my imagination. He was interested in *me*! This man made of memories was opening his pages so that his past, present, and future beckoned. For a split second I was blinded by happiness. I felt as though I might dematerialize and envelope him completely. I was ready almost to slip out of myself and leave my mind behind, with its analytical reasoning that kept trying to determine the safest route, the route that in the end led nowhere. If only I could say aloud, "Kurt, I'm so scared of this happiness, but it's you and me, and I'm ready to figure it out," everything would be okay.

But I was too late. At the mention of its name, that overactive, analytical part of my mind woke up and marched out of its room. Taking stock of the situation, it shook its head in dismay. With that,

my breath caught in my throat and fear crept in, wrapping its fingers around my neck. Who was I kidding? I wasn't ready for this. Could Kurt even handle my emotional skittishness?

As I struggled to loosen fear's grip, a new and more horrible thought occurred. Was this moment created and sustained by nothing more than the freeing flow of alcohol through our veins? My mind, part of it anyway, nodded smugly –not even condescending to sympathize. That the sensations coursing through the whole of my body, awakening every cell and nerve ending so that I felt alive as never before, might mean nothing staggered me. I hurried to dismiss the doubt. He's had as much to drink as I have, I thought, and I'm fully aware of what's going on. I know exactly what I'm doing, and what it might mean, and he's twice my size so he *definitely* knows what he's doing. This isn't the alcohol speaking. This is our moment of truth.

I looked up, suddenly worried that he might have seen the rapid succession of thoughts passing through my head. He was looking at me with such intensity that I immediately looked down again.

"Look at me," he said softly.

I did, for a second, and then I closed my eyes and leaned into his hand again. The very real pressure of his hand reassured me, and the spreading warmth slowed my thoughts and eased my mind. I looked up at him, and this time I held his gaze.

"How about I walk you home?" he said, and I knew what he meant. I nodded.

I leaned on his arm, and he kept me from falling over the contrary curbs that kept grabbing at my ankles. He was warm against me, and I felt safe as we made our way through the shadowy streets. I led him up the steps to the door of my apartment building, and he followed me through to the inner glow of the lobby. When I finally stood in front of my room, fumbling with the keys, I could feel him behind me. I paused for a moment, leaned back against him, heard him sigh. Then I unlocked the door.

I set the keys on the kitchen counter and lit a candle, my heart flaring up so that I could hardly see the little flame flickering before me. His impatient arms were around me then, so strong, and I could feel every part of him pressed against me. I turned around to face him, my arms wrapping around him, and he kissed me. For the first time since I was sixteen, when I had kissed a boy and hated it, I didn't maneuver my mouth away or lead his lips to my neck instead. This time I kissed him back, fully, without reservation, until the light weaving around us pulsed with the violence of a volcano, softened into music. Hot, lovely, wonderful.

"Hello, Ani," he said, and I beamed up at him with such happiness that he repeated it. "Hello, Ani." Over and over again, "Hello, Ani. I can't stop smiling."

I kissed the corners of his mouth, tasting to see that his happiness was real. It was! Oh, for joy, it was! Because of me, Ani. Seeing his happiness amplified my own. I pressed closer, my leg climbing up his thigh and my hand kneading the back of his neck, and the heat, the pressure –all of it– terrified me with how good it felt.

"I've dreamed about this for a long time," he whispered into my ear.

His hands moved to my belly, to the skin just above my jeans. One hot finger traced the boundary –like a scout ... or a question. I couldn't stop the shiver from racing up my spine. That spot was so dangerously delicious. His fingers found the button of my jeans, playing with it, pulling at it, until my waistband opened with a *pop!* A world of intoxicating possibilities spread out before me –the colors brilliant and blinding and making me dizzy. Kurt could take me there. He could lead me through the small door of my dark room into the open-aired expanse of sensation and freedom. What better guide? What better time? What better way to step out into my own?

But suddenly, I was jolted back inside my head where immediately the analytical part of my mind with the loud, loud voice began listing off a whole slew of possible outcomes –pregnancy, regret, shame, and a broken heart, to name a few. I then became conscious of the cold counter biting into my back, until soon our jeans were no longer gateways, but just jeans. And our bodies were no longer luminescent, but just bodies –bodies in need of a shower and a good night's sleep.

No, no, no! I wanted to silence that voice. To feel again the musical heat of his touch. To lose myself in just being with him.

But I'd already made up my mind. I wasn't going there, not now. I'd decided beforehand –long ago– and that was that. No matter how much I wanted it. Or him.

I gently, so very carefully, took his hands captive in my own and moved them up along my waist. There I freed them. I kissed him again, biting his lip and letting my hands travel up his arms and under his sleeves.

"You're making it so hard," he said quietly.

"I'm so sorry," I whispered.

What would our lives have been like if I hadn't stopped him? Would we have laughed over TV shows and talked with strangers and argued over what to hang on the walls? Would we have roamed and travelled and finally put down roots? Would we have had a son who looked like him, or perhaps two girls whose ringing laughter filled our home and hearts with unfathomable delight? Or would we have separated after two months or two years only to follow our current paths? What I really want to know is, would he still be alive?

I was but one moment of the hundreds, thousands, millions that filled his life –but anything is better than picturing the blood and the dust coating his newly grown beard as he lay broken under the blazing Afghan sun. Dear, dead Kurt –neither of us could have known where our lives would lead. But even if we had, would the conclusion be any different?

Kurt breathed out softly with his eyes closed. "Let's just lie down then," he said. He took another deep breath, and when he opened his eyes, they were brimming with something I could not quite decipher. My mind grew more alert. I wanted to follow our connection to that perfect, immaterial space wherein everything could be felt and understood. But I was drowning in my uncertainty, my inability to decide whether this was right –whether he and me together as a pair, a couple with a future, was right. My head was swimming. I didn't know what I felt, what I wanted. If only there was more time. If only he'd be patient and keep reaching out to me. But what if all this was nothing but a chemical moment, the birthplace of a regret that would rise up and haunt him, embarrass him, and later me too? I was at such a loss. Terrified, hopeful, already steeling myself.

"Nothing will happen," he whispered. "I promise." The sweet innocence of his intentions was clear. He was sleepy. He wanted to lie down. He would ask nothing. Expect nothing. Except only to lie down. Next to me. I nodded.

He led me to the living room –his warm hand, his large, warm hand engulfing mine– toward my makeshift bed. I felt a flash of embarrassment at my pile of blankets as I knelt on the floor and spread them out, endeavoring to make space for two. As I ran my fingers over them, smoothing them out, I just knew it'd be so uncomfortable for him. But there was nothing else for it, so we laid down together, somewhat awkwardly –his arms were so big, his barrel chest huge. Lying beside him was like lying next to a wall. I felt like such a child. How should I position myself? With my head on his chest, his arm? Cuddled up close or sprawled across him? I shifted, trying to be subtle while hoping he was too sleepy to notice, before eventually settling on my side with my back to him. He moved in, curling around me and putting his arm over my waist. Its wonderful weight comforted me. I inhaled slowly, deeply, but my mind raced. I felt desperately awake. With happiness suspended and no mattress to ease the rigidity of the floorboards, I found it impossible to relax, to let sleep overtake me. So, I pretended. I lay still and absorbed his heat until I heard his breathing deepen into snores that made me smile. I listened to his breathing and I felt him sleep and I felt him dream. Slowly my muscles softened. I lay awake all through the early morning hours. Then, when light tentatively began peering into the room, I felt him stir and quietly rise. I remained where I was, eyes closed. He got up and moved about, then came back and knelt beside me, pulling the blanket up over my shoulder. What did his face look like just then? Was his expression gentle or tinged with regret? I didn't dare open my eyes; they would've been intrusive in their need to know just what this was to him. Without a word, he left.

When the air stopped moving and all that filled the room was early morning quiet, I pulled myself up, stretched, and sat against the wall next to the window. I stared out at the time-weathered fountain in the little courtyard below and at the spreading ivy tinged with morning light that was every minute growing stronger, and I thought. Fear and happiness wrestled within me, knocking over chairs and making a ruckus that echoed in my ears. Would he consider the previous night a mistake? And if not, if he was happy and hopeful because of me, was I ready? Ready for what, I couldn't say, but it felt like such a very big deal. Not caring was so much easier. I almost missed my freedom already. What was wrong with me? Did I want to be lonely forever?

He called a few hours later, and we met for milkshakes. He wanted to make sure things weren't awkward, he said. Of course, that's only natural, I thought. Right? Or was this what regret sounded like?

"Awkward? No." I smiled as if to say, "Don't be silly." And then I focused on my milkshake –those straws are never large enough. I didn't feel awkward. Curious, and most definitely confused, but not *awkward*. In fact, I could've acted as though nothing had happened. Perhaps that would be necessary, in the presence of some, to protect his job –him being the Resident Director and me a student. Could he get fired if things continued between us? We'd have to conceal our feelings from everyone, which, the more I thought about it, would be rather easy for me as I did that naturally. But what if he thinks I'm indifferent? If I could only bare my soul and tell him everything! But I didn't. I didn't say anything. I kept quiet, looking for some clue as to where we were headed. I was playing it safe, I realized, bracing myself should he decide to downplay his desire as a casual side effect of one drink too many. "Tequila!" he laughed at one point, and I shifted uneasily. I had no idea –*no idea*– what to make of any of this.

We met again later and walked through several fine furniture galleries, laughing at the oddities we found. Kurt knew the sales associates in one of the stores, and they greeted him like a long-lost friend. He said he was still considering the couch he'd looked at earlier. He showed it to me, and we plopped down.

"Buying a couch is a big deal, you know," he said.

"Oh?" I raised an eyebrow.

"Well, of course. It's a sign of commitment –that you're settling down. You don't buy a couch and then pick up and move again."

"Still deciding whether to stay or leave, huh? Restlessness is a hard thing to shake." I looked away. The uncertainty of our situation was driving me insane. I wanted to jump up and shout, "Out with it already!" Instead, I leaned back and made little patterns in the cream-colored suede fabric.

"So, what do you think? Do you like this one? Could you see sitting here after a long day and saying, 'Honey, guess what Johnny did *ta-day*?"

I laughed, but I knew we weren't talking about the couch; we were talking about us. And Kurt was still deciding. I felt tired then, lacking the energy to convince him. All my creativity withered under the suspicion that I was failing an exam. Being witty was not something I could do effortlessly or on command like he could. I sighed and tried to relax into the softness of the couch. It was a wonderful couch, really. Then we stood and left.

# Chapter 8

The next weekend when my brother John arrived, I could hardly contain my excitement. I showed him as many of the highlights as I could in the few short days he was there. "This is Pike Place Market, this is Westlake, and this is Kurt." Being infinitely curious how they would interact, I made dinner for the two of them on the second night of John's visit.

We ate pasta in my small kitchen and afterward went out for drinks. We stayed out only long enough for a couple of shots and for Kurt to lean over and ask me to dance with him. He said it playfully, but my face flushed red, and I was suddenly self-conscious. I stammered, and he laughed, ordering another drink and saying it didn't matter. But it did. He admired confidence, and I'd lost mine. He admired the ability to shut out the world without caring what others thought. But I did. I cared what he thought. I was afraid of making a fool of myself in front of him, of being ungraceful and boring. And nothing could be more self-defeating.

I wanted so much to reach out and touch him –his arm, his knee, any part so long as there was contact. But I couldn't. What if my touch was unwelcome? I sat, reserved, thinking that if he was just patient enough, I could be coaxed out of the uncertainty in which I now found myself. But that was asking a lot, I knew.

Back in my kitchen late that night, having said goodbye to Kurt a few hours before, John and I started discussing relationships and sex. I had just made myself a cup of tea when he surprised me with the revelation that he was no longer naïve on the subject. I was taken aback. His religious views were similar to mine in that he wanted his faith to be about a relationship rather than ritual. He, too, wanted to determine what he believed and why –only he didn't overthink it like I did.

I let the knowledge of his lost virginity sink in for a moment, and then asked, "Do you regret it?"

"Yes," he said. But he said it matter-of-factly, without any weight or darkness in his voice or manner. Questions filled my head, but I simply stared. This was my little brother ... my little *Christian* brother.

After moment or two I asked, "Was it at least worth it?"

He thought about it. "No ... no, I was disappointed."

I furrowed my brow, surprised. We were quiet for a few minutes; then he looked at me. "Always be true to your beliefs, Ani," he said, his voice serious, despite its usual lightness.

I stared off into space, getting momentarily lost in my thoughts, and then the mood shifted, and I stood up and stretched.

"There were some benefits, though," he said as I stacked the plates in the sink and ran warm water over them. I looked back over my shoulder to let him know I was listening. "After the mystery was gone it allowed me to focus on other things –things that matter, like personality and stuff."

"Things you should've been focusing on from the start," I said. He grinned, and our conversation turned to other topics.

I SPENT THE FOURTH of July with my brothers in Coeur d'Alene, Idaho. Before the trip, when I had stopped by Kurt's office to see him, I found a group of people surrounding him. Instead of talking to him as I had hoped, I tried to act as though everything was the same as always. He was looking down, as though deep in thought, and that's how I had left him.

I half-dreaded the conversation that was building up inside me –the need to know if anything existed between us. If there was indeed nothing, I would let go and move on. I truly believed I'd be okay with any outcome, but I hoped there was *something* we could build on.

Late Sunday afternoon, I finally headed across the street, through the alley, into the lobby, and up the stairs to the ninth floor. My heart started pounding and my legs began to wobble at the thought of facing him.

*Just be honest with him*, I told myself. *Tell him ... tell him how he fascinates you and that you're attracted to him –in* every *way.* A warm glow spread through me, even as my heart pounded louder with the thought and implication. *Tell him how you're afraid of happiness, but that you'll find a way through your fear. You'll find a way to let go, to get close. If you're good at anything it's adapting to people, and if he can just be patient, you'll gain back your confidence. You just need a little reassurance.*

Yes, I thought, the two of us could work, if he wanted us to. That's all I needed to know –whether or not he wanted this ... us. No matter what happened, I'd be fine and would make the most of it. I was strong, resilient. I just needed to know where we stood. There was nothing wrong with that.

Arriving at his door, I paused to catch my breath –I should have taken the elevator. Why hadn't I taken the elevator? I could almost hear the ticking of a clock somewhere. My anxiety had winded me. I stood there, somewhat aghast at the vulnerability I felt. I took one more deep breath, considered leaving, and then knocked on his door.

Immediately I could tell things weren't the same. He invited me in, and we made stupid small talk that I found excruciating, although I tried not to let it show. I tried to act as casual and nonchalant as I could. I waved away his offer for something to drink. I nodded as he talked about the lack of anything good on television. I stared out the window and watched the sun descend as the pressure escalated inside me. When I could stand it no longer, I blurted out the question that was raging within. It was like breathing out a bomb, and I waited, weakly, for the explosion to sound in my ears.

"Where do we stand?" he repeated. He considered the question for some time. I steeled myself, knowing what was coming. I'd felt it, almost, from the first morning after.

"Well," he said at last, "I guess we don't."

A deafening roar. All my thoughts lost their cohesiveness then, and I heard only a portion of what he said next —something about the "timing" not being right and that maybe he "just wasn't ready for the commitment."

I felt a need to explain how this was a first for me —this whole caring about somebody and not knowing how to act.

"Look," I said, "I ... I know I have a hard time getting close, to people, and ... and I *am* attracted to you, in *every* way. And I know it won't always be like that —the getting close part, I mean. But I do like you and know that if you would just, if you could just give me a little time ... or something ... I think maybe we could be happy. And this, this is what I'm afraid of —not of being happy with you— but of the happiness itself ..."

I trailed off and stared at my feet in despair. Everything was coming out wrong —little jumbled bits that didn't make any sense. I couldn't think. I couldn't seem to straighten out my words to say what I wanted them to mean.

If he was softening a little, I couldn't see it.

"I've thought about this for a long time," he said, as he took another breath. "And it's not the age difference," he was quick to add. "It's ... well, for one thing, you lack *goofiness.*"

I was almost angry until it struck me what he was talking about. Yes, of course, I thought —the tiring need to be witty.

"And social grace," he added. He thought about this a minute longer, and I looked up, so I could see his face. "Well, not social grace, exactly, because you have dignity. You have your own sort of self-confidence, but something is missing."

He didn't have to explain. I understood. I thought of *The Way We Were*, the movie with Barbara Streisand and Robert Redford. "I'm not pretty enough, am I?" Streisand had asked Redford. "What I mean is, I know I'm pretty, but I don't have that social elegance that you need."

"No, you don't."

Redford had looked so matter-of-fact as he said it. Stupid, sad movie. I hated it.

But now, in this sterile room, that scene was being replayed between me and Kurt. Why should the need to work a room matter more than the "style of one's soul"? An old friend had once told me he loved the style of my soul. I had felt so beautiful with him, so fun and clever. But you couldn't help who you did or didn't love.

And that's when I finally knew. After all those many months of wondering what I truly felt for this man, I at last knew. I *loved* him. So much so that my heart was breaking into a million jagged pieces at the rejection he was laying out before me. *Kurt –I love you!* rang out in my head, *only you don't love me back.* The pain was almost more than I could bear. I couldn't breathe. I couldn't seem to get in any air at all, much less *think* coherently.

He paused for a moment, almost as though waiting for me to convince him to change his mind. How could he be so calm when such turmoil raged within me? –turmoil confined behind my placid countenance.

I sat there, stupefied, trying in vain to make sense of my thoughts.

"I've even talked to my mother about you." He offered the words as though they were some sort of consolation. And maybe they were, because I realized as he said this that at one point his interest in me had been real enough to discuss with someone who mattered to him. But knowing I hadn't foolishly imagined everything didn't make me feel much better.

"I think you'd make a great wife, and you'd be a great mother. And I told her that. But, personally, I don't know if I'm ready for that."

There were so many things I wanted to say just then –things like, "Why are we both trying so hard to figure it all out *now*?! We can figure it out together, when we're ready." And, "I'm scared too. I'm restless and non-committal too, but that's okay. We can take it slow."

But I didn't. I didn't say any of those things because I was altogether incapable of speech. I sat there, feeling helpless, but trying not to let it show –doing everything I could just to be strong enough to keep from breaking down right on the spot. Perhaps, though, that would have helped. Perhaps he thought me emotionless, and he needed to be convinced I had true feelings for him. Maybe he needed to see some passionate emotion to know that I wasn't aloof, apathetic, or cold.

"And then there's the sex thing. I think sex is groovy."

I considered telling him how much I wanted him. But I couldn't. I would never use sex as a means to hold onto him. The thought alone felt wrong and manipulative. I offered no intelligent reply.

"If we got married tomorrow, you'd have sex that same night?" he asked.

"Yes," I managed to get out.

"See, *that's* a mystery to me."

"But marriage is about so much more than sex," I insisted. "It's a sign of commitment, born from the desire to share a life together."

"The decision to share a life together takes time. It isn't arrived at lightly."

"And sex is?"

"Sex is fun. And it lets you see if you're compatible."

Sex is sacred, I thought. And what about pregnancy and STDs? These risks loomed larger outside the safety of marriage.

He seemed to be waiting for a response, but I didn't know what to say. I got up to go. I had stayed too long already. He offered to walk me home. I gave him a bitter answer in reply.

The tears I might have cried got lost somewhere inside me, building up and sloshing around until my thoughts felt sluggish and my head heavy with the pressure. I stared straight ahead, not seeing much, as I walked home and up the stairs. In a daze, I unlocked my door, sent my keys sliding across the counter, and curled into bed. I welcomed sleep, grateful to let it come and steal everything away –all my confused thoughts and swirling emotions and the numbness gripping the whole of my body. I slept late into Monday morning. And then, upon sitting up in the gray, empty stillness, my grief and heartache came spilling out. For two whole days I cried, until I was drowning in a flood of emotion of which I hadn't believed myself capable. After all the time I'd spent wondering whether it was even possible, there it was: I loved him. And I had lost him.

I thought about going back to him. I could pour out my newly acknowledged feelings and maybe he'd respond. But even as I thought this, I knew I'd never do it. He'd already given me the easy let-down. Desperate as I was, I wasn't going to try to force his hand the other way.

My thoughts kept scattering in the days that followed, so my body did the talking. My chest felt like it was capsizing. My stomach filled with rocks that rolled and lurched and dragged me to my knees. I wanted to vomit or scream or find some other way to expel them, but I couldn't. So, I alternated between the oblivion of sleep and the mind-numbing relief of busyness.

*Pointless*, I thought as I vacuumed the floor. *Pointless*, as I cleaned the bathroom and folded laundry. *Everything's pointless. Even this misery. Come on, come on! Get up! Get going!* The rational tyrant within me pointed to food, to the computer, to the door. I made myself eat. I sent out resumes and went shopping. And slowly, I felt a resolute determination taking shape within me.

I wrote to Leo about it.

*Ani,* he wrote back, *What the fuck? eh? Reading your emails is disturbing in the least...It sounds like you are trying to figure things out to the extent that you don't know what side is up anymore...It seems like I say this every time, but you seriously just need to chill out...is that possible or what?*

*First sex...now of course my views are a little different and I would appreciate this not going any further, not that I think you will run out and tell the parents but...anyways...John is right...sex is always going to be disappointing the first time...always...for everyone...regardless of who you are...It takes practice and knowledge to turn it into the awesome experience it is...But John is also right in saying that sex becomes such an issue before it happens that it consumes everything in the relationship...After you get that out of the way you can really concentrate on the person themself...Not only that, but in a serious relationship it is hard to have true heart to heart intimacy without opening yourself completely to the other person...and sex is the way this intimacy is achieved...Don't mistake me and think that I am advocating sex with just anybody...it has to be in the context of love...true long term love...but it helps to take the relationship to the next level...Personally, I would never get married without having sex...If you are not compatible once intimacy is introduced then that needs to be discovered before the marriage vows are taken...Once again don't think that I am advocating wanton sex, but I do think that true intimacy can only be discovered through complete openness in a relationship...*

*Please dear god don't take this wrong and go out and throw it all away...I just want to give you an idea of how the other side thinks...*

*Now as far as what happened with Kurt...what happened with all that?...we went to Wilmington NC over the 4th weekend and one of our real good friends is getting married to a guy who is 10 years older than her...Not really as big of an age gap as one may think...just seems more severe when it is my sister, but it is not weird or unnatural or anything like that. More common than you would think...so what happened with you and him? You lock up and just decide to chuck the whole caboodle? Just don't know...hmmmmmm*

*Another thing you need to think about is that you are always saying, oh How I want to live. What the fuck is this? If you want to live, just freaking live...What do you want? Do you expect some white knight to come off the mountain and show you the way? What way is this anyways? It can only be your way...This is your life...We define our reality and how we live each moment. What more do you want? It sounds like you have a good, somewhat rewarding life in Seattle now...seize the opportunity with both hands and live! What scares me is I wonder if you need great loss or tragedy to feel like you are experiencing life... Forgive me, but you sound sometimes like every other disenchanted American who looks out from their opulence and wishes for something to take them out of their misery...Think about real misery, this life does not offer any promises...We have to be happy with whatever peace and beauty we can find...We, unlike 85% of the rest of the world, have the education and tools to constantly change our life to however we see fit...Use these tools to create your reality...*

*Well, enough of my rambling, and once again I hope you know me well enough that you know that I do not mean to offend...but I am not going to sugar coat the way I feel about things, and I know you can appreciate that...I hope you are doing well and things work out ...*
   *Your loving brother, Leo*

TIMING IS EVERYTHING, or so they say, and I would have to agree. Change the sequence of events in a life, and everything would be different. We would be remade.

"*If you want to live, just freaking live...*"

Leo's letter and my broken heart spurred a re-evaluation of everything I had been holding onto for so long. I decided it was time I grew up. Instead of being so terrified of making mistakes, I determined to step out of my head and out of my safe boundaries. I would make careful choices, while trying not to over-analyze, and I would learn from whatever happened, without regret and with my eyes wide open. I think I saw myself as something of a Solomon or a Siddhartha, who each set out to discover the meaning of life through exploration of the world, spirit, and body. Each, in his own way, seems by journey's end to have found his answers, his peace, and his harmony. That is what I desired. More than anything. However, I was unprepared for the shadows that I found, not without, but within. I had sensed them, guessed at them, but never before had I understood their strength or scale. I would soon come to learn what Nietzsche meant when he wrote, "I am that which must constantly overcome itself."

# Part 2

Who never has suffered, he has lived but half.
Who never failed, he never strove or sought.
Who never wept is stranger to a laugh,
and he who never doubted never thought.
–Rev. J. B. Goode

# Chapter 1

My watershed moment. With what perfect clarity can I recall the sharp distinction between the long, slow months before and the rushing swirl of months that followed that moment of decision. It stretched out into a fine, thin line –a dissecting, dividing line that split my life into a before and an after.

Conscious of the importance surrounding my decision to let go and live, I nevertheless believed that I would remain the same inside, my soul untouched by the external forces that lurked beyond. The familiar light of my innocence followed me around like a friendly titanium halo that I thought would survive no matter what stormy consequences should fall upon me. I believed also that the great love I felt for my family, my God, and my religion was safely rooted within me. I just didn't understand everything, that was all. But with experience would come understanding, and with understanding, an even greater love. That was how I would grow. Or so I told myself.

Therefore, believing myself cloaked in spiritual, if not personal invincibility, I felt ready, eager even, to embark on a journey of discovery. Because even though the beautiful sun blazed bright in my world, I knew there were places its rays didn't reach. There were places where what was good and right seemed of little consequence. And for the people who existed there, it was all they could do just to survive. I would go there, I decided –I would explore, interact, learn, and discover. After all, I reasoned to myself, if I hadn't known the safety and shelter created by my family and my religion, would I still believe as I believed? Would my definitions of what was good and right still be the same? Would I still be "saved"?

Then too, I wondered, who could appreciate God's love more fully –the one who was holed up in her study creating a picture of God through meditation? Or the one who went out into the world and could then still see God despite what she saw surrounding her?

And so, standing atop my watershed and looking down at the slopes on either side, I decided I would still seek God and truth and the meaning of things. But I was no longer going to do it from the safety of my tower. Like the Lady of Shallot, I was going to step out and experience life. And although conscious that I might well be calling the curse down upon myself, I felt compelled. As though faith untested wasn't faith at all. I imagined myself one day saying, "Yes, I've been there too, but this is *why* I still believe as I do."

I considered it a good plan, despite the risks. I unleashed my compassion and curiosity and resolved to be *mostly* careful, and, especially, not to hurt anyone.

So how was I going to initiate my plan? I started with the most obvious act. Sex –that mysterious, irrevocable act. Having grown up thinking sex was sinful or sublime depending on the when and with whom, I decided I was going to remove both its halo and its devil horns and treat it as a mere physical, if intimate, act between two people. I would find someone who would be kind and gentle, and yet who wouldn't think I'd given him or owed him the world for what we'd just done.

His name was Andy.

"TAKE A PICTURE OF SOMEONE famous?"

I was returning home one Saturday morning after taking pictures in the city when his voice, soft and deep and playful, stopped me.

"Why?" I asked, turning to look at him. "You famous?"

He was tall, tan, and maybe a year or two younger than me. His dark brown hair had warm highlights from long hours in the sun. There was laughter in his blue eyes, and he had an easy, good-natured grin. His open, unassuming manner put me at ease, even as I noted his huge, black duffle bag and scuffed-up cooler. Homeless, but harmless, I thought.

He jumped up onto a sidewalk planter and began a series of theatricals, so I made a show of taking my camera from around my neck and snapping a few pictures. He jumped down again, all eagerness and energy.

"You want to hang out?"

He stood there, so tall and broad-shouldered, looking for all the world like a kid wanting a playmate. He was beautiful, really –his dark hair framing a face that faintly resembled Jim Morrison. Or rather, Val Kilmer playing Jim Morrison. He stood, watching, waiting.

Curiosity sparked within me at the chance to haunt and inhabit someone new. To see the world through his eyes. So, I smiled and said, "Sure," and he led the way with long, boyish strides. Stopping abruptly, he turned back to face me with a, "C'mon!" and I ran the few steps to join him.

He talked. How he talked! –jumping from one subject to another as though starved for social interaction. Four months earlier, he'd driven a couple guys from his home state of Colorado up to Seattle. Upon arriving, they stole his wallet and his car, and he'd been living on the street ever since. He described the best places to eat, to sleep, and to watch people when you're homeless. He described his family back home and the people he had met in Seattle and his detailed plans for the near and far future.

He absorbed my attention as we walked to the pier. There, the sunlight sparkled off the water and fell in patches around us, warming the wooden planks and occasionally spotlighting us.

At twenty-two, he exuded boyish energy, along with a sort of sweet, trusting innocence that I found refreshing. He wanted nothing other than shared time, and because of this I found myself relaxing into the moment.

At the end of the pier, I leaned my back against the railing while he settled onto a wide, worn bench. A slight breeze cooled my neck as I watched him pull the contents from his bag and share their stories in show-and-tell fashion. His bag had the faint, stale smell of homelessness, like a well-worn t-shirt that's been forgotten under a pile of junk in the back of a car. Not acrid, really, just thick. But he smelled good. Clean.

Was his lack of recent social interaction responsible for the undue significance he gave each of these common, discarded, and rediscovered items? I wondered how homelessness would change me, change my friends. I watched him, transfixed, until something he said startled a laugh out of me. He fed off my delight. Free of inhibitions, expectations, or hidden intentions, he seemed so different in every way from Kurt and everybody I knew. I smiled, watching him.

He told me his full name. "Andy," I repeated quietly as he chattered on. He ran his hand through his thick hair and adjusted his sock a little, looking around and laughing, and then he tried to guess my name, Rumpelstiltskin-fashion. Or maybe not, seeing as how no claims were made on firstborn children. Shaking my head and waving my hands through my laughter, I finally told him.

I turned around after this elaborate display of all he owned and looked out over the water. He came and stood behind me. I sensed him, felt him, as he moved closer, until at last he was holding me, the hesitant lightness of his arms seeming to ask permission. I let him.

He smelled like lotion. When he stepped back enough so that I could move away if I wanted to, I stayed. He seemed harmless. And lonely. And in a way, I was lonely too.

In the previous weeks, my feelings for Kurt had fallen like a landslide, deep into my belly. I had done my best to wall them up into a perfect little compartment, which I buried even deeper, out-of-sight. I could almost ignore them as I focused instead on interacting with the world, with Andy. Neither of us was asking or offering anything, other than shared time.

We walked again, soothed by the comingled sounds of water and traffic. Lazy gulls floated above us, peering down unconcerned as they waited for someone to spill their fries or share a sandwich. We weaved in and around groups of happy tourists as we passed little diners and ice-cream shops that left the air smelling sweet and salty.

Spotting the fountain down by the aquarium, Andy shot me a grin and raced ahead. He stripped down to his shorts and jumped in. I watched in wonder as he splashed about. I snapped pictures as onlookers stared and a few women laughed behind their hands in embarrassment. He was having such a good time and the water looked so refreshing under the hot July sun that soon several little boys ran up and joined him, their laughter lively and loud.

Andy climbed out suddenly, dripping water across the pavement as he chased down a bus to retrieve a toy left onboard by tourist's child. He returned, handed over the treasure, and when he looked at me, his smile reflected the sun. Not a care in the world. I clapped and cheered, and the tourists around us joined in.

And now, a quick montage of the rest of our first day together:

There we are eating peanut butter and jelly sandwiches in an empty courtyard while flipping through the pages of his notebook. He tells the story behind a page filled with stick-figure sketches, and I laugh, covering my mouth with the back of my hand so as not to spray peanut butter chunks everywhere.

Next, we're inside a music store, our heads crowned with earphones. We're laughing, dancing, and swapping in a tangle of arms and cords. At the same instant, we glance up and lock eyes. I smile. He grins back. A moment later I pull away, browsing from a distance until, connection lost, I spy a book about Rodin. I wave my Jim Morrison look-alike over so he can admire *The Thinker*'s fine and fetching figure. He poses straightway for me –replicating a man lost in thought, chin on his fist. I laugh and snap my shutter before pulling him up by the hand and out into the evening air.

Next, we're in a movie theater, shoulders pressed together as we sit breathless in the dark. Our faces are lit by moving colors. We don't share popcorn. Instead, he picks up a kernel from the chair beside him and shoots it, basketball-like, into the cup holder ring a couple seats down from us. He looks at me, whispers, "I hate it when people litter. Don't you?" and turns back to the screen while I surreptitiously start tossing any popcorn I can find into his lap.

Now we're facing each other on a quiet street under tall, dark buildings punctured by yellow windows. The sidewalk is sparkling, and the streetlamps are casting moving tree shadows at our feet. The cool night air raises the hairs on the back of my neck.

"So," he asks, "can we hang out again?" And with that, the mood shifts and my montage ends.

Upon hearing his question, I took a mental step back and considered him. He was nice. Being with him was nice. Where was the harm in seeing him again? "Yeah, okay," I said finally. "But–" and I wondered whether I should even say anything– "I'm not one for getting close."

"As in, you're not looking for a relationship."

"Yeah. Friends only."

"Hey, I get it. I'm good with friendship." That easy smile again.

I gave him my number before heading home through the darkened streets.

I had no idea whether we would, in fact, see each other again. In a small way, I think I wanted to "save him." Typical.

When I told John about it later, he interrupted me with a quick, "Be careful." Before I could protest, he added, "He'll see you as a project as much as you see him as one."

A *project* –the word made my skin prickle. Was that how I viewed Andy? I hated the idea almost as much as I hated the idea of being anyone else's project. No, I insisted to myself, he was just fun, and if we saw each other again, we'd just hang out.

Andy called on Tuesday, and I met him after school that night. I found him lying on top of one of those ventilators that blows up hot air in front of big buildings. I climbed up there with him. We were alone and warm on top of a dusty world.

Everything else became dark and far away as we talked and laughed. He reached out, his outstretched hand a shadow in the dim light, and traced the curve of my cheek. Before I could become uncomfortable under the intimacy of his touch, he let his fingers slide gently down toward my neck and shoulder. "Clavicle," he said softly, tracing the bone, his fingers moving lightly. His voice named the adjoining bones, the route within my body, all sheathed in moon-reflected skin that shivered beneath his touch. "Pectoral," and he named the adjoining muscles. I barely breathed and my mind was quiet as his sensual fingers traced their anatomy lesson across my skin. When I smiled at him, his relaxed grin caught the glow of the streetlamps, and his eyes shone like stars.

"I'm starting a new job tomorrow," I whispered. "Will you walk me home when I get off?"

"I'll walk you home," he said softly. "Every single night."

I climbed down from the vent and looked up at him.

"See you tomorrow?"

"See you tomorrow."

"HERE, WOULD YOU LIKE these?" I handed Andy two tickets as we walked together several weeks later. "Someone at work gave them to me, but I have a shift that night."

He held them toward a streetlamp so he could read them. "The Crocodile? Is that the bar in Belltown?"

"Yeah, on Wall Street, I think. Just past First Ave. I've never heard of this band, but the guy making copies was cool."

"Does that happen a lot –people giving you stuff?"

I shrugged. "Yeah, I guess. The perks of making copies in downtown Seattle." I grinned at him.

"You like your job then?" Andy asked, pulling his coat tighter against the cool, late summer night air.

"I love it! Copy X is surprisingly fun! I mean, I wasn't expecting it to be bad or anything, but still, my coworkers are pretty awesome, and there's no manager hanging over us on the swing shift. Everyone's free to just hang out and do their jobs. And you should see some of the people who come in."

"Oh, yeah? Like who?"

"There's a Vietnamese man who says he's returning to his country to become the next president. He keeps asking all us girls if we want to go join him in the palace."

"I bet you were tempted."

"Haha, no. This other guy looks just like a troll –shorter than me, with this huge, thick, hairy neck and beady eyes and hands the size of baseball gloves." I gestured, showing him just how big. "And you should see this model who comes in. He's completely in love with himself. If one of his comp cards messes up, we can't throw it away because he thinks someone might steal it out of the trash. Like we're going paste it up in the backroom or sell it. He acts like he's doing us a huge favor every time we help him. But that's what I love most, I think –the variety of people."

I loved passing notes back and forth with the friendly deaf man who came in to use the computers. I loved the soft-spoken artist who ordered piles of postcards displaying his brilliant, beautiful work. I loved the musicians who came in to print band flyers and who invariably passed along free tickets. I loved all of them.

"Everyone has a story," I'd say to my coworkers, practically bouncing with excitement.

"That'll change," they told me. But I waved away their knowing pessimism with a laugh. How could I not be fascinated by everyone?

"But the weird thing," I said, looking at Andy, "is that despite how different they all are, they feel familiar. It's almost like I know them. Understand them. Like family."

"Shit. I don't understand my family."

"But you love them, right? They're familiar to you?"

"Yeah. Some of them."

"Well, that's how I feel with these people."

"You love them?"

"More like, I feel connected to them somehow. Does that make sense?"

"Not really. I thought you couldn't get close to people."

"I don't. Not easily anyway. But this isn't closeness, exactly. I'm not going to invite any over to my place for dinner or hand over my keys and ask them to housesit when I go on vacation. More like, I feel like we're all part of something."

"As in one of those 'we're all waves in the same ocean' sorts of things?"

"Not 'waves' exactly. I like my individuality too much. But maybe one ... picture. Or one living tree, each of us the leaves, connected and part of a living whole."

"I don't know what tree you're looking at. The only one I can picture has its leaves all shredding each other."

"I know, right? Humanity and unity aren't exactly synonymous. I mean, there's times I don't even like people all that much. But what if we could be?"

"United?"

"Yeah. I mean, don't you ever feel it? Like there's something connecting us?"

"You and me, maybe," he said with a grin. "I don't care about anyone else."

I grinned but looked away, wishing I could explain myself better.

"Honestly, Babe," Andy said, and I looked up at the softness in his voice, "the only connection I care about is this one." His finger moved in the air between us. "This is all the picture I need."

THE NEXT DAY AFTER school, I met him in the park. After tossing my backpack on the grass and adjusting the camera strap around my neck, I asked him if he'd help me take some motion shots for my fashion class.

"You want me to tear off my shirt and run circles around you?"

"Appealing as that sounds, I had something a little different in mind," I laughed, wrapping a scarf around my waist and handing the ends to him. "Here, hold these. We'll spin ourselves around, and I'll shoot you with a blurred background." I could see everything so clearly in my mind. It seemed so easy. "Like this," I said, raising my camera as we slowly started orbiting each other. "Okay, a little faster...Perfect! That's it!"

The camera's cold metal frame smacked my forehead, causing me to wince, and my feet seemed to be made of lead. But we began picking up speed. In the too-small frame of the sliding, shifting viewfinder, I caught glimpses of his beautiful laughing mouth and shining blue eyes. I clicked away, the rapid shutter releases sounding loud in my ears.

"Wait!" I said, laughing, "Not so fast--*whoops*." I stumbled, vision spinning, and caught myself on his shoulder with one hand, the other wildly clutching the camera. He reached out to steady me, and I grinned up at him.

"Don't stop," I breathed out, "Keep going!"

We started spinning again, the world streaking by. The scarf dug painfully into my sides, making me feel heavy and light at the same time. Suddenly we were caught in a vortex of swirling trees and leaves and flying hair. Wisps of sunlight reached for us, but we were too fast. The sounds of birds and traffic faded away until all I could hear was our breathing and the pounding of my heart. And tiny bells of happiness. Reaching my free hand out to him as we spun, I unsteadily traced the curve of his jaw with the tip of my finger. So beautiful. So fleeting and so beautiful.

Then suddenly, I lost my balance again and fell, pulling him down on top of me. I scrambled back to my feet before the spinning in my head could stop. "Again!" I shouted, happily, dizzily. He grinned at me like I was the strangest, craziest girl he'd ever seen. His face shone, delight spilling out, and I couldn't help but laugh in response. He laughed too, which made me laugh harder. "C'mon, faster," I said, giggling to the point of hiccups. I couldn't shoot for how hard I was laughing and hiccupping. We tripped and twirled, until we finally fell to the ground, holding our sides and trying to breathe through our happiness.

"You're awesome," he said, his voice a whisper.

The grass tickled my cheek as I turned to look at him, smiling and trying to catch my breath. Sunlight played across his face, warming his skin, his hair, his mouth. I took a deep breath and sat up. Rolling the scarf into a ball, I shoved it into my school bag. "Here," I said, holding up a soccer ball and a Frisbee, weighing them on either hand. "Which one?" He pointed with his chin, and we spent the rest of the afternoon racing across the field.

Afterward, feeling happy and tired, I took him to my apartment for the first time.

He casually set his duffle bag down and looked around the small living room.

"So," I said, waving a hand dramatically at the desk, bookshelf, TV, bowl chair, and my pile of blankets under the window, "this is my room. The bedroom is my roommate's, but she's rarely here."

I watched him for a moment, feeling both cautious and curious. But when he looked at me and smiled, my worries melted away.

After dinner that night, I turned from the sink where I'd been washing dishes and asked him, "Can you slow dance?"

"The only slow dancing I've done was at my high school prom," he said, his voice soft and deep.

"Then you're good to go," I said, pulling him up and placing his hand on my waist. He stepped closer, his arms wrapping their warmth around me. He was so ... relaxed. I'd say accommodating, but it wasn't even that exactly. He was just so fully present, willing to try anything and content to be in the moment. I leaned into him, head to his chest, feeling safe and warm as I listened to the rhythm of his heart.

"You're the perfect height," I told him, nestling my head under his chin.

"For what?"

"For me ... right now."

I traced his golden dark skin –how the sun loved him– and looked up at the dark brown hair falling across his broad forehead. Such blue eyes. Perfect lips.

It was getting late.

"You need to leave," I said, suddenly backing away. I looked down, then up again. He quietly asked to stay.

"No," I said. "You can't stay the night." We stared at each other, neither of us sure what to say. Then he picked up his bag.

Part of me wanted to reach out a hand to stop him, but I was afraid. Not of him, but of him getting used to an easy arrangement that I might find difficult to undo later. "When you get your own apartment," I said. When there was no longer a risk of dependency. I softly shut the door behind him.

That Friday, his voice full of enthusiasm, he described the job applications he'd submitted, his new voicemail system, and how he was going to get his ID.

"That's so great!" I said, absorbing his excitement.

Halfway through making dinner, I noticed that he'd fallen asleep –sprawled out in the middle of the floor, a sweater I'd left lying on the chair pulled up into a pillow under his head. It was late. I ate in silence, watching him sleep. He was so sweet, so gentle. A child. A man. Caught in limbo.

I decided not to wake him, and instead draped a blanket over his shoulders. I quietly lay down opposite him, tucked away in my pile of blankets under the window. In the beam of streetlight shining between us, I watched the dust motes dance to the soft sounds of his breathing until I, too, fell asleep.

OUR SHARED MOMENTS had piled one upon the other, creating friendship ... creating trust. His way of always listening –even when he didn't seem to be– disarmed me. He'd bring up something I had said days earlier –a thing I'd nearly forgotten– and I'd turn to him in wonder. He still liked to talk, but not with the overwhelming rush of words as when we first met.

He also had a way of touching me that was as natural as breathing –as though he wasn't fully conscious of it, and yet, all so *very* conscious of it. My fingers reached out, almost of their own accord, curious about his many textures. Where we touched, we glowed. I traced the soft and scratchy stubble along his chin, the smooth edge of his brow, and the curve of his full mouth. So sweet. So beautiful.

Yes, I thought, he'll do.

I didn't love him. I didn't see myself ever loving him. But he was gentle and kind. He was a tool, and I used him. Selfishly. Tenderly. I was curious and expectant and vulnerable too, but mostly, I was selfish.

He touched his forehead to mine, silently, reverentially, and the hair on the back of his head tickled my palm as I embraced him. His hands slid up my back, freeing me of my shirt. Then they slid down, past my ankles, until soon I lay white in the darkness. He was all breath and heat and gentleness as he leaned closer. My eyes stung at the sudden sharpness of the pain, but I let my hands feel his smooth, strong back and his sweat-drenched hair. I tasted his mouth. I inhaled his breath. And though all the world was shifting, I felt the same.

Afterward, as he lay on me, next to me, his deep breathing giving way to sleep, I thought about God and eternity and this thing called morality. If I'd just sinned, I felt no different. If I'd just surrendered my future to the dark void of faithlessness, I nevertheless felt whole. All that was different was a word, the word attached to a mere physical trait. I was no longer a virgin.

My choice was conscious. Not to reject God, or the religious teachings of my youth. But to experience life, and the ability to choose. I wanted to love God, but not unknowingly. I wanted to have the faith of a child, but not the mind of a child. I wanted to stand not on tradition, but on my own two feet. So, I took a chance, and was, for the first time, willing to make a mistake for the sake of growing.

And I did grow. I grew up.

# Chapter 2

In the weeks that followed, I felt no regret. In fact, I felt stronger, more confident. Walking down the street I even felt ... powerful.

I fluttered on the outskirts of Andy's world over the next couple months –flying close, but never forming an attachment. He introduced me to his world –led me on a tour through the lives of the homeless. I had no idea –for everything I had seen while walking through the city, for all the faces I had stared into and the sounds and smells I had pushed through– I had no idea. He showed me the best places to sleep –the warm, dry places. Not that he always found such a place. He often slept when he could, where he could. Once, while walking with Yoshi late one night, I found him curled up on a bench down by the pier. The streetlamps glowed an otherworldly orange as I knelt in the rich brown shadows next to him. "Andy ... Andy," I called softly. He was so embarrassed, and his words were all jumbled up with sleep that I left him there, telling myself his life wouldn't always be the way it was then. It would be better. Soon.

Later he took me to the diner where he could earn a free meal by bussing tables. He was so proud when he bought me lunch that day. He took me to the place that offered free showers and laundry services, and then together we walked to the Department of Licensing to get him an ID. The ten bucks were nothing. Everything. He'd pay me back, he said.

The nights I worked, he walked me home. We'd talk and hang out, and then he'd disappear off into the darkness. We'd meet again in the mornings and head out together. As we walked, I noticed how people looked at him, treated him. Because of his bag –his badge of homelessness. No respect. Scorn. He spoke of an "us" versus "them." He felt alienated, shut out from the rest of the world. From society. I listened with wide eyes as his speech sometimes drifted a little too far off center. His situation was changing him.

Together though, we were optimistic. With his new ID, he found work through Labor Ready, an employment agency. Long-term goals took shape within him, and he talked excitedly about his plans.

"Everything's coming together for you," I said, feeling so happy.

But as time passed, I began to worry. He was so gentle and sensitive. When he got angry or frustrated at the way things were going, the mood passed in a moment. At social events sponsored by Seattle's shelter for street youth, he got along well with everyone, and no one ever hesitated to approach him. Even so, he stood alone –not tied to any clique or group. Nevertheless, he was easily influenced, and I soon noticed a tendency to drop all for the sake of pursuing some new plan that offered the possibility of quicker rewards.

"I'm working for you, Babe," he said. "I mean, I'm doing it for me –to help myself. But you're my motivator. I want to be worthy of you."

I could've cried. For the briefest of moments, I considered –truly considered– the possibility of an "us." But then the tender possibility slipped, and I began to distance myself.

He hated his job. It started at six a.m. in Kent, a city twenty miles south of Seattle. I rarely saw him, but he called or emailed when he could. He described everything, including the people he met.

"They can help me get on my feet," he wrote, "I can do that with you, but I *can't* do that with you. You see? I don't want to be a burden or for you to be the one supporting me. I'll work with these guys; get a little money so I can get on my feet, and then I'm gone."

# Chapter 2

In the weeks that followed, I felt no regret. In fact, I felt stronger, more confident. Walking down the street I even felt ... powerful.

I fluttered on the outskirts of Andy's world over the next couple months –flying close, but never forming an attachment. He introduced me to his world –led me on a tour through the lives of the homeless. I had no idea –for everything I had seen while walking through the city, for all the faces I had stared into and the sounds and smells I had pushed through– I had no idea. He showed me the best places to sleep –the warm, dry places. Not that he always found such a place. He often slept when he could, where he could. Once, while walking with Yoshi late one night, I found him curled up on a bench down by the pier. The streetlamps glowed an otherworldly orange as I knelt in the rich brown shadows next to him. "Andy ... Andy," I called softly. He was so embarrassed, and his words were all jumbled up with sleep that I left him there, telling myself his life wouldn't always be the way it was then. It would be better. Soon.

Later he took me to the diner where he could earn a free meal by bussing tables. He was so proud when he bought me lunch that day. He took me to the place that offered free showers and laundry services, and then together we walked to the Department of Licensing to get him an ID. The ten bucks were nothing. Everything. He'd pay me back, he said.

The nights I worked, he walked me home. We'd talk and hang out, and then he'd disappear off into the darkness. We'd meet again in the mornings and head out together. As we walked, I noticed how people looked at him, treated him. Because of his bag –his badge of homelessness. No respect. Scorn. He spoke of an "us" versus "them." He felt alienated, shut out from the rest of the world. From society. I listened with wide eyes as his speech sometimes drifted a little too far off center. His situation was changing him.

Together though, we were optimistic. With his new ID, he found work through Labor Ready, an employment agency. Long-term goals took shape within him, and he talked excitedly about his plans.

"Everything's coming together for you," I said, feeling so happy.

But as time passed, I began to worry. He was so gentle and sensitive. When he got angry or frustrated at the way things were going, the mood passed in a moment. At social events sponsored by Seattle's shelter for street youth, he got along well with everyone, and no one ever hesitated to approach him. Even so, he stood alone –not tied to any clique or group. Nevertheless, he was easily influenced, and I soon noticed a tendency to drop all for the sake of pursuing some new plan that offered the possibility of quicker rewards.

"I'm working for you, Babe," he said. "I mean, I'm doing it for me –to help myself. But you're my motivator. I want to be worthy of you."

I could've cried. For the briefest of moments, I considered –truly considered– the possibility of an "us." But then the tender possibility slipped, and I began to distance myself.

He hated his job. It started at six a.m. in Kent, a city twenty miles south of Seattle. I rarely saw him, but he called or emailed when he could. He described everything, including the people he met.

"They can help me get on my feet," he wrote, "I can do that with you, but I *can't* do that with you. You see? I don't want to be a burden or for you to be the one supporting me. I'll work with these guys; get a little money so I can get on my feet, and then I'm gone."

"I want to be able to take you out," he added. "To dinner, to music concerts, to a little country fair fifty miles from here. You and me, Babe."

It was beautiful. Touching. Distressing.

I cared about him and wanted to help him, but I couldn't ignore the fact I wasn't emotionally close. Which meant I was using him. And he didn't know it. I began to think that helping him return home to Colorado would be the best thing. For both of us.

I MET LYMON AT THE school's computer lab near the end of August. Sitting at either end of a long table with no one between us, I tried to finish my assignment but couldn't focus because Lymon was one of those people who, when he glances in your direction, you *feel* his eyes as much as see them out of the corner of your own. The first time he rose and approached me –a black shadow looming toward me from the right– I half turned to him with a polite smile and gave his question a quick reply. He returned two or three times more to ask other, obvious, questions. The repetition was almost painful. The last time he approached, I stared at him fully, taking in his dark eyes and the shaggy black hair that hung down across his broad, pale forehead, creating shadows that shuddered with his nervous movements. With my attention fixed so directly upon him, he looked down, smiled, and returned to his seat. I stayed until the lab closed at six. Then I packed my bag, and he followed me out, introducing himself and making small talk while we walked back to the dorm where I'd planned on visiting some friends. I listened to him and answered politely while noticing the peculiar way the skin of his neck drooped a little, giving him the look of one who wasn't fully held together. He asked if we could talk a little longer. He was new, still meeting people, and would love to make me dinner.

I hesitated. But my curiosity –as yet unjaded and still interested in hearing everyone's story– quietly persuaded my caution to relent, and so I agreed.

He looked far older than his twenty-seven years, and I was surprised he had chosen to live in student housing. His major was multi-media, but his passion, he told me as we entered his room, was his music. He was the lead singer and guitarist for his band, and he wrote the music to their songs. Pulling out a scuffed guitar he started singing. His voice was ... *eh*, but he could play.

Propped on the floor with my back to the small couch, I observed his peculiar manner. He wasn't comfortable socially. I mean, he wasn't exactly shy, but he seemed to be hiding something, sounding off little warning bells in my head. Still, I wanted to peer inside his brain, and so we started talking, sharing ideas. When I told him about growing up as a missionary kid, he said he was a Christian too, and he pulled out some prayers he had written. They had all the fervency of true sincerity. Not that it was for me to decide one way or the other, but it was just that everything he said, everything he did carried an aura of falsity –as though he were spreading out a thin layer of ice over the deep, dark pool of his soul, through which, if I ventured too far, I could fall and find myself in a freezing horror. Why then did I stay? I was a student; he was my subject.

He described his views on relationships. He had created a timeline for himself: wouldn't date a girl before knowing her a month, wouldn't consider marrying her until such and such a time after that, and so on. I stared at him, seated now at his kitchen table, and hoped he wouldn't notice my amusement. Pacing oneself was one thing, but a timeline?

Before I could say anything, he added, "It's really great meeting another believer. I don't get the chance to talk about religion very often, especially not with Christian girls."

I felt the need to burst his bubble.

"I'm not who you think I am. I love God, and I want to do what's right, but my faith is changing. I used to obsess over all the do's and don'ts, but now, after spending so much time being terrified of making mistakes, I think that sometimes we have to just live, even if that means making a mistake. Not that I want to disregard God or the rules laid out for us. More like I want to explore life, with all its good and bad and shadowy parts."

"Meaning?"

"Meaning I used to think I would go to hell if I did certain things. Not that good or bad deeds determine salvation, because I believe faith in God is a relationship. Or at least it should be. But I felt so much guilt, all the time, over everything. I thought maybe I wasn't really saved. In fact, I don't know how many times I asked God to come into my heart –again– just to be sure. But now, after being so hung up on morality, I think that God understands us, what drives and motivates us, what our weaknesses are, and why we fail or do things that are 'wrong.' I think that instead of standing over us, waiting to condemn us, he sees everything and loves anyway."

"Why are you telling me this?"

"Because I don't want you to think I'm something I'm not. I'm not a saint. A Christian, yes, but not a saint. I slept with someone for no other reason than because I decided I needed to grow up. I don't even have feelings for him. He's sweet, but I have a hard time getting close to people. If I feel guilty over anything, it's that, because ultimately, it means I'm using him."

"Who is this guy? What is he like?"

I paused a moment. It really wasn't any of his business. But then I answered, "He's *good* ... thoughtful, kind, treats me with respect. We met when he was homeless. He had driven up here with some people who stole his car after they got here. But he's got a job now, and things are looking up. I think I see him as something of a project, which is condescending, I know. He's so much more than that. I just mean that I want to help him. It feels good to help him."

Lymon absorbed all this and then asked, "Do you regret your lost virginity?"

"Well, first off, it's not *lost*. I made a conscious choice to give it up. And do I regret it? No. Maybe I should, and I want to do what is right –to please God, to grow ... but what's done is done, and I wouldn't change it. And I can honestly say that I love God no less."

The conversation shifted to other topics then, and still, my curiosity pulled at me. I wanted to look around inside his head, as though inside an oddity shop. With his own articulate willingness to express himself providing entry, I explored his thoughts, looking for take-aways.

Soon the conversation centered on religion. For all that was religiously contradictory about him, he knew the Bible. These are the most dangerous types, I thought. But perhaps I could use his knowledge despite his persona.

Let me explain. Lymon came at a time when I wondered, despite all my assertions, whether I might unknowingly be walking away from God. I didn't think so. It didn't *seem* so. But maybe I was turning my back on God without even realizing it. Everything seemed just as it had before, but this did little to reassure me. Did God's love and grace truly blanket all? Or was it possible that I was slipping away, imperceptibly ... my downward slide so slow as to escape my notice? Or maybe it was neither, and my actions –which seemed so monumental to me– were inconsequential. Or maybe, and this thought unnerved me most of all, God had never been there to begin with. Or at least not in the way I imagined. So, I looked for signs. I listened. I even listened to Lymon, bypassing his biases and calling on his knowledge, to see if perhaps he could be an unknowing, not unwilling, messenger. Unfortunately, although maybe not surprisingly, he was not.

But I'm getting ahead of myself. Lymon and I decided to have a Bible study. Yes. A *Bible study*. The time and date set, I got up to go.

THE FOLLOWING FRIDAY night, I met Lymon in the dorm's band room. His group had just finished up, and excitement poured off him.

"What do you do when all your dreams come true?"

"I'm sure I don't know," I said, smiling as I watched him with cheerful curiosity.

We took the elevator to the eighth floor, and I followed him to his room. He dropped his bag and guitar in the corner, and we settled down across from each other –him sitting on one side of the small room, me on the other with my back against the wall. We decided on a passage, and, after reading through it, I looked up to find that he was flipping through the pages of his Bible with a bored expression.

I leaned down closer to my Bible. "What do you think about this verse?" I asked, and I read it aloud before referencing another verse in the New Testament. "See how they echo each other? I love how the Old and New Testaments tie together. Everything points to the coming of Christ. And his gift of eternal life."

He looked at the passages, nodded, and we began discussing the rest of the chapter, each of us becoming more animated as we talked.

"You know ...," he said after a while, and he laughed in that way he so frequently laughed: a little bit nervous, quite a bit telling, but only somewhat unsettling. "You know, I've never met a girl who studies the Bible the way you do."

"You need to meet more girls. Besides, what other way is there to read the Bible?"

He shrugged, and we sat there in silence for a few minutes. Then I looked up and asked, "Do you believe in predestination?"

"Where did that come from?"

"Nowhere. Just curious."

"You mean, do I think a loving God would only choose to save a select few and deliberately send the rest of humanity to hell? Why would anyone *want* to think that?"

"I agree, but for the sake of argument, is leaving it up to people really that much better? I mean, there are those doing all they can just to survive, who don't exactly have time to sit around pondering the meaning of life and the existence of God. Are they going to hell because they haven't gotten around to accepting God? And those who have chosen not to accept, do they even have all the facts? Would they have chosen differently if born into a different family, a different culture or time or religion? Should they be punished *forever* because of the choices they're making now, in this fleeting lifetime?"

"You don't think much of people, do you. And so, what? Eliminating free will is somehow more compassionate? What about the people in hell? Sucks to be you? And that's it?"

"I'm not saying I believe in predestination, but a lot of Bible verses hint at it. Look at all the analogies Jesus uses: sheep, referring to the saved, goats to the unsaved –no choice on their part, and you never read about a goat becoming a sheep or vice versa. Or how he says we were 'dead' in our transgressions. The dead don't resurrect themselves. He even comes out and says in the book of John, 'You did not choose me, but I chose you.'"

"He's talking about his disciples there."

"Okay, but what about Romans 9:11-24? 'Prepared for destruction'?"

"There are just as many instances of the Bible telling us to choose –Old and New Testament. The prodigal son chose to return."

"Yeah, but he was already a son."

"'Now choose life' –over and over again. And 'choose for yourselves this day whom you will serve.'"

"Day-to-day living?"

"Do you just not want to believe we might have a say?"

"No, it's not that. What about those who make the *wrong* choice? The stakes seem disproportionately high: eternal damnation for failing to recognize and accept the one true God? How could anyone who truly knows God reject him? And yet, how often are people given the chance to truly know him when so much is obscuring the view? It's not like God is making himself visible."

"Isn't he?"

"*Is* he? That's just my point –there's so much room for interpretation. Or misinterpretation. Those who do reject God, are they truly rejecting him or just the tainted version of him presented by fallible Christians? It seems like some sort of haphazard, spiritual survival-of-the-fittest."

Lymon studied me for a moment before answering. "Ultimately, it comes down to this: 1 Timothy 2:4-6, God 'wants all men to be saved and to come to a knowledge of the truth. For there is one God and one mediator between God and men, the man Jesus Christ, who gave himself as a ransom for all men.' You gotta have faith in God's love, girl."

He was right. I knew he was right. God's love was an ocean I wanted to dive into. Maybe such an immersion would extinguish the nagging question that burned at my heels –the question of how a loving God could condemn anyone to hell. I'd been told that God didn't owe anyone anything. That it was his grace alone that offered life to those who accepted it. Others suggested that hell wasn't a literal place, but a separation from God. Perhaps only a temporary banishment. Did this fit? Or were people adjusting the narrative to suit their individual tastes? Was this what Seneca meant when he said, "to mankind, mankind is holy"? Was I elevating humanity by trying to negate hell? Or was humanity elevating itself by creating something, *someone* to believe in?

"You know what else gets me about that?" I asked.

"About what?"

"About faith. Or maybe not faith exactly, but more like focusing on a particular thing. That's what we're told to do, right? To meditate on God's word? On his love. Are you familiar with the story of *Rasselas* by Samuel Johnson? No? Okay, so it's about this prince who lives with all his brothers and sisters inside the palace grounds in some fictional country. He and all of them have everything they could possibly want –the best food, the best teachers, material goods, entertainment, all of it. But they're forbidden to leave the palace grounds –for their own safety. Rasselas, one of the princes, starts to get curious about what things are like in the rest of the kingdom. So one day he sneaks out, along with one of his teachers and a sister. The three of them go off and have all these adventures, meeting people and learning about life.

"Anyway, one of the people they meet is reportedly the wisest man in all the land, although, supposedly, he's become something of a recluse. Rasselas's professor manages to meet and befriend the guy. After they've been friends for a while, the old man starts looking like he has something to tell the professor, but he can't quite bring himself to it. Then, one day, he says, 'I need you to do something for me.'

"And the professor says, 'Sure, what is it?'

"'I have this responsibility that's become too much for me. I'd like to hand it over to you, if you are willing.'

"He then goes on to describe how he controls the weather all over the world. 'It's up to me whether it rains in Africa or shines in the east,' he says. 'Any misstep, and there could be droughts or floods. People could die if I'm not careful. It's exhausting.'

"Meanwhile, the professor is thinking, 'okay, this guy is bonkers,' but he asks for time to consider. Then he goes back to Rasselas and the princess and tells them all about it. They decide the guy has been alone for too long and that he needs to resocialize. Maybe being around other people will help him see the error of his thinking. So they start having the guy over for dinner and engaging him in conversation.

"It works, and sometime later the guy realizes how ridiculous it was to think he could ever control the weather. He tells them, 'It started out innocently enough. I used to daydream as I looked out the window at the clouds. Almost as a game, I started to think, *wouldn't it be fun if I could control the weather?* In my mind, I'd arrange the clouds, with their rain or shade, so that everything was equitable. I spent days, weeks –months!– giving myself over to this daydream. Until, one day, I started to believe it. Little by little, it changed from a harmless pastime to an overwhelming, all-consuming burden, devoid of all reason.'"

I paused a moment and looked at Lymon before continuing. "And this is my point–"

"*Finally*!" he said, laughing.

I grinned and shook my head at him as I said, "Oh, come on, it's a good story."

"Okay, sure. Go on."

"My point is that we can convince ourselves of almost anything if we think about it long and hard enough. It doesn't matter if the thing is good or bad, true or false. If we dwell on it long enough, we're going to start believing it."

"There are worse things to dwell on than the Bible."

"But that doesn't make it true."

"Yeah, but if you start thinking like that, where does it stop? How could you be certain of anything?"

"We have our senses, our reason, our logical thinking–"

"—well, some of us do."

"Hey!"

"I didn't say *you* didn't."

"*Anyway*, it's not that I need empirical evidence. It's just that I need more ... more than just my one-sided attempt at a closer relationship with God. That's how it feels anyway: like I'm reaching out into empty space. Does that make sense?"

"Yeah, I guess. But do you think maybe it's the choices you're making that are keeping you from God?"

"Maybe. But honestly, I felt that way before I did anything overtly 'sinful.'"

He thought a moment, then shrugged. "I'm sorry, I don't know what to tell you."

"It's okay," I said, looking away. "It's my own thing I'm working through."

As the conversation moved on, I found that Lymon's faith, if that's what it could be called, didn't seem the kind that could be weakened or worried by the questions that were troubling me. The questions I had withheld even from my own parents for fear of ... what? That my doubt would spread to them? Or that they wouldn't be able to answer, and the "I don't know" would hang between us, dark and ugly? Or maybe that they would answer, and I would find the words insufficient? Whatever the case, I felt no such need to withhold from Lymon, and over the next two hours, we discussed grace, morality, the self, and the soul.

After a while, he said, "You know, we're evenly matched."

Something in the air shifted then, and I stared at him for a moment. "This isn't about that," I said. "It's not about changing the other's views. It's about sharing perspectives and ideas."

"It doesn't matter —you'd hate to admit it if you were wrong anyway."

"We're discussing, not debating. And anyway, if you showed me I was wrong about something, I'd be the first to admit it."

"Hardly. You like control too much. You don't see it, do you? You say you can't get close to people, but it's because you refuse to *let* yourself get close. You're afraid of losing control, of letting go."

"You're right —I don't want to lose control. That's when things happen —things you can't take back and you come to regret. It's when people lose control that they become the victim. So yes, I like to be aware and in control of myself. What's wrong with that?" I waited a moment, but before he could respond I added, "And by no means am I controlling you, or anyone around me. And really, what does that have to do with getting close to people? It doesn't stop me from getting to know them, and if I found the right person, I'd be all for 'letting go.' But until then, I'll openly confess to holding certain people at arm's length. It's better than hurting them. I'm tired of hurting people."

"And holding them at arm's length doesn't hurt?"

"As long as I'm honest with them, what else should I do? Say goodbye and lose the friendship? What good does that do anyone?"

We stared at each other silently a moment, my chest heaving slightly. I didn't know why I felt so defensive. I closed my eyes and leaned my head back against the wall.

"Look," I said finally, "I've tried to get close to people, and people have tried to get close to me. They've said and done the sweetest things —one guy even typed out the entire story of *Rasselas* for me just because we talked about it once. I mean, he could have just bought me a used copy if he wanted, rather than typing out ninety some pages. I've seen chins quiver and eyes tear up, and I felt *nothing* in response. It's not about letting go. It's about not feeling anything in the first place."

I thought about Kurt. I had felt something for him, briefly, but now those feelings were locked away. Inaccessible.

"Take a chance," Lymon said, and I lowered my eyes away from his gaze, which was too direct and making me uncomfortable. Closing my Bible, I set it beside me and sat up straighter.

His suggestion turned into a request. "I mean, I feel something here. You're impacting me in a huge way –surely that makes you feel *something*."

The only thing I felt was sorry for him. I'd just explained the pointlessness of others trying to get close to me and here he was telling me that even though this was only our second meeting he was affected by me.

His voice grew more intense the quieter it became. "You'd have to be either inhuman or psychologically disturbed to feel nothing!" His voice was almost a whisper.

With a half laugh I blurted out, "Then can you recommend a good doctor?"

"I'm a smart, talented young man," he said, his voice slowly returning to normal, "and I'm a Christian –so me telling you you're impacting me should touch you in some way."

Thoughts of Andy kept returning to me. He didn't ask for anything. He didn't try to fix or figure me out. He was simple. Sweet.

I left shortly after four-thirty that morning. The more we had talked, the more I saw that Lymon's mind carried things through to extremes –when he wasn't excited over possibilities, he was paranoid. There was something familiar about the way he overanalyzed, and I viewed my self-same tendencies with new disgust. Was it possible that Lymon was the person I could become if I wasn't careful? –or maybe who I already was?

I considered this thought as I walked home, and over the next few weeks it returned often, waving like a little flag on the edge of my awareness, demanding attention.

LYMON AND I MET AGAIN a few times after that. He never liked it when I brought up Andy. Ever quick to work in the Christian angle, Lymon insisted on Andy's lack of character because he was at my apartment late into the night. It had the "appearance of evil." Never mind the fact that Lymon and I were often alone together way into the wee hours of the morning. I would have laughed at his many double standards if I hadn't been so disturbed by the sincerity with which he pursued them. He insisted that I wasn't being "sensitive to the Holy Spirit" and that I needed to be "careful about disobeying God by socializing with worldly sinners like Andy." The voice in my head told me he was spiritualizing his jealousy, but I saw no point in expressing that thought aloud. I endured his self-righteous patronizing because he felt like a case-study that I wanted to observe for a little while longer. With detached curiosity, I made mental notes of his behavior so that I could be on the lookout for anything similar in myself.

Once he got upset when I became lost in my thoughts and forgot to say anything for several minutes. He said I wasn't being a true friend since true friendship was about give and take.

"Friendship doesn't give you a license into my thoughts," I said.

"But friends *trust*."

"Trust is earned."

"Well," he said, stopping me. "I'll be very privileged when you feel comfortable enough to share your thoughts with me. You keep them locked away, but maybe one day."

*Maybe*, I thought. But not with *you*. I was beginning to understand that he was the type that uses abuse to hide his own insecurities. Why, even that afternoon he'd made a comment that was specifically chosen for its cutting effect.

I had told him he seemed to be going through a checklist with the people he met –as though he were filling a job position– and he had replied, "My time is limited, and I'm at the point where I don't want to waste my time on friends who aren't going to build me up as a person."

"And you –do you build up?"

Ignoring me, he'd said, "And *you* –well, after our first meeting I wrote in my journal that you were going to be a *project*" –with what perfectly nasty precision did he pronounce the word!– "what with your inability to get close to people and all. I wrote that you have a whole lot of potential but would require some effort."

"A *project*?!"

"–But that was before. I've since realized I was too hasty. We're similar, you and I."

*God forbid*, I thought. But upon hearing him turn the word "project" around on me, I suddenly saw myself and my actions with a new, disturbing clarity. That his condescension should stir up such sharp indignation in me was an irony I couldn't fail to notice. His arrogance, which I so despised, was not unique to him. I shared it. And hearing the word –despite his carefully chosen poison, for had it been unencumbered by spite I'd have felt the sting all the same– hearing the word showed me the callousness of such a comment and made me ashamed of my own insensitivity. What a disgusting way to treat someone.

Andy was not my project. He was so much more. I felt a burst of affinity for him. Yes, I was condescending to look at him as an innocent who needed help, which I was only too willing and eager to give. But unlike Lymon, my condescension was colored with compassion. That mattered, right? Detached feelings aside, I truly desired Andy's happiness. Not that this justified anything, but I could work with this. I could alter my mindset into something better.

Andy. I could help him go home. Away from me, away from the friends in Kent who didn't know the meaning of the word. Away to family and familiarity. Away. Away. I would miss the sweetness of his manner, his unassuming tenderness, but I could help him regain his footing.

And as for Lymon, I would learn from him. For a little while longer, I would watch his manner and movements for what they might say about myself, about people in general. I would be on guard. I would be open and ready. And I would learn.

ANDY CALLED ON SUNDAY. I told him about Lymon, about school and work. Phones are so inadequate at times. Unable to read his expressions, I felt handicapped. He listened, said little, and then with a burst of feeling, he said, "Sometimes I want to just come and take you off to Colorado, or some place."

I pressed the tiny phone to my ear, and like the ocean's echo in a shell, I heard the roaring of empty space.

Four days later he returned to Seattle.

"I'm going back to Colorado," he told me. "That's what everyone suggests –you, the lady at the homeless shelter, the priest, my family. My sister says they can support me better if I'm there. I'll have a place to stay and already have residency, so I can go back to school when I have enough saved." He leaned in close and wrapped his arms around me. I felt his breath on my neck. "I think something bad will happen if I stay here," he said, his voice almost a whisper. He kissed my cheek as I sat there, quiet and pensive. He thought I was missing him already. Maybe I was. I wasn't sure exactly what I felt for him, but one thing I did know – "It'll be good," I said at last.

The next day we said goodbye at the Greyhound station. It was going be a thirty-two-hour ride of crying babies and bumpy seats. I wasn't conscious of feeling much as I handed him a bag of books, sandwiches, and snacks. But as I rubbed at my eyes, I thought about how sweet and unassuming he was. His sensuality was natural and unaffected, and his feelings were uncomplicated.

I would miss him, without a doubt, but I understood, with a pang of guilt, that his departure provided me with an easy way out. Shoving that thought aside, I focused instead on feeling optimistic for him. I forced a smile and waved. He was going home.

# Chapter 3

Labor Day weekend came and went.

Andy called to say his homecoming had been sweet, if unremarkable. We laughed and listened and joked. And with inexplicable ease we each settled into our separate, but ordinary lives in which he was no longer homeless, and I was simply a long-distance friend.

The following Sunday night I sat across from Lymon at his kitchen table. On the table before him lay my American Literature Anthology book –a heavy and expensive red textbook I was somewhat quite attached to. I'd wanted to show him an Edgar Allen Poe story about death and the limits of personal will, but he kept stopping to ask too-personal questions like, "So where did Andy sleep when he stayed over?" to which I would reply, "Goodness –just read the story already!"

As the directness and intensity of his questions gradually increased, I started to get nervous. To divert his attention, I pulled out my little notebook, one I carried everywhere, and handed it to him, pointing to a poem. Then I walked over to the sink at the far end of his tiny kitchen to get some water. Setting down the glass, I thought I heard something –I wasn't sure what, but my skin began to crawl. Turning around slowly, I noticed he had dimmed the lights in the living room. He suddenly appeared in the kitchen doorway, mumbling something about wishing he had some candles. Something about the room and his manner wasn't right. I stood with my back pressed against the hard edge of the sink, hemmed in by the oppressively close walls that seemed almost to be moving, pressing in one breath at a time. My hands slid up to the counter behind me as he stepped closer. I felt so young just then, so foolish and naïve. And angry. I didn't want this. Or him. My dread grew as he moved forward slowly, deliberately, looking by turns from the book to me. My eyes searched for an escape, but his big, bulky shape blocked my only way out.

"What are you thinking about?" as he took another step.

"Nothing. Just waiting."

"What are you waiting for?" taking one sliding step closer. My fingertips started trembling. They were cold, freezing. I felt suddenly cold all over, and my fingers, clenched now against the counter, wouldn't stop shaking.

"For you to finish reading." I looked past him again, hating the narrowness of the kitchen. They were all like that —every kitchen in that dorm. So horribly narrow. And Lymon was rather tall, rather shaggy and slithering and still filling my only way out. The blood running through me was turning to ice, sending goosebumps running along my arms and making my legs feel cold and stiff within my jeans. A shiver ran through me. I was freezing in my fear.

"Wow!" he said when he finished reading, now less than two feet away. I was trapped in that corner, heart racing. Surely, he knew what he was doing, how too terribly close he was —why then didn't he stop?

"Do you feel what I feel?" His voice was low. Again, that secrecy. Maybe he didn't realize the awful affect he was having on me; maybe he lacked experience; maybe he was just stupid. I wasn't going to stay to find out.

"I don't know," I said, trying to make my voice sound casual, although it came out distracted as I searched for a way to squeeze past. "What do you feel?"

"I feel like gravity is pulling us together."

I shot him a glance. "You don't even really know me!"

"Not for lack of trying. You need to open up."

"C'mon," I said, staring at his chest as though to push him back, "I learned early on that people aren't really interested in what others have to say. I'm tired of trying to entertain, of trying to be interesting. I'd just as soon listen. For years, that's what I've done. I'm not going to change now. You're up against a long history of habit."

"You just need to practice."

Something lurked within him, casting shadows, shifting about inside him, barely visible at the backs of his eyes.

As a kid I loved snakes. Catching them, holding them, studying them. I once heard a story about a cat who had caught a snake, pressing it down between its paws. Any sudden movement and the claws shot out, triggering the cat's predator instinct. I've seen people do this –you run; they chase. A knee-jerk reaction as the predator instinct takes over. So, what the snake did instead was to move slowly, almost imperceptibly, until, with patiently controlled effort, it was out of range. Then in a flash, it was gone.

I made my voice light. "Yeah, maybe so, but it doesn't happen overnight."

He shifted his weight then, and I saw my chance. With affected nonchalance, I ducked under his arm and made for the open space of the living room, the dim-lit dying room. He followed and with an air of false casualness handed back my notebook. His hands were cold and clammy. I'd have preferred them to be hot and sweaty. A horny guy is easy to handle, but a guy who's nervous and uncomfortable with himself, a guy like Lymon, couldn't be trusted.

*Can he see how fast I'm breathing?* I wondered, as I struggled to hide my fear lest it excite the predator within him. It was all I could do to hold myself together –to pretend that everything was fine, so that I could leave before anything happened ... before his furtive urgency escalated into something beyond my control.

"Do you want to dance?" as he stepped closer again. What was *wrong* with him that he should look at me like that?

"Nah," I said casually, feigning lightheartedness despite my near-suffocating fear. "I'm not really any good at it." Thoughts of Andy flitted through my mind. How good and *safe* he was ... how good it had felt to dance with my ear pressed against his warm and protective chest.

I threw my notebook into my bookbag and pushed in the many papers that had spilled out, while keeping a quick and cautious eye on him and trying to control my breathing. He appeared put-out, which was fine –as long as he didn't try anything. I firmly declined his offer to walk me home by saying I had people I needed to visit. Stay calm, remain calm; he won't react so long as I am calm, I thought. Then I burst out into the bright freedom of the hallway, quickly shutting the door behind me and taking in a huge breath of shaky air. I escaped into the elevator, slamming the gate closed, and stared at my shaking hands as the tired machine lurched and began its slow descent. I closed my eyes and breathed. One ... two ... three deep breaths. My fear felt irrational –he couldn't have done much in a thin-walled dorm room. But I was terrified, truly terrified, in a way I'd never been before –not even walking home alone from work late at night through the dark and deserted streets.

Two floors down I knocked on Jimmy's door, not realizing it was past midnight. Jimmy was the warmest, safest, sweetest person I knew in the building, and I needed someone friendly before I choked on my panic. His was a safe place, a soothing face. I'll feel better soon and then I'll walk home, I thought, and everything will be okay.

He was half-dressed, with a toothbrush in his hand. But his face, his beautiful face, was a picture of concern when our eyes met. He glanced down at my still-shaking fingers. I shoved them into my pockets.

"What's wrong?"

"Nothing. I just wanted to talk." I smiled, straining for sincerity, and followed him into the room. He sat me down and knelt in front of me.

"Ani, don't mess with me. What's wrong?"

"Can we just talk bullshit for a little while?" I turned my head away, not meaning to sound so pathetic and pleading. I wanted to brush away my weakness and be done with it.

He nodded. "Of course." So, we did. We talked about homework and school and a whole lot of nothing, and it was perfect. My breathing gradually relaxed, and my heart rate slowed.

"I got scared," I said at last. I looked up at him and saw a tiny version of myself reflected in his eyes. I told him about Lymon. "He didn't touch me, thank God, but I felt so threatened." The tremor had returned to my fingers, so I rubbed my arms. "The way he looked at me!" I shuddered.

Jimmy's eyes grew liquid as he stared at me silently. A healing light swam in the corners. I reached a hand up halfway, as though to touch his cheek. Then I dropped it in my lap, laughing with embarrassment as I said, "No, don't cry. You're sweet, Jimmy, really, but please don't cry. It's nothing." I looked away, unable any longer to meet his eyes, filled with their flowing sensitivity. I felt grateful and so relieved to be cocooned in his concern.

He walked me home and hugged me at the door. When I climbed the hallway steps in the darkness, I felt his sweetness still. And by the time my head fell against my pillow, all my worries were faint, and far-away.

I REALIZED THE NEXT day that I'd left my American Literature book on Lymon's kitchen table. I'd paid sixty some dollars for it, and I loved that book. Still, when Lymon called the next day, I didn't answer. He called three more times. And then he knocked on my door. That I was at home was obvious —what with the lights on and the TV blaring. I shivered as I ignored him.

He called again. My phone's cheerful melody echoed throughout my tiny apartment. I stared resolutely at the TV. I heard his voice receding down the hallway as he left me a message.

I listened to the message several hours later —right before I went to bed. Motivated by incredulity, I listened to it three more times so I could copy it down.

*Yeah, hey Ani. Listen, uh, you know, well, basically you're a fucking loser, and I think you're a liar and really lousy Christian and shitty friend so why don't you do us both a favor and don't bother me anymore. Don't call me cause, uh, I don't have time to waste on someone like you. All right? So, uh, I hope you understand where I'm coming from and if you don't it's your problem. And uh, anyway, whatever else I can't remember to say just know that I mean that as well, all right? Later.*

Well, that was interesting, I thought. Knowing him, I mean. Another case study now concluded. Only, he still had that book of mine.

VOICEMAIL:

*Ani, uh, please don't bother me anymore. I told you to leave me alone and not to come by to see me anymore. I really wish you would respect that.*

*You're a game player and a white-trash ho. My first assumptions about you were completely accurate, and I don't have time for any more projects in my life. You're an extremely weak person. You're also morally deficient and I have no res–, you have no respect for yourself and it's no wonder that you aren't respectful of anyone else.*

*You're selfish and incredibly dense in your logic about life in general. I feel sorry for you. Um, I do have pity on you though, but not at the expense of my own sanity and well-being. So please understand that no contact with me means no contact whatsoever, not by any means. Any attempt to do so will be construed as harassment from this point on.*

*I've given you plenty of opportunities to redeem yourself. Three strikes is all you get and now you get the boot. Please leave me alone and do not bother me anymore. Not through a third party, not in any way. Please be respectful of that –okay? You're just not worth it, and I don't want to be around you.*

*You're a lousy person –no, you know what's worse, you're a horrible person and I don't want to be bothered with you anymore. You now go, like, hurt and bother other people but leave me alone.*

*Thank you, bye.*

–and all because I knocked on his door with Jimmy in tow to ask for my American Literature book back.

"I left it by your door that night I stopped by," he said, calmly enough.

"There was no book by my door." I folded my arms across my chest and stared at him.

He glanced at Jimmy; then back at me.

"Don't you listen to your messages? I asked you to leave me alone."

"Happily. I just want my book back."

"I said I left it by your door, so I don't know what else to tell you." He shrugged.

"Could you please just check, just in case?"

He stared at me, unmoving. Seeing I was getting nowhere, I turned and left.

Jimmy was walking me home when Lymon called again to leave that wonderful message. We took turns listening to it and laughing. When my laughter became more subdued, Jimmy hugged me.

"You okay?" he asked. "Just remember we love you for a reason."

"Thank you," I said, smiling up at him and thinking how kind and sweet he was. His presence was so refreshing.

How was it, I wondered, that I ever gave Lymon the time of day? I was so foolish. I mean, *obviously*. But in a way, I was thankful. It was a warning: what to avoid in myself and in others. Unfortunately, I was still learning.

# Chapter 4

Through the windows of Copy X, I watched the buildings on the other side of the street catch fire with the sunset. The September days were getting shorter, and the heads that bobbed down the street now wore hats that half hid the flying hair.

"Hey, Tommy!" I called as I leaned with both elbows on the counter. Tommy was early thirties, tall, heavily built. He kept his head shaved and wore a goatee. He looked the type to watch Monday night football holding a beer in one hand, a sagging pizza slice in the other while yelling at the referee and laughing with his buddies. He walked up behind me, a half-open ream of paper in his hand.

"What's up?"

"What do you suppose Mr. Laminate is doing?" I nodded toward the front of the store.

We both stared at the man in question. He must have had five sweaters on under his black coat. He looked the same every time he came in –arms sticking out a little because of all the padding. We called him Mr. Laminate because he had laminated his driver's license so many times the picture was almost unrecognizable. Earlier, when he had asked us to laminate it once again, it had barely fit through the rollers. And now, he was standing in the middle of the room with his hand up in the air, as though screwing in a light bulb.

"Huh," Tommy grunted as he offered me a Creamsaver. "Beats me." And he turned back to his work.

Someone on one of the computers started waving frantically. I stepped out from behind the counter to go help the woman. Our local Barry Manilow look-alike reached out his hand to me as I walked by, and I slapped his palm lightly with my own.

"When are you going to let me take you out for dinner?" he asked me on my way back.

"When are you going to find someone your own age?" I returned with a grin.

"Oh, c'mon now. They're all too *old*. With wrinkles and dyed hair and fifteen grandchildren. I'd never date someone my own age. But *you* ..."

Just then a woman with a short skirt and skinny high heels logged onto a computer next to him, and he forgot all about me. I smiled as he leaned over and introduced himself.

The windows were dark and the machines whirring when I returned to the counter a few minutes later. Looking pleased with himself, Tommy showed me his latest stop-action movie featuring several Star Wars Lego figures fighting a dramatic scene in which one of them lost his head –the little thing soaring across the screen of his laptop in comic slow-mo gore. When I heard the front door open, I looked up, still smiling, in time to see my whole life change, redirected by the entrance of suited man with way too much caffeine in his system and blue grey eyes that flashed about, absorbing everything.

His cell had just died and by his voice and manner this was no good. He evidently had places to go, things to do, and could he please use the telephone? I smiled and pointed him to the window overlooking Union Street. He looked all around for a minute, searching, and so I walked over.

"Here it is," I said, pulling it up from the low windowsill behind a desk no one ever used. "We like to keep it hidden."

"What's with the shoes?" he asked me, glancing down at my feet.

"What about them?"

"They look like bowling shoes."

"I know. They're so ugly, they're cute. Like bulldogs. I love them."

He smiled, and I left him then. "Back in ten," I told Tommy. It'd been a slow shift, mostly just kids asking me to make change so they could catch the bus, and now I was hungry. Two bites into a sandwich and Tommy leaned in through the door. "Someone's asking for you," he said. Wiping my mouth with the back of my hand, I followed him out, puzzled.

Mr. Caffeine-in-a-Suit had finished his call and was leaning on the counter by the cash register. His eyes were quick, alert, seeing everything. But it was his mouth I noticed. Before relaxing into a smile as I drew near, I saw its firm, hard set. The lower lip was slightly fuller than the upper, giving him a determined look.

"Thanks," he said, "for letting me use the phone."

"Of course."

I smiled and studied him, my hands in the pockets of my blue apron. He had freckles. I liked them. They reminded me of the warm summertime freedom of childhood.

He was hesitating. He was going to ask me out. I waited, glancing at his curly dark hair. It was just curly enough not to be called wavy. He spoke, and I dropped my eyes down to his.

"Would you, uh, would you like to get coffee sometime?"

His whole manner was confident –only his voice was nervous. The flattering kind of nervousness, I thought. As though, while being sure of himself, he wasn't sure of my reply. I liked this. I liked that he didn't assume I would say yes. He reminded me vaguely of someone I used to know, with those blue-grey eyes and those freckles. Only this man was a bit older than my friend and older, too, than my own twenty-four years. And, unlike my friend, he carried himself in such a way that left no doubt he was successful at whatever he did for a living.

"Sure," I said with a smile, still studying him.

"What times are good for you?"

"Mornings."

His gaze was steady, still a little nervous, while he thoughtfully chewed the inside of his lip.

"Tell you what," he said, reaching a decision. He paused to read my name tag. "Here's the deal, Ani, I leave for Chicago in the morning, but I'll be back by the weekend. Here's my email address–" he reached for some paper, "–and ..." still writing "and here's my home phone." The hesitation over that last part was almost imperceptible. "My name's Derek, and I'd love to meet up with you. Sometime soon."

Eye to eye. Green meets grey. Brown meets blue. The future was in that look. A future I couldn't comprehend.

"I look forward to it." I folded the slip of paper and stuck it in my apron.

He shot me another quick glance, and then with a pleased smile and wave he was gone.

IT WAS NOT LOVE AT first sight. Time did not stand still, and sparks did not flash through the air between us. But there was curiosity. Always, the curiosity. The same curiosity I felt one time when I glimpsed, half obscured down a narrow alley, the colors and curves of a mural. The slanting sun reached only part-way down, adding mystery to the lines that flowed into each other, fluid and bold and *alive*. The image beckoned to me, and my feet responded, carrying me closer despite all that might have been lurking in the shadows. I felt the same curiosity another time when, walking through a lonely forest, I spied a color so vibrant I ignored the "PLEASE STAY ON THE PATH" signs and stepped closer, ferns brushing my legs and leafy branches clutching at my shoulders.

Curiosity as the need to know more. A brief excursion, a sight-seeing dalliance, a minor detour, before returning to my original path. Who was he? What did he do for a living? What was his world like? With Andy I'd peered inside homelessness. Perhaps this man with his fine suit and easy confidence would take me for a stroll through affluence. Curiosity has its own pull, the strength of which can be just as powerful, just as stimulating and consuming and ill-advised as instantaneous attraction.

I emailed him the next night –a short little thing asking about Chicago, whether he liked it, blah blah, I hoped he was doing well, goodbye. A few days later, on Saturday, in the middle of my unopened emails was the subject line, "Time, wine, and cheese." His friend was having a gallery opening that night –would I like to go? I called him; we set a time. He would arrive in an hour.

Heart thumping wildly, I hung a dress over the bathroom door and flew into action with my brush, eye shadow, and lip gloss crowding the sink before me. What did people wear to gallery openings? Leaning toward the mirror, eyebrows raised, mouth open slightly, I darkened my mascara and wondered vaguely if my eye shadow was too dark and whether I needed a sweater and how late I'd be out. But none of it really mattered. I was too excited. I threw on some shoes and danced about on one impatient foot trying to buckle the clasp before running down the stairs to meet him. There he stood on the front steps, suited up in front of a huge Cadillac, saying I looked ravishing and leading me to the passenger door, which he opened with quick precision and a confident smile. Everything he did was decisive, deliberate, executed with energy. He knew what he wanted and pursued it without wasting any time over-thinking. What was there to consider? His mind was made up, his choice decided, and now was the time to act, to live, to grab hold of everything he wanted. I stared in amazement, smiling and clutching my purse. I rather liked the fearless speed of his certainty.

The gallery was packed. We were overdressed, but it didn't matter. All that mattered was us. We were everywhere. Derek was everywhere. We circled the place three or more times, talking together, talking with everyone. "Hello! How are you? This is so-and-so. I know her from such-and-such. We're good friends of the artist. Speaking of which, where is she? Isn't this incredible? I have to tell her what I think." Then to me, walking again, with him just ahead, "See anything you like? Anything. Say the word and it's yours. Nothing much draws me. Wouldn't exactly fit with the Picassos at home. Or the Rembrandt. You should see them and my Chihuly sometime –they're exquisite."

His dropped names failed to impress.

"Chihuly? Who's that?" I asked, leaning closer to study an ornately-framed painting of a bare-breasted lady with red, scaly claws.

"What?! *Chihuly?* Only the most famous glass maker in possibly all the world. You've never seen that piece of his in Benaroya Hall –the massive work of genius hanging in the lobby? And you, the *artist!*"

"Okay, sure, I've seen it. It's, uh, interesting. And massive, you're right."

"He's huge in this area. He's got a whole museum down in Tacoma."

"What drew you to the pieces you've got?"

"I see them as an investment."

"But you *like* them, right?"

"The glass pieces. Not so much the Picassos."

"Why do you have them then," I cut in, "if you don't like them?"

"Why do I have them?" with a smile, not unkind, "because they're *Picasso.*"

"I don't understand that. I see no point in displaying art I don't like. I'd prefer something I can lose myself in, even if it's by someone unknown."

Something ahead of us caught Derek's attention, and we side-stepped a laughing couple as we moved forward.

Derek's restless nature seemed unable to remain fixed on any single point, including me. He was captivating with the force of his energy. I'd never met anyone quite like him. But in his full-forward energy he left everyone behind to the extent that he couldn't see them or their reaction to him. I guessed the references to his wealth and his overall success were meant to impress me, but that they had the opposite effect was quite lost on him.

*We're going to be temporary*, I thought. But instead of a desire to distance myself, I felt an odd sort of freedom. If he couldn't see me, he couldn't be hurt by me. Our time together would be unencumbered by emotional entanglements.

So, I stayed. I watched him. I walked with him. Around the room, around the building outside as he smoked and explained how the perfect age for a couple is found by taking the man's age, dividing it by two and adding seven to get the woman's age (he then told me his age, and of course our ages, thirty-four and twenty-four, fit the formula precisely. Had he done a background check on me? And how depressing that the formula never worked for the same two people for more than a year), and around the gallery's circuit once more.

One of my friends from school showed up. He seemed so good and sweet and normal by contrast. Not that Derek wasn't, exactly, but everything about them seemed opposite. From the way they moved to the things they said, I saw them as existing on two, entirely separate planes. My friend regularly spent time with people he trusted, and it showed. His face was happy and his words thoughtful, kind. Derek's expression was cynical and alert, and while he was charming, his attention felt as though it were directed towards each of us as roles rather than as individuals: artist, date, strangers never to be seen again. I looked from one to the other, feeling aligned to neither.

We left then. Away, away. Off to some adventure. I was ready. I was safe. I was a Solomon study –yes, yes, lacking the wisdom, to be sure. But that's why I was there. To gain, to grow, to know. I was going to look through Derek's eyes and see the world as he saw it. And I was going to become wise and the whole process would be horribly exciting.

"Want to go dancing? Or sailing? Or ride in an elevator shaft? You think I'm kidding? I'm not."

No, he wasn't kidding. He was serious and direct and ready to take me there. I laughed.

"Show me, then," –which was precisely what he wanted to hear.

We drove to the condo of a friend of his named Paul, who was away at a concert. Apparently, Paul had a grill he didn't mind Derek using. I waited in the car, flipping through the music selection, while he ran up to check on the place. The car was a rental, his BMW having been in the shop for thirty-two weeks, he said. The BMW was a special-made car designed for some big wig I had never heard of, and now it was Derek's. He said it came complete with bulletproof windows and a sunroof in front and in back. A one-of-a-kind, he said, and I nodded with a very contained smile as he said this and many more amazing and wonderful things. He said ... my goodness! the things he said! He spoke of the condos he bought people, the cars, the artwork –essentially the *money*, the *money*, the *money*. He was rich. Filthy and fabulously wealthy. Not so much as to be conspicuous or to rob him of his anonymity. But enough to carry him on the waves of freedom. He could go, do, see, and be as he wished, when he wished. There could be no mistake –he left room for no misunderstanding– he was financially successful. Possessed as well, and this I noted with far more interest, of a tireless need to allude to his many attributes –material and personal. It was the most marvelous display of self-flattery I had ever seen. Had he not been so terribly amusing to hear and watch, he would have been pathetic. What possessed him to go on this way? I figured it must be born from an irresistible need to prove that he deserved attention ... that he amounted to something. Instead, his magnificent horn-blowing did nothing more than drown out the effect of his words. But he was oblivious. As though he'd learned long ago not to notice the reactions of those around him. He was the actor and I his audience, and this suited both his need for attention and my desire to watch and learn. He plunged straight ahead, and I had only to cling to his coattails to see the world and its responses through his eyes. He didn't need to fix or figure me out, nor did he need me to be entertaining or witty or to act sophisticated. He could do all that for the both of us, and he didn't care what the rest of the world thought about it. We met each other in the moment –just as we were– with a liberating ease.

He returned to the car then, startling me with the sudden opening of the door, and said as he climbed in, "It was messy, but I cleaned it up. Let's go to QFC and get something for the grill." He started the engine and began backing out.

"What do you want to eat?" he asked, still looking over his shoulder. When I was quiet, he glanced at me. I shrugged and smiled. "Alright," he said with a laugh, "we'll see what they've got."

We picked up shrimp, marinated steak, salad, peaches, wine, and he bought a bouquet of lilies. I hoped he wasn't expecting me to cook. I had been known to burn tea. In fact, I think the only thing I'd never burned at least once was cold cereal.

We returned to Paul's place, which was on the sixth floor of one of those formal "luxury" condo buildings with the fake-or-real? flower-filled lobbies and quiet elevators. The hallways sported tastefully bland carpeting and recessed lighting.

"I'm not the greatest cook," I said, as soon as we set the brown paper bags on the kitchen counter. "Just so you know. I don't want to create any false expectations." I turned toward him and smiled as I tore open the bag of shrimp. He already had a cutting board and knife in hand, with the peaches spread out before him. He smiled back as he sliced up a few and tossed them into a pair of glasses.

"I'm the grill master," he assured me, pouring the wine over the peaches and handing me a glass. I took it and swirled it around –watching the light ignite the beautiful deep red.

"Well then, I'm in luck." And we clinked our glasses, staring at each other a moment, before setting out all the food.

Once everything was in place and the grill was heating up, I walked around the small living room, pausing in front of the little black furnace with its little fake fire. Glancing up, I was instantly captivated by the painting above the mantle.

"Schrödinger's cat," Derek said, and I felt him at my elbow. "You familiar with it?"

"No." I stared at the angles jutting out and tilted my head back and both to see both sides.

"The cat, you see, is either dead or alive or both, depending on how you look at it."

The painting illustrated the principal perfectly. On the left side of the six or so angles that jutted out was a full-fleshed cat, but on the right was a cat's skeleton. I stared at it as though hypnotized, while he explained.

"You put a cat in a box," he said, "along with a radioactive atom that has a half-life of, say, an hour –half-life referring to the midpoint of time it takes the atom to decay, after which a little mechanism is set up to trigger the release of poisonous gas which will prove fatal for the cat. After an hour, at this midpoint, there is a fifty-fifty chance the cat is dead –or still alive. Now some people would like to say there's a formula out there that will determine the outcome, or probability, ahead of time, which will lead to predictions of the future in every sense. Einstein said no, you don't and won't ever have all the information you need for such a thing, and that therefore you need to interact –to open the box and see for yourself whether the cat is dead or alive. But Schrödinger, on the other hand, he said the two outcomes exist simultaneously, in two different quiffs, or representational realities if you will."

"Dimensions?" I asked, turning towards him.

"More like alternate universes. The alive cat universe and the dead cat universe. But again, they're both only representational."

"What do you mean?"

"Meaning, they both exist only in your head –each a picture of what could be, not of what is."

"But what does it matter if the cat is ultimately dead?"

"It's not about that. It's merely illustrating a specific point in time –one in which anything is possible, if not probable. At this moment, this one exact moment, the cat is both alive and dead. And there's no nice little formula to determine which is the reality."

I looked up at the painting again, and felt a sudden, inexplicable affinity for the cat. It was a sensation I didn't quite understand; an idea I could not fully dissect into its many classified parts. But I was intrigued, and deeply moved.

While the grill slowly coaxed the steaks to perfection, Derek showed me the online game he'd helped create. My online gaming experience consisted solely of postcard chess and solitaire, but I knew plenty of enthusiasts. I asked questions and played the role of inquisitive audience as he gave me a virtual tour. Apparently in conjunction with the game, which he could not believe I had never heard of before – "I mean, I may have, I don't know," – he had just opened a software company. He was pushing his ideas, several of which were in the process of gaining patents, towards several companies, which explained his trip to Chicago and the one he was planning to take to New York the following weekend.

I was all fascination, with enough disinterest to maintain objectivity. He answered my questions, only too happily, and I wondered again at his need to self-promote. And yet, perhaps this need wasn't so unique. Everyone needs that, don't they? –to be heard, seen, and appreciated?

Derek retrieved the steaks and handed me a knife and fork. The living room where we sat was dim, affording an intimate view of the city-lit night through the adjoining balcony.

"You know, from the first time I met you I knew you were intelligent and complex."

I was unprepared for this kind of mental flattery, and wary too, but I liked it.

"How could you?" I asked.

He looked at me, intense even when relaxed, from where he sat reclined on the brown suede couch. I sat opposite him, on the matching loveseat. I noticed again the firm set of his mouth, and I felt the brightness of his blue-grey eyes. I wanted to step out of time so that I could move closer, unperceived, and study the freckles across his nose and the patterns within his eyes where the blue and grey mingled before merging. I wanted to run my fingers through his dark curls and touch this face that was both hard and gentle.

"We're different from other people," he said, his plate resting untouched before him on the low table and his arm slung along the back of the seat.

"Everyone tells themselves that." I looked away and swirled my wine, my eyes drifting up again towards the alive and dead cat.

"Do they?"

"Yeah sure. Who wants to be mediocre? We each set up our own self-inflating idea of who we are and how we're different. Special."

He laughed in disagreement. "Why do you have trouble admitting what you are? We *are* different –you've felt it, I know you have. I've been watching you." I wanted to believe I was unique –to claim his compliment as my own and believe he meant what he said. But seduction coming from him made me suspicious. He was a man used to having his way. So, even while wanting to believe that he found in me something different from all the other girls he'd met– I felt certain I was still just another girl to him, someone he'd soon forget.

"Say you're right," I said, grinning at his self-assured conviction, "what does it matter? What's the good of being different when our lives are so short and there's so little lasting difference any of us can make? Is it just something people tell themselves to make them feel important? Because that's worthless."

"Eternity. Make the most matter for eternity, is that it? I have my own ideas about that."

"Like what? Do you believe in a soul? In an afterlife?" I leaned forward a little.

"Hardly. However, you'll have to wait till after dinner."

I picked his plate up from the coffee table and handed it to him. "Then let's eat," I said.

"That hungry, huh?"

"This tastes *amazing*, don't get me wrong, but I just really want to hear your ideas."

We ate only a little, rising and leaving our half-empty plates on the counter by the sink. I rinsed off the knives, washed my hands, turned around, and then he was there, kissing me. I leaned into him, kissing him back, feeling his hands move, everywhere. I held them, diverted them, ran my fingers up his arms and through his hair. I felt the sensations, the heat of his mouth on my neck, the pounding in my chest. But I *felt* nothing. Of course. How could I? This man, this Derek person, was still a stranger. Hearts that feel too soon are feeling only their own creation. I knew this, believed this, but still hated the numbness within me. Would I remain disconnected from everyone? Always? Being conscious of my own detachment made me feel desperately cold inside. I couldn't feel; I couldn't care; I could do whatever and it wouldn't matter. It didn't matter.

I felt him against me, on me, and soon we were on the couch with his hand sliding up under my dress. I eased it down, pressed it against the cushion, tasting him, smelling him. We were wild, our skin hot and our breathing fast. Inhaling everything, inhaling each other.

We eventually got up, me straightening my dress and him running his fingers through his hair and taking a couple deep breaths.

"Let's take a drive," he said. "I know a great place up in Queen Anne where the view is incredible."

And it was. We stopped by my place on the way, so I could change into jeans, and then away we flew to Queen Anne. There he kissed me again. I'm doomed, I thought, never to feel a kiss. I liked to be touched, immensely, but always I was waiting. Watching. Wondering what would happen next. Mind, heart, and body all disconnected.

"Is it okay if I fall in love with you?" Derek's face was lit by the streetlamp outside my window, his eyes intent. Too intent to be joking.

"Don't be silly. You don't even know me."

"Oh, but I know a lot. You're beautiful, unflappable, intelligent." He leaned toward me a little. At least he was looking into my eyes, rather than at my mouth, my chest, my hair. And I found I could look back, unafraid to hold his gaze. I wasn't worried about what he might see –the thoughts laying bare my skepticism, the thoughts revealing how comical I found his self-inflation. Proud, self-absorbed people couldn't be hurt, I reasoned. Or if they could, perhaps they needed it.

"I'm not the kind of girl you want." I half-smiled at him, and then pushed back against my seat and laughed. "I'm small town."

"Hardly."

I thought of Kurt.

"The last time I got close to someone, I felt vulnerable and insecure. Nothing happened, in the end, because apparently, I didn't have enough 'social grace,' or something like that."

"Don't you hate that? You open yourself up to someone and they abuse it!" He was indignant on my behalf. I smiled, finding it sweet.

He lit another cigarette and then blew a stream of smoke out through the top of the window.

"God! You're beautiful." He tapped the cigarette against the ridge of glass, and I watched the ashes dance away in a swirl of wind. "Have you ever been in love?"

"No," I said. Had I? Did Kurt count? My confused, jumbled feelings never got the chance to straighten themselves out into anything real. That's what I told myself, anyway, as I watched the brilliant ember at the end of his fingers swing and fly.

"I find that hard to believe. A girl like you," he shifted in his seat to face me more directly "–how can it be that you're not snatched up?" He looked at me like I was the unclaimed prize –the inspiration and jewel he had been searching for all his life.

I laughed out loud. "Do you practice sincerity?" I asked. I really wanted to know.

"No!" He looked taken aback. "I mean everything I say."

I hated small talk and everything that felt like meaningless flattery. Being "romanced" in this way felt fake.

"You told me yourself you like to take girls out in your free time. How you buy them cars and then report them stolen when things go wrong" –he had said that as if it were the most natural thing– "The word for that is *player*."

He looked shocked and made some comment to justify himself.

"Look," I said, "I just don't see the point of setting up illusions for myself or anyone else. You find me interesting; I find you interesting –let's leave it at that."

He studied me a moment.

"Okay," he said. "Okay." And then he began describing the volunteer work he did with Seattle's homeless kids, feeling, I guess, a need to polish up his persona. Said he'd been homeless himself, at one point, before becoming unofficially adopted by the man he now considered his true father. He'd hated his stepdad –the only dad he'd known up until the time he left home at the age of fifteen. He'd lived on the street then, sleeping on rooftops, but only for a short while. When the man and his family befriended him, they gave him a place to stay. He later studied at the University of Washington, after which he secured a job at Microsoft where he worked his way up from menial tasks to computer programming. Now he owned his own business. Type A personality all the way.

"I'm ADHD," he said, a just-so-you-know sort of add-on.

"I would never have known," I said, laughing. His attention was truly everywhere at once. It seemed to work in his favor though, the success he enjoyed surely owing to his energy.

"What can I say, I'm a workaholic."

We returned to Paul's building, and with a smile he pulled out a key that looked like an iron rod the size of a pencil. An all-access elevator key.

"How did you get it?" I asked, unable to hide my curiosity.

"When a building's on fire, how do the firefighters get in? It's impractical to carry a set of keys around –impossible. So, when a building's first built, they put in a firebox with an all-access key inside. These keys work for all of Seattle. *This*," and he paused for effect, "is the key to the city."

I stared at him. He stared back.

"So...what you're saying is, you stole it?"

He pulled himself up a little straighter before turning around to face the elevator. "I own a building," he said over his shoulder. I wasn't sure whether to believe him or not. "You want a set?"

"No," I laughed.

After getting out on the second floor, we waited for the elevator door to shut again and then Derek slid the key into a hole in the door. When it reopened, he lowered the elevator box until the top was below us. He stepped onto it, turned to me, and held out his hand. I hesitated only a moment before taking it and climbing in after him. Surrounded by glinting steel and twisting cables, I looked up and wondered aloud about our chances of getting crushed against the ceiling –blood oozing down the sides, people stepping in it maybe. He assured me there was plenty of space at the top. At least, if memory served. He seemed to recall that one of the shafts cut it kind of close. The doors shut, and I braced my feet, my body, as we began our ascent.

Heart thumping, I waited for our box to pick up speed. It didn't. I looked around, at the walls sliding slowly down, at the ceiling creeping slowly nearer. I could push my 1984 Honda Civic faster than this.

"They aren't all this sluggish," Derek said, "We just happened to pick the slowest go-cart in the lot."

It was just as well. We listened to the people getting in and out of the second car. A crying woman choked on her words as a comforting, encouraging stranger told her she deserved better and who needed men anyway, she should just buy a dog, and something else, but by then they were out of earshot. A couple of drunk guys got on next, all laughter and swearing and banging against the walls like they were wrestling to see who could fall out into the hallway first. I leaned over and knocked on their wall as it slid past us.

"What the–?" a guy's voice said. I cracked up. He knocked back, but when I stretched out my arm, I could no longer reach the receding box. Hand over my mouth, I could barely contain myself.

Derek stared at me. "You're the first girl not to get freaked out by being in here."

I looked away. He'd done this before, and with who knew how many girls. I was obviously one in the middle of a long succession. I knew he was romancing me. Everything about the night made that apparent. I wondered if this usually worked for him –his many offers to buy paintings, cars, and flowers, along with the peach-slices-in-wine and flattery and the near-death experiences in a harmless elevator shaft. It was all rather amusing, honestly. And strangely, I realized I didn't care. I was here to look inside his head, inside his world, to feel my heart race and my skin tingle. I was using him; we were using each other. So long as I remained conscious of this, I decided it didn't matter that he was someone I'd never in a million years want as a lifelong, or even long-term, companion.

We returned to the condo. I gave one last look at the elevator, giggling at the thought of the confused guys. I was still giggling as I tossed off my shoes by the door. He watched me, smiling. "God! You're so ... *pure!*"

And then abruptly his manner changed. I stopped mid-stride. He had something to say, something he needed to tell me. I waited. He stalled, furrowed his brow, paced. But whether his difficulty in finding the right opening words came from its importance or was manufactured for effect, I couldn't tell. He proceeded to tell me a story, one completely incongruous with everything else about that night. He'd been to prison, he said, his demeanor all remorse and sorrow. He stepped out onto the balcony and rested his arms on the railing. He'd been innocent, of course, but something had happened there. And it was all because an old boss from Microsoft had asked him if he knew how to get drugs.

"Now I don't do them myself –don't like them, don't need them– but what other people do is their own business. So, I gave him the number of a dealer, and when this dealer got busted, part of his plea bargain was that he'd name names. My boss was caught and denied all, saying he'd gotten the number from me. 'Derek! Derek gave me the number!' His lawyers being better than mine, and the justice system being what it is, I went to jail for two years, while he got off. Two years because a kilo was involved, which made it a federal offense."

Derek looked away then, and he seemed to fold in on himself. "I became a murderer," he said, his voice a half-whisper. I waited in the silence. I couldn't tell if he was going for an Oscar or if he was being serious. If he was serious, why was he telling me? And if he wasn't serious, why was he telling me? Goodness, I'd only just met the guy, and here he was revealing every mother's worst fear for her child –all that was left was to ask if there'd been an ax involved. And yet ... his manner was like someone who'd seen something horrific and who was still grappling with how to respond. Like someone looking for guidance. For forgiveness. Or, at the very least, the chance to get it off his chest. But why me? Why now?

"That's what jail did to me," he said, leaning out into the night. He shifted his weight.

"First night there," he said, "I was in a house –that's what they call the cells, 'houses'– with three other guys. Two in the bunks, me and another on the floor. In the house next to me was a black man, all by himself. This black man calls over to me, 'Hey kid.' 'Yeah, what?' I say. 'You like it over there?' 'Yeah, guess so.' 'Want to come over here?'

"Now they tell you when you're in prison not to look anyone in the eye and to go along with everything. So, I said, 'Yeah, whatever,' and he handed me a piece of paper to sign. This is what we wrote requests on –if we needed toilet paper, or wanted to move, or whatever. So, I signed it, and he handed it to an officer. 'Kid!' the officer was at the bars, 'kid, you cool with this?' 'Yeah, sure,' I say.

"Then it got loud. 'Black man's got a new wife,' people were saying.

"Along comes this man, Vinny. Now Vinny's a convict, but here he was walking around free. No shackles, nothing. Vinny runs the place. The officers want something done, they go to him. He'd been there since he was fifteen –nearly twenty years ago.

"Vinny came up to my house. Called me. 'Look,' he said, 'you want to go through with this?' 'No.' 'What are you in here for?' I told him, and he was all, 'Man, you shouldn't even be here. How are you on the other side?' I stared at him. 'I mean, do you got a house?' 'A couple,' I say. 'A car?' 'Yeah.' 'How many?' 'A few.' 'Money?' 'Yeah, man, I got money.' 'So will you watch out for me?' 'What?' 'Look, I get out in two years. Been here since I was fifteen. I don't know what it's like out there. Will you look out for me?' 'Yeah, yeah, I'll look out for you.'

"And he handed me an ice pick, a small one. 'Wait, no,' I said. He stared at me –like this" –and Derek bugged out his eyes to show me– "but I just stared back, so he took the pick. 'Alright,' he said, 'but you better look out for me.'

"I cried that night. Seriously, I cried. I was in for two years –I didn't want to do twenty.

"The next morning, the doors open. Everyone comes out into the walkway. Now the walkways are only about two feet wide. Vinny comes up and goes into the house next to mine. The black man is just getting out of bed. All stretching and yawning. Vinny goes up and slams the pick into his forehead –right between his eyes. He comes out and looks at me. 'Finish it,' he says. I'm scared as hell. I go in there, and the man, he's huge, he's shaking, and I pull on the ice pick till it comes out. Blood all over my hands. I put the pick under my arm and am wiping my hands on my shirt, trying to get the blood off. I just know everyone sees what I am. What I did. The server in the cafeteria –he could see it. I knew he could see the blood under my fingernails. Everyone had to see it –I was a murderer. That's what I'd become.

"Later that day the officer comes to my house. 'Derek,' he says, and I'm shaking. He has to know, and I think, 'it's over for me.' I go to the front. 'Get your stuff.' I get my stuff. 'You asked to move next door, right?' 'Yeah,' I say, 'I did.' 'Okay, let's go.' The door slides open. I go next door. The door slides shut. Blood still on the floor.

"And that was my first morning."

Derek took a deep breath. The air around him buzzed a little, like radio static. I strained my ears, but the message, if there was any, was indistinct. I waited, staring, having no idea what to say. He was nearly bent over at this point, as though something in his stomach was contracting, pulling the rest of his body inward. He was sick. Hating himself. Hating what he had done.

"I got out two years later," he continued a few moments later. "Vinny got out a year after that. Let's just say he's doing very well. He owns a house. He owns a Harley. I'm looking out for him. I'm taking *good* care of him.

"To this day though, I hate blacks. I was never prejudiced and know they're not all the same, but that's what prison did to me. In there, they're animals. I hate them. Every time I see one on the street, I want to fucking run over them. I hate them."

What does skin color have to do with anything? I wondered. Is he really so lazy that he needs visual cues on which to hang his biases?

He leaned heavily on the balcony railing, apparently still reeling from the relived memory. Again, I wondered why? Why had he told me? Was he looking for sympathy? Did he want me to know what he was? And just what was he? And, really, two years in prison because of a *phone number*?

I straightened, narrowing my eyes –an act he couldn't see. Maybe he was a murderer, or the casualty of a screwed-up situation, or maybe he was just a liar. But what really unnerved me was that ... I didn't care. In my detachment, I felt safe. Which was strange to me because I'd never felt that invincibility which supposedly accompanies the young. In fact, I'd never seen myself living past twenty-five. But here, with Derek, I didn't feel personally threatened. Not like I had with Lymon. I wasn't picking up anything from Derek other than a need to confess. For what purpose, I had no idea.

His remorse stirred up a small measure of sympathy, which pulsed alongside my skepticism. But I wasn't going to justify what he'd done. The most sensible option was to cut him off. Completely. He clearly wasn't someone I wanted to get attached to. Ever. I could leave, I thought, should leave, right then. No explanations needed.

Why then did I stay? Because he was a new and fascinating subject, one unfamiliar to me. Besides, I thought, I don't get attached to people anyway, so why not study him? Despite his words, his confession, I wasn't afraid of him. There was nothing in his manner that made me uneasy. Even knowing what happened to the curious cat, I was undeterred because I felt both alive and dead already –and this combined state lent me a sense of protection.

How was it that after so many years of trying to be strong, smart, and careful should I suddenly be so reckless?

He looked at me.

"Do you think less of me?"

"But you didn't do it yourself."

"No. I'm a murderer." He turned around and went inside.

"I'm sorry," he said, "But I feel sick. I always do when I talk about that." He clutched his arm around his stomach. He went into the dark bedroom and sat down on the bed, squeezing his eyes shut.

"I'm sorry," he repeated.

And again, I couldn't tell if he was sincere or putting on a show. I suspected he was playing it up. He seemed to expect comfort of some sort, but I was on guard, suspicious, and stayed where I was, leaning against the door. He was, after all, on the bed.

Finally, he got up.

The conversation turned to other things and before long we were laughing again in the living room and then drinking wine and eating cheese in the kitchen. It was getting late. I saw all the possible routes before me –the one leading home, to my secluded room and solitude shining the brightest. Opposite me, Derek was leaning against the counter.

And that's when I touched him. I reached out and touched him where it mattered most to a man like him. He breathed in sharply, and immediately responded. He pressed me to him, and our hands were everywhere. Our lips, on the move. This was earth and flesh and blood and heat.

We moved to the bedroom, this borrowed room.

"We don't have to do this," he murmured into my hair. "I don't want to do anything unless you're sure, absolutely sure."

I was sure. He was older, more experienced, and I was curious. I wanted to see what it was like –what *sex* was like– with someone well-practiced. I wanted to explore all the many ways a body could feel and a heart could beat, while I tasted his skin and heard him breathe. I wanted to *ignite*.

I asked, somewhat awkwardly, if he had protection. He fumbled around in the drawer next to the bed until he found a condom. And then we made love. No, that's not correct. It wasn't love, most certainly not love-making. There was passion, yes, heat and contact between two people experiencing each other intimately. But it had nothing to do with love.

Afterward, I lay with my head on his sleeping chest, feeling it rise as I listened to his heartbeat. I wondered how it could beat so fast even during sleep. Did he ever truly relax?

When he awoke, I awoke, with sunlight streaming in through the window. I got up and checked myself in the bathroom while wondering what I was supposed to do, how I was supposed to act. If there was morning-after etiquette, it was unknown to me. I took a deep breath and entered the kitchen, where he smiled and offered me a plate of freshly sliced peaches. I returned his smile and began eating in silence while he picked through the shrimp and cheese left over from the night before. Then he drove me home.

When he dropped me off, he kissed me. He fingered my earlobe –I'd lost an earring.

"Let me love you," he said. I looked at him, raising my hand as though to touch him. He was impossible. Ridiculous. I almost liked that about him. I quickly climbed out. And then he was off.

Back in my room, I curled up in my chair and gazed out the window, my breathing quickening when I thought of where I'd been and what we'd done. Part of me thought he'd call again, but another part of me thought he was gone forever, already a memory. I didn't really expect him to call. When no feelings are involved impressions fade, and I felt nothing toward him, except curiosity. I couldn't imagine him feeling anything toward me. All his talk of attraction, of wanting to love, felt like sentimental small talk, designed to lead and leave. We'd simply had an experience. Besides, he seemed to have no ties whatsoever. Hadn't talked to his family in years, he said. Prison had hardened him, and he was used to getting his own way. I felt the truth of it. There could never be a "we," an "us," a future. Nor did I want there to be. We were opposites; time spent together was a contradiction. Guys like him weren't influenced by girls like me.

"Girls like me."

And just what did that mean? Derek had called me pure; he called me innocent. Had I ever been either of those? And now? I thought back to the picture of Schrödinger's cat. That's what I felt like, only in my case, *morally* dead and alive.

I decided there was no neat little moral formula to decide or discover who or what is "good" or "bad." Eternity could never depend on morality when everyone is simultaneously good and bad, even if to varying degrees. Instead, the only possible coexistent is grace. But given by whom, or by what, I no longer knew.

# Chapter 5

He called.

I was at work, and he asked if I wanted a ride home. Eleven o'clock and there he was —standing perfectly straight and eager in front of a huge Chevy Suburban. I crossed the street, and he immediately enveloped me in a hug so tight, his arms wrapped so fully around me, that for a full minute I was conscious of nothing other than the wonderful pressure of his body against mine and the soft, clean smell behind his ear. I could have stayed like that forever.

Pulling back, he opened the passenger door for me and then quickly stepped around to the other side. We flew through the streets while he told me all about his day, pausing for a moment to ask about mine and inserting how much he had missed me. I watched him talk, watched the pedestrians jump out of the way, watched the city lights flash by; I leaned back and took it all in —everything. And I smiled.

He arrived at my building, pulled up to an abrupt stop, and said, "I brought you something." He opened the back of the Suburban and started pulling out a computer.

"This okay?" he asked, pausing a moment to look at me. I wasn't sure. The last thing I wanted was gifts with possible strings attached, and my current computer wasn't all that bad —the speed slow and the screen fuzzy, but nothing I couldn't live with. "I mean, I have about thirty of these things at home," he added. "I'd rather you take it than have it sit around in my garage."

"No strings?" I asked, studying him.

"No strings. Look, it's going to waste. This way it's getting used."

Inside my apartment I watched him build it. He showed me where each of the components went. All of it a puzzle that fit together perfectly.

"Now let's get your internet connected."

"The cable service people already tried to hook up my computer. It didn't work."

He fixed that.

He was leaning back to survey his work when he got a call from a half-drunk Paul, who'd just gotten pulled over.

Derek turned to me. "He's afraid the cops might snag his car, so if you're cool with it let's go see what's up."

A few blocks away, two cop cars with flashing lights filled the tiny parking lot of an apartment building, blocking the exit. Derek pulled up alongside the curb, and I stared past him at a white Ferrari caught in a vortex of red and blue lights. A tall, slim man with hair past his shoulders leaned against the door, chatting amiably with two officers. They looked as though they were all out having a midnight tailgate party. One of the policemen pointed to the car, as though asking a question, and the man uncrossed one of his arms for a moment and leisurely gestured while explaining his answer. So, I thought, this is Paul.

Derek started to get out of the car and was promptly told to get back in. He settled back, elbow on the window, and watched with focused intensity.

"It's always good to have a witness around with cops," he told me in a quiet aside.

After a while, the two policemen came over. One of them, a tall, slightly overweight man who shuffled a little, proceeded to explain himself. Unnecessarily, in my opinion. "Thank you for staying put," he said. "I couldn't have a bunch of people pouring out of a car when I didn't know who you were or what you wanted. Your friend Paul here was going eighty downtown. He's free to go now, though I'm still not sure his car is legal given all its alterations." He glanced back at Paul's car, shook his head, smiled at us, and walked away.

Everyone pulled out then, with Derek following Paul back to his condo.

"Such polite cops!" Paul said, leading us inside. He was all flirtatious energy as he immediately began searching out something to drink.

"You know the first thing they said when they pulled me over?" He snapped the cap off a beer and offered it first to me and then to Derek when I shook my head. "They said, 'Thank you for stopping. Did you know Seattle law forbids any officer from engaging in a high-speed chase downtown?'"

"Seriously?" Although he sounded animated, Derek's attention was elsewhere. He stood by the computer, leaning over it.

"Yeah. Like they *wanted* me to outrun them. I guess having a Ferrari's not all bad." And he winked at me. "Bad tags. That's all. I was going at least eighty, and they just wanted to look at my car."

He smiled again and walked over to me, stopping closer than was comfortable. "So, Ani, huh? Been hearing a lot about you. I'm Paul. It's so nice to meet you." I took his extended hand, shaking it, and he held on, gently, seconds passing, still smiling. His face was more handsome than I'd first thought upon seeing him in the dim parking lot, and he was even somewhat charming, but in a smooth, sliding, slimy way. I withdrew my hand and sat down on the couch, leaning over the armrest where I could watch Derek. Paul seated himself across from me.

"How'd you two meet again?"

I told him, feeling distant. I glanced over at Derek, at where he sat with his back to us as he typed away in front of the glowing screen, fully absorbed.

"Looks like I need to go make copies." The corners of Paul's mouth twitched, as though he were thinking things, imagining things, things about me.

"Oh, you wouldn't believe the things we can do there," I said absently. "That's one of the things I love about my job. All the creativity and ideas and of course the people."

"People like you? –someone you could introduce me to?"

I smiled but didn't answer. Instead, I crossed my arms and looked away. The room felt small, like a box –like a box with an atom-trigger whose half-life was unknown. He leaned forward.

"Cold?" he asked. "You sure? Cause I've got blankets –a whole bed-full of them. I could get you warm." –another winking smile– "Okay. How about a drink then?"

I nodded –anything to make him leave. He was too much –his smiles, the oily sound of his voice, the way his eyes touched me, roved over me, shone with just enough good-natured sensitivity to seem sincere. His unrelenting inuendoes, despite his almost affable charm, were making my skin crawl.

He jumped up, rummaged through the kitchen. "Looks like the only thing I've got besides beer is wine." He held up the bottle.

I nodded and said, "A little, please," as I raised my thumb and forefinger.

"God, look at you –you're so cute. Derek, she's just too sweet." He brought over a glass and held it out, managing to touch my fingers lightly as I took it from him.

"So, Derek treating you right? Cause if he's not you can call me anytime. I'll treat you like a lady deserves." He smiled, with one corner of his mouth sliding up in a way that could almost have been called endearing, were it not so smarmy. Still looking at me, he sat back in his chair, both arms spread open wide along either armrest.

"Where's your harem tonight, Paul?" Derek asked, glancing over at him and then swinging his chair around to face us. "I hardly ever see him without *at least* three or four girls hanging on him."

Paul shrugged, as if to say, "Guilty. What can I say?" He was all good humor and barely contained sensuality, some of it spilling out onto the couch beside him where his hand was rubbing, rubbing, as though he couldn't stand not to be touching something. I wished he wouldn't stare at me like that.

"And you know why," Derek continued, "it's because he usually makes between nine and thirty thousand a month just in commissions."

"Oh, is that why?" I said. Paul's mouth slid up into a smile again.

"So, this guy, a friend of a friend, is getting married," Derek said, scratching his shoulder and then leaning back with one elbow on the desk. "He'd been seeing three girls for several years and now, after all this time, he's finally tying the knot. I asked him, 'How'd you know, man? How did you decide which one?' Turns out he'd given each one fifteen thousand to spend on him.

"The first one went out and bought him a complete entertainment center –massive screen, well-placed speakers, the works. 'Because I want you to have the best,' she says. 'You deserve the best.'

"The second one had surgery –she got the implants, removed the crow's feet and wrinkles, got the bikini wax, everything. 'Because you should have the best.'

"Now the third one took her money and happened to invest in just the right company at just the right time. She cashed out with several hundred thousand dollars' worth which she put into a safety deposit box and gave him the key to. Not only that, but she gave him the mutual funds which she had reinvested in and told him she kept a hundred fifty for herself, because she did all the work. 'You deserve the best.'"

Derek looked at me. "So, which one did he marry?"

I looked from him to Paul, who was grinning, and I gave an exasperated sigh.

"Of course," Derek said. "The one with the biggest tits."

"Men!" I said, with a show of disgust.

"Hey, we're not all like that," Derek said, holding up his hands in self-defense. "Not all women care only about money, and not all men think only about sex. Just the majority of us."

I crossed over to him and slid onto his lap. He wrapped his arms around me, and everything felt so natural, as if we always sat like this, our bodies fitting comfortably together. "So, we're all just using each other?" I asked as I kissed him.

"Not all of us," he said quietly, still kissing me. He pulled back then and looked at me, his face serious. "Not with you, I'm not."

I didn't buy it. We *were* just using each other, and I figured we'd be fine so long as we didn't pretend otherwise.

I slid off his lap and circled the room. Paul got up and told Derek about this problem he was having with the computer. With Derek's attention once again absorbed, Paul put on some music and held his hand out to me.

"No? Don't want to dance? But it's so much better than dancing alone." He danced for me, showing me just how much fun it could be.

I slipped around him and stood behind Derek, resting my hand on his shoulder.

"You ready to go, Baby?" –he was already calling me "Baby," as if he'd been doing so for always.

"Mm-hmm," and we drove back to my place –back into the sweet, dim seclusion of my room for another night of pressure, of pleasure, of drowning in my hair.

# THE CREOSOTE BUSH

LATE THE NEXT MORNING he took me out for breakfast at a wonderful, grungy, little diner that was all sunshine and moist air scented with bacon. We sat in a little booth near the front door. Peaches and cream pancakes for me; a Heineken, a Camel, and a pile of eggs with sausage for him. We ate while discussing religion, morality, and science. I sat back and watched him as he described his stepdad –the fire-and-brimstone brand of Christian who is all conviction and no compassion.

"My mom met him while pregnant with me," Derek said. "I wished she'd just had an abortion. It would have spared us both. I hate him. *Hate* him!"

The man wrote inspirational and religious self-help books, and never missed an opportunity to teach his family the importance of trusting God and sharing the message with others. "God doesn't want you to have a new pair of shoes, son. You just gotta trust that when the time's right you'll get them." So, Derek's feet were cold. And sore. And then there was his dog.

"I loved this dog! My first ever. I'd wanted him so badly –*begging* until by some miracle I got him. And I took good care of him too –nobody else had to do anything. We were best friends, truly, doing everything together. I was probably about eight or nine at the time.

"Then my dog started getting into the neighbor's yard. This neighbor guy hated the dog –threatened to shoot him. I did what I could. We kept him fenced in. But then one day he got out. Somehow, he made it into the guy's yard –chasing a rabbit or something, I don't know. And the guy ... this guy grabs his gun and shoots him. He shot my dog!

"I was at school when it happened and when I got home, I didn't know where he was, where my dog was. He was always there to meet me. Always. So, I go all over the yard, all over the neighborhood,

193

looking for my dog, calling him. And nobody says anything. Nobody tells me what happened. I keep thinking he'll show up any minute –my poor dog– that he's fine, just lost, and I'll find him soon. "This goes on for a couple of days and the guy, my neighbor, actually starts to feel sorry for me. So, he tells me. He says, 'Kid, I shot your dog.' Well, shit, I'm beside myself. I don't come out of my room for anything. I'm just sobbing my eyes out. I mean, I was a kid! And this dog was my best friend.

"Finally, my dad comes up to my room, and I'm thinking, 'This is it. He's going to try to comfort me, for the first time ever.' I actually believed that –that maybe this would bring us closer together, or something. And you know what he told me?"

Derek paused, lips pressed into a hard, thin line. I held my breath, fearing the answer.

"He told me that he knew I was suffering, and hurting, but that now was the perfect time to go share God's love and forgiveness with the man who'd shot my dog! I couldn't see straight, my eyes were so swollen, and he wanted me to wipe my nose and go hug the man and tell him everything was all right. Like it was *nothing!*"

Derek's hand popped the table, making the forks and knives clink against the plates. I jumped, eyes flitting from his hand to his face.

"He always made me feel like *shit*. And my mother too. I could forgive him for what he did to me, but not what he did to my mother."

I stared at Derek, at his resentment, and I felt his hurt twist inside me like a cold knot.

I had always abhorred the notoriety of hypocritical Christians –perpetuated by violently-religious Bible-thumpers whose chests expand with righteous condemnation as they shout their views on the love of God and the certain hellfire that awaits those who reject such gracious generosity. Such infamy impacts people.

Christianity wasn't about condemnation or sin or the select few. I believed it was about the love of something –*Someone*– greater than us for us. And about returning that love. Even with all my doubts, my heart kept returning to the promise, the reassurance of God's love. Because of it, I still felt that somehow everything would be okay in the end.

Back then I couldn't see pain without wanting to do everything I could to ease it. Compassion for Derek swelled within me. I surrendered to the feeling fully, without doubt or hesitation. Maybe because I could do so from a distance. The warmth of it made me feel alive and connected to him. I didn't expect to change him, but I wanted to help somehow, to make life better for him. For *everyone*.

I leaned toward him. "That was wrong –what he did was wrong. I'm so sorry it happened. Nobody, especially not a child, should have to go through something like that –not ever." I rubbed the back of his hand. "But that's *not* Christianity. It's callus and uncaring, but it's not *Christian*."

He shook his head, still disgusted. I reached my hand up and touched his cheek. The slight stubble felt bristly under my fingertips. He looked toward me, and his eyes softened.

"I'm sorry," I whispered.

"You had nothing to do with it. Don't apologize."

"I'm sorry it happened. I'm sorry it hurt you." I stared at him, willing his hurt away.

He reached up and took my hand in his.

"Doesn't matter," he said. "But I'm never going to be like him. I'm never going to have anything to do with church or any of that hypocrisy."

"Like me?" I asked.

"What?"

"Like me –a saint sleeping with a sinner." I gave a small laugh, but the sound quickly disappeared, leaving behind a faint unease.

He kissed me, and I tasted the cigarettes and sausage. Not unpleasant. I opened my eyes and smiled at him.

"You're young," he said. "You might not always believe as you do now. With a little more education, especially at a state school, you might even change your mind a little sooner."

"Oh?! And your way is so much better? Cynicism and bitterness? No thank you. I prefer my unassailable peace and joy." I grinned at him.

We both looked up as the waitress came and cleared our plates away, leaving behind the check. Derek slid his card onto it and then leaned on the table, one arm propped up, with smoke trailing out of the fresh cigarette between his fingers, the other hand resting next to his elbow on the table.

"You never told me your idea about the soul or the afterlife," I said.

"What?" He looked over at me, his eyes intent and piercing, but gentle. He was seeing me, and it felt nice.

"Your idea," I said, "The one you were going to tell me after dinner the other night. About what you believe happens when we die."

"Hmm." He was silent a moment. He bit the corner of his fingernail distractedly.

"Please?" I smiled and raised my eyebrows. He seemed to be gathering his thoughts. I waited, watching his lips move as he thought. Those lips had trailed across my skin the night before, sending shivers along my neck, my shoulder, across my ribcage.

His eyes met mine again, and I tried not to blush.

"Okay," he said. "So where are memories stored?"

"The brain."

"Yes. But more precisely, in the cells and synapses of our brain. Now, once we die, these don't just immediately disappear. In the time it takes for them to decay, I believe it's possible to 'relive' our memories even after we're dead."

"Like a dream?"

"Exactly. It's very much like a dream, okay, because –that's a great example– because you know how in dreams there's no sense of time? At least no real sense. I mean, hours, days, can go by in the space of a few minutes. Shit, I've built entire houses in my mind. Back when I was in solitary I'd start with a hammer and a nail and work my way up, board by board. Unbound by time, your mind can do anything. So, while our bodies are decaying –all the atoms and energy being transferred, absorbed into something else– we're experiencing parts of our life, our memories, all over again. Heaven or hell depending on the life you've lived. And since there's no sense of time, this is your eternity. Forever in a moment. Maybe we're conscious of it, maybe we aren't. You see?"

"But alone?" I asked. "How sad. Without interaction, what's the point? I don't want to spend eternity in some mental movie where all the people I'm talking to aren't real, are just memories. I'd rather die and be done with it. For good. Completely. I mean, that's depressing."

He blew a stream of smoke into the air. When his eyes met mine, they were blue and grey and beautiful. "Have you never had a memory you wished would last forever?"

I could only stare at him, trying to recall one such moment. Dust particles danced in the sunlight between us. There was green in the blue of his eyes.

I gave up and laughed, "It's not as though you could choose your eternal moment."

197

He shrugged. "Maybe not," he said, "but how we think and act creates a sort of overarching frame of mind, which then determines our narrative. We're doing it now."

"Creating our own realities?"

"Essentially, yes."

"But where are the absolutes?"

"Do there need to be absolutes?"

"Life isn't all subjective. There must be commonalities."

"Our external environment may be the same, but we each have our own point of view. Take Milton's *Paradise Lost*. Satan climbs out of hell and makes his way to paradise only to find that he's brought hell with him. It's inside him and he can no more escape it than he can escape himself."

"That's a scary thought," I said, studying the table. The sunlight turned the surface into a mirror, so that it reflected a lone flower, perched in its vase at the center of the table. "But I suppose it goes the other way too. Some people carry joy with them, even into the worst circumstances."

"Like you?" His tone was a bit teasing.

"I can only hope. I've never experienced anything too terrible, so I wouldn't know." Maybe by trying to see more of life, both the good and the bad, I'd see more of myself as well.

We were both quiet a moment. As I sat thinking, he began describing some articles he had read recently regarding neuroscience. I didn't hear much of what he said at first, but his mind for detail was extraordinary, and soon I was listening to him in absorbed silence.

"You're quiet," he said at last.

It was an observation, not an accusation. I knew there was nothing wrong with being quiet, but even so, I thought of Kurt and wondered how Derek would take my silences.

"I can get rather dull sometimes," I said.

"I don't want you to entertain me," he said, looking at me, "I have enough energy of my own. You know? I'm my own hurricane, and you're the eye. Calm. I need that. You give me peace." He pulled me to him, and I nestled into his shoulder. "You make me happy."

When I looked at him, I saw that he meant it. I met his smile with my own.

# Chapter 6

As the weeks passed, we became inseparable. Derek was like that fun childhood playmate who I raced off to be with every day after school and during the long, hot summers. The one who made life feel full and turned everything into an adventure. The one who was just as excited to see me as I was to see him. We didn't need rhyme or reason or a plan to be together. Only the present moment. That was enough. That was everything.

Only we were most definitely not children. He took me to restaurants with glass walls overlooking the bay, and I took him to the Irish pub where I liked to play chess with Yoshi and Jimmy while listening to live music. Derek embraced me in an alleyway that was all sunlight and shadows, and we kissed to the sound of a bluesy saxophone piece played by a street musician just around the corner. We ate ice-cream at the pier and hit up happy hour at McCormick and Schmick's where we stuffed our faces with huge burgers and fat fries. And we stayed in too, spending long hours in my room surrendering to sensation.

During those moments, we were conscious only of each other, of the sound of our breathing, the feel of our heat, the blood coursing through our veins. Every inch of my body came alive when he slid down and showed me what my body could do. What it could feel. He was so gentle then. So tireless. So patient while something deep inside my belly uncoiled. At his touch, galaxies were born. They spun out from me, enveloping me and lifting me up. Their swirling stars created constellations that danced in the air. I'd watch them slowly fade as I drifted back to earth, feeling wonderfully lost in my own trembling body.

Until then I had been starved, muzzled by my scruples. I had been careful, cautious. I had wanted to do the right thing, wait until the right time. And I was glad I had. But I was no longer willing to live inside my head. My constant over-thinking had felt like a tangle of webs getting caught in my hair and restricting my body. I wanted to be free. To let my body move and feel. I still wanted to be careful. I still wanted to do the right thing, which is to say, I didn't want to hurt anyone. But Derek and I wanted the same thing —the experience of being alive, together. I felt we were safe in what I considered mutual utility.

JUST HOW MUCH IS COMMUNICATED along the invisible threads connecting one person to another, I cannot say. But sometimes those threads thrum in my chest, and I wonder. Like that time Andy described his hot tub dream the day after Derek and I got caught naked in one. "It's our anniversary," Derek had told the security guard who was doing his midnight rounds on the rooftop. "I was installing one in my backyard," Andy had said from where he sat in Colorado, eating chips out of a bag and regaining all the weight he had lost while homeless.

Then there was the time Derek suddenly stopped and asked, "What is that? Something's not right. There's something toxic over there." I was lying on my belly on the floor of my room, feet in the air, and when I looked over my shoulder at him, he was looking past me, toward my desk. Moments before, I had glanced at the trashcan underneath and seen the crumpled-up note containing Lymon's voicemail. The memory of it, of him, had nauseated me and made me feel cold. With my back to Derek, I wondered how he could have picked up on it. Was he truly sensing my agitation? Or had he seen the note earlier? Had he gone through my trash? I hid my confusion with a laugh and asked what he was talking about.

"Something is affecting you –something bad." He came over and started shuffling through everything on my desk.

"I don't know what you're talking about."

Unsatisfied, he knelt and reached into the trash. When he found the piece of paper, I reached for it, but he pulled his arm away.

"What's this? What *is* this?" His voice, his body, everything about him was intense.

"Nothing. Just a message. A stupid voicemail."

"Ani, this is affecting you –I can feel it in your whole body."

Physical intimacy makes you sensitive, he had said a few nights before –opens a sort of telepathic door. Was that true?

I took back the note and tore it into tiny pieces as I told him –briefly– about Lymon.

He was pacing now. "You want him gone?"

"*What*?"

He had to be joking. I laughed at the absurdity of his question.

"Do you want him to disappear?" He was serious.

I stared at him, unbelieving, for a few seconds. And then, "No, of course not! He's just a stupid guy –that's all. He'll grow to become a bitter old man –alone."

But I couldn't stop staring at him. Was he serious? Probably not. Not really. Not truly. But what if he was?

"Let's go see my friend Javier," he said, abruptly changing the subject. "Want to?"

"Okay," I said slowly. I picked up my purse and followed him out, still staring.

As we drove out of the city, Derek said casually, "So this guy we're going to see, he ... gets me stuff."

"As in drugs?" I asked, no longer interested in this little drive.

"I mean, I could get a prescription for Ritalin, but this is easier. Speed is just another methamphetamine. With my ADHD, it slows me down. Gets me to calm. I'm not going to push it on you. Don't worry. We'll just be a minute."

Javier's place epitomized nearly every small-time drug dealer's house I'd ever seen on a crime show: non-descript neighborhood; a souped-up car with gleaming, over-sized rims; huge TV; expensive stereo equipment pushing out of every corner; and the bonus of a little dog in a spiked collar yapping around at our feet. Everything else was in shambles. Piles of clothes lay in the corner, pizza boxes and chicken bones filled the sink, and the carpet was coming up in the entryway and along the walls, which were dented here and there and scuffed with long black marks. All this was only barely visible though in the dim light of the naked bulb above us.

It was past midnight. The three of us drove to another house. Derek gave Javier some money and Javier went inside. Derek and I talked about nothing for a little while. I kept looking around, feeling conspicuous. I didn't belong there. Part of me wanted to go home. Another part wanted to pull out a notebook and make observations, as though this were some sort of behavioral study for my ongoing research.

Javier returned shortly after. I didn't see anything on him, of course. No little white baggy like you see in the movies. Not that he'd be waving it around, but I still felt like sliding down in my seat. I didn't know anything about speed. I had no interest in drugs. Was Derek into other drugs too? At a gas station we picked up foil and beer before driving back to Javier's place.

While Javier fished around for an extra light bulb and a pen, Derek pulled out –yup, there it was– a bag of white crystals. He set it on the oven, which stood unplugged in the middle of the kitchen floor.

"Speed calms me down," he said again, as though to normalize what he was doing. "I would go get prescription drugs from my therapist, but I haven't seen him in a while –I'm not ready to tell him about you yet."

Javier returned with a bulb. I watched, feeling more and more detached, as Derek poked out the end of it with the pen and then took the pen apart, so he had an empty tube. After pouring in some of the speed, he held a lighter under the bulb, and I watched the crystals liquefy and the inside get all hazy. He breathed in deep using the tube, holding his breath several seconds before handing the makeshift pipe to Javier.

"I'm not going to get you hooked on this stuff," he said to me, his voice sounding weird because he was still sort of holding his breath. He exhaled, and Javier handed it back to him.

"Not interested anyway," I said. I had absolutely no desire to experiment with drugs, not with all the stories I'd heard of the mind and body-wrecking effects bumping around in my head. Plus, the idea of dependency on anything, or anyone, made my skin crawl.

"Everybody likes to try –but we won't go there."

Not everybody, I thought. Goodness, what was I doing here?! I was in the house of a *drug dealer*! A long, long way from Kansas. Why then did it all seem so very natural? Had my childhood experiences of being repeatedly thrown into vastly different environments deadened my ability to be shocked, even by what was morally unfamiliar? Or was it because I had seen the moral failings of strangers, loved ones and even myself to the extent that my judgement, while it existed, was nevertheless tempered with a sort of laissez faire detachment? Was this detachment a defense-mechanism? I stood there, emotionally and mentally removed from what was going on. An outsider with an insider's view, I felt no need to either interfere or participate. As a resident assistant at the dorm, I had spent most of my rounds asking people to either turn down their music or to put their weed away. A single smoke-filled room would make the whole hall reek, and the incense they tried to mask it with only made things worse. But Derek was a grown man. I doubted he'd pack it up on my account. What were we to each other anyway? Not long-term prospects. So, while there's a big difference between weed and hard drugs, I figured any objections on my part would be futile, and as for me, I'd be on my way soon enough.

"So, you guys hear about the girl who was murdered here a couple nights ago?" Javier had his head tilted back as he spoke. He dropped it down and looked at us. "Her boyfriend caught her cheating, and he shot her three times. She came running to our door –I wasn't here– but she came knocking and no one would help her. Well, one guy tried, but he got shot too. She ran back over to the door of her building, and he shot her as she was trying to get inside."

I stared, almost forgetting to breathe.

"Let's go see if there's any blood." Derek started out the door and across the street. Javier followed.

*See if there's any blood?* What were they –boy scouts poking at a dead sparrow? I trailed behind. We were all morbidly curious, drawn in by the story and needing props –the scene of death to make it more vivid. More real. "This is where it happened."

Prayer candles stood melted to the sidewalk outside the door of the apartment building. Through the glass we could see into the entryway where the carpet had been taken out, a huge bald spot in the hallway. But no blood, no deep brown stains remained. Nothing but a story sending picture reels through our heads.

Having worked in an ER, I had seen my fair share of death and gore. And now, standing on the cold concrete patio in the emptiness of night while rubbing my arms for warmth, I could almost see her in my mind –the poor girl lying there on the ground with black holes soaking her clothes as her blood pooled out into spreading black mirrors beside her. What must it have been like for this girl in the moments before she died –when she was screaming with terror, her heart racing, her adrenaline sparking lightning stabs of electricity through her chest as she clawed at the door with numb and useless fingers, desperate for shelter, for safety, for someone –anyone– to help? In that moment I was her. And I almost choked.

"We used to see her all the time. I helped her carry her groceries up once." Javier was smoking a cigarette now. "Yeah, she was *fine*. I couldn't say nothing, I couldn't speak, she was so hot. She was cool, too, you know? Sometimes she'd flash us from her window." He laughed.

We all stared at the dirt for a while. Javier rubbed the back of his neck, and I pushed at a rock with the tip of my shoe. My heartrate gradually returned to normal.

"Hey man, you got your scooter with you?"

Derek went to his trunk and pulled it out, and that was that. No more about the girl, no more solemn silence. Now everything was engines, speed, sound, and speakers.

Derek's manner was that of an older brother, with Javier hanging on his every word and movement with open-faced admiration. As I watched the two of them adjusting the sound system Javier was building for his car, Derek pointing out ways to make it better, I moved about them like a shadow, fascinated. My whole life I'd viewed the world as consisting more or less of two spheres, one light and one dark. I was familiar with the safe, bright, and happy one filled with family dinners, Sunday mornings, and a clear-cut, conventional path leading all the way through life and into eternity beyond. But the other side? The dark and shadowy one with back-alley doors and late-night activities usually involving drugs, distrust, and danger –that one was a complete mystery to me. One in which I was an outsider who didn't speak the language or know the customs. And this bothered me. But why? Because despite only ever knowing warmth, acceptance, and the promise of good to come, I felt something akin to survivor's guilt. As though, why me? What about the others who were suffering, some for no other reason than parentage or bad luck? Perhaps by witnessing life's struggles and grit, I would be able to better appreciate the good that existed. That my lack of experience was a luxury not granted to all was not lost on me. Yet here I was … sticking out my foot and dipping my big toe into the "other side." I was cautious and a little excited. And completely unaware that I had so far yet to go to reach a place that didn't even exist.

GRADUALLY, DEREK INTRODUCED me to more of his friends, although "friend" really isn't the word for what these people were to him. They all either needed or offered something that he was only too happy to give or receive.

I liked the My-House-Is-A-Warehouse girl. Or rather, I liked her place. Wide, wooden platform steps led up to the door –the kind you might see outside a foreman's on-site office. Inside, the expansive living space was lined with bookshelves and sculptures and taller-than-me artwork leaning against the space between the huge windows. There were maroon couches you could live and die on arranged around a large Persian rug topped by a carved wooden coffee table. The wide, open room was lit with candles and strings of colored lights.

I wanted to paint in pajamas and write novels here. I wanted to build a giant blanket fort in the middle and sit inside with all my friends drinking tea and telling ghost stories. I wanted to turn up the music and dance until I was too tired to move. I wanted to lock the door to the outer world and escape into my own inner one here.

I might have envied the woman who lived there if not for her detached and empty eyes. She was late twenties, petite, with short bleached blond hair framing a beautiful and intelligent face. Her clothes boasted the casual, understated style found in the small boutiques downtown and on Capital Hill –unique, well-made, expensive. But despite the eclectic beauty on and around her that made her other visitors laugh and talk excitedly as though they had just gained entry to an exclusive club, her expression remained flat, disinterested. Her replies were automatic, and her movements mechanical. I felt, watching her, that I was looking at someone who had lived centuries, someone for whom the world no longer held any appeal. When I looked at her, all the warmth left my body and a dark, heavy sadness crept in.

Apparently, she threw incredible parties, but that night there were only four or five other people. I was glad for this. We didn't stay long, an hour maybe, during which time I sat curled up on a loveseat trying to look inconspicuous while Derek tweaked her security system. The others passed around a blue and red glass bong and occasionally leaned over to look at the camera feed Derek was working on. They spoke about the coming nights, the lost nights, how daytime was something to be endured. The girl sat, impassive, unaffected. Even when she answered Derek's questions, she didn't appear to really care.

"She seems so empty," I said to Derek as we were driving home. "Beyond sad, beyond *any* strong emotion. Just ... empty. It makes me hurt inside."

"She doesn't know what to do with herself anymore," Derek said.

"But how?" I asked. "There's so much to see and do."

"She's done everything she wanted to do. Everything she wanted to try. Live the dream long enough and even the best experiences become monotonous."

"But there's got to be something else she wants to do," I insisted.

"Some people actually reach their goals. Now she's trying to figure out what's next."

"What about close friends, family? What does she care about?"

"Not everyone has what you have, Ani."

"Yeah, but ..."

"She'll find her way."

I stared out the window, unsatisfied and wishing I could do something for her. But even as I clung to the idea that the components of a meaningful life lay free for all, waiting only to be discovered, I also realized that without truly knowing her or her history, any words I might offer would come across as hollow.

A few weeks later, we met another woman who I inwardly dubbed, Ms. I'm-a-Grownup, because of her large, tastefully furnished house, professional wardrobe, and perfect appearance. She was in her late thirties and had schedules and a briefcase and high heels that clicked when she walked. She made important phone calls that got things done and had a voice she used specifically for dictating orders. In short, she had achieved a sophistication I didn't see myself ever attaining. At first glance she seemed to embody the upper-middle class woman who is successfully balancing career and family. Her two daughters, aged twelve and fourteen, were sleeping upstairs when we arrived late one night. I felt a bit like a child myself and kept my elbows tight against my body so that I wouldn't knock over a vase or break something valuable.

Derek was there to clean her computer of spyware. Apparently, she was in the middle of a nasty divorce, but only once or twice did her composure slip. Otherwise, she was all steely resolve.

She mostly ignored me as we sat in an upstairs den lit by a single Tiffany lamp. The windows beside me were large and black, reflecting the room back to me. I leaned toward the coffee table and picked up a pair of silver balls from a shallow tray.

"Baoding balls," Derek commented from where he sat working at the desk. "You know what they're for?"

"What?" I asked, rolling them around in my hand and liking their weight.

"Women put them in their vaginas and hold them there while going about their day. They say it strengths the muscles down there."

I quickly returned them to their tray.

"Oh, don't worry. They wash them after."

He was teasing me, probably, but my skin still burned with embarrassment.

"I've made you blush. I'm sorry," he said. "Here, I'm almost done."

Ms. I'm-a-Grownup rose from where she'd been regarding me with obvious wonder at my apparent youth and gullibility.

"What did you find?" she asked, turning her focus to him.

He showed her, and as he did, her hand slowly rose to her mouth. Her eyes glistened as she took in the extent of the malware. Derek reached up and gently touched her arm.

"This is what I've done," he said, explaining each step. "He won't get in again."

She nodded. Then she put her hand on the desk and supported herself a moment.

With her eyes closed, she confided in a whisper, "He's gotten to Alexa too. He's using my own daughter against me."

Derek leaned back in the office chair and studied her as she began describing the things her older daughter had said and done. Her voice was a string, unspooling. Somewhere deep inside her, the other end was unraveling. I listened, feeling a part of me crumble.

"I can't trust her, my own daughter," she said, choking. "I've lost her."

Her pain echoed through the house. Sorrow and emptiness swirled together like smoke behind curtains and around picture frames and flower-filled vases. Something scuttled in the shadows. I couldn't quite make it out, but the hairs on the back of my neck prickled. I blinked my eyes, trying to clear them, and then jerked my foot back as something darted by. And there, squeezing behind the perfectly polished mirror frame, what was that? I shifted uncomfortably, wishing we could leave.

I looked back at the woman. "There's still hope," I wanted to say. But my hope, when cupped in my hands, felt very small. I clasped it to me, but in that moment felt helpless to share it.

I GOT READY IN A STATE of fevered hurry. He was taking me out. I would look the part, act the part, *be* the part. I'd been to a club before. In Arizona. It didn't count. The country-western club, with its cowboys who either couldn't dance or else boasted of their skill being so great they could make *anyone* look good, had felt "safe." My two girlfriends and I had mostly laughed over drinks while discussing Mr. I'm-So-Hot, whose unadulterated self-praise as he swung Savannah about on the dance floor had left us in stitches. So yeah, it didn't count.

Tonight would count. It would be safe, but barely. I would look sexy, or at least sexy enough. And I would dance. Not some choreographed line dance where everyone kicked their feet in unison –no offense to those who love it; my clumsy feet just can't seem to follow the rules. No, tonight I would dance like I danced in my room when the lights were low, and the music flowed through my veins. When I didn't care what other people thought –when I just *moved* inside the music.

Another layer of eye-shadow –dark on the outside. Another strand of hair twirled in mousse –the kind that smelled so good, even after years of sitting in my bathroom cabinet rarely getting used. Dark lip gloss. Black pants. High heels. A passable shirt. I was sexy and powerful and alive. I was ready.

He stared. He smiled. I smiled back as I slid into the car and he shut the door behind me. Then we were off, finding a parking spot, stepping across the street, pulling out ID's – "yes, it's real, all Arizona licenses expire in fifty years. Yes, yes, crazy, I know"– and into the black. Bar to the left, booths to the right. Dance floor ahead. Tables and people and flashing lights. Hot and wet and moving.

Derek pushed through to the hallway in back. I followed close behind, feeling him, feeling hot, feeling everyone. I handed my coat to the woman in the cloakroom before turning to Derek who pulled me close by my hand. Sitting on a stool, he looked around as he took out his pipe. Cop, cop, dealer, user, dealer, he said. I looked where he looked. Maybe, definitely, it didn't matter. His lighter flared. The white powder bubbled. He inhaled. He offered. I shook my head. He shrugged and blew out a stream. I ran a hand through his hair. Kissed the edge of his jaw, my cheek touching his and feeling the slight stubble, the thrilling sandpaper of sensation. He inhaled. He pulled me close, lips to lips. My pounding heart and ... pause. Eyebrows asking permission. I nodded. He kissed me then, and I breathed in his air, his drug, his speed. The warm inhale carried a slight chemical taste, like the lingering trace of an electrical fire. I didn't feel anything. No sudden racing of the heart. No sudden need to explode with energy. Only awake. Awake. Awake. All. Night. Long.

Dancing, dancing, as the hours passed. Ceaseless energy. The screen overhead flashing scenes from anime I didn't recognize, from the black and white past, from places long ago and far away, bright, vivid, and exotic. And the music never ever stopped. It was pounding and electrifying. I wanted to dance the world away. Long after the alcohol was capped, long after the wolfish young couples and laughing groups of friends had cleared out, long after the sun had sunk beneath our feet, we were there. All of us who just wanted to move together inside the music. Awake and alive and soaring.

I was self-possessed and perfect, free to move and feel and be myself. There was no one to make me doubt. Only a man who liked to watch me dance. Derek took what I offered and didn't care if I sometimes missed a step or laughed too loud or shyly glanced away. We existed together in the moment, and that was enough. Derek could leave after, to be seen no more, and I would be fine. He wasn't Kurt or Jimmy or any of the others. He was no one I'd ever known before, and I was free to not give a damn. For once, I didn't overthink.

Derek returned from having a smoke outside, the cold night air still clinging to his hair. He drew close, until we were inches apart. We danced like that, mirroring each other's movements while the teasing space between us challenged our ability to resist touching the other. We started laughing at the same time as we fell into each other. Still entwined, we claimed a table and kissed for hours. For always. I pulled out a clove, and he lit it. I blew smoke rings the way he had shown me late one night out on a rooftop, and I let the smoke curl in thick ropes that drifted up toward the ceiling. We kissed again, and I tasted him; I craved him; I pressed up hard against him.

A flurry of fire appeared suddenly above us, and I laughed. Two small, lithe brown women with glowing skin wove fire stripes over their heads and around their bodies as they danced on two joined tabletops. The tassels on their skirts and bikini tops swayed and caught the light, joyous, like the faces of the women. They were lovely, ecstatic, their bodies liquid grace.

Derek turned away from them as he looked at me. "They can't hold a candle next to you." I shook my head at his flattery, but smiled, feeling warm. His warm breath caressed my ear, his warm hand traced the skin beneath my shirt, just above my waist. I felt awake. Awake. I rose and danced again, feeling the energy around me like an embrace. It flowed over my skin and rolled up my body, and I reveled in it. And when the sun rose with thin, grey light sneaking between the buildings, we stepped out into the crisp Sunday morning air and drove somewhere new, where we ordered fresh drinks and danced amid fresh faces.

By mid-morning we were back at my place, blood racing and bodies laughing, alert, calling to each other. Time stood still, and we absorbed each other. I absorbed everything. So, this is what it was like. To be in another world, another body, letting go in fearless, breathing passion.

HOW MANY NIGHTS DID we do this? How many Saturdays did we dance until dawn, losing ourselves, before going over to Havana's –the gay bar that reopened early– for more dancing, more kissing in some dark corner while our glasses shivered and gleamed on the table beside us?

Christianity speaks of losing one's self as a way of letting go –submitting, surrendering, yes, yes, and only then truly finding ourselves.

On the dance floor, conscious only of my own breathing and the heat –the heat!– all around, I would lose myself. I *felt*. I felt alive as my racing mind slowed and my senses took over. I welcomed the relief! I was young. I was powerful. I was *alive*.

In the mornings, after everything, we'd sleep, wrapped up in blankets in the middle of my floor. Or he would sleep, and I would lie there, listening to him, trying to match my breathing to his while wondering how his slumbering breath could come so fast.

I could always tell when I'd inhaled too much of his drug the night before. A few breaths of second-hand speed and I wouldn't even notice it. Too much, however, and I wrestled a demon through all the long hours that followed. I'd feel the effects first in my lips. I wouldn't be able to stop licking them –as though they were parched, cracking. And then I couldn't get enough air –no matter how deeply or quickly I sucked in each breath. Then, too, there was the occasional hyper chatter –like that day I polished off a bag of Chex Mix on a work break without realizing it had been inadvertently spiked with some of Derek's white powder the night before. I assailed every customer with jokes and laughter and an up-close buoyancy that left them grinning and bewildered.

But the worst side effect came on those mornings I lay beside Derek trying to sleep. Plagued by my desperately dry mouth and the inability to slow my breathing, I'd toss about until the blankets were a tangle around me. I once heard a fly scream as it tried to extricate itself from a web. Maybe it was just the high-pitched whine of its tiny wings, but it sounded like screaming. That sound filled my head every time I ran my cottony tongue over my thick lips and tried to stretch each breath into something longer. But no matter what trick, what effort I employed, each breath got snatched away by my gasping need for air. I'd get up and pace. I'd guzzle water. But I was a hurricane in a bottle. It was maddening. I'd finally bury my face in the pillow and cry for sleep. But sleep wouldn't come. In its place was a humming in my ears that grew louder, an insistency that something wasn't right. That what I was doing wasn't right. The moral weight of my current lifestyle slowly bore down on me. Softly at first, and then heavier and heavier until I felt some part of me would soon be crushed. The good part. The hopeful, optimistic, idealistic, sweet part. These were the only times I felt truly ... guilty. As though –enlightening though my experiences were– I might be *consumed*. As though, if I stayed on this course much longer, that assurance that I had always taken for granted, that everything would be okay, that everything had purpose and meaning, would erode, and I'd find my fingers slipping from the hand of God until we were lost to each other. This thought terrified me.

NEARLY EVERY NIGHT in the many weeks that followed, Derek picked me up from work an hour before midnight. A couple times he met me during my lunch break, and we'd zip away toward the pier to watch the sun sink a little, listening to the waves and feeling happy. Or we'd fly away down the street and eat pizza while sitting at an outdoor table and watching the endless stream of people flow by. I picked up the check occasionally, so he'd know I didn't expect him to pay for everything –I could pull my own weight. I wasn't dependent. I could handle my own.

I looked forward to these lunch breaks until the time I was a half hour late getting back to work. Then we met only after my shift was over. Time couldn't fly fast enough. Eleven p.m. and I'd dash across the street into his waiting embrace. In those moments, when we drove off through the deserted streets, the city was ours. We'd stop at an all-night diner or explore hidden nooks of the city. Or we'd talk, usually staying awake until two or four in the morning.

Mornings were difficult –I began putting off going to the darkroom and was finding it increasingly hard to take classes seriously, what with everyone seeming so ... young, and the information so impractical. Who was I kidding? Photography was fun –I loved it!– but as my *profession*? I was in a state of flux, but although I didn't have the foggiest idea of what to do or where to go next, surprisingly it didn't matter. The loud, healthy beating of my heart, combined with my sheer confidence of will, made me powerful. I was POWERFUL!

I was living an experience, conscious that it was unlike anything I'd yet known, might ever know; that it was *significant*. I didn't understand fully *why* my new situation was significant or what it would mean down the road, but that was okay. I could figure it all out later. Now was the time to *live*!

And I was. And it was wild. I mean, how do you respond to someone who says, as he's driving you to work and you're worried about being late, leaning forward a little as if that'll help speed you up, "I know you want to work –to be your own person– but ... you know don't have to."

I flinched, expecting him to hit the pedestrian who had just walked out in front of him –him going so fast, the pedestrian staring straight ahead, oblivious. But he missed, everyone was safe, we were on our way. I might even actually clock in on time–

"What?!"

"You don't *have* to work."

I stared at him, unbelieving. Then I laughed. "Oh no, no thanks. That's sweet, really it is, but I don't need –or even want– a sugar daddy. Besides, I like my job. I love the people. I love the customers, the projects, the ideas, and creativity. I need that stimulation. I thrive on it."

He shrugged.

Then later, as we were digging into each other's Chinese food with chopsticks, "How would you like to go to Thailand? To live."

I nearly choked. How could I take him seriously? I truly believe that for the whole two minutes we talked about it he was actually sincere. An escape oversees could never work –for him or me. To go with him anywhere felt like I'd be cutting ties to everything I'd ever known for an excursion that would be unsustainable. And then what? I was not about to let myself become dependent on anyone, much less a man with whom I'd be only temporarily involved. It'd never do for him either. He needed constant stimulation, a stage and audience with whom to interact. And yet, it's as though he would get caught up in these little bursts of fancy, as though he fully believed it was possible for us to escape together and live out some sort of indefinite vacation-like fantasy in paradise.

Derek did what he wanted, when, where, and how he wanted. For no other reason than because he wanted to. For him that was all the reason he needed –despite the circumstances, regardless of the consequences. That was how he lived his life.

I visited friends in the dorm occasionally –especially Jimmy, his roommate Will, and Will's girlfriend, Stacy– and I'd feel like I was returning from the moon. They joked and argued and threw food at each other while playing video games and watching *Buffy* and *Cowboy Bebop*. Surrounded by their carefree happiness and good-natured banter, I wanted to tilt back my head, eyes closed, and just bask in how natural and normal it all felt. But while refreshing, their company also left me feeling like a foreigner or a long-absent voyager, for whom the everyday has become novel and unfamiliar. My friends became my tether, pulling me back to earth. Around them, my eyes cleared and my spirits lifted.

I never told them much about myself though, or about Derek, until one night when Jimmy walked me home. I confided bits and pieces, surprised at the relief it brought. He listened, all sweet attentiveness.

"But what about you?" I asked, feeling suddenly embarrassed by his wrinkled brow and silent absorption. "How are things going?"

He described his class projects, the dorm parties and the girls he'd met –"she waited until we're drinking beers at her place to tell me she's engaged –can you believe that?!"– and then he brought up Kurt.

"He says you're the most confusing girl he's ever met."

I felt a sudden pang, a longing ache to see and speak with him again.

"How so?" I asked.

"Because you're so conservative with the guys you like and so carefree with the guys you don't." He looked at me a moment, and a flood of emotions I didn't understand washed over me.

"You and Kurt share a special bond," he said casually, but with a glance that seemed to see through my feigned nonchalance. "I think he just wants to see you happy."

"Has he said anything to you?"

"No, it's just what I see." He smiled and shrugged.

"Do you think I should tell him what's been going on? Would that be weird?"

He turned to face me at the front steps of my building. "Not at all. Go see him. It'd be good for both of you." He hugged me then and said goodnight. I leaned against the doorframe and watched him retrace his steps into the darkness.

DEREK AND I SPENT ENOUGH time together to fill oceans. Restaurants, the state fair, dancing, and drives. And hours spent exploring each other's bodies. We were together morning and evening, between work and school. Nearly every waking moment, and every dreaming moment too. I was thrilled; I was flattered; I was exhausted.

He'd begun to creep into my time and my space with phrases like, "let's see if we can increase your internet speed" or "let's go furniture shopping because sleeping on your floor is killing my back" or "let me see if I can fix the computer problem your roommate asked me about" –so thoughtful, so sweet. Only it wasn't. Don't get me wrong, I was appreciative. But he'd make these suggestions at the most inopportune times. Like when I wanted to do something he didn't want to do. Hours later I'd look out my window to see the sun sinking, my day wasted. I felt myself getting absorbed into a world of "let's do this" or "let's go here" –a world not my own. I was like a frog being slowly boiled alive, unaware at first what was happening.

I pulled back one night and shook my head. I was staying home. I was tired and wanted only to watch a movie. He didn't like movies. I knew he didn't. Because of his ADHD, he said –his short attention span. He was restless. I didn't care.

"You're used to manipulating, aren't you?" I asked.

"No," he answered with that oh-so-serious face that I still couldn't take seriously. "I don't ever want you to feel like I'm manipulating you. Because I'm not." He clinched his lips together and his chin moved. "Okay?"

"Okay." But I didn't fully believe him.

DEREK often said he couldn't comprehend the love I felt for my family. Familial bonds were foreign to him, given his own experiences.

"I have no happy memories from before I was fifteen," he had said, gradually revealing more about his stepdad and childhood. My chest tightened as he described the verbal and psychological abuse by his stepfather, whose joyless religion Derek disavowed, fought against, hated. After his stepdad kicked him out of the house when he was fifteen, a compassionate ophthalmologist welcomed him into his home. Derek came to consider this man his true father, the man's sons his adoptive brothers.

The two sons –one in his late teens and the other in his early twenties– worked with Derek in his software company. He took me to meet them one night –after which Derek and I sat alone on their couch, eating ice-cream and watching television.

"If you were old," Derek said, lifting the spoon to my mouth and watching me, "if you were old and couldn't feed yourself, I would feed you."

*Awww!* I thought. Next, he's going to tell me that he's going to buy me a unicorn and together we'll ride off into the rainbow.

I laughed, but quickly covered my mouth so as not to wake the family who was by then sleeping upstairs, the time being around one or two in the morning. Strangely, they all had to get up early for work, like normal people.

They seemed like a happy family. When I'd met the sons in the computer-lit office, they'd been telling jokes with the volume turned way up as they saw who could make the other's character die a more gruesome, blood-splattering onscreen death. Extra points for head shots, of course. The father seemed a little distant though. He was polite, kind even, but he didn't approve. This made me uneasy. Otherwise, they all seemed happy, close. And their home was beautiful. Lived in, but stylish and comfortable.

I still had not been to Derek's house.

He brought up his secret again –one he had mentioned the previous morning while we ate breakfast in the little diner down the block.

"I've been afraid to tell you because I don't want things to change."

I just looked at him, more curious than anything else. It should've been obvious, but I didn't have the faintest idea what his secret could be. I thought he was being melodramatic. Again.

"Worse than your murder story?" I asked.

"Much, much worse."

# Chapter 7

"I have this friend, my best friend, who's terminally ill."

Compassion flooded through me. Derek was sitting on my olive-green bowl chair, rubbing his knees and clearly having a difficult time telling me this. It was late the following night, dark, just us –and he was shaking.

"She has extreme schizophrenia and doesn't even really know me anymore. We've been married now for eleven years and found out only three years ago." He rushed on, "There were the warning signs, of course, but we didn't know. I mean, I knew she hated people, but some people are like that –I didn't realize until later that it was because she was always 'hearing' them talking about her."

I waited, expecting an avalanche or a tidal wave to come crashing down, crushing me with the weight of the word "married." I waited. But nothing came. Instead, I grew smaller, and smaller, until I was the size of a fly, crawling over the words "adultery," "mistress," and "betrayal." They were mountainous. Too big to be absorbed. And Derek. He was very, very far away. A talking giant.

He continued, telling me how they'd met at the university. She was his tutor –brilliant, with a Ph.D. in physics and a Master's in math, or something like that. They'd slept together, lived together, until one day she'd told him to reel in or cut the line because she was tired of waiting. Loving her, but not "in love" with her, he married her –those were his words– and she'd been amazing, supportive, and, he said, crazy.

"When she wasn't painting the neighbor's brick house using milk and a roller while wearing only her overcoat, she was freaking out at the sight of magazine covers because she knew –she *knew*– each one was really a picture of her that had been digitally altered to mock her. She thought everybody was laughing at her, hating her. She'd hear incessant screaming and yelling in the room next door at hotels, insisting on another room, a new room, fifteen new rooms. I didn't hear anything, but her hearing was always better than mine. We'd try room after room, but none were good enough, none were quiet.

"I did what I could. I tried to handle each in stride. I supported her, accommodated her –even the time she called Nordstrom's –that's back when I was working as a contractor on their security system– and told them I had videotaped myself sexually abusing children. It wasn't true, of course it wasn't true. A delusion, a sick piece of paranoia, but you just can't undo that sort of damage. They don't want to believe it; they want to think it's not true, but ... they're not sure. Everyone looks at you differently –always– after a thing like that."

I listened, imagining. From a distance, I saw the horror in his eyes as he recalled each time he had stood before her, confused and not knowing how to act, how to respond. The frayed edges of his voice caught in his throat as he described her suffering, and I swallowed hard as I thought, what if it were my mother? Or brother? Someone I loved? How would I feel watching them lose touch with reality?

And yet ...

"Once, during a moment of lucidity, she told me, 'Derek, I understand how hard this is for you. It's okay if you see other girls.' I told her, 'No, I can't. I don't even *see* them –I've seen only you for the past eight years of our marriage.'

"'Derek,' she said, 'it's okay, I want you to. You're a man and you have needs. But please, please save your heart for me. Don't give that away.'"

I leaned back, incredulity returning me to my normal state, and I furrowed my brow. Derek looked at me, his eyes pleading for me to understand. They were wide open, vulnerable. "That's why you scare me," he said. "I feel things for you that I've never felt before."

I shook my head. "No, don't say that. Please."

"I love her. I do. But I'm torn. Part of me wants so desperately to have her back –the real her– and the other part knows she'll never get better and hopes that she would just die. Ani, look, I know that sounds horrible, but it's not even her anymore. When she's not doped up on medication, she stares at me with these crazed, hate-filled eyes."

He grimaced at me with his eyes bugged out and his mouth in a snarl, showing me what it was like, the face of this woman he no longer knew. Then he looked away again and clinched his mouth shut.

"I don't know what I'm going to do. I want to take care of her, to do right by her..."

He looked at me again and sighed.

"I had to tell you –wanted to sooner but had a hard time. Paul didn't think I should. But I had to –I have to be honest with you, you understand?"

I just looked at him, my brain on overload. I numbly watched as the edges of my vision turned gray.

"I love my wife," he said, "but I never had that gushy, puppy-dog love. I'm feeling things with you that I've never felt before. And don't say, 'you don't know me,' okay, because I know enough." He took a deep breath. "I'll understand though if you don't want to see me again."

He dropped his head and then raised his eyes to meet mine. I was sitting on the floor next to him.

Standing to my feet, I yelled, "How dare you! Your wife needs you now more than ever and all you can do is try to make me feel sorry for *you*?! As if *you're* the victim here?! You're not a victim, Derek. You're a liar! And a coward! I don't feel sorry for you. Your wife, yeah, but not *you*. I don't want anything to do with you! Ever! Get out!"

Only I didn't say that. Instead, I sat still as a statue as I struggled to make sense of the conflicting thoughts and emotions tumbling around inside me. The moral outrage I expected to feel lay bound and gagged by my confusion. How was it possible that an unknown woman could be so deeply connected to this man with whom I was so intimately involved? How could I have changed so suddenly from girlfriend to mistress? I didn't feel like the "other woman." I felt the same as I had before: detached and almost ... curious. As though, upon finding myself in a gallery I had heard about but had never seen, I was too distracted by the images looming above me to find the exit.

I could see his wife. Imagine her from a distance. The portrait of her suffering was tragic. Sympathy swelled within me, pressing against my chest, churning within my stomach. What she was going through must be terrifying!

But alongside this river of sorrow and sympathy for her was a stream, small and trickling, but moving all the same, flowing from me to Derek. He was selfish and deceptive, but not malicious. What would it be like to watch the person you love waging a war within their own mind? Becoming a new person? Creating a new, disturbing reality?

Compassion. That's what I felt. I felt compassion for his wife. I felt compassion for him, too. It welled up within me, blinding me to my role so that I felt instead like a clinician. As though I might be even able to help them. The two of them. Foolish girl that I was, I thought, I can switch from lover to friend, maybe even nudge him back to his wife. I can turn this around, I thought. I can still do good.

I reached out. I put my hand on his knee but didn't say anything. Dust particles drifted in the air around us. We sat frozen as they settled on our hair, our skin.

Finally, I said quietly. "Okay."

"Okay what?"

"I'll see you again."

"Really?" The word came out in a rush. He leaned forward and wrapped me up in that squeezing tight hug of his. Startled, I just sat there, until at last he let go and left me to my thoughts.

THIS, *this*, is the only thing I regret from my time with Derek. That he was married. For this I can make no excuses. Why didn't I end things immediately? Or at the very least, the next day, when I'd had time to think? And why wasn't I angry at his betrayal? How could I stand to be near him knowing there was someone else? How could I do that to her? To myself?

The next time I saw him, I felt odd. Still numb maybe, or maybe just ... *blank*. No matter what I called myself in relation to him, we were adulterers. A part of me was horrified. But the other part of me felt the same as I had before: uncorrupted.

Was corruption something that happened little by little or all at once?

What did it even mean to be "good" or "bad"?

"Human constructs –that's all those are," Derek said later. "Like time. They're labels that serve a purpose but are only ideas."

"I don't know. I think they're more than that. I think we call people 'good' or 'bad' based on the sum of their actions."

"But not all actions carry the same weight. Ani, listen, you're not a bad person."

"How do you know? I mean, I realize it's not actions that save us, but maybe they're a reflection of who we are. Maybe I'm just a bad person."

Derek scoffed. "You're a lot of things, but you're not a bad person."

I wasn't going to take his word for it. Still, when it came down to it, I felt neither good nor bad. I was just me −a girl selfishly trying to experience sensation while questioning the teachings of her youth. I hated the cold and uncertain feeling I got when I caught myself thinking that heaven seemed more like an ideal than a very real possibility that all have an equal opportunity to grasp. *We're all good! We're all bad!* −I thought. And grace? How does it qualify −when some have not even heard? When they've been programmed by their childhoods, their cultural environments to believe that some *other* ideology is the real and right one? Either grace is granted to all, whether or not they've consciously accepted it, or there is no such thing.

I had often been told that the miracle of grace is that it is undeserved. No one *deserves* salvation, they told me. But damnation? −do we deserve that? Because someone loses sight of or never saw God to begin with, should they be written off forever?

I shouldn't have been surprised at the growing distance I felt with my God. I'd just discovered the man I was sleeping with was married and instead of immediately exiting the relationship, I had hesitated. Perhaps it was only natural that I should find myself shifting away from my beliefs and the person I'd been.

My choices had brought me to this point, but regardless of how or why I made them, I had to take responsibility for them. Every choice has a consequence. And the choice to do right lies always ahead, no matter what choices came before.

*Please, God, forgive me!* I prayed. *Help me to be strong. To do the right thing. Because I want to do right, and I need you. I need your help.*

I felt my prayer go up. And up. And up. Into the silence. Perhaps it is still rising, a transparent thought bubble floating through the cosmos.

Did God hear? Was he present? I wasn't ready to give up my faith. I clung to it still, but I remembered hearing that Nietzsche once said something to the effect that those who conclude there is no God must either give in to despair or make their own way. If there was no God, I thought, then I could do anything *–anything–* and it wouldn't matter. *Nothing* would really matter. Was humanity's moral code nothing more than a socio-political construct enabling us to progress without killing each other off? Or was there something else to it? Something outside the bounds of what I'd been taught that I had yet to discover?

What was there to strive for, to live for, if not an eternal, loving relationship with God and those around me? The single, short journey of today? A better world for tomorrow? Should I live for myself or for those I love? Or, maybe, for all of us together? –the whole, of which we are each a part? At my best, I had felt the invisible threads tying me to the rest of humanity, to the world. Empathy, wonder, and connection coursed through those threads, assuring me I wasn't alone. But at my worst, I had felt different, separate, with a desperate longing to crawl into a hole and fade away. During those times, hope was what pulled me out. Not just that tomorrow could and would be better, but that there was something larger than myself, something meaningful.

I would not give in to despair, I thought. Existence possessed meaning. Maybe not the way I had previously believed, but I would find it.

I WENT TO SEE KURT.

He greeted me from behind his desk with a huge "Hello!" and I basked in the comfortable familiarity of his presence.

"What brings you here?" he asked.

"I have a favor to ask," I said.

"Of who?"

"Of you."

He looked surprised. And good. And healthy. And wonderful. "Yeah? What can I do?"

"Can we talk?"

"Sure. About what?" I could see his heavy leather cowboy boots sticking out from the side of the desk where he had his legs stretched out, ankles crossed. He always leaned back when someone stopped by, offering his full attention. When he straightened up and started shuffling papers, we'd know the conversation was over.

"Um ... stuff. My life's been ... interesting lately."

"In what way?"

"Later, if that's okay."

He smiled, shrugged. "Of course."

"Tonight?" I asked. "Or would sometime tomorrow be better?"

He chose that night.

He offered me juice when I arrived at his apartment –always the conscientious host– and led me to his beautiful, new, cream-colored suede couch.

The couch surprised me, although I had heard about it from Jimmy. Kurt had said buying furniture was like making a commitment. In his own way, and despite the way he still spoke of moving out of this "dull and dirty" city, he was putting down roots. I silently cheered for him.

We talked about nothing at first. A home-decorating show flashed on the TV, which we made fun of for a while. Then he asked what was up.

"I've been trying to guess all day," he said. "Let me see –is it because you're thinking of having sex?"

I laughed, not allowing myself to wonder how things might have been different had I gone to talk with him before Andy, before Derek. I told myself he had made his choice, and any earlier discussion of sex would've felt too much like I was trying to change his mind, rather than figure out my own.

"No," I said. "In fact, since I last saw you, I've slept with a homeless guy and a millionaire."

"Damn! I knew this was going to be good –with you it had to be interesting."

I told him everything ... nearly. Andy. Lymon. Derek, of course. I described meeting Andy. I repeated conversations I'd had with Lymon. I even mentioned how Derek had essentially offered to make him disappear. I glanced up at Kurt as I said this. He was sitting with his head resting against his wrist, just watching, his eyes bright and piercing.

"Pretty wild, huh?" I asked. I dropped my eyes to the floor, feeling suddenly self-conscious. My emotional vulnerability began stiffening my joints so that I felt awkward and afraid to move. I started to say something, but hesitated.

"Don't stop. Keep going."

So, I kept talking, feeling both uncertain and relieved as everything from the past few months poured out. He smiled. He asked questions. I answered, and he asked more, curious and sitting forward a little. Encouraged by his attentiveness, my words came out with increasing speed. That was his gift –he was fascinated with people's interiors and could coax out our secrets. And I so desperately needed to talk to someone, to get it all out. I confessed things I had told no one else, knowing Kurt would understand, that he wouldn't judge. I wanted nothing from him other than to share with someone I trusted. Someone objective, who I respected. And this is what I told him when he asked why, why him, why all this.

But it was getting to be too much. I could see it in the gathering tension around his brow. He had heard enough. I could hardly contain myself though! There was more, much more, straining to be said. I tried to reign in the words, even as they slipped out, until finally, finally, I ground to a slow halt, nearing choking on the unuttered word, 'wife'. A few breaths later, I couldn't believe I'd almost been about to.

I turned my head and looked out the far window. I took one more calming breath and collected myself. Then I turned back to him and gave a little shrug. I was done. That was all. What did he think?

"I think you've been far too generous with your trust," he said. His eyes were warm, gentle. He studied me thoughtfully. "I personally don't see the need to waste time on something I don't see as long-term. But I'm older. I've had my experiences, and you're still young. Maybe you should milk the situation for all it's worth. You could get a new car out of it, or something." He grinned.

"This isn't a game show!" I laughed. "And besides, it's not about that. It's never been about the money."

"I know." He nodded, becoming serious again. "I know."

"But listen," he added, "be careful."

"I am. I am being careful," I insisted.

"I'm sure you are. But there's questionable things about Derek —for instance, his whole attitude toward the Lymon situation."

"Yeah." I nodded, knowing it was true but needing to hear him say it —to hear someone who was real and safe and solid say that I was stepping out too far.

"There's that and the fact he does speed. You don't want to be linked to someone like that should something go down. And two years just for giving out a dealer's number? You don't get that much even when you're dealing directly."

It seemed to me Kurt understood the world in a way I never would. I nodded again. "You're right. I know you're right." I stared down at my tapping foot. "But it's been one hell of a ride."

"Sounds like you're living a movie." His voice grew quieter as he said this. He sat for a moment, studying the darkness beyond the window. He pressed his lips together and did a little, forced half-grin. It was a quick up and down movement of the corners of his mouth. He dropped his arm and stretched his neck from one side to the other. Then he looked at me. "But listen, I don't think you should fuck him anymore."

"I'm being careful," I said softly. "There's freedom in using someone who's using me. Then it's just an experience. For both of us."

"That's what I mean." He leaned forward, resting his elbows on his knees. "It's going to warp your ideas of intimacy."

I looked down and slowly nodded, understanding. He was right. I knew he was right. Already intimacy seemed like something out-of-reach, something only other people had. Even before Derek. And now... now when I didn't care ... when I wanted only sensation, now I felt more detached than ever. Like I was watching myself. Studying myself. Becoming my own personal lab rat.

"Did you ..."

I looked up at him and waited for him to continue. He was staring at the floor.

"Is it because of me?" he asked. "Did you change your mind about sex because of me?" His eyes darted up to meet mine, and he was worried.

Yes, I thought. But also no.

I shook my head. "No, not really. I just decided I needed to grow up. That's all."

He looked at the floor again, studying the pattern between his knees. I needed to reassure him somehow.

"I've always respected you," I said. "Always. That's why I came to you." I watched him. "But I don't make my decisions because of you or anyone else. That's the point really. I want advice. And knowledge. And hopefully one day wisdom. And then, after thinking it out –whether it's about sex or God or my future– I want to move forward as best I can. That's why I did what I did. Not because of you. But because I had to stand on my own two feet."

His expression relaxed as he leaned back again. He looked so good sitting there on his soft, new, cream-colored couch. Things were right, as they should be, around him.

"Thank you for this," I said, feeling both nostalgic and quietly happy just to be near him. "I knew you would be honest with me."

Our conversation drifted after that. He described his visitors from earlier that day with smiling lightness. Their little girls were "out-of-control!" –jumping on his bed with shoes on their feet and cookies in their fingers. Germs and crumbs –just the thought made Kurt shudder.

How I had missed talking with him like this! Familiarity shone from his smile, and there was tenderness as he spoke of his sister and nieces. My happiness swelled, stirring up confusion. My old feelings came rushing back, and I experienced a moment of panic before I had them pressed safely down again. They no longer belonged to me, with me. He had made his choice. We had both moved on.

I had come to him to clear my head, and it had worked. I felt grounded again. I even very nearly made up my mind never to see Derek again. But as I was leaving, I knew: I wasn't ready to let go.

Even so, after talking with Kurt, I saw Derek as just another man with his own insecurities who wanted to be cared for. This explained his attraction to me, I thought. I listened, I cared, I empathized –from behind my bulletproof window. Compassion can be attractive, especially to those unaccustomed to it.

"Thank you for loving me," he was always saying.

"I never said 'I love you,'" I always said back.

"You don't have to –I see it in your eyes."

Sometimes he would change it up a bit: "Thank you for being my girlfriend."

"I'm not your girlfriend."

"Well ... thanks for being my friend."

"Okay. I can handle that."

I was Derek's chimera –a composite creature created from my adaptability and his desires. I could see no possible happy ending for us. But, for now anyway, I found the fairytale fun. And, quite honestly, rather liberating.

# Chapter 8

Slowly, almost imperceptibly, I began to open up to him. I'm not even sure how exactly, especially considering the number of times I vowed to myself never to see him again. Rationally, I knew I should end it –this little thing that was nothing. That'd been Kurt's advice, and I had agreed with him. But I couldn't quite shake the curiosity, the fascination, the pleasurable pull I felt when exploring new situations and sensations with Derek. So, I hesitated, and everything just kept on happening.

Everyone around me at school felt young, innocent almost. Such innocence felt like a memory. Not of childhood, not exactly. But of a time before disillusionment. Back then, I wasn't ignorant of evil or suffering, but I clung to the good. I believed that everything would always work out okay. Now, I wasn't so sure.

But still I hesitated.

After work one night, Derek met me at midnight, and we drove through the city. Everything felt so dark and empty, but shimmering and alive too, as though all the secret creatures who shunned light and other people were free to emerge and haunt the streets. Rather than feel afraid, I felt like I was one of them. Like I was free. I remembered spending the night at a friend's house once and getting up in the darkness, pulled by an invisible force –the glow of the moonlight on the floorboards perhaps, or the Tiffany nightlight in the recessed den, or the way the house creaked as though getting comfortable. Whatever it was, I rose in response and padded silently through the house in the solitude of early morning. My senses felt unveiled, alert to every small sound, every tiny movement, every creeping shadow. I felt liberated and strangely safe, cocooned in the darkness, as though I could finally discover what had been hidden from me during the day.

I felt the same that night with Derek. He used his all-access keys to gain entry to various apartment buildings. Keiko was moving out in December, and I was hoping to find a studio for myself while wishing lofts weren't so expensive. We peeked into shadowed corners, tip-toed down sleeping halls, talked to strange people with missing teeth and ravaged hearts.

Sometime after two a.m., we ate dinner at the 13 Coins. Our high-backed booth felt like a private room, sheltered from the rest of the dim and fragrant restaurant. I watched Derek toss balls of butter at the backsplash across the aisle from us, trying to get them to stick, while a local dinner theater troupe filed past, some still in performance dress. Loud and laughing and colorful, they settled somewhere behind us, out of sight. I smiled and looked out the window. Headlights flashed and streetlamps blinked above shadows that twisted and churned, and I thought, *what a strange, but marvelous world I am travelling through.*

The sun was just coming up when we left and drove to the pier. The Alaskan viaduct rumbled overhead as we parked and climbed into the back of the Suburban. The city before us, the bay at our backs, we burrowed into each other and watched the golden rays spread and fill the sky. Saturday morning.

Shirts discarded, lying together, we clung to each other with a sort of desperation. What strange chemistry was at play, weaving our time and our bodies together with such ease? Heartbreak hung like a specter at the edge of my vision, ever present. But for now, I was hopelessly happy.

Lulled by the soothing, muffled sounds of traffic and the gentle touch of his fingers in my hair, my eyelids began to feel heavy, and my breathing slowed. Dreams danced, blending with the world around us. Derek stirred, pulled out his ADHD pills. He held out three little capsules to me. I looked at their tiny red and white beads, feeling relaxed and untroubled, then looked back at him. Non-addictive, he said. They'll help. I shifted a little and took them. Then we settled back into each other as our voices drifted softly through the air between us.

"This is nice," I said, "just holding each other."

His face was open, his expression sweet. The hard corners of his mouth had melted into a soft curve of happiness and vulnerability. His eyes, too, were warm. He had blinked away their usual cool glint in the brilliance of the rising sun.

He caught me studying him and smiled. My heart surged.

"Thank you for loving me," he said, voice soft.

"I don't," I said, just as softly.

"Call it what you like –thank you for adoring me."

"We're temporary," I insisted, as much to myself as to him. The words echoed in my mind. We were temporary. The warm, happy, fuzzy feeling that we'd been wrapped in moments before began to evaporate.

"Sometimes, I feel like we're in this little bubble, outside time, and it's just us and nothing else matters. When it's just us, it feels so ... natural. But we can't sustain this. We want different things. Even if you weren't married, we're impossible. This very moment is impossible. I–"

I shifted out from under him until we were facing each other.

"I don't know what I think about God and morality, but I know that all this is wrong. Every time you turn your back on your wife –that *matters*. And I'm enabling you."

I put my palms to my forehead and rubbed.

"I know," he said. "I know. I wish things were different."

I dropped my hands and looked at him.

"Even if you weren't married," I said, "we still wouldn't work. All your friends are cold and hard, and you are too. At least you can be. I don't want to be like that. Plus, the drugs and the alcohol and everybody suspicious of each other –I don't want that either. I know I'm naïve, but maybe that's not such a bad thing."

"It's not. It's part of what I love about you."

"I want so much for you to be happy," I said. "I want to be the one to make you happy. But when I'm honest with myself, I know it shouldn't be me."

Leaning forward, he brushed my hair back from my forehead. I leaned into his palm.

"But it is you, Ani. You're the one who makes me happy. Maybe it shouldn't be you, but it is."

I could have lost myself in the sound of his voice, the press of his body as he touched his forehead to mine and pulled me close.

The minutes ticked by, becoming hours. People came and went. They parked their cars alongside the Suburban; they led their children by their tiny hands; they checked their teeth in the tinted windows, never guessing that a half-naked couple lay entwined in each other's arms just behind the glass. None of them mattered. The sun was high, stretching into noon, and though my mind was alert, I felt warm and relaxed. I felt *good*.

We stopped by Paul's place after that. He was still in bed –it'd been an all-nighter for him too. I stood on his balcony and felt the rushing wind carry my words and whisk them away, until my little song faded into the larger blend of shouts and horns and never-ending engine noises. I felt my heart soar. I felt it race. It was racing. Rather fast. Faster than normal. I stepped back inside, mentioning it to Derek and feeling the edge of worry. He raised his hand to my neck, and then held my wrist. Two seconds later he dropped it, saying my pulse felt normal.

"Besides, it's been a long morning."

Back home alone in my apartment an hour later, I headed straight for the shower, craving the heat and pressure. I needed to unwind. But this shower, no matter how hot, no matter how hard, was just not doing it for me. I couldn't relax. Quite the opposite. My heart was beating faster, and I couldn't slow it down. I tried deep breathing. Slower breathing. I tried hotter water, longer. I tried everything I could think of. I was making it worse, I knew, just by thinking about it. What good was an imagination when all it entertained you with was scenes of exploding organs and parents finding out their sweet, sheltered daughter had died due to a horrible, pill-induced heart attack? So unnecessary. So pathetic, and tragic. A daughter lost –because of her own stupidity. It would be such a shame. My parents would be heartbroken, their disappointment complete. Premature aging, grey hair, and sagging, drooping eyes, because of *me*.

I jumped out of the shower. I started pacing. Something to drink. A glass of cool water. Oh, and some milk –that was supposed to help, right? More pacing. No, I should sit. I should be sitting down, relaxing, trying to calm myself. Nope, more pacing. Hand to my throat. *Feel* it! My veins were jumping! My heart thumping against my shirt. Surely it would tire soon. Or collapse in on itself. Or worse! It would burst, spraying blood all over my lungs so that they'd find me –someone, Keiko maybe?– would find me with blood oozing out of my mouth and my eyes staring in a wide, gruesome expression. Keiko would need counseling.

I sat down. I looked at the clock on the oven. The green numbers –were they buzzing? was that buzzing I heard?– burned into my eyes as I counted the beats in my wrist. Oh my goodness, it was over a hundred. Still counting. My pulse had never been this high before. Mid-seventies, usually. Almost one hundred and thirty! My pulse was a hundred and thirty. I counted again, once more, just to make sure. My hands were shaking. I stared at my trembling fingers, still counting. Yes, it was close to a hundred and thirty. Could people die from that? How high was dangerous?

I stood up. I walked to the bathroom mirror. Yup, my eyes appeared dilated, and I felt light-headed.

I was all alone.

I started, just then, to panic.

I called Harborview Medical Center and was transferred to a nurse hotline and then cut off. I called Swedish Medical Center next and then 911, who transferred me to poison control. I was very casual with them, saying I was just curious if it was at all possible that someone could maybe die from taking a couple of Ritalin pills when they weren't actually ADHD? My heart was beating a little fast, I said, and I just wanted to make sure it was okay. Nothing serious. What do you think?

"Were you trying to hurt yourself?"

"No, no. I just wanted energy."

Both Swedish and poison control suggested I go and get it checked out.

I grabbed my purse, slipped into my shoes, and hurried out the door. I skipped down the steps, flew out the lobby, and stepped with remarkable speed through the alley and toward the dorm. I called Kurt. He didn't pick up. I tried twice more. I made it to the building and tapped the elevator button several times. And then a couple more times, just to be sure. Once inside, my hands drummed the wall behind me as I hummed. The door dinged. I got out and rushed to Kurt's door, knocking rapidly. No answer. Where was he? I needed him. I *needed* him! I could trust him. He would be understanding and kind and, where *was* he? Was he avoiding me?

Still shaking, I took the stairs to Jimmy's room. He was all concern. I stared at the floor, the wall, embarrassed. Stacy, his roommate's girlfriend –oh, my goodness! she was so sweet, just look at how sweet she was– immediately insisted on driving me to the ER.

I joked with her on the way –trying to pretend I wasn't really as stupid as I appeared to be– but by this time I was *terrified*. I was going to pass out any minute, I just knew it. All I could think was –not like this. Oh, dear God, *not* like this!

We were nearly at the hospital when I called Derek. It hadn't even occurred to me to call him sooner. I needed someone I could trust, like Kurt. Like Jimmy, his roommate Will, and Stacy, or even Katie –pretty much anybody but Derek. Besides, these people all lived closer.

I asked him for the name of the pills.

"Why? Because I'm on my way to the ER," I said.

"Turn around." It sounded like an order. "You don't need the ER. You're going to be fine." His voice was quick. Abrupt. He told me I was overreacting.

I held out my phone, stared at it. Didn't he care? Even if I was overreacting (which, okay, maybe I was a little), where was his empathy?

A few minutes later, unable to take any more of his abrupt directives, I hung up.

Three hours later, after being given Valium, some water, and a long, condescending talk about "substance abuse," I was deemed free to leave the ER. I was fine. Stupid maybe, but otherwise A-OK.

As I walked home from the parking garage, all I could think about was Derek's response. No concern, no sympathy, only fear of his own implication. It was a reminder, I thought. We were using each other. That was all.

HE CALLED THAT NIGHT –sometime past eleven. I was on the phone with my brother John at the time, having just told him what happened. "You need to drop Derek like a bad habit," he said. "But it's your life, Ani."

Derek was calling on the house line, meaning he was at the apartment's front door. I had a phone to each ear.

"Yeah?"

"I'm downstairs," came his voice, "Can we talk?"

"Alright," I said. "Be down in a minute."

Back on the other line, John asked, "Was that Derek?"

"Yeah, why?"

"Ani, your voice totally changed. It was freaky." He was breathing fast. He was serious. I tried to play it off. He gave me more warnings.

Once off the phone, I stood for a moment by the kitchen counter. The lights above me turned my eyelids pink as I listened to the sound of my breathing. I missed John so much my chest hurt. I wanted to pull him through time and space to be with me. Or better yet, travel to his side so we could watch the stars flash across the huge Arizona sky above our parents' porch as we discussed all the tiny details that made up our ideas, our lives, our reasons why.

Downstairs, Derek's soft side was nowhere to be found. His expression was cold, and his eyes hollow. He stared about him, aloof, and I despised him and his drug, the drug that transformed him, hardened him, stole him away. He said he was ashamed of having given me the pills –especially after he had promised everything would be fine. No one had reacted this strongly before, he said, and of course the circumstances hadn't been typical. Lack of food, lack of sleep, my slight frame. So many factors. He felt defensive. He had been scared. I had used my cell phone, and cops can listen in, and if he was caught, he could go back to jail because he was a felon.

I felt my stomach clinch. Empathy, that's all I wanted. I turned and headed up the stairs. As I reached for the door, I heard his car drive away.

DEREK CALLED ON TUESDAY night, and I gave in. I had not realized before just how completely he had come to fill my life. Every morning, every night, between classes, and before and after work, we were together. Monday, not hearing from him at all, I felt the silence like a void, a vacuum, that drained my room of color. I tried to step around it by keeping myself busy. I turned the TV up loud and drank my weight in tea. I paced and showered and hid myself under blankets until I lost myself to sleep. I hated missing him this way. It was illogical. Weak. Even worse was the relief I felt when he called. And now, he was trying to make up. "Okay," I said. "Okay." All resistance gone.

He drove me far out of town, toward a destination he refused to reveal. I felt my fear only vaguely. Neither of us talked much as he drove, and drove, far out into the darkness to nowhere. He could do anything, leave me anywhere. But I didn't care. I truly didn't care. I wanted only to ease the ache that was growing within me.

A man with the last name of Banks was telling his "Sarah Cole" story on the radio. The man's voice, along with the detail and emotion with which he told the story, enthralled me. Derek too, for he was unusually quiet and still. By turns bitter and sweet, the story penetrated us each in the darkness, and we clung to every word as we raced along the night tunnel of the freeway. Something about how the darkness hugged the car both isolated us from the rest of the world and insulated us.

We were nearing the end, the beautiful, poignant end of the story, when the radio signal broke up and threatened to disappear. I sat forward in consternation, almost beside myself –unable to relax until, finally, the static died away, leaving the sound mercifully clear once again. It was a heartbreaking story of impossible love. Love now glorified as a memory –appreciated only in retrospect. I held my breath and tilted my chin just far enough up so that the swelling tears would not spill over. And then it was gone –story and sorrow and solitude.

Derek swung onto a road that led around the airport, and then, finding the perfect spot, he pulled over just beneath a hill that led sharply up toward the runway. Blinking towers rose far above our heads on either side like impassive giants who had gathered to discuss affairs far beyond our limited understanding.

"The planes follow those lights," Derek said, pointing, as we got out of the car. "One'll pass over soon, and when it does, we'll see every scratch and dent and bug smear marking up its underbelly. And the noise –the noise will rattle our teeth."

Unexpected delight washed over me, filling the empty space inside my chest until I felt almost tipsy. I grinned at Derek as I stepped into his open arms –into that oh-so-wonderful tight embrace. I closed my eyes and inhaled him. He felt so solid and warm. Happiness spread through me at this small surprise. This happy distraction in which I could forget ... everything. Everything except the fast thrumming of his heart and the press of his arms around me, sheltering me from the gathering cold.

We heard the sound then, a far-off distant rumble that tickled our insides. We turned, arms still wrapped around each other, and lifted our faces up toward the bit of sky at the top of the hill.

The first plane came with such roaring, rushing speed that my heart pounded, my ears drummed, and my hair thrashed around as though alive. The massive plane passed so close I felt I could have reached up and touched its belly. If I had, the passengers would have felt my fingertips tracing the soles of their feet, and they would have wondered at the sensation.

I squinted my eyes against the wind as I threw back my head and laughed. I opened my arms wide as my laughter flashed like lightning from the car to the sky to the hill to us again before getting lost in the sea of sound that rushed around us, tossing our hair, and expanding our chests. We were blinded by the blazing lights. Blinded by euphoria.

Chilly air settled over us in the silent darkness of its wake. He pulled me closer. Two more planes roared over us with shooting, streaming lights, and we clung together, laughing and happy.

Back in the car, I grinned at him and held his hand over the consol. I felt connected and breathlessly happy. I could almost forget the reality of our situation, as though it were only him and me, with all our faults and pasts behind us, meeting each other as we were right at that moment, fully accepting and intimately personal as we rejoiced in who we were and what we were to each other. It felt like an alternate dimension we could step into, leaving everything else behind.

But we could never stay there for long.

THE FINAL DAYS OF OCTOBER carried with them a deepening chill.

In an email to Leo, I described the pills and the hospital, and he put things into a different perspective.

"What did you think was going to happen? You take stuff like that and naturally your heart is going to feel like it's going to explode. Derek knows you can't get hurt from the amount you took so of course the next thing he's going to worry about is why you didn't call him sooner and whether the cops are going to be on him."

This was the first time I considered the possibility that Derek's lack of concern might be justifiable.

In the summer between 5$^{th}$ and 6$^{th}$ grade, I spent my days scouring the Texas desert for living creatures I could claim as my own. I considered myself lucky the day I found a huge rock that looked like a promising hide-out. I set my two-liter coke-bottle-turned-terrarium beside me on the ground before carefully lifting one dusty edge. Excitement shot through me when I spotted at least five scorpions dancing beneath, startled by the sudden sunlight. Two ran off before I could even take a breath, but the rest froze with fear or indecision. I found two twigs that I held together like tweezers and maneuvered with a skill that amazed even myself. I managed to get the first two scorpions up and into the narrow mouth of the coke bottle. The twigs slipped a little in my hand, and I had to keep readjusting them as I moved in on the last little scorpion. The sand-colored creature was about an inch long, and it wriggled wildly when I pinned it to the dirt. One twig slid sideways, and I dipped my thumb to straighten it. Instantly, the tip of my thumb exploded with pain. I jerked back, knocking over my make-shift terrarium and landing on my bottom. I was up in a flash, silent, but eyes watering. I had the presence of mind to replace the rock, carefully, before I picked up the coke bottle, checking to see who was left. Then I raced home.

Back at camp, I washed my hands and grabbed some ice, wondering all the while if I was dying. Just how bad was scorpion poison? Was my racing heart, sweating body, and shaking hands due to shock and fear or was the poison working its way through me? I debated telling someone, but then I'd have to admit what I was doing. My mom knew I caught scorpions. She'd almost fainted the first time she'd heard the scratching noises coming from the bottle beside my bed when she was tucking me in one night. But she didn't know how I caught them, and for some reason I didn't think she'd approve. My mental mind games that afternoon were strenuous, but I finally decided to risk being called stupid in order to possibly save my life.

I was fine, of course. But before being thoroughly chastised and reassured by my mother, my eleven-year-old self had considered both outcomes of living and dying equally plausible. Stuck inside my own over-active imagination, I had had no idea what to believe. The same was true with the ADHD pills. Could I have died? My brother didn't think so, and he knew more about these things than me. Derek didn't think so either. But still, I'd been so scared. Shouldn't Derek have shown some concern? Perhaps if I had discussed Derek's reaction with someone else, they might have offered support or additional insight, but I didn't discuss it with anyone else. And so, in the light of day, when the only lasting effect of the pills was a whopping medical bill and a strong sense of my own stupidity, I thought, maybe my brother is right. Maybe Derek knew I'd be fine and was understandably worried about illegally sharing his drugs with me.

Of course, there was still so much else my brother didn't know, and perhaps if he had his response would have been different. But as it was, I told myself I'd had unrealistic expectations. I had overreacted and gotten emotional. I needed to be stronger. I needed to be cooler, calmer, more controlled about all this.

But is it really so bad to be emotional? Is it so horrible to be vulnerable? No, of course not. If only I'd known that then.

# Chapter 9

November in Seattle occasionally offers up days of unexpected beauty. Sunlight comes in sideways, lighting up window displays and the smiling faces of those skimming along the shining sidewalks. Everything glows with a happy, expectant vibrancy as the light passes through the few remaining red and orange leaves to play with the strands of hair escaping from the knit caps and colorful scarves that have re-emerged from the backs of closets and the bottoms of drawers. As fall embraces winter, a sort of cozy warmth blossoms out, moderating the coming grey drizzle with the promise of hot cocoa, inviting interiors, and a festive holiday season just around the corner.

Derek met me before work one such day, and together we drove to the Firehouse Café. The sunlight that poured in through the café's windows spilled over me as I walked around looking at the black and white photos hanging on the bright red walls. Older men and elderly couples filled the booths, smiling and at ease with the world. Happiness sparkled around us. Derek and I laughed as we ate, until an older gentleman walked up and demanded to know who had given us permission to have so much fun.

"Stop it!" he said, smiling. "You're not allowed to enjoy life this much."

"I can't help it," Derek said. "I love this girl."

"What?"

"I LOVE this girl!"

"I'm a little deaf. What'd you say?"

"I LOVE MY ANI!" he yelled, and I laughed with one hand spread forward across the table –trying to support myself under the weight of so much happiness. The man grinned, laughed, and looked back and forth between us. Then he shook Derek's hand and was gone.

Just as we finished our burgers and fries, Dean Martin's voice filled the air, and I heard "That's Amore" for the very first time. I reached out my hand to Derek and whispered, "Listen ... isn't it great?" He pulled me up, his eyes on mine, and took me in his arms. With the music flowing through our hair and across our skin, he twirled me around and dipped me down before pulling me back up into an embrace. I felt like I was floating, and I laughed, my hand on his chest. Memorizing the words, memorizing his eyes, the soft blue light in his happy eyes, I echoed the chorus in an out-of-breath whisper as we leaned into each other. We were both so *happy*! His eyes contained within them oceans of blues and greys and reflected sunlight that spilled out, joining the dancing patterns on the walls. Clouds gathered at our feet, and the birds outside sang like it was the middle of May –everyone so happy for us. All the little old couples and even the smiling ghosts peering out from the picture frames around us clapped in delight and cheered for us. Sunlight flooded the room, scattering cobwebs and dispelling gloom. Shadows didn't exist. Not here. Not now. They were gone, melted away. We stayed like that, swaying together while Dean Martin serenaded us. And in that moment of ecstatic happiness, I felt an eternity bloom within me.

Work that day was great!

THE HENRY ART MUSEUM at the University of Washington was filled with tall, open spaces and unremarkable art the day Derek and I visited. Finding little to interest either of us, we chose instead to sit on the steps outside, where he could smoke. The sun was remote, whispering its secrets from behind layers of clouds. But the scene before us was alive with color and the animated faces of students. I leaned over as a girl with a green vinyl jacket and a red hat came skipping down the steps past me, fingers dancing and head bobbing to a beat only she could hear. I could just make out the guitar riffs of two guys playing under an overhang at the far end of the courtyard. Derek sat in front of me absorbing it all with a relaxed and confident air. When he turned and looked up at me, he smiled with such open-faced happiness that my heart hiccupped. I stared at him a moment, just taking him in. I could almost forget. I could almost pretend that we were not, in fact, betraying prior ties.

As we turned our eyes again to the courtyard before us, I wondered, *what makes a person fall in love?* Is it mental? Chemical? Is it a mix of time and place? Of stars aligning? Is it sealed when you look up to find that someone is *seeing* you, and when, in that moment, something inside you responds and connects?

"I love you," I said suddenly, the words slipping out impulsively into the space behind his ear.

He leaned back, surprised. "I love you too, Baby." He smiled and kissed me. Goodness! –but he was so beautiful like this: relaxed, with his blue-green eyes filled with such sweet softness. I touched his lips and traced his eyebrow.

It was true, I loved him. I felt a bit like a rabbit peering out from a dark hole at a wide, open meadow filled with sunshine and carrots and every possible delight, all the while knowing that if I ventured out too far, I'd get shot to bits. But it was love, nevertheless. I hadn't thought it possible. And for such a man. Yet here I was, hopelessly, irrationally, in love. Those three little words, spoken honestly, unexpectedly, were a revelation to me.

We sat silently then, my arms around his neck, while we stared out over the wide, white steps leading down. I closed my eyes and felt the warm press of him, the cool November breeze on my face. The truth of those words, spoken so openly, felt as unsettling as it did extraordinary.

BURSTING OUT INTO THE cool, fresh air the next day after class, I caught sight of Derek walking away from me –long, dark coat and confident stride giving him away.

"Derek!" I called, and I ran a few short steps after him, as though to catch hold of the thin trail of smoke he left curling behind him, so I could reel him in.

He turned, startled. "Hey Baby!" He smiled and opened his arms to me. I walked into them, leaving behind classes and grades and the increasing alienation I felt when on campus. The warm press of his cheek against mine, the solid feel of his back beneath my fingers, the whole of his body was alive and present and calling to me.

We slid into his car, the sky growing overcast as we did, and he leaned over to kiss me before saying, "A friend of mine asked for some help –she thinks she's been bugged. Want to come with me while I check it out?"

"Okay," I said, pulling on my seatbelt.

He related the backstory as he drove. He had dated her a few years ago when she was studying photography, like me. Theirs had been a simple relationship: he bought her stuff; she slept with him. This worked well for both until, ironically, he caught her cheating. Then he reported the car he had bought her stolen, and they naturally wanted nothing more to do with each other.

Until she called him, sobbing and terrified and asking for help. She believed her boyfriend had tapped her lines and her computer, and she thought there was a good chance he wanted her dead. Not knowing who else to turn to, she had called Derek.

The thought of someone being so afraid in her own home, of her own lover, twisted my insides. The boyfriend was a dealer with an extensive network and a suspicious mind, Derek said, and he named the missing persons. I don't remember what the girl had done to piss the guy off, but he had grown tired of her, wary. Hence the spyware, the taps.

She met us at the door to her building, and led us down, into the basement. At the bottom of the stairs she waited, thin and trembling, for us to catch up. Her hair said, "look at me," but her expression said, "please don't." The dark brown strands, glossy in the hallway light, fell around her shoulders and over a cream-colored, suede jacket. This was accented by trendy boots, perfect nails, and expensive, but understated, jewelry. Were it not for her darting eyes, she'd look like any other beautiful girl one might see downtown on a Saturday night. But those eyes, slanted only slightly –they never stopped. Always checking behind, around, over her shoulder, up along the ceiling. She pointed as she walked.

"There. You see it? That cord is new. It doesn't belong. And look ..." She walked along, leading us down the hall and still pointing. We followed the line, past the other doors, past the other hallways. It led us, directly, without turning, without distraction, to her door –the only door in which it had any interest.

She looked at Derek helplessly, tense and shaking. "Can you do anything?"

We stepped inside. The room was large, with brick walls and pillars. Lights and veils hung from the ceiling, casting warm, rich tones on the cushions and paintings that leaned against the wall. I walked around, amazed. The place was an artist's haven. So much open space, one large room with the living, sleeping, and eating areas all comfortably merging into one another, with art and candles and a simple desk and a simple bed inviting you to lounge here, away from the rest of the world. How do you even find places like this? I wondered. It must have cost a fortune.

She led Derek to the computer, and he went to work –searching and destroying. He talked as his fingers flashed across the keyboard. "Why don't you go stay with your mother?" Her mother, a short, open-faced Filipino woman who smiled out from the picture frame on the desk, lived in Hawaii and was concerned, although ignorant of the details, and was arriving the next week.

"I can't. He'd find me."

"You'd be farther away. And no threat to him. You'd be safer than you are here."

She stared silently at the ground. Then, to turn her thoughts, she looked at me and offered me a drink. I followed her to the kitchen and watched her rummage through the open shelves.

"Your place is incredible," I said, taking the glass she offered.

"Thanks," she said quietly, as she sat down on a barstool, leaned her elbows on the counter, and started twirling a strand of hair around her finger. Her mind was elsewhere.

"These yours?" I asked, bending toward a collection of framed photos.

"Most of them. A few of the paintings aren't."

"I love them. The contrast is perfect, and the faces are beautiful. Your work is amazing."

"You're sweet." She looked up briefly and smiled just a little.

"Ani's studying photography downtown," Derek said from the other side of the room.

"Oh?"

"Yeah, just for a little while longer. He said you went to the same school."

"Feels like so long ago. That was a different life." Her thin arm, with its delicate light brown wrist, dropped to the counter. It lay there a minute, looking so small, as though too weak to move. I felt a burst of compassion. I wanted to hug her. She couldn't have been much older than me and was used to laughing –I could see it around her mouth, and at the corners of her eyes. But now all the light was gone.

"It's going to be okay," I said softly.

She looked at me with shining eyes. And then she *really* looked.

"I used to be like you," she said in quiet wonder. "I even taught Sunday school." The laughter that followed was bitter, and I knew that in a minute she'd be crying.

"I was a *Sunday school* teacher," and the tears spilled out, falling freely on the counter and splashing her arm. "...a Sunday school teacher."

I didn't know what to say. What *could* I say –hypocrite that I was? Even my empathy –as great as I can assure you it was– even this was overshadowed by the self-inflating thought that, no, I was different ... and I would *not* become like her. I would get out, get away, before I found myself sobbing in regret.

"It's okay," I said again, but this time neither of us heard the words.

# Chapter 10

We are all capable of monstrosity –I believe this. I believe that given certain circumstances, shaped as much by the laws and people present as by those that are absent, and influenced by all that has been given and withheld, any one of us can find ourselves standing atop a mountain of rubble and ruin, with the weapon responsible still smoking in our hand. And no matter how shocked, how horrified, our good and honest reaction might be, the crime still lies before us ... within us. It lies there now –a seed of potent possibility.

When I see such stirrings within myself, I shudder. But when I lean in for a closer look, when I poke and prod this ability for interior and exterior devastation with my focused attention, I also begin to understand my strengths, weaknesses, triggers, and what I can and cannot control. Understanding this about myself provides the first step for change, for improvement. It also fosters compassion, which I can turn towards others. When I see someone else atop their own mountain of rubble, I wonder, how did they get there? What would I have done in their shoes, with their history? What might have led to a different outcome? Consequences and accountability each have their place, but if I can look inside and see myself, or look outward and see another, then I can begin to understand and perhaps even say, "Ah, so this is why ...." This is why we act, think, and make the choices we do. We are none of us alone. We are all striving together, sometimes weak, sometimes strong, but always fallible, and yet persisting.

"SO, WHY ARE YOU STILL with this guy?" –John's utter contempt coated his question.

How could I explain what I couldn't even acknowledge to myself: that something irrational and primal in me responded to Derek? Part of me came alive around him. Why him? Why not with someone who I admired, respected, and was proud to introduce to everyone I knew? I hated that I was learning how to feel, hurt, and live inside the company of another woman's husband.

"I want to leave him," I said.

"Then just do it already."

"Right, because it's that simple."

"Yeah. It really is."

"Being with him has been a whole new experience. It was fun at first. Exciting even," I said.

"I'm sure it was."

"No, really. Because of him, I'm seeing things differently –a side of life I'd heard about but had never experienced. But now I'm like, why did I ever want to? Some of the people I've met seem so empty. Their lives, their expressions, everything about them. They're paranoid and experimenting just so they can feel something, and it makes me so sad. I don't want to end up like that. I thought I was immune. That my faith would keep me safe, or that somehow I'd remain untouched by it all. But it's getting to me. I hurt for them, for the world, but I'm not sure I have the answers anymore. Not that I ever did, but I had peace, at least. And the sense that everything would be okay. But now I ... I just don't know. And what makes it so hard is that even though I don't want to be with him, I've become invested. I didn't expect to. I didn't expect to feel *anything*. I don't even know what it is I feel, but I can't seem to shake it. How could I care so much for someone who's so wrong for me?"

# THE CREOSOTE BUSH

Because he was my whirlwind. At least, that's what I thought at first. Wind whipped my hair when he came near. Objects swirled around us, and our bodies moved with grace and power. Our spirits soared, uncontained, as we flew down busy streets, stepped through crowded rooms, and explored the hidden recesses of the city. We crashed into desire and burned off our energy until there was nowhere else we wanted to go, nothing else we wanted to do, and we'd return to my room and curl up tightly together and sleep until the winds grew and strengthened and raged again.

Then I realized that, no, Derek wasn't the whirlwind. The whirlwind was mine. It had always been there, stirring up a restlessness in me long before I had met Derek. It had been there in Arizona, urging me to jump in the car and drive, no destination in mind, to somewhere new, somewhere far away. It had urged me to stand, arms raised, under the hammering monsoon rain while thunderclaps shook the ground and lightning flashed across my vision. It had been there the night I'd gone to Kurt, hoping for a prowling partner. But instead of walking the streets, we had talked in his room until, gradually, the storm inside me had subsided.

But with Derek, I could let it out. When we first met, I thought I had nothing to lose. Inexperience, social awkwardness, undefined expectations for the future –none of that mattered around him. I was free to live in the moment with a partner whose energy gave shape and direction to my restlessness. When the tumult came pouring out, we rode it together. And the release was exquisite.

"I'm afraid of what comes after," I told John. "Of the silence." Silence had never bothered me before. It had always felt light, soothing, and peaceful. But the silence that crept up in Derek's absence was oppressive. It bore down on me, seeped in through my ears, my nose, my mouth. It got stuck in my throat and grew there, choking me, before squeezing down into my chest and settling its heavy weight in my belly. In those moments, the whirlwind was tiny. A distant hum.

"I know I can't go on like this," I said. "It's not safe –physically, mentally, emotionally. But I don't know how *not* to keep seeing him. I thought I was stronger. Less stupid. That's what you're thinking, isn't it, that I'm stupid?"

"I don't think you're stupid. You're definitely smarter than this, though."

He was right. I knew he was right –it needed to be over.

And yet ...

"You're the first woman I've ever wanted to grow old with."

Did all men say that? I wasn't sure, but I could almost believe him. Despite our impermanence and the utter lack of trust, I could almost picture myself by his side in what could only be considered little holidays from reality. Derek had said a great many things though, and only a few of them had the ring of sincerity. What scared me was that as time went on, it was getting harder for me to tell the difference.

Talking with John was like momentarily getting away –away from the growing gloom of Seattle. I needed to distance myself further. I had never planned on staying long-term in Seattle anyway.

"I'm thinking of coming home," I said.

To which John replied, "About time."

THANKSGIVING APPROACHED and my great aunt and uncle invited me to spend the holiday at their house, just south of Seattle. Derek offered to drive.

He called late the morning of to say he was coming soon, but that things had gotten manic at his house just then. His wife had flipped out –something about him not helping enough.

"And that was only the start of it. Her mother came over, and they both started laying into me saying I needed to help out, do some work instead of dumping it all on them. I don't know what they expect. I was already doing all the cooking preps, stuffing the turkey, making the salad –*everything*, already, myself. I don't know what they expect me to do."

I listened impatiently, glancing over at the oven clock. If I left now, if I started walking to the bus stop now, I could still make it the thirty miles south well before dinner. Everyone was going to be there –all the relatives on my grandmother's sister's side who I'd met for the first time this last year. Kids and cousins and food and ... if I didn't leave soon, I'd be late.

"Look," he said, "I have to go, but I'll call you back soon –as soon as I get a chance."

"Are you sure? I can take a bus, no problem."

"No. No, of course not. I can do it. I insist."

I waited. Oh, but what a beautiful day! The sun was shining, actually shining, and I longed to go outside and *do* something. I could walk. I could walk through the city and smell the sunshine and see the happy faces of the people in their colorful scarves and holiday glow. I could walk toward the bus stop –just to be ready. In case. In case he didn't make it.

Time passed. He didn't come. I waited longer than I meant to, longer than I should have. Finally, I got my things together and headed out, not meaning to slam the door behind me. The sound echoed through the lonely-quiet halls.

As I made my way to the Second and Union bus stop, I pushed away the angry-hurt tears that I didn't understand. It was my own fault for trusting him. For *being* with him. I was on my way. It was no big deal. Not really. I'd still see my family.

The bus came at three-thirty and by this time the glorious sun was setting. Leaving me. At least the windows on the bus were huge, and I could watch the sun as it sank. So beautiful. A gift. I slid down into my seat, leaning against the window and feeling the warm light fade as I watched the people around me. Families stepped onto the bus with hot, just-bought turkeys. Homeless couples clung to each other. I saw Mr. Laminate from Copy X. He stared, so I smiled and turned my face to the window. I caught a few people's eyes in the street. Some held my gaze, one guy winked, others went on their way. People ... it's all about people.

What was I doing? Derek was *married* for goodness' sake. I should have left the moment I learned of her. I didn't know what about her condition was true and what wasn't, but none of that mattered. She was no less his wife, and he was no less her husband. He was trying to live a new life, a separate life, without the shame of abandoning her –her, the woman who had written him every day he'd been in prison, who had gifted him the sports car he'd always wanted, who had supported him despite everything –despite his self-absorbed insecurities, despite his arrogance, despite everything he got himself mixed up in. And now, because she could no longer take care of him and his needs, he was bored. And lonely. And needy. And playing the victim.

And me –I was nothing but a mistress. Shame flooded through me when I thought of Derek's wife. She was experiencing a multitude of horrors that no one should ever have to endure, especially not with a betraying husband who magnified, rather than soothed away, her paranoia.

But still I made excuses. Still, I justified. Because I, too, was selfish and weak. I'd had no idea just how weak I was. No matter my misguided motives, no matter the outcome, I was responsible for my actions. And Derek was responsible for his.

I squeezed my eyes shut a moment and told myself everything was going to be fine. Fine. Fine. I didn't want to think anymore. I looked up and stared off into the distance until I was numb.

My phone rang.

"Now before you hang up–"

But I didn't care. I was no longer angry. I was merely a million miles away.

"Yes?"

He launched into a story about how he'd had to go buy more medication for his wife after she lost control and smashed the phone. During which time the turkey caught on fire and the fire department came and broke down the door, and ...

I listened to him, my mind trying on various emotional responses but liking none. I heard him apologize. He was sorry. So very sorry. I rubbed my forehead with my palm. His life was a mess, and there was no room for me inside it. I was the mistress who would come second, always, because, in truth, I didn't belong there in the first place.

He drove me home the next day and, noticing my silence, began shooting me glances. What's up? Something up? But I couldn't answer or explain my agitation. He grew quiet too, watching. He rolled his shoulders a few times.

"I said I was sorry, now tell me what's up. I can't help you unless I know what's pissing you off."

But I couldn't. I wanted to talk but had no idea how to go about it.

Finally, I said, "I've been thinking about going home. To Arizona. To stay." I said this casually while staring out of the window. Then I reached for the radio as if it was nothing –what I had just said was nothing, an off-hand observation with no bearing on anything whatsoever.

"You know I couldn't go."

"I know," I said, quieter this time.

We said nothing after that.

THE NEXT FEW DAYS WERE silent. Then he came. When I opened the door, he stood, watching, gauging my reaction. Somehow, I couldn't stay angry at him for long. Tension between us was like an itchy wool sweater that I had to shrug off as soon as I could. I smiled –I couldn't help myself– and he embraced me with that old familiar hug that was so tight that it was all I knew for the next forty-five seconds. Then it happened again. Some failure to agree, to communicate, and the line was drawn in the sand once more.

I told myself my love was altruistic, even if my behavior was not. Because if my love was altruistic, then it could also be good. Pure. I wanted this to be true. Not that I felt evil. I hated that Derek was married and that I found it so difficult to leave him, but beyond that I was simply living, breathing, acting out my choice to understand more of the world. What I was doing was wrong, but it wasn't my intention to abuse God's grace. I was going to make things right. Soon. I needed only to find the courage, the strength.

"Let him go, let him go." I heard it when he kissed me. "Let him go," when he made love to me with the fierceness that I craved. "Let him go, let him go, let go, let go, let go."

I did. I let go and I gave in to his touch. To him. To the slight buzz of the alcohol, the smoke, the desire to hurt myself and not care. Come cancer, come time, come all and take me. Only let me live now. Because for the first time I don't care, I'm not afraid, and this is remarkable. What does this mean –that I don't care? That I can hold my head up and pour myself into the moment, filling it up with me and reveling in my ability not to care if I am destroyed because this abandon makes me free, makes me powerful. Oh God! What does this mean?

And then suddenly, I care. I stop drinking. I stop smoking. Because I think I may be pregnant. I don't know for sure. Even after the pregnancy test purchased from Target tells me there's no baby, I'm not sure because it could be wrong. What if I'm pregnant?

I tell Derek I'm worried –that I'm worried about getting, about being, pregnant, despite our precautions. He says there's no question. Abortion, the only option. I tell him no way. There's no way I'd get an abortion. I'd keep the baby, and he'd never have to know. But, of course, he'd need to know. "Why?" I ask. "So you could wish it was dead? I won't allow it. If there's a baby, I will love and protect it, and it will never be thought of as a mistake."

We argued. We made up. And the next thing I knew it was Christmas. I don't know how it happened, but suddenly there were lights, mittens, and wreaths everywhere. Even the train set was back in its familiar corner window display at the Bon Marché, charming all with its innocent circuit. The warmth and happiness of this time of year reminded me of family. Of togetherness. This year I would be staying with my great aunt and her extended family, some of whom I'd be meeting for the first time.

Derek came over the night before I was to catch the bus for the holidays. It was the sweet him. The soft and gentle him. He must be off his drug, I thought.

Our evening was quiet. Subdued. I couldn't remember the last time we'd sat together like that, cross-legged on the soft carpet with the candle on the kitchen counter flickering a little and making the room smell warm and sweet while the rain glittered on the black window. When I unwrapped his gift, I stared at it a minute, surprised, before looking up to catch his eye. A little herb-growing kit. Despite all the times I had gushed over the colorful planters in doorways or had paused to touch the petals in some flower shop, I never thought he had paid much attention to my love for plants and growing things. His gift felt unexpectedly thoughtful.

We curled up next to each other and listened to the barely audible rain as it fell in the courtyard. His heartbeat thrummed against my shoulder blades. I stretched my neck to better feel his breath.

He slid his hand over my waist and down to my stomach. Such warm hands, always. Ever so softly, ever so gently, he traced my belly button with the flat of his palm.

He's thinking about a baby, I realized. We don't even know for sure, and yet he's thinking about the possibility.

That struck me as strange somehow. The lightness of his touch confused me –he was thinking about a baby ... a baby in my belly. All arguments for abortion and inconvenience aside, he could actually visualize this baby in the dark.

I'm probably not even pregnant, I thought. I tried to imagine what it would be like ... how my family would react. I shuddered. And what about school? And work? And Derek? –how could I ever hope to fully separate myself from all-absorbing Derek if a child connected us?

Oh God! *Please*, don't let me be pregnant! Please, God, I'm so sorry. I don't want –I can't– be pregnant. Not now, not like this.

I felt myself shrink beneath Derek's arm. I wanted to shrink and shrink away until I was small enough to crawl off into nowhere.

Instead, I fell asleep.

THE PLACE AND PEOPLE were foreign. My great aunt and I smiled occasionally at each other over our glasses of eggnog, and then we'd go back to talking to whoever happened to be sitting next to us as we reclined in our separate corners of the room. But I felt utterly alone. The host joined me for a while, telling me about the music classes he taught and listening to my delight over the little twirling angels that chimed over the candles. The heat made them fly, made them sing. This man, the host, was my great aunt's nephew. I have no idea what that made his relation to me. But he was nice. So nice. Too nice. He suggested we go see the new Frida Kahlo movie together. I didn't know why he should be expressing so much interest in me. I was on the verge of unease when his children entered the house with sudden noise and laughter. The daughter –or was she a daughter-in-law?– wore a lovely shirt that draped stylishly across her expecting belly. The eyes of all who greeted her mirrored her radiance. Everyone so happy. Everyone curious and excited and eager to know the date, the sex, and every possible name picked out.

Her baby was wanted. Her parents were proud. Their home was open and warm and full of hope. Full of many tomorrows in which there was nothing to hide. Nothing of which to be ashamed.

I was a shadow –a dark spirit that spread a slight gloom over the objects and people surrounding me. I looked away from the woman. I turned my eyes instead to my own belly. My baby, if I were pregnant, would be met with silence, with delayed acceptance. Even so, I would wrap my baby in love, and make sure that it, too, just like this other baby at the center of all this bliss and brightness, would be embraced with just as much pride and promise.

I looked up again –not to the woman, though, and not toward my great aunt. Instead, I stared across at the empty space in front of me. And because I felt so alone, I felt myself grow smaller, and lighter, until soon I was the size of a moth floating up toward the ceiling. As I passed the angel at the top of the Christmas tree, I grabbed onto her and held on for dear life. And there I stayed, watching everyone move about below me in the sparkling golden light of the room. Their laughter came easily, and no shadows obscured the light in their eyes. I'm sure they were not without their secrets, fears, uncertainties. But each appeared cushioned by the knowledge that everything would be okay.

I used to be that way too, I thought. The memory made me ache inside, and I clung to my inanimate angel, feeling far removed from everyone.

# Chapter 11

Derek and I continued to spend all our free time together. We sampled new restaurants and bars; we took long drives to anywhere and everywhere; we laughed and kissed in the photo booth at the zoo until the father who waited outside with his little girl was sufficiently shocked; and we did whatever else caught our fancy –like the impromptu photo shoot at Value Village.

At first, the idea of entering a thrift store repulsed him, and he sulked. Then he picked up an old football helmet and a couple of picture frames, and the next thing I knew he had his own one-man show going in full swing for everyone present.

How he loved his audience! As I watched him swing his plastic sword and speak from behind the giant picture of Jesus, I knew now I could believe him all the times he had said he loved me. I was his friend, after all. His encourager, comforter, companion, and above all, I was his audience. Of course, he loved me.

But his inability to empathize with the people around him left him disconnected. The giggling child who stood in front of him was not a shy girl who he'd just helped to emerge from her shell, she was simply faceless applause. The gruff and dirty man in coveralls who was chuckling in spite of himself was not a man scraping pennies together to buy his apathetic son a decent pair of shoes, he was only a spotlight. And I, I was not a woman who was being torn apart by her raging inner conflict. I was simply *there*.

# C A LEGORRETA

BECAUSE I WAS SIMPLY there, I hesitated only slightly when a customer from work invited me to a dinner party at the Showbox, a club where he worked. I wasn't interested in the guy. He was soft-spoken and sweet, but not my type. However, I had never been to the Showbox before, and the idea of an invitation-only dinner for the music world intrigued me, so I said yes.

When I told Derek, he elaborated on just how badly I was treating the poor guy by using him this way. He was right, of course, but I wrote off his protests as the product of jealously and reminded him again we were "just friends." I, too, it seemed, could be selfish and cruel.

Derek dropped me off and said he'd wait for my call afterward. I thought I'd only be a couple hours. I should have told him I'd walk home. Or maybe I did, and he insisted on picking me up. I don't remember. All I know is that five hours later, while he was phoning me repeatedly from Paul's place, I was still waiting for the Modest Mouse concert to start. After another hour I finally excused myself. I declined my date's first offer to walk me home, but he insisted –so sweet and reserved was he, barely taller than me and thinner. By the time he dropped me off, I didn't feel comfortable walking to Paul's place. It was too late. I tried calling Derek. No answer.

An hour later I heard a knock. I crawled out of bed and in the dim light of the living room walked to the door. No sooner had I opened it then Derek had his arms around me, squeezing tightly as he said over and over in a rushing flow of words, "You're here. You're here!" He started crying, then yelling. "I've been waiting seven hours –seven fucking hours– for you. Calling over and over while you're out with some ... *guy*! Why didn't you call?"

Then he got angry.

"Seven hours, Ani!" He was really yelling now, and I was sure everybody in the building could hear him. I'd never seen him like this –desperate, frightened, and relieved all at once.

He started crying again.

Suddenly he lunged for the kitchen counter and grabbed a bottle of wine. Before I could stop him, he whacked himself in the head with it. I heard the sickening thud and froze. He doubled over, bottle still in hand, and stumbled. I stared in disbelief for a full second, completely shocked, until he swung it against his head again. I lunged, but wasn't in time to stop him, and he fell to the floor holding his head and crying. He reached for the bottle again, but I shoved it out of reach as I tried to hold his hands down. I kept my voice low and asked him –pleaded with him– to calm down. "I'm sorry," I said, "I had no idea it would go that long."

I smoothed his hair and stroked his forehead as the tears streaked his face. The room had taken on an otherworldly light, and my hands moved as though in a dream.

How could I begin to understand the absolute contradiction of Derek's many moods? One minute he'd surprise me with his thoughtfulness, saying things with an insight that touched and bewildered me. The next he'd be cold and cutting. Then, without warning, he would throw himself into a moment of passion unlike anyone I'd ever known –as though that moment was all he knew, was all he felt. And it didn't matter that he would feel something very different the next day, the next hour, because here and now he was truly in love. Here and now, he was truly sorry. Here and now, he was truly broken and abandoned and all alone in a world he wished he had never known.

With a quick reversal of feeling, he got up to leave. "I can't stay here."

He stumbled toward the door, but I scooted over and got in his way.

"No, Derek, please don't go. Not like this." I sat with my back against the door. I stood up and put my arms around him. "Not like this, please."

He buried his face in my neck like a child and cried, "You hurt me." His hot, wet nose tickled my skin. "How could you hurt me like that?"

I felt so confused. His reaction was too much. How could it be real? Was it real?

"I'm sorry. I'm so sorry."

I held him, rocking a little. Pulling back, I looked at his matted eyelashes and shining cheeks. He wore an expression of utter pain and vulnerability. A curl of dark hair was sticking to his fevered forehead. I pushed it back, running my fingertips along his hairline and down his jaw to the edge of his mouth, whose corners were dark and sharply beautiful in the soft, low light of the kitchen. *I* did this to him, I thought, as I rubbed a tear away with my thumb.

But how many times had he done the same to me –making plans and then abandoning them as I waited, hurt and angry, while the sun set on another wasted day of broken promises.

"This is how I felt," I said softly, "all those times you didn't show up."

"Thanksgiving was out of my control."

"I realize that, but there were other times."

"So, you were punishing me? Is this your way of getting revenge?" He was getting angry again.

"No, no, of course not. I left as soon as I could. I'm sorry."

"Why didn't you come to Paul's place?"

"I was afraid."

"Why?"

"Why do you think? Belltown at midnight isn't exactly safe. And anyway, I tried calling, but no one answered. I'm sorry."

He settled into a subdued sullenness.

"Let's get out of here," he said.

"Why? Let's just stay here. Let's just go to bed."

"No, I need to get out. Come with me, please." His head was hanging. He looked exhausted.

"Okay," I said quietly.

He started walking out the door. I began to follow him but realized I had forgotten my keys. I turned around quickly, grabbed them, and was almost out the door when a thought stopped me. I nearly dismissed it, but desperate people do desperate things. I hurried over to my desk, hunted for a pen and paper, and started writing the date, time, and that I was going out with Derek. I had almost finished when Derek opened the door. I quickly stood up.

"What are you doing?"

"Nothing." My reply came out too fast.

"What were you writing?"

"Nothing." –how could I not think of *any*thing else to say?

I walked back to the kitchen counter and picked up my purse. Derek tried to pull the piece of paper out of my hand.

"What did you write? Were you writing where you were going? Why? ... were you afraid? Are you *afraid* of me?"

"No ... I just ..."

"*You're afraid of me*?!"

"No, Derek. It's just that you're not acting like yourself."

He started crying again. "I would never hurt you –*never*." He held me for a moment and then spun around and walked out the door. I ran after him. "Wait!"

I caught up with him on the stairs.

"Derek, wait a minute." I touched his arm. He stopped, not looking at me. I took a step forward and wrapped my arms around him. We held each other for a moment, letting everything else fall away.

Then we hurried to his car. I drove as he held his head and moaned, "I've got a goose egg."

A chilling, blood-quickening song we both loved enveloped us. I turned up the volume until my skin vibrated. I wasn't driving, I was flying. With no destination in mind. I shot through a red light and sped between and around the cars in my way. I wove through the city and headed for the interstate. Faster. Faster. To nowhere. No future ahead. Nothing behind. Only now. Only us. We were alive, driven by emotions that made our hearts beat out of our chests and our bodies want to glide, weightless, above the earth.

As the song slowly faded, I noticed the fuel tank was almost empty. The real world always has a way of catching up. I turned the car back toward my place, and my pulse reluctantly slowed. Derek sat slouched in his seat. He looked over at me.

"Why can't we just run away –just the two of us –to some little bungalow somewhere?"

I smiled at him, the corners of my mouth giving way to sadness.

Pulling up in front of my building, I parked and looked over at him.

He sat, staring at his hands.

"I have cancer," he said, not looking at me.

"What?" I asked, my voice little more than a whisper. This had to be just another story.

"I had cancer a couple years ago and they cut it out. Now it's come back. I have a biopsy on Wednesday to find out if it's malignant."

I kept staring at him. "Derek, you say a lot of things, but–"

"Want to feel it?" He reached over and took my hand and placed it on his lower back. This wasn't my first time feeling the bump beneath my fingers. It was the size of a man's thumb. Before I was even aware of what was happening, tears blurred my vision.

"Let's go inside," I said.

Once inside my room, we held each other in the darkness and slept.

# THE CREOSOTE BUSH

HE SLEPT A LOT OVER the next few days. He had done this before, whenever he stopped taking speed for any length of time. But my obsessed mind interpreted it as a symptom of his illness. I'd seen it before –when my best friend's dad did nothing but sleep in the months before his cancer killed him. Was he dying? Was Derek dying?

I watched him sleep and I heard him cry out for his wife, and my heart broke. Needing to escape my room, I ran out into the stairwell, where I hugged my stomach and cried.

My mother called, and I tried to clear my voice, to pretend that everything was okay, but then I gave up. "I'm so afraid, Mom. I'm so afraid he's dying." I could barely speak the words, and I couldn't seem to catch my breath. Vitality such as his couldn't just slip away, could it?

I don't remember what all she said. Perhaps she hushed me with that nonsensical salve that feels so good during times like those: *It'll be okay. Everything will be okay.* Spoken like a promise. Believed because I wanted it to be true. Until I forgot it a minute later under the weight of my anguish.

A few days later, Derek and Jimmy helped me move into my new place, a studio that overlooked a parking lot and the monorail that ran along Fifth Avenue. Derek slept while Jimmy and I carried up the last of the bags and boxes. When we were done, I thanked Jimmy, wanting him to stay even as he turned to go. As he headed out the door, all the sparkling light particles gathered about him, trailing after him like stardust until I was left standing in gloom.

I turned back to survey my new place. It was sweet and perfect. I sighed and locked up, heading down the back stairs to where Derek sat sleeping in his Suburban.

We drove to the international district where we ate potstickers and talked quietly while sipping our soup. He nodded off a few times. I smiled up at the waiter, Derek paid the bill, and we cracked open our fortune cookies.

"'Make serious decisions in the last few days of the month,'" he read, leaning heavily on his elbow.

"Mine says, 'You find beauty in ordinary things. Do not lose this ability.'"

He smiled and leaned over to kiss me.

Back at my place, in the freshly made trundle bed, he fell asleep. I lay down next to him and listened to him breathe. Above us, feet thudded softly. Unintelligible voices sent their scattered notes drifting through the floorboards. Somewhere a faucet dripped. I lay there, soaking up Derek's warmth while listening to the sounds of life all around. Then I slept too.

I HAD JUST FINISHED another photo shoot with Terrance, and the sun was setting as we started walking back from Sixth and Union toward the Westlake Center. Derek called and offered to pick us up. Terrance agreed, and I told Derek where we were.

After throwing my stuff into the back seat, I climbed in next to Derek. From the back, I heard Terrance breathe out a soft word of admiration.

"Nice BMW," he said to Derek, still taking in the details.

This was all Derek needed to launch into a long description of everything that made this car unique. I rolled my eyes, but Terry leaned forward eagerly as Derek explained how the sunroof could open in the front and the back -*at the same time!*- and how the windows were bullet-proof (was that even true?) and how the guy who had owned it before had special-ordered it so that it was one-of-a-kind and he was also some big-wig that everyone was supposed to have heard of. I didn't get why Terry was so impressed.

After dropping him off, I said, "He's a great guy and all, but he's obsessed with making it big as a model or an actor. He wants the big house and fancy car, but he hasn't even paid me for the last time I shot him."

Derek turned towards me, the line of his mouth suddenly serious. "That's not right. You should go get it."

"It's not that big of a deal. Besides, I like shooting him and I can use the pictures for my portfolio."

"I'll go get it." His hand was on the door.

"Honestly –it's not that big of a deal. If it really mattered to me, I wouldn't have done the shoot today."

He looked at me briefly and then pulled out into the street and headed towards the freeway. The sun looked like it was being pulled down by invisible hands. As night took over, Lake Union's glassy surface lit up with cheerful, multi-colored lights. The water seemed to be waving at me. I smiled in reply.

"I've got something special for you," Derek said. When I turned to him, he was grinning, but not looking at me. "I think you're going to like it."

I watched him, waiting, and he glanced over at me, looking like an excited kid. He seemed to be trying to build the anticipation by not saying anything, as though I should guess and plead with him to reveal the surprise. But I just sat there, enjoying his excitement. Unable to take the suspense any longer, he shifted and pulled out a little plastic bag. He handed it to me. It took me a minute to realize the tiny, brown, withered things inside were mushrooms.

"They're all-natural," he said quickly. "Harmless. I thought you might like to try them."

He was right, I was curious. I'd heard stories and wondered what type of hallucinations I might have –whimsical, frightening, revealing? I flashed him a grin before opening the bag and taking a tentative whiff. They didn't smell like much.

With his free hand he reached over and took the bag from me. Setting it on his lap, he pulled out a piece, and then another, until he thought he had the right amount. He handed them to me. Looking back and forth between me and the road, he waited, still grinning. I held them up and studied them.

"Do it already."

"Don't rush me."

I slowly placed the first piece into my mouth and began chewing. Then I shook my head violently and grimaced. It was so nasty. He laughed and handed me a bottle of water. I ate the second one as he swallowed his first.

"How long does it take?"

"Not long. We should be there soon."

We were meeting some of his friends at their house, and when we arrived, he told them what we'd taken. They laughed, and Derek and I escaped together into their kid's room upstairs. The room was dark and empty –both kids being away at their grandmother's house.

As we sat on the floor in the dark, surrounded by pictures of space shuttles and the indistinct outlines of toy cars and plastic action figures, I kept waiting for the hallucinations to start. I had heard all about how the experience was like being awake inside a dream. What would I see? Would my visions be scary? Illogical? Would I discover the secret to the universe?

The minutes ticked by, but nothing happened.

*Figures*, I thought, feeling mildly disappointed. I resigned myself to sitting it out while Derek had his high. With a sigh, I glanced around until my eyes came to rest on the shadows under the desk and along the wall behind it. Something peculiar was going on over there. I wasn't sure what, but I became increasingly intrigued. I found myself wishing Derek would stop talking so I could figure out what I was seeing.

"I'm dying," he said.

I glanced up, then back at the shadows.

"I'm dying," he repeated.

After the fourth time, I assured him, "You're not dying," and I tried to tune out his voice so I could focus. I needed to focus so I could see into the shadows. I needed to concentrate. I couldn't concentrate –not with him babbling like that. What was he going on about?

"You're not dying," I said again, looking at him and realizing I could see the same mysterious something in the shadows behind his ear.

"Look at me," his voice was small.

"I am looking at you, and you're fine," I said distractedly.

"No, my skin is withering away. I'm dying."

I ignored him. I had to concentrate. There in the shadows, behind his ear and everywhere, were little, turning gears –each spoke, each rim, consisting of a thousand tiny rainbows. And they all fit together perfectly –each one turning, turning, all of them turning, so that the turning of one meant the turning of the others. Everywhere I looked, it seemed, these tiny rainbow gears were turning, connected, so that no single one of them could do anything independently. All they could do was turn, together. The whole world: tiny, turning gears. I wanted to lay down and just think about that for a while.

"I've died," Derek said, interrupting my thoughts. "I'm dead."

I wanted to bury my face in a pillow and scream! He wasn't dead! I had to focus on my rainbow gears. There was something to them, something I needed to figure out. If he could just be quiet!

"I'm dead. I'm actually dead." Now his voice was flat, matter-of-fact.

He wasn't going to stop. After a final, fleeting look at the shadows, I refocused my eyes on Derek. He had grabbed a blanket from off the bed –when had that happened?– and had draped it over himself –so that he was a shapeless mound of sullen self-absorption. Bidding my rainbow gears goodbye, those happy little stars, I crawled under the blanket with him. And suddenly we were kids again –children sitting cross-legged and facing each other.

"If you were dead, could you feel this?" and I kissed him. "We're alive," I whispered into his ear. "We're sitting in a child's room, talking to each other."

His eyes grew wide, and he held out his hand, turning it, as though watching something slide up his arm. "What's happening to me?" –a slight edge of panic.

"Nothing. Nothing's happening to you, Derek."

"Something's happening ... I'm being born."

I stared at him, missing my rainbow gears and rubbing his shoulders.

"I'm a baby," and he wrapped his arms around me. "We're kids again."

"I know, Derek. I know," I said, rocking him.

We stayed like that a long time –holding each other under a blanket on the floor of a kid's room, until gradually, Derek grew up. Then it was me and Derek the man. We walked back downstairs, hand in hand and blinking in the hallway light. We were greeted with bright-eyed curiosity and offered little white pills, which we waved away, saying we needed to get back. We left, but not before Derek had described every minute detail of his incredible death and rebirth.

NEW YEAR'S EVE.

I'd made reservations at Fernando's –a restaurant whose view of the Space Needle would allow us to watch the fireworks up close. I'd taken care of everything. All Derek had to do was show up.

The reservation was at nine. By eight-thirty I was writhing. I considered going alone.

Then he called, sounding sleepy. "I'm on my way."

Fernando's was everything I'd hoped: candles and lively people in lovely clothes, elegant staff offering elegant drinks, and the sound of a piano just audible over the happy hum of conversation and tinkling silverware.

Derek became instant besties with the couple next to us –they thought him so wonderfully witty. They had kids our age, they said, as they took pictures of us throwing streamers around each other. We posed with them in our ridiculous plastic top hats and feathered crowns, and everything felt celebratory and surreal, as though we were all play-acting.

The three main courses consisted of tiny fancy bits that tasted wonderful despite their miniscule size. I had the duck, and he had the chicken something or other. We laughed over the small portions and joked with our doting neighbors, who showered us with good will as they smiled at how "very much in love" we two were.

We got up two or three times to smoke and dance in the barroom. Derek still wasn't feeling all that well, and his energy came in spurts. Whenever his head started to droop, I changed the subject to distract him.

"So, Derek," I said one such time, "supposing we were going to have a baby –a boy, let's say– what would you name him?"

We both knew by now that I wasn't pregnant. I'm not sure who was more relieved.

His head popped up. "Spike!"

"Try again."

"Not Spike? Why not? Spike's a great name."

I turned my head away in mock exasperation.

"Okay. If not Spike, then ... Rawhide!"

I wrinkled my nose. "You're fired!"

"You can't fire me ... Let's ask her." He motioned to a passing waitress.

"So, she's pregnant" –the girl smiled at me in delight even as I waved my hand in denial– "so she's pregnant and she says to me, 'what do you want to name the kid?' And I say, 'Spike!' That's a good name, don't you think?"

The girl had been leaning toward us, but now she straightened up as she realized he was joking.

"She says, 'You can't name a child Spike!'" Derek continued. "So I say, 'How about Rawhide?'"

The girl was laughing.

"And can you believe she fired me?" Derek held his palms up in feigned bewilderment. "She *fired* me."

The girl walked away, looking back over her shoulder and still softly chuckling. Derek repeated the whole process with a woman and her friend who walked by and then with the couple when they returned from the bar. Free laughs for all.

Derek grew tired. The couple noticed.

"Is he all right?" the man asked.

"Not feeling too well," I replied with a small shrug.

"I have cancer." Derek said bluntly, turning his head toward them.

"Oh my," said the woman. "That's awful."

Derek looked as though he might die right then and there. I folded my arms across my chest and leaned back.

"Well, is it malignant?" they asked, all innocent and compassionate concern.

"We find out in a week," Derek told them, and he continued to look at them with large, trying-to-be-brave-but-failing eyes, feeding off their attention as he mournfully described the worst possible scenario.

"That's awful," the woman repeated.

Yes, it was awful.

"Well, we wish you both the best," the man said with forced brightness, to cheer us all up.

"Thank you," Derek said. "You both are just wonderful. Aren't they, Baby? They're just wonderful."

It was almost time. "We should be going to the roof soon," I said, taking a deep breath and looking from one to the other with a big smile.

"Oh yes," they agreed, and we all started talking about the fireworks and what was going to happen and how exciting it all was.

Just before midnight, everyone was herded through the kitchen, up a back stairwell, and onto the roof. Derek and I leaned against the railing –the Space Needle looming above us. Everything was loud laughter and shouts and drunken happiness as people crowded together on the roof with us, on the roof below us, in the street, across the street, and everywhere in every direction. The music started –distorted and blaring– and then the top of the Space Needle exploded. Derek squeezed me tighter as the sky blazed with brilliant color, showering us with rainbow-colored sparks. Glowing with the ever-changing light, our bodies formed a single happy pillar in a sea of chaos.

We drove back to my place after that, curling up together for a few hours of solitude on my squeaky bed. He left at three in the morning. I was barely awake when I saw him getting out of bed and putting on his shoes. I was reminded again how my time with him was borrowed. Or rather, stolen. I did not lay awake contemplating it, however, because I was so very, very tired.

EYES CLOSED, I LEANED my head against the cold window of the bus as I made my way toward the Northgate Mall. I was trying to feel the dappled sunlight on my face. The sun was there, bright enough, but that day, try as I might, I couldn't feel its warmth. I might have spent the entire bus ride watching shadows dance across my eyelids had I not been startled by the most beautiful sound –the sound of children laughing. I looked up to see a whole long line of them, joined together by their hands, boarding the bus. Their bursts of laughter, like fireflies, lit up the darkness around me. The brilliance of their faces dazzled me. I didn't know where to look or whether I should just close my eyes again and soak up their joy. These children seemed to radiate all that was good and right and lovely with the world.

Something caught in my throat –an emotion immense and choking. I turned my face away, until my nose was pressed against the cold, hard glass. My eyes stung as I realized I felt like an outsider who no longer belonged in that bright realm of ebullient joy and unsullied security. When exactly had my world become so dark? My peace and quiet happiness, which I had taken for granted these many years, were now gone, along with the assurance that everything would be okay. My faith had always kept them close, had kept the darkness at bay. But now, with my faith crumbling and my relationship with the God of my youth slipping away, I felt despair creeping in. I *missed* my God. I missed the reassurance that believing in him had given me. My faith was the one thing I had thought would never change. And now ... now as the bus screeched to another stop and the children clambered down the aisle and out the front of the bus, all the light fading away behind the last noisily happy child, I wondered if I could ever reclaim it.

# Chapter 12

The following Friday, I fidgeted in my room as I waited for Derek to arrive with the results from his biopsy. When I finally heard him honking outside my window, I rushed to the window. He stood, waving like a madman –all smiles and energy.

"Come see my new car!" he shouted up at me.

Only then did I notice the silver BMW behind him –the sports car he'd talked so much about, the one he'd recently ordered. It was sleek and flashy, with a longing –intrinsic or my own?– to find freedom in movement. "Come," it seemed to call. "The expanse awaits."

Not now, I thought, pulling my sweater around me as I half ran, half fell down the stairs. First, I needed to know exactly what the doctor had said. The bars of the iron gate at the bottom of the stairs broke Derek up and made him look as though he were floating. I hurriedly pushed open the door, and, unable to contain myself any longer, I blurted, "*Well*?! Is it benign?"

"It's benign. I have surgery next Thursday."

With a burst of joy, I reached forward to embrace him.

"Baby," he said, "this is Max –the man who sold me the car."

I slid back and squinted over at the stranger, who felt like an intruder. We nodded politely. Then Derek grabbed my hand and pulled me to the car. I heard nothing of what he said about its features –except that it had seat warmers. "Really?" I said. "That's cool." Derek jumped up out of the car and looked across the hood at Max.

"I get the special edition BMW, and all she cares about is the seat warmers," he laughed.

I stared around me and inhaled the new-car scent, wondering why I felt so deflated. I wanted to hold Derek, to talk with him and celebrate, to tell myself that everything was going to be okay. That we were going to be okay. But this car and this strange man felt like a distraction.

"I'm really happy for you," I said softly.

"Me too. Imagine driving around in this? I don't get it for another two weeks or so, but Max here insisted on a test-drive."

"That's great," I said, as we both climbed out.

"Hey, we've got to get it back, but I just had to show you."

He gave me a quick hug –I barely had time to lift my arms– and then he was off. I waved goodbye, knowing he wouldn't see me, and slowly walked back up the stairs.

A COUPLE HOURS LATER I heard voices outside my window and then his whistle –that loud, piercing whistle that woke me up and interrupted my thoughts, the one that jarred my peace of mind.

I walked to the window and peered down at him.

"Hey Baby! I've got some people I want you to meet."

I didn't want to meet any more people. I wanted only to turn my music up a little louder and go to sleep. Instead, I walked down the stairs –no longer feeling powerful, or sexy, just tired.

I faked a smile as he introduced the couple standing before me, who, as it turned out, lived in the same building as me. Derek had met the guy a few days earlier and had just now bumped into him again. He suggested we all go out to eat.

The four of us climbed into Derek's car, and he drove like a maniac –the techno music shaking the speakers and making us holler to be heard. My thoughts kept slipping out of view. I made mental grabs for them while wondering at Derek's need to impress these people.

At the restaurant the guy came and sat next to me. He was friendly. Polite. Well-groomed and well-dressed, no doubt a very hip, very successful computer expert, or some such. I didn't really care. We talked while watching Derek and the girl, whose personality and manner matched his. Wild, theatrical, saying anything and everything that came to mind, they flirted with as much energy as humanly possible. The guy, by contrast, was subdued, sweet even. But I had nothing in common with him, or the girl. I closed my eyes and sipped my drink, silently seething.

The girl's sudden laughter jolted me. She had her hand on Derek's shoulder and her head thrown back as though his joke, the crass, tasteless joke that I'd heard a hundred times before, was the funniest thing she'd ever, ever heard. And Derek was just as absorbed by her as she was by him. For the first time since being with Derek I felt ... jealous. The feeling rose slowly from somewhere deep in my belly, until I was hot all over with it. Jealous! After all the times I'd watched him flirt, knowing the kind of man he was but not caring because I flirted too, and we were both only using each other –consciously and ecstatically using each other– *now* I was jealous.

She was my opposite in every way –loud, dark, extroverted and provocative, shameless and unapologetic. I felt bland next to her. I watched them draping their arms around the other's neck, both laughing and leaning into each other, and my anger gave way to nausea. After all, how could I justify my anger when I was a mistress? So now I just felt sick. My stinging pride made my cheeks hot and my skin itch. Even when Derek praised me in front of them, even when he held me and kissed me passionately so that we dipped almost to the floor, my whole body ached. I felt utterly disposable.

We drove. First to Gasworks, where Derek proceeded to saw into a lock that was keeping us from driving down further while the girl sat in the back screaming with delight until a woman threatened to call the cops. Then on to the house of Chihuly, the glassmaker –or so Derek said, although the building looked more like an old warehouse. We sat ourselves down on the docks of a nearby waterfront restaurant. I stared out over the sparkling water, trying to ignore Derek's female carbon-copy as she performed a non-stop one-woman show in which she chattered on in different accents, took pictures, and then danced around with a broom before throwing it out into the water.

Derek leaned over to the guy, winked, and said, "Quite a woman you got there!"

I immediately excused myself to go to the bathroom.

The guy had said earlier that he hadn't had this much fun in a long time. Fun? What had we actually done besides watch Derek and the girl try to outperform one another? It might have been entertaining if it wasn't so sad. Why was Derek trying so hard to impress these people he barely knew? His endless boasting of the things he'd done and the people he knew disgusted me, and I didn't understand his insecurity ... his insatiable craving for praise and recognition.

We drove back to their apartment –"Look, Baby! Look, she's changing. She's taking off her shirt ... *in the car*!"– and I stared out the window in silence the whole way there.

When the girl complained of a headache, Derek asked for a phone. He called Javier –for some "medicine." I stared in amazement as something in me finally snapped.

Derek and the girl took off to get the speed, and I headed the other way, thumping down the front stairs to the lobby. I felt as though I might explode. I was suffocating. In this building. In this relationship. In my skin. I almost slipped in my haste and clutched at the railing. Then I jumped the last few steps. Bursting out into the cool night air, I stopped and turned my face to the sky. It bent down and kissed both cheeks.

I roamed the city before entering the bright lobby of a movie theater where I bought a ticket. The isolation I felt upon finding my seat was both comforting and punishing. I tried to hold myself together as the movie flashed before me. Everyone else was laughing. Cute little couples and groups of kids crunching their greasy popcorn –all laughing.

Why? Why should I care what Derek did? We'd both been only using each other. Now was the time to say goodbye and enter again the real world, my world, and get on with my life.

I walked home, showered, and went to bed. It was over. I had only to tell him.

DEREK SHOWED UP AT my work on Monday night, bubbling over with excitement. I stepped outside the front door and stood with my arms folded tightly across my chest as he told me the "great news" of what he'd done. He'd decided not to buy the sports car because it didn't make him feel young like he thought it would –"like I do when I'm with you," he said, he actually said. Instead, he took the money and started a program for homeless kids in Portland.

"That's great, Derek," I said, shivering in a way that had nothing to do with the cold.

"Well, can I have a hug?" he was all smiles and energy.

"No." The chills were getting worse.

He was taken aback. "Why?"

"Because I don't want to see you anymore. I'm moving back to Arizona."

I watched as the knowledge of this settled over him, changing his expression.

"Arizona ... that's good. But let's not be hasty."

I shook my head.

"You've said before you wouldn't see me," he said.

"Which is why I have to cut all ties and leave town. This is hurting me too much."

"I'm not hurting you." He was growing more insistent, desperate.

"Then I'm hurting myself. Either way, leaving is the best thing for me."

"For *you* –that's all you've ever cared about. You think the world revolves around you." His voice grew louder, angrier.

High above me, a piece of the sky cracked, fell. It shattered against the pavement, sending little shards flying into my skin. I shifted my feet. They hurt; everything hurt. I turned my head away and rubbed my arms.

"Fine," he said, with an edge of malice. "If you really don't want to see me, give me all my stuff back –everything. Everything I ever gave you."

I looked at him, shocked, I couldn't believe he would use material objects –none of which I had even asked for– as a bargaining tool. I had always been wary of exactly this, and yet, now that it was happening, I realized I had thought our relationship had been above that.

"Sure," I said, the absolute shallowness of his request strengthening my resolve. "I was under the impression those were gifts, but if you really want them, fine."

"I don't want them. I'm only going to give them away. But if you really don't want to see me, give them back."

I stared at him, remembering all the times he had said, "You're so non-materialistic. That's why I like to give you things." Now here he was using a pile of junk as leverage.

I turned away abruptly and walked back inside the store, feeling something dark and heavy grow and stretch inside my chest. It swelled against my ribcage as I stumbled for the breakroom. It swelled as I threw up a hand to support myself against the cold, gray lockers. It swelled until I felt I could no longer breathe. Then, suddenly, it collapsed in on itself with an overwhelming force that robbed me of all thought and understanding. My insides felt like they were being ripped, torn from their seams, as the inward gravity pulled them down into a dense, tangled knot of anguish so profound that I gasped for air.

It was done; we were done. *Finally!* but –heaven and earth!– why did it have to feel like this? There was no fighting this thing in my belly. There was only containment, which I managed after some time and much wrestling. I spent the rest of my shift stalking composure.

Action is the enemy of thought, they say, so as soon as I got home, I started packing. I included even the small things –the funny little Pez dispenser that had made me laugh and kiss him on the cheek, the cowgirl hat I had never much liked anyway, the silver flip-top lighter.

When it was all piled up in my hallway, I stood for a moment, staring. Well Derek, there you go: our memories reduced to trivialities.

He called around three in the morning.

"I have your stuff in my hallway," I said. "You can pick it up anytime." I felt numb, on the verge of cracking. My thoughts skidded out to space and back again. A jumble of incoherency. I squeezed my forehead with my hand. I just wanted to sleep. To bury it all with sleep.

"What do you have in your hallway?"

"I don't have time to give you an inventory –but you'll need your truck." I liked the nice, sharp sound of the "k" in "truck." Anger felt good and when I latched onto it, it solidified into something cold and hard. Something I could wield. I continued, "You know, I'm glad you asked this because it's therapeutic. It'll make forgetting you so much easier."

"Years from now you'll realize what a dumbass you are." And he hung up.

I fell back on my bed and stared up at the ceiling. Was this really the sum of our relationship?

I let my thoughts go then. I didn't try to gather them in or organize them into neat little files. I watched the anger fade and everything grow farther away as I fell into the numbing darkness of sleep.

He never came by. I kept the stuff in my hallway, just in case.

THE DAYS, THE WEEKS that followed were excruciating.

Tucked away in my room, I tried to stifle my sobs so that no sound should escape those thin apartment walls –those oh so thin, translucent walls. But they slipped out. The sounds slid under the door and down the stairwell. They echoed and shook and rolled back to me –ghosts of my sorrow blending with and amplifying my pain until there was a multitude all howling and raging and weeping in a chorus of misery. Hush, hush! I clamped a pillow over my head. I buried my face in my sheets. Hide. Drown. Disappear. How I hated that consciousness of mine, the sensation of other people watching ... listening ... being aware of me. Why should I care? Why shouldn't I pull the pillow from my face and let the surging tears echo and splash into every corner of the building so that everyone knew exactly how I felt? Because Derek didn't care, and it was that very lack of consideration for the people around him that I despised most. So, I tried not to disturb my neighbors. Or at the very least, I tried to keep my sounds, the eerie sobs of a stranger, low enough that they might easily be drowned out by a TV or stereo.

I lost five pounds, and then ten. I tried to eat but couldn't. I couldn't do anything except pull myself out of bed to go to work, which alone was a welcome distraction.

Once, when I was out in the customer self-serve area, a beam –a flash of silver– cut across the street and through the window, blinding me in its brilliance. Sitting there so quiet, so perfect in its stillness, was a silver shark, one exactly like the BMW Derek had said he'd decided not to buy. Could it be? Was he here, over there, mocking me, missing me, making me lose my mind? Or was it another's? Similar, but different?

I stared, stumbling about the store, doing my work, mumbling out the helpful tips to those who asked, and all the while, I was watching, waiting for the owner to step forward to claim the car. But when? Why was it taking so long –what business did the owner have here, now, for so long? I paced the store, my thoughts constantly interrupted by customers. Why the questions? Always the questions! Were these people really so helpless? Pressing copy, pressing total, hearing the cash register pop out with a ringing ding into my stomach. Always watching.

And then, gone. I looked up to see a void where the car had lingered only moments before. Its sudden absence disturbed me more than its haunting presence had, for reasons I couldn't articulate, and I excused myself to the breakroom.

I mustered composure while friends and coworkers sympathized. Tommy: "I never liked him anyway." Friends from Arizona called to check in, and I visited other friends at the dorm. Katrianna insisted that I stay with her for a few days, so I packed my bag, hoping to reclaim my sanity, and knocked at her door. Her roommate opened the door wide with a smile.

"Ani!" So sweet. So welcoming, gesturing me inside with a dainty hand.

I stepped around the three or four other people filling the room and settled myself on the floor on the far side of the bright living room. I wanted to become a cat and curl up in a corner. Instead, I hugged my knees and made myself small. Katrianna gave me a sympathetic smile and continued with a story that she must've been telling before I arrived, of how she'd been sitting on a bench watching a crow on a telephone line. Transfixed by its bright eyes and sharp head movements, she wondered what the world must look like through its eyes. She sat focusing with such intensity that she couldn't say exactly when her perspective shifted, but suddenly she looked down to see herself, staring back.

"It was electrifying," she said. "I was seeing everything in a whole new way –light, colors, details. The tiniest details, things I've never seen, never noticed. Not even about myself. When it took off, my stomach lurched, and I was flying! I could see and feel everything –wind, leaves, voices– and it was incredible." The crow dipped out of sight behind a building, breaking the connection. "But it was unlike anything I've ever experienced, so vivid and mind-altering."

I rested my cheek on my knee and imagined seeing everything from a bird's point of view. What would the world be like if we all could see through each other's eyes?

By the end of the third night, I returned home with a longing for my lonely sanctuary. I busied myself with work and packing for my upcoming move to Arizona. All the while, thoughts of Derek hounded me. I wanted so much to see him again. To find peace. Closure. Despite its illusory nature, closure felt like more than just an idea. It was a crystalline butterfly whose wings of light faded in and out of view. With the right timing, I could reach up and catch it. *Why not?* I thought, and I devised a plan.

## THE CREOSOTE BUSH

THE NEXT DAY BEFORE work, I bought a marvelous little backgammon set for Derek, as he often played the game online. After having it gift-wrapped, I dropped it off at my apartment and headed to work, where I began composing the email I would send. Drawing on all my inner melodrama, I agonized over the wording while distractedly quoting prices and pointing out directions. I could hardly wait for my shift to end so that I could pour out my romanticisms onto my computer.

Finally, walking back to my apartment, I began reciting what I thought was the perfect email when the temperature suddenly dropped fifty degrees as Derek himself flew out of my building's front door, breezed by me, and headed toward his car, which sat on the far side of the street.

"Derek!" I called out after him. He only half-turned, as much surprised to see me as I him. "Derek, I ... I have something for you."

"What is it?" –his tone brusque.

"A gift."

"A gift?" The caustic edge to his voice seared me. He stood straight as an arrow –feet close together and arms stuck to his side, ready to fly.

"I, uh," I stumbled over my words, which kept scattering. Why couldn't I stop shaking? What was wrong with my body? I squeezed my fists and rubbed my arms, but my teeth and limbs kept knocking.

With the large flashlight he held in his hand he flashed a window –*her* window. He looked like a caged animal, restrained by invisible bars and unable to leave. He whistled –and the piercing, abrasive sound made me flinch.

"Derek, listen ...," but I didn't know what to say. All my carefully composed words had fled. "I needed time," I said, trying to hurry. "We can't be together, but I still care about you. I need ... I need closure. Please, can we just talk for a minute? The gift's upstairs. It'll only take a minute." I looked at him with pathetic hopefulness. Time was slipping by, and this was all wrong. Everything was all wrong.

"Why should I go? Get it yourself and bring it to me."

My desperate illusions came crashing down around me. I could almost hear the little pieces shattering as they rained down on the sidewalk at my feet. I stared at the pavement in despair.

The girl arrived, and again I tasted the bitter sting of jealousy. My stomach churned, and my throat tightened. Derek pulled her close by her elbow and then draped his arm awkwardly over her shoulder. It was meant to be a statement but came across as hollow. There was obviously no physical warmth between them. After a moment she pulled away and stood just apart.

"Can we speak alone?" I asked quietly.

"What?" –the movement of his hand to his ear short, abrupt.

"Can I speak with you ... alone."

"She can hear whatever you have to say."

He used to say that about me.

I looked at her, hating the way I felt in her company. She was filing her nails, looking bored. This irritated me. How could she be so calm, disinterested?

She was everything I could never be –no matter how I adapted or changed my color to fit the occasion, I could never match the vibrancy of her hue. Comparing myself only made me feel small and self-conscious, but I couldn't seem to stop. My jealousy overshadowed everything. I was superfluous. This girl had taken my place at his side. She was absorbing his attention and energy. Regret and insecurity clogged my throat so that I found it difficult to swallow, to breathe.

I started to turn away when Derek stopped me.

"I talked to Kurt the other day."

Instantly alert, my body went rigid. I felt a rushing sense of panic. He had no right to talk to Kurt.

"I visited him to ask advice, you know, and we talked for over two hours. I thought, since you two had dated–"

"–I never said we dated–"

"–since you'd had your 'thing,' maybe he could help me know what to do. He denied ever having anything but a purely business relationship with you. He looked at me like I was crazy."

Derek couldn't have said anything more hurtful to me. I respected Kurt, considered him a friend, and I couldn't bear the thought of him losing respect for me.

I had to leave. This conversation was going nowhere. I hurried up the steps and into my building.

Halfway down my hallway I stopped, overcome by an irrepressible need to see Kurt. My blurred vision was turning the walls and the floor beneath me liquid, but I reached out a hand to steady myself and spun around. I had to hear for myself just what had happened.

I stumbled down the back stairs. The whole way there I hoped Kurt was still in his room, still awake. He usually went to bed early and now, surely, it must be well past midnight. "Please, please, *please*, let him be there!" My throat constricted when I saw his light was off. I ran to the end of the block, craning my neck to make sure. Relief flooded through me when I saw the blue lights of his TV flashing.

With my face hidden by my hair, I pushed open the door to the lobby. Eddie, the security guard, asked how I was. I gave a short answer and stepped into the elevator.

Upstairs I knocked on his door. No answer. Please, oh *please*, come to the door. I knocked again, a little louder. The minutes passed. I was disappearing. On the verge of giving up, I tapped once more, and *this* time he answered.

"Ani!" –he was genuinely surprised. "Are you okay? Are you crying?"

"No," but my voice broke. Suddenly he was all concern. "Come in, come in."

He led the way to his kitchen. "Want something to drink?"

"Water, please." And then I couldn't bear it any longer –"Is it true? Did he come to see you?"

He stopped and looked relieved. "Is that what this is about? Yes," and he held up his hand as if to reassure me, "but he's so full of shit I don't take anything he says seriously."

He sat me down at the little table by the kitchen window –the place where we had once spied on the people in the building opposite, joking and happy; the place where I had looked at pictures of him while loving him, laughing with him. That felt like ages ago.

I looked up at him. Dear, sweet, wonderful Kurt!

"I couldn't stand the thought of someone I respect losing respect for me," I said quietly. I dropped my gaze and studied the table as he sat down opposite me. The air felt cool on my wet cheeks.

"I feel so stupid," I said. "I thought I was safe. Separate. I thought I could learn more about people and maybe even show him a brighter side, a happier side of life. He's gone through so much. I *hurt* for him." I avoided Kurt's eyes, so gentle and full of understanding. I tried to squash down the vulnerability that rose in response to his silent attention.

"That just makes you all the more sweet and beautiful for caring."

How could he be so kind when I felt so misguided and weak? Gratitude surged within me. I took his words and tucked them somewhere deep and safe inside my chest. "He can be thoughtful and sweet," I said, not sure who I was trying to convince. "But it's like he has two personalities, and the one ..." I looked around the room, thinking, remembering, and then dropped my gaze and shook my head.

"Ani, you should have seen him. We only talked for twenty minutes or so, but it was enough to see he really loves you."

"*Loved* me."

"No, he loves you still."

He told me how Derek had pretended to run into him as he was walking to the gym one morning. How he'd obviously been waiting. Derek had asked what he should do. He'd made a big deal over the stuff I still had in my apartment –fourteen hundred dollars' worth. Kurt had asked why it was such a big deal when he had just made a point of explaining how he pulled in six figures a year without having to do any work. "Let it go," he had told Derek.

And now he said the same to me. "Just let it go."

"But is it so wrong to want closure?"

"No, but it's unrealistic."

I wiped my eyes. "My make-up's smearing," I said, suddenly self-conscious.

"Get out!" and he pointed toward the door.

A laugh slipped out of me. He laughed too, and at the sight of his smile something inside me relaxed a little.

"I'm sorry you had to talk to him," I said. "How embarrassing."

"He told me all about his company and actually offered me a job–"

"He did not!"

"Yeah. I was polite, but after a while I said I had to go –we were both wasting our time."

"Unbelievable."

I stole glances at Kurt as we kept talking. He was so beautiful. Remote, but beautiful. I asked him about his plans and his family. He still wasn't sure what he was going to do long-term, but he seemed more-or-less content. He took satisfaction, he said, in the impact and influence he was having on the students.

"I'd like to think I'm making a difference," he said.

"You are. You most definitely are," I said. Oh Kurt, you have no idea. Everyone you ever met –we are all better because of you.

I left soon after, drawing the warmth of his memory around me as I walked home.

DEREK MESSAGED ME THE next night. He wanted to meet. For breakfast. I fell back against my bed and stared up at the ceiling. I should say no. My mind was telling me to say no.

"Okay," I typed back. And we set a time.

The next morning, we drove to a nearby diner. Surrounded by the mid-morning bustle with its coffee and bacon aroma, I played with the steam rising from my mug of tea while Derek ate. He offered me a piece of toast, which I used to nudge my eggs, but I wasn't hungry. Instead, I watched him eat and when he had finished, I handed him his gift, which he opened with a grin. He slid his plate forward and began setting up the little backgammon board.

"Thank you," he said. Then he turned toward me and leaned close. "Thank you," he said again, his voice soft against my ear.

"Oh, hey," I said, to distract myself from the competing desires to stay and go. "I developed the negatives of you from the thrift store. They were entertaining. In a good way."

He leaned back to look at me. "I'm surprised you developed film of me."

I shrugged and swirled the remaining tea in my mug as I said, "I'm thankful for our time together. I just ... we're just different."

He looked past me, at nothing. "Okay."

"But I care for you. I think I always will."

His eyes returned to mine. "I miss the closeness we had."

"Me too," I said.

"Distancing yourself from me was probably for the best though. We want different things, and you don't trust me. You think I'm self-centered and unable to empathize with less fortunate people, which is untrue, but you're right —we can't be together. I have very good memories about us though —you have to know that. I miss you so much sometimes, it kills me inside."

"I miss you too," I said, wanting so much to touch him, wanting so much to be somewhere else, far away. I took a deep breath as my mind scrambled about for something different to talk about. "So," I finally said, "what are your plans?"

"My plans...I dunno." Derek thought for a moment. "I'm selling my interest in the company for a sum large enough to buy a third world country almost. I think after that I'm just going to disappear into the jungles of Asia."

He shifted then, turning his head so that he was facing me, but not quite looking at me. "There's something else, Ani. That girl, from your building, she's my daughter."

Before I could respond, he continued, "Her mother was the second girl I'd ever been with. I'd just started my freshman year at the U, and she was a junior. I met her at a party. She had been in a fight with her jock boyfriend and was crying. I consoled her like a dipshit. It was that night, and the following night. That was it. She got back together with her boyfriend and said she had forgotten my name."

Derek frowned at the table. "I'm extremely mortified by the entire thing."

"But how did she even find you? Are you sure it's not a scam?"

"She's not asked me for a single thing. Nothing at all. We also had a blood test last week at her insistence."

"Did you get the results?"

"Not yet. I remember her mother though. And it's weird because when I took her to my grandfather's shop without saying anything, he knew immediately. It's also weird to me but cool at the same time how fucken loyal and protective she's become. She throws away my smokes and tells me to put on my seatbelt."

He shot me a sideways glance. "She *hates* you though. Says you fucked off the best thing that ever will happen to you. But what would you expect her to say?"

A weariness settled over me. "I hope things work out the way you want," I said. I reached for my purse. "I should get back. I have to work soon."

"Of course," he said.

When we reached his Suburban, he paused beside the door. "Let's talk a minute," he said. I took a deep breath as he slid into the backseat. "Please?" he said. He never could hide his desire. I got in anyway. He was a black hole pulling me in despite all my mental attempts to scramble away.

He kissed me, his hands on the prowl, and my resistance melted. I leaned into him, hating him, hating myself, but –don't you see– I loved us too. I didn't care what might happen. I could fall into the abyss and I didn't care because the falling felt sweet and painful and consummate all at the same time. He held me, so tightly, and heat spread through me as his hands traced the skin of my back. One hand slid around to the front and slowly started unzipping my pants. I closed my eyes. He kissed me again, with more urgency, and I breathed into his ear, "Let's go back to my place."

He pulled away, only to lean forward to kiss me again, and again, and then we were each in the front seat, heading back to my room, my bed. I sat with my head resting against the back of my seat, staring out the window. I didn't care that this was a bad idea. There was something wonderfully and deliciously self-destructive about desiring him this way –like swimming late at night during a thunderstorm. Yes, I could get struck by lightning. Yes, *let* me get struck by lightning. There was an exhilarating freedom in the absence of fear, of caution.

But then, halfway to my apartment, he said he had a meeting. I wasn't surprised. Why be surprised when he'd probably only been satisfying his own pride? No, I didn't care. This was for the best. I had to work in half an hour, and besides, I was leaving soon –for good.

"I'll call you tonight," he said as I climbed out.

He never did. In fact, that was the last time we spoke in person before I left Seattle.

# Chapter 13

"Ani! Hey, Ani!"

I couldn't see at first who was calling my name, but then I spotted Terrence half a block away on the other side of the street. I raised my arm and smiled.

"I've got something for you," he called.

I pointed to the crosswalk behind me, and he nodded. Then he turned suddenly as though responding to something behind him. Someone was walking up to him from the opposite direction. It looked like Derek, although that didn't make sense. But sure enough, it was Derek, looking aggressive. What was he saying? I couldn't make out the words, but when Terrence raised his arms defensively, I thought, *Really? Good heavens, what now?*

There was a break in traffic, so I jogged across and made for the two of them, my camera bag bumping my back as I ran.

"Look man, you don't know what you're talking about," I heard Terrence say.

"Where's the fucking money? She said you've got her money."

"Dude, I hardly know you. It's got nothing to do with you anyway, so back the fuck up."

"Hey!" I yelled, still running, still getting whacked in the back as I ran, but neither seemed to hear me.

Terrence started backing away, but Derek made as though to stop him. Terrence shoved him, hard, and Derek lunged for him. That's when Terrence swung. The impact of his fist knocked Derek back several feet, and it was as he was bent over stumbling that I saw the girl. The Suburban had been parked alongside the road the whole time, but it wasn't until she climbed out that I registered it.

She had a knife.

"Stop!" I half screamed, but everyone was yelling, and no one heard me. I was almost there.

Her face was wild with rage as she ran at Terrence. Seeing her coming, Terrence grabbed Derek and used him as a shield. The girl looked unhinged. She nearly stabbed Derek trying to get at Terrence. Derek wrenched himself away and grabbed the girl's arm as he ran for the car.

"I'm gonna kill you. I'm gonna fucking shoot you," Derek shouted over his shoulder.

Terrence turned and ran.

"Fuuuck!" he yelled as he passed me.

When I looked back, I saw the Suburban had jumped the curb and was headed toward me. I screamed, throwing up both hands.

I knew the instant he saw me. He slammed on the brakes, but it was too late.

The Suburban hadn't seemed like it was going that fast, but when it hit me, the force emptied my mind of everything. The next thing I knew, I was staring up at the sky, fighting to breathe.

"I can't, I can't..." I tried to say, but no sound came out. I tried to pull in air as my panic mounted.

We used to go fishing on the Rio Grande when I lived in Texas. All we caught were these little grey things, which we flung up on the rocks. I can still see the horrible way they would writhe and gasp, their little mouths opening and closing as they slowly suffocated.

I couldn't breathe. I tried to suck in air, but it wasn't working, my chest wasn't working. There were so many people shouting, and my heart was pounding inside my ears. I felt tears rolling down the sides of my face. Then with a wrenching, wet gasp I managed to suck in a breath. The pain was immediate, sending sparks behind my eyes. A moment later, I passed out.

I HAD A TRAUMATIC PNEUMOTHORAX, which, I found out, is a punctured lung. In my case, it was caused by one of my broken ribs. I awoke in the hospital to find a tube sticking out of the side of my chest. "To help with air drainage," they said.

I also had a concussion, a chest contusion, two broken wrists and a broken elbow. Everything hurt, even with all the medication.

I was surprised by all the people who came to visit that first week in the hospital. Katrianna, Terrence and Jimmy, Will and Stacy, my great aunt and several other relatives, an Officer Stiles, and Kurt.

I was still staring at the officer's business card and desperately hoping I wouldn't have to testify like she said I might when Jimmy walked in.

"Hey," he said, stopping just inside the doorway to look at me.

I set the card aside and tried for a smile. "It's not as bad as it looks."

His eyes shone for a moment, but after a quick swipe of the hand, he said, "What? You look great." He pulled a chair close to the edge of the bed and reached into his backpack. He took out a chess set and spread it open between us. "But don't think I'm going easy on you just because you look like a mummy who got hit by a car. Oh wait, not a car. A big-ass Suburban. You never were one to do anything halfway."

I watched him as he set up the board. His long fingers were graceful in their quick movements. The pieces made little tapping noises as he set them down. One tipped and started to roll. He caught it in a fluid motion, replaced it, and offered, "You first?"

The familiarity of the game, his voice as he spoke, his half grin as he thought of something, all of it felt wonderfully comforting. A distraction from the pressing gloom.

A despair I couldn't even articulate had settled over me. The nurse had said this might happen, but somehow the overwhelming hopelessness engulfing me felt like much more than the aftereffects of shock. I felt broken, body and spirit. I wanted to retch –to just get it all out. All the misery, the growing self-loathing, and wretchedness welling up inside me. Maybe then I could stand, wipe my mouth, and get on with my life.

In the silence following Jimmy's visit, I gave myself over to my thoughts. After everything, after all my efforts to gain understanding, I realized I had no more answers than when I had started. Fewer, in fact. It was dawning on me that I might never have all the answers. I had stepped out of my safe tower in order to search them out –expecting to see God fully or not at all. Instead, I saw people living, striving, loving, and learning in a world in which God exists in bits and pieces scattered throughout the messy chaos of life. Was this enough? If nothing lay beyond this life, if no loving Lord was waiting to greet our souls into the afterlife –would our striving together in the face of our fleeting, fragile existence be enough to make it all worthwhile?

I looked up at Kurt as he entered, feeling first surprised, then self-conscious. I wore no make-up, and my lips were chapped. I didn't want to think about what my hair must look like. And then there was everything else. I looked down, feeling exposed, and hated my insecurity and the way it made me wish I could talk to him from the inside of a box. But he was here. And that mattered more than anything else.

He stood frozen, unprepared for this bruised and bandaged version of me.

"Ani," he said, voice soft.

"Hey, Kurt."

He took me in, and nodded, before pulling up a chair beside me.

"You should see the other guy," I said, trying for humor.

"I'd like to see the other guy," and for a moment his voice was cold and his expression hard.

A surge of emotions flooded through me –gratitude, affection, sorrow, and regret. And weaving through them all was desperation. "I've been trying to decide whether it was worth it," I blurted, ditching all small talk as he settled himself in his chair.

"What? Getting hit by a car?"

"No, I could've done without that. I mean everything else. All the choices that led me here."

"Did you get your answer?"

I looked down, fingering the edge of my blanket. Would I do it all over again? I regretted not leaving when I learned of Derek's wife. She was put through a hell that I had helped create, and I had to own my part in her suffering. But as for the rest? I had glimpsed a small portion of the human experience, and although the ground now shifted beneath my feet in a manner precarious and unsteady, I was glad to have started the journey, even if I still didn't know where the path would lead. I could never have ignored my questions or smothered my doubts. They weren't the problem anyway; they merely signaled the existence of one.

The pursuit of answers had also shown me truths about myself, the knowledge of which was uncomfortable, but invaluable. Because how could I have hoped to grow when mired in self-delusion? I needed to know that although curious, compassionate, and sensitive, I could also be selfish, detached, and weak. I contained within me the propensity for every kind of action. I was like an Arizona sky on a late summer evening with its rolling layers of orange, red, violet, blue, and black. And grey. Light grey, dark grey, slate, pewter, and fossil grey. Lavender grey. Ash grey. Grey tinged with pink. A shifting grey full of light and shadows that ultimately gives way to the clear, black, star-studded night sky. Our window to the universe.

"So, what now?" Kurt asked, and I looked up.

"Back to Arizona in a couple weeks, once I get the okay. And then ..."

"That's not what I meant."

"I know. It's just ... I don't know."

When I had first set out to see and understand more of the world, I had fully expected to find God's plan and purpose fusing it all together. This belief that God understood, and was there, with watchful eyes and a guiding hand, had always reassured me in the face of the nagging worry that somehow the pieces didn't fit so well together. But lately my faith had begun to feel like a woolen security blanket that's been washed too many times in hot water. I had been told that doubt would ultimately strengthen my faith. But now, even after prayer and fasting and reading my Bible, I saw only pointlessness.

"I'm afraid," I said.

"I know it. I can see it."

He reached out and with the lightest touch traced my cheek. I could have cried at the gentleness of it. I leaned into his hand, wanting him to stay, dreading when he should go.

When he settled back, my face felt hot and cold at the same time. I took a breath, flinching a little.

"I used to think that no matter what, I'd always believe in God," I said, glancing at him before looking down at my lap. "I mean, I know people change. I knew I'd change. Grow. But I thought my faith would be the one thing that would always stay the same. I had such peace then, even with all my questions. There's a certain comfort in believing God has a plan and purpose for our lives. That everything's going to be okay in the end. That despite tragedy, it all *means* something. Life means something. I felt safe in the knowledge that I was here to *do* something and then I'd go to heaven after. But then I thought, what about all the people who are dying every day, with and without God? People in the middle of doing things, leaving their lives and projects unfinished. The child who's shot, the father dead in an accident, the cancer patient, the senseless death and sorrow everywhere? I mean, I know I can't see the big picture and all, but sometimes death seems completely random and pointless. Sometimes life feels that way too. The idea of a master plan or individual purpose feels like a fairytale. Or at least something granted only to a few. Maybe I'll do something for God or the world or maybe I'll die tomorrow. There are no guarantees. And then I think, 'Well, what if life is so small and eternity so huge, that all of our troubles and pain disappear in the light of what we have yet to experience? Would I then ask how a loving God could let people suffer on earth?'"

"Life's not all suffering. You're just going through a hard time."

"I know. Really, I do. I just ... I feel it so much sometimes. Ever since I was a kid. Like when I read that news article about the murdered girl or saw the face of that Israeli soldier in the magazine or when I saw a woman with her mascara running as she choked, just choked. I get sucked into the feeling of being there with them. No ... of *being* them. And I feel sick that things like that even happen.

"I get that there's suffering. I do. Some of it is outside our control, like sickness and the weather. And some of it is just because people suck and do horrible things. I read somewhere that evil is the absence of good, the corruption and fragmentation of what once was whole. And this makes sense to me. Whether the good is God or love or that ... that *thing* connecting all of us, it makes sense that the farther we move away from it, the worse off we're gonna be."

"It's the price of freedom."

"Free will?"

"Yeah, the freedom to make choices."

"But do we really?"

"Really what? Make our own choices? Of course, we do."

"I mean, yes. But how much of what we think of as being a 'free agent' is really only the result of our nature and nurture? I mean, if I had different parents who gave me different genes and raised me with a different mindset, would I still think and act the way I do? We all live as though exercising free will. We must. And ... I guess the consequences are the same regardless."

I sucked in a deep breath. Stars exploded around me as the pain bit into my chest. Everything hurt. I took in another sharp breath, and the pain intensified. I tried to slow my breathing, but the more I tried, the more I needed air. I shoved the panic down and closed my eyes, trying not to cry. I focused on the hum of machines and imagined I was floating on an endless sea. Floating, floating. Everything soft and gentle. Slowly, the pain subsided. I opened my eyes.

"I know this isn't a perfect world," I said, looking down at my blanket through watery eyes. "I know we're imperfect creatures and that suffering is a part of life. I'm even okay with this. Because I don't think I'd fully understand or appreciate anything without the contrast provided by its absence. Like right now, when everything hurts, all I want is to feel normal. Just *normal*." I squeezed my eyes shut again until the calm returned.

"I appreciate things, I do, but not as fully as when I've been without them. I love tea and chocolate, but I *really* love them when I haven't had them in a while. Or those huge burgers at McCormick and Schmidt's–" I looked up at him and smiled "–they're good, but when I'm super hungry they are *the most amazing burgers in the entire world!* I appreciate everything more by contrast. Even people. I'd like to think I make the most of my time with others, but I don't. I try to be conscious of them, of how good it feels just to be near them, but I feel it so much more when I have to say goodbye. Then I want to soak up everything about them. Every moment becomes vivid. As though individually and perfectly framed. And it's like this with everything. Life, joy, and peace are best understood and valued in light of death, sorrow, and turmoil. I mean, it's even how we see. Without shadows and darkness, we wouldn't be able to make out anything. I don't think I'd even know myself fully without experiencing both pain and joy. Interacting with the world shows us ourselves. God and other people too. We know them better when we see them react to good *and* bad. Is this ... am I making any sense?"

"Yeah," Kurt said. "And no. Are you saying you lost your faith because of the suffering in the world which you believe *had* to exist?"

"No. It's not that. It's the idea of *eternal* suffering. That some are damned because of choices made for them or by them in their fallible, finite form as a human being. Billions of souls condemned for eternity because of something done in this brief life? How could any of us desire a heaven in view of a spiritual graveyard like that? Even if hell isn't a literal fire, even if it is separation from God or just oblivion, that still doesn't fit with a just or loving God. I mean, *forever*?"

"What if it wasn't forever?"

"Like purgatory?"

He shrugged.

"But where does it talk about that in the Bible? How do we know it's not just another idea created by people to alleviate the weight of hell?"

"So, what? Nothing?"

"I don't know. No. Not nothing. Because I still find myself praying to him ... to God. I just don't know who exactly or what that is anymore."

I looked down at my hands. They didn't look like my own. The color was off, and they looked fatter. Ugly. My eyes slid down to Kurt's hand, the one resting on my bed close to my leg. I felt the urge to clasp his hand like it was my lifeline.

I was terrified of the inevitable crumbling of everything meaningful unless I reclaimed my faith –or *a* faith– in something. Whether we believe in God, ourselves, or another person, in the will to power, the desire to leave the world a better place, a full abandonment to hedonism, or simply in the decision to ignore that which is less than ideal, don't we all need motivation of some sort to keep our feet moving one in front of the other? And surely it couldn't all be subjective, could it? Was there an Absolute? If so, how did I find it?

"Without a higher Power," I said, "without a point to all this, I feel as though nothing would matter. Nietzsche said there were two possible reactions when confronting the meaninglessness of life: despair or joy. My reaction would not be joy."

"He also said, 'if you are not a bird, beware of coming to rest above the abyss.'"

"To keep going I feel as though I need to choose," I said, "but ..."

"But what if it's the wrong choice?"

I stared into his eyes –large and warm and filled with compassion. I half expected him to spell out the answer. I wanted him to, feeling like the child who asks, deeply serious, if Santa is real –while inwardly, Hope and Disappointment cling to each other, biting their nails as they await the answer.

"How can we know?" I asked.

"Do you have all the information?"

"Will I ever?"

"Does anyone?" He stared at me a moment before asking again, more quietly this time, "Does anyone have all the information?"

"Some think they do."

"Dogma isn't the same as having all the information."

"But isn't that where faith comes in?"

"Perhaps, but give yourself room to grow –whether that means closer to God or in a completely new direction, just keep moving forward. Ideas change and evolve. Allow them to. For now, start with what you know, and build up."

DEREK TRIED MULTIPLE times to contact me in the weeks that followed, but I refused to see him, or even to take his calls. One early voicemail overflowed with sorrow and remorse that dripped out of my phone and onto my bed as he described his version of events. He had gone up to Terrence, very politely, of course, and on *my* behalf, to ask for the money. He said Terrence had immediately gotten defensive, and that as he was turning to leave, Terrence had hit him hard on the back of the head. Then the girl –his "own flesh and blood, seeking only to defend" him– got involved because "she wanted to protect me –she adores me."

"When we finally got back into the Suburban," Derek said, "I could barely see –my head was hurting so bad, and I just wanted to get away from him. I couldn't see where I was going, with my eyes all blurry and shit, so I just started driving. I never meant to hurt anyone –least of all you. God, you've got to believe me. Please, Ani, you've got to believe me. I'm so sorry."

I was so tired. I almost didn't care anymore. I just wanted to be done with it all.

In the end, I didn't testify, or even press charges. Terrence did though, and Derek was charged with gross negligence. His cell time was lengthened by domestic violence and tax evasion charges following a nasty divorce. But this was almost two years later, justice system being what it was, and by that time I was long gone.

Once released from the hospital, I began distancing myself –from school, from work, from friends. Whether lying on my bed or wandering through the city, I rarely left my head. Slowly I began to untangle my thoughts. Then I got the okay from my doctors, and I packed up my stuff and prepared to leave town.

The evening before I left, Kurt stopped by to say goodbye. In a room lit only by streetlamps, we talked late into the night. He was so sweet, so empathetic and thoughtful that I could have cried. A stillness gradually settled over us, and we sat, thinking and feeling and content just to be. When I looked up, I saw that he was staring at me. I didn't want to be seen. I wanted to be comforted, encouraged, *loved* in that moment. But to be seen was too much. I studied the curve of his mouth, the lovely line of his jaw. I wished I could run my hands down the length of his back. Say something, tell me you'll miss me or make a joke even, only don't look at me like that, I pleaded silently.

"Smile for me."

His request caught me off guard. I struggled a moment at so simple a task. Why should it be so hard? Surely, I could do this one little thing for a man whose words and kindness were helping to sooth away a hurt that I had not yet even fully acknowledged to myself. With great effort, I created one curve and corner at a time. I can only imagine what he thought of the process, but I had a full smile at last and I hoped he could see through it and into the growing determination that lay behind. This determination was due, in part, to him. Kurt was a reminder that there were good people out there worth knowing, whose very existence made others better. I thought of Jimmy, Andy, and Neva. Of my parents and brothers and yes, even of Derek. I gathered my memories of them and held them to my chest, and I felt ... full. Whatever else I did or did not know, I could at least say that relationships were what mattered.

"You know," I said, "before I came to Seattle, I had this idea that the world was made up of two parts: a light side and a dark side –the gritty underbelly, so-to-speak. And I thought that everyone more or less existed in one or the other. I thought I needed to experience both in order to fully appreciate all I had."

I stared out into the night at the scattered lights and shadows weaving together across the deserted parking lot.

"The idea of a darker side used to scare me a little too. I thought that if I explored it, I could somehow confront and demystify it. And I think maybe I felt like I had some of that darkness inside me, a wildness that didn't fit with my idea of how a good Christian girl should be."

I glanced at Kurt, to see if he understood. His gaze felt like a warm hand on my cheek, and his eyes were clear and expectant.

"Did you ever read *The Book of the New Sun* by Gene Wolfe?" I asked.

He shook his head.

"There's this part where it says that every person is like a plant with a part growing up, toward the sun, and another part, the roots, digging down deep into the darkness. Those roots are what give the plant the strength to grow.

"We exist in both the light and the dark simultaneously. Everyone. And we *need* both. Together they provide balance. I don't mean good and evil, exactly, because we can't use the term 'evil' to blanket everything in the darkness. Darkness includes doubt and struggle and fear and grief. At one time or another, we all experience these. More like ... joy and suffering, etermity –goodness, I can't even talk– *eternity* and impermanence, success and failure, doubt and certainty. The whole mix.

"I think the best any of us can do is try to reach out to each other and grow. Together. To understand more was always my goal, and sometimes I think it's the ultimate goal.

"Christians believe that God knows everything already, that he's omniscient. As the Maker and Sustainer of heaven and earth, how could he not be? But then he sent his son, Jesus, to live and die as a man. Jesus knew what was going to happen, that he was going to suffer and die, but as he's waiting for the soldiers to come and arrest him, he pours his heart out to God and pleads, 'take this cup from me.' Because he was *afraid*. Even though he was God in the flesh, he was terrified. To the point of sweating blood. He overcame his fear, of course. He said, 'not my will, but yours be done,' but he *felt*. He felt his fear, his dread because it's one thing to *know* about suffering; it's another thing entirely to experience it. Our bodies and our lives are powerfully influenced by our histories and the world around us –just by being human. Just by being alive.

"Joseph Campbell once said, or maybe he was quoting someone, I don't remember which, but he said, 'Man's search is not for meaning, but for the experience of being alive.' For me, those two things go together. The times I felt most alive, and the greatest meaning, were when I was fully interacting with the world around me. With people, ideas, nature –*all* of it.

"I grew up being so terrified of making a mistake, of doing or being evil. But maybe the dark isn't something to be afraid of. I mean, yeah, I'm going to run away from the guy waving around a knife, and I'll do my best to alleviate the suffering of others, but maybe the good and the bad exist together as a way to understand and appreciate what it means to be alive. What it means to *be*. Together they give each other context. They give each other meaning.

"No single one of us is alone. Buddhism talks about the interconnectedness of all things, and Hinduism refers to the oneness of all life. There were even some early Christians who referred to God as an 'intelligible sphere whose center is everywhere and whose circumference is nowhere.' Whatever the case may be, all I know for sure is that together we share it all. The joy and the heartbreak, the triumph and the defeat, killing and being killed, loving and being loved –all of it. Together we cradle new life as it draws its first breath, and together we kiss the forehead of our loved one who lays dying. We feel the exhilaration of pushing our bodies to their limits and also the helplessness of watching these bodies deteriorate bit by bit. Together we progress under good leadership and suffer under the bad. We feel proud; we feel embarrassed. We feel peace and rage. We feel exhaustion, despair, hope, and determination. Together. No single one of us can experience everything on our own, but together we share it all, the joy and the pain and everything in between, and we are stronger for it. We don't have to be afraid, and we don't have to escape. Because suffering is not the final word. By embracing life, I embrace all of it, the good and the bad, the light and the dark, you and me. We're all part of something. We're the ultimate creosote bush."

"Creosote bush?"

"Yeah. In Arizona, there's this bush that makes the desert smell so good when it rains. That's not the point though. There's a ring of them, several in fact, and it turns out they're connected by the roots. A single living organism. Some of these rings are estimated to be thousands of years old. Many bushes, one plant. I think that's how it is with us. There's you and me –thank God there's you and me– but there's also us, we, all of us together. Individual parts of a whole. And the good and the bad, the light and the dark, it's how we experience life. It's how we grow. How we understand. Sometimes life is so hard, and other times it's so, so beautiful. No one is ever lost or alone because they're part of us and we're part of them. Connected, and growing together. I think this is what I believe in."

Kurt didn't say anything for several minutes. The white and red lights of a car streaked by, but inside my room all was quiet, save for the sound of our breathing. I held my breath and listened to his soft inhales and exhales. He was a warm fire on a winter's day, filling my entire room.

I heard him shift in his seat and when I met his eyes, he smiled and nodded.

"You give me hope," he said.

I stared at him, confused.

"Hope for what?" I asked.

"Just hope."

Still, I pressed him. "For the future? For *humanity*?"

"Just hope."

Then I understood. Hope doesn't point to a far-off fulfillment. Hope *is* the fulfillment, the goal, the happiness and strength to persevere –in and of itself. In giving him hope, I had given him something right then and there.

I nodded and sighed. Something inside me relaxed and let go, leaving me lighter. "You too," I said.

HOPE.

For some, religion gives that hope. I've seen it. I've seen the change in people's lives and the new light shining in their eyes. They no longer fear the void –neither the one within nor the thought of what comes after. For others, it's love –love of a person, a place, an idea, or activity. For me, it's connection. The ties that bind lovers to each other, parents to their children, believers to their God, friends and siblings and teachers to their students –all the countless ties that bind one to another and to the world around them– this is what gives me hope. I believe we are connected, all of us, to everything.

## THE CREOSOTE BUSH

And the more I try to see and cherish all the beautiful souls and this beautiful world with its network of invisible threads, the greater my understanding, my purpose, my love.

# Chapter 14

Sitting across from Kurt and seeing him smile as we talked was something I thought I'd never do again. But here we were. I watched him, amazed, and I saw more than just the man who'd been my Resident Director at art school. More too, than the man who'd fallen asleep beside me on my makeshift bed in my downtown Seattle apartment that night I'd said, "No, I'm not ready." I saw more than the man who'd always respected my person, my thoughts, and my ideas as they shifted and evolved. When I looked at him in this moment, I saw the man I'd loved all those years ago. The man I loved still, would love always. The man who, despite the fact he'd never be mine, would nevertheless be there always, in my thoughts.

"What are you thinking about?" he asked, as he pushed his now-empty plate to the side and rested his arm on the table.

"The way we used to talk," I said, "in your office and that time in my hospital room and in my apartment. I was trying so hard to figure everything out back then, and you never tried to tell me what was what. I felt like I could tell you anything, and you'd just listen and ask questions and share your perspective. I don't know if I ever told you how much that meant to me."

The thought had occurred to me that maybe I shouldn't have come, unannounced, after all these years. But he was exactly as I remembered him. A few pounds heavier maybe, but the warmth in his eyes was still there, along with the same glint of stubble along his chin. His broad shoulders stretched the fabric of his shirt so that the faded red cotton looked soft and inviting, just like I remembered. I felt such gratitude to be there in that moment with him, to see his face and hear his voice. Even if only for a few hours.

Katie was the one who'd told me he had left Seattle for a sunnier locale. "He owns and runs a bar now," she'd said, "in Texas." That was two years ago.

"Did you ever find what you were looking for?" Kurt asked.

"What I was looking for," I repeated, laughing. "The meaning of life and all that?"

"Yeah, and all that."

And just like that, it was like we were back in his office in Seattle, talking with the old, familiar ease. What was it about his expression that seemed to pull conversation out of me, making me want to pour out all my thoughts and ideas, just to hear his take on them? Was it the interest lighting up his eyes? The way he leaned forward a little as though to better hear me? Or was it the memory of how I never needed to tiptoe around any subject, because he always responded honestly and without judgement? Maybe it was all of these.

"Well," I said, "for a while after I left Seattle, I embraced the oneness of everything. And it was great. But I also began to feel desperate because I thought if only more people saw their connection with each other and their environment, there would be so much more harmony. Together we could do more to nurture life and our planet. We could–" I lowered my voice for dramatic effect "–end global warming and achieve world peace. And it would all be wonderful."

Kurt leaned back with a smile. "Sounds nice."

"I know, right? But I felt powerless to help. To do anything. What could I do that would make any difference? And then, even if humanity were to somehow achieve harmony and world peace, then what? Could we sustain it indefinitely? How long before something new came along to shake it all up? A natural disaster, internal dissenters, an alien attack, gradual apathy, who knows –but *something's* bound to come along eventually, and we'd have to start all over. Like an Etch A Sketch or ants in an ant farm –no matter how pretty the picture or intricate the tunnels, if something shakes it up, you have to start all over.

"I also wondered how far the oneness extended. Was it our planet only, like the idea of Gaia? Or, if there is extraterrestrial life, does our oneness extend to them? To the far reaches of the cosmos? Is there a limit?

"And then one day I experienced something –nothing magical or profound, but something that shifted my view a little.

"I was at a playground with a friend and her kids. When she got up to go tell her son to stop throwing bark all over the place, I stayed put. The park is fenced-in and bowl shaped, and the bench where I was sitting was on the outer edge, so I could see everything within the circle of it. The wind started to blow, swirling the leaves all around, and the whole place felt like the inside of a snow-globe –secure, self-contained, with everyone doing their own thing. And I thought, this is how the universe is. We don't all have to go in the same direction or do the same activity because everything is as it should be. Right now. Does that make sense?"

"I guess, but I don't get what you're driving at."

"Okay," I said, thinking. "Everyone inside that playground was sharing the same space, but we were each experiencing it from our own individual vantage point. Kind of like players in a first person POV game in which the only point is to play. Like World of Warcraft. Did you ever play that or any of those other online role-playing games?"

"Some. Not really."

"Same here. But what made me think of it is how each person plays their game their own way. Some of my friends were all about leveling up as fast as they could. Others were happy just to hang out in one area and collect things. Both ways are okay. And life is that way too. Some people want to 'level up' as fast as they can; others are content just to be. We don't have to change anyone's mind or convince everyone else to do things a certain way –the 'right' way– because unity isn't the same as uniformity. All we have to do is 'play the game.'"

"Play the game?"

"Yeah. I don't mean that in a superficial way. I just mean we have to ... be present. Experience life. Engage with it."

Kurt's expression was hard to read. I shifted, feeling inarticulate, and tried a different approach.

"Did I ever tell you about the time Yoshi and I were talking about the Sims?" I asked.

"No, I don't think so."

"So one night he told me all about this video game back in Japan –not the Sims, but something like it where you play ordinary people living ordinary lives doing ordinary things. And he started getting all depressed because he thought, how do I know I'm not a simulation being played by someone else? And if that's true, what if *they're* a simulation too, a game within a game? Where does it stop?"

"Okay."

"I've heard about others who think this way too –that our existence is being played out within a program. But to me that implies an inside and an outside, and I don't think there's anything external in the sense that they mean. More like, what if everything exists within a self-created, self-sustaining system? Life, our planet, other planets, other life, the whole universe from the subatomic to the galactic –*everything*– contained within a single whole. Some people call that whole 'God' or 'Brahman', but whatever you want to call it, it implies a sense of unity and interconnectedness. That's nothing new, of course, but here's what felt new to me: maybe heaven or enlightenment isn't the ultimate goal. I mean, I get that it's the personal goal of many. But collectively, maybe the goal is what we're doing right now – living our lives. Because doing this creates understanding through experience."

I looked at him, searching his eyes. "It's like what we were talking about my last night in Seattle," I said, "how Jesus knew he was going to die ahead of time, and how knowing and experiencing are two separate things. In the Garden of Gethsemane when he's faced with imminent death, he's afraid. The son of God, *afraid*! And that's my point –is it possible to fully know *anything* while lacking the experience of it? A med student may know every function and disorder of the human body, but does that mean he's ready for surgery? Or to see someone shoot past on a water slide, is that anything close to feeling the wind and water against your own skin? Or fire? Does knowing about fire bring the sensation of heat to your cheeks or the crackling to your ears? I could go on, of course, but do you know what I mean?"

"I do."

"Not that we have to experience everything ourselves. We can't. No one can. But together we are. Every possible scenario is being played out in every possible way on every possible level. It's universal self-discovery.

"Maybe that's why everything exists: so that the whole may experience, through each individual point of view, every possible experience –living, dying, creating, destroying, struggling, *life*! And the struggle is what makes it all possible. It allows us to see who we are, who we could be in the best and worst scenarios. Struggle is necessary to define us. To define everything. Struggle and suffering create the contrast by which we see and appreciate and give value to things."

"I get what you're saying, but I think we could all use a little less suffering."

"Oh, me too! A lot less suffering. Seems like there's so much senseless hate and violence. There's no whitewashing or justifying it. But good can come from it."

"I see your optimism has returned," Kurt said, smiling.

"I'm glad you didn't say naïve idealism."

"Well, the jury's still out," he said, still smiling. He looked at me directly then. "So tell me," he said, "how can good come out of something like the holocaust or cancer or the death of a child?"

I held his gaze. "No holding back, huh?" Although, of course, that was one of the things I loved about him.

"Why would I?" he said. "The universe apparently doesn't."

I breathed in slowly while trying to gather my thoughts into something I could articulate.

"I could speak of humanity's ability to survive, to heal, to come together and say, 'what must we do to make sure this never happens again?' Or I could point to the altruism shown by all those who have risked their lives to help and protect others. But all of these combined could never justify the death of six million Jews. There is no justifying the holocaust or cancer or death, other than to say suffering exists not in part, but in whole. To live in a world where only a little suffering exists would be the same as living in a perfect one. Which is to say, we'd always be in danger of slipping into complacency, or at the very least, a gradual lack of appreciation for what we have."

"That's so much easier to say when you're not the one suffering."

I nodded and looked down at the table. There was no ignoring or downplaying the overwhelming amount of suffering in the world. "It is," I said, taking a deep breath and meeting his eyes again. "But at least I can try to help ease the suffering of others. We can help each other. We can give strength, and we can receive it. Because we aren't alone, and we don't have to suffer alone. We are all stronger together. Or we could be."

"And just because there's suffering doesn't mean we have to sit back and take it," I continued. "We can fight it. We can try to make things better. We *should* try to make things better."

Kurt still looked skeptical. "But to say suffering is necessary is to say that it's good."

"It serves a purpose. I don't think that's the same thing. Suffering allows for growth. For discovery. It wakes us up to what we have."

"We can have all those without suffering."

"But not to the same extent. A year ago, I found out my best friend has a brain tumor. I love this friend with everything in me. And I love being with this person. But when I found out about the tumor, I started appreciating our time together so much more. I should have from the beginning, of course. Ideally, we should all value our time together. But in the face of loss, our time together becomes so much more precious, and we appreciate each other that much more."

Kurt sat still a moment, thinking.

"In Christianity," I continued, "it's a given that God is perfect. The Bible talks about how in the beginning there was God. Just God, who was and is and will be. I used to wonder about that –how could he have existed *forever,* without beginning or end? The idea of him being outside time and surrounded by nothingness *terrified* me as a kid."

Kurt smiled and nodded. "Yeah, me too."

"But thinking about him like that now feels a bit like thinking of a computer in a white room. The computer might possess complete knowledge and be capable of running an infinite number of simulations, but it will still lack experience, sensation, appreciation. Does that sound blasphemous? After all, you're still a Southern Baptist, right?"

Kurt leaned back and gave a little wave. "Labels serve a purpose," he said, "but as soon as you give something a label, you create a boundary with walls keeping some people in and others out. Just say what you gotta say."

"Okay," I said. "So what better way to understand everything than to run through every possible scenario? Not theoretically, but in actuality."

"That makes it sound like you're saying God was somehow incomplete or lacking."

"Does it? I guess, but only when viewed in terms of a beginning and an end. And God is without beginning, containing everything within, always. When I say 'God,' by the way, I don't mean a man in a white beard somewhere. I just mean the whole or the Absolute."

"Got it."

"Time is largely considered a human construct, so maybe it's as some say, that the past, present, and future are happening simultaneously. To imagine the very beginning or end is beyond my comprehension, and anyway, with the relativity of time, there's only so much we can know from our vantage point. But maybe we don't need to know what preceded this universe. Maybe it's enough to know that everything just is –here and now, then and always. Everything contained within a single system."

"Where does that leave us?"

"That leaves us with our own unique vantage point, but still connected to something greater than ourselves."

"And after?"

"You mean when we die?"

He shrugged and nodded.

"We continue, in one way or another. That same friend I mentioned with the kids at the playground told me about a time when they were visiting a battle site and her son said, 'a lot of people died down there.' He started talking about how he'd been a doctor and had tried to save some of them. My friend's a Christian and didn't know what to make of this. It's anecdotal, I know, and whether he was remembering or just imagining, I couldn't say. Some people think we're like a spark that can go from one candle or lantern to the next. Others say no, we're simply the candle or lantern that houses the spark and gives it expression. For my part, I don't know. But this whole not knowing, not being sure if we come back or move on or something else –I think I'm finally okay with that. It used to bother me a lot, but now it's just fun to think about. I mean, maybe these bodies are our avatars –gloves we inhabit for a little while. Maybe we were once single-celled organisms, living out our whole existence at the edge of a pond –a pond that was our universe. Maybe we've had wings and scales and fur. Maybe you and I have met before, and maybe we'll meet again. Who knows."

"If that were the case, what about our memories? They mean nothing?" he asked.

"No, not nothing. Although honestly, I can't remember half the stuff I did last week, let alone years ago. And are memories alone what defines us? What I mean is, would you define yourself as your collection of memories or as your point of view?"

"Don't the two go together? Without our memories, we wouldn't be whole. And without a point of view, there'd be no one to make sense of the memories."

"Yeah, maybe," I said. "It's hard for me to imagine one without the other. But what got me thinking about it was a couple novels I read recently. Both described how scanning our brains and uploading the content into a digital system will bring about a form of 'immortality.' To me though, unless the same consciousness, or point of view, is somehow also transferred, the uploaded version is essentially a clone. If I upload a copy of myself, I may be passing on my memories, but as soon as that copy emerges, it becomes a separate entity. And our paths, if I'm still alive, will diverge. I won't be able to see what my copy sees, and she won't be able to see or experience what I see. This sort of copying may be a great way to preserve history and memories, but that copy is not 'me.' She will become her own person, shaped by her future experiences. In a similar way, I think, to how I may pass on my genes, but my child will be his or her own self. Do you see what I mean?"

"I do. But maybe you think that way because you identify with your physical body."

"Maybe. I mean, I do like this body, aging and all. I love what it can feel and do. But as soon as something goes wrong with it, I'm like, what is this thing I'm trapped in? Why is it making these sounds and feeling this way? And why does it look so much older than I feel?"

We both laughed.

"Anyway," I said, "even if a brain is scanned, will the uploaded version behave the same inside the digital realm? Can a computer ever function the way a brain does? One day, perhaps. I don't know. I can see, though, how the idea of talking to a copy of a dead loved one would appeal. In a way, it might feel a bit like having them back. But still, I don't think it would be the same thing. It would just be a copy, a projection."

"So what about point of view?"

"What?"

"Do you think a continual point of view is any different?"

"Oh yeah. So by point of view, I just mean –and this goes without saying, I guess– our individual perspective. Like when someone gets amnesia, that person retains their point of view, more or less. Or like the characters in the movies *Memento* and *50 First Dates* –it's still 'them,' despite their memory loss. There was another book I read recently about a seventeen-year-old girl who has short-term memory loss and every few hours or so she 'resets.' She writes herself messages on her arms and has a notebook, and the whole time she's trying to figure out where she is and what she's doing while clinging to a single memory that may or may not be real. That type of short-term memory loss seems like it'd be so terrifying. But while the book *is* suspenseful in parts, the story isn't dark because the character herself is so bright and optimistic. She's funny and brave and ... *herself* –despite her lack of memory. If that makes sense."

Kurt nodded, and I continued. "I've always identified so strongly with my memories –for better and for worse. Memories ground us. They give us a narrative we can build on. Plus, to think of someone I love, or even myself, losing those memories is horrifying. But it'd still be them, at least in part, and it'd still be me, wouldn't it? Even if in altered form?"

"To some extent maybe. But I'm sure you've heard people say, 'he's just not himself' or 'she hasn't been the same since' when referring to people with dementia or a brain injury."

"Yeah, but does changing the personality change the point of view? Are they the same? It's like that conversation we had about *The Three Faces of Eve*? Remember?"

"I do."

"You said each of her personalities were aspects of her. So, a single point of view, just colored by different lenses? What about a body swap? There are so many examples of this in books and movies –either someone's mind getting inserted into a new body, or someone waking up in someone else's body, or an alien taking over someone's mind. Sometimes they can access the previous person's memories, sometimes they still have their own, sometimes not. The common thread though, is the point of view. Which is essentially the awareness of the present moment. And that's what it's all about, right: the act of being aware? The reason I'm asking is because I think there is more to our existence than just our bodies and even our memories. We are the universe experiencing itself, to quote half a dozen others. Maybe our individual point of view is a one-off, or maybe it comes back, like in a video game where we move through the story using an avatar. If that character dies, we get a new one. I don't think someone on the outside is playing me because I don't think there is an outside. I think it's all self-contained, with our points of view allowing us to experience and add to the narrative."

"So when we die, you think we forfeit our memories? That's depressing."

"Wasn't it Walt Whitman who said something like, 'We were together. I forget the rest'?"

"I don't care," he said, laughing. "I still don't want to lose my memories."

"Same here actually. I mean, who does, right? Maybe they aren't lost forever though, especially not the ties between us."

"I should hope not," Kurt said. "It sounds alienating."

"Not necessarily though, because we're still connected. Being part of something doesn't mean we have to lose ourselves to it. We can gain everything by it. And honestly, if we do come back again and again, what would we do under the weight of so many memories?"

"Build on them," Kurt cut in.

"On the knowledge maybe. But the memories of heartbreak, betrayal, and regret? Too much of those and we lose our willingness to take risks, to see what could be. Even today, I almost didn't come to see you. I wanted to. I hoped we could talk. But I was so nervous. How would you respond to me just showing up? Would we get the chance to talk? Would it be awkward? What if we had changed too much to relate to each other?

"It wasn't like that when I was a kid. Not as much anyway. Any worry I had was pushed to the side by the belief that what was about to happen was going to be *great*! Even when disappointment followed, which, of course, it sometimes did, I was still so eager to try, to believe that the best could and would happen. Most of us lose that, I think, as we get older."

"That's only natural though. It's part of growing up. Reality sets in and we start to understand our limitations."

"Yeah, but don't you miss it? That feeling that *anything* is possible? Back then, every emotion was all-consuming. Not tempered by reservation. Childhood is an impetus, powered by excitement. It offers a fresh start, unburdened by previous loss, failure, weariness. It allows us to see the world with new eyes. To feel wonder at something as simple as the color and texture of a butterfly's wing. Or to see the dark hollow of a tree and feel all shivery at the thought of what might be living inside. Such optimism, such wonder, curiosity, and imagination, is a gift. Perhaps one that comes at a cost."

"So, no heaven or hell?"

"I get that people believe a lot of different things. But regardless of what comes after, we are each creating our own heaven or hell through our actions, and we carry that with us, inside us –like Milton's Satan in *Paradise Lost*. We can't escape it any more than we can escape ourselves. What we do affects us, internally and externally –not irrevocably, but I think change requires conscious effort. Which is essentially karma, I guess."

"So why not just become a Buddhist?"

"Because I value attachment and the experience of existence, suffering and all. And maybe that's not at odds with all of Buddhism, but that's just it –there are so many different interpretations of every ideology with each group saying, 'this is the right way and that is the wrong way.' To varying degrees, of course. And to say I am *this* or *that* feels like I'm putting a box around myself. Kind of like what you were saying about labels and boundaries. There are so many things I love about Buddhism, and Christianity, and Hinduism, and many other religions and worldviews too. But it seems like each one has become its own rigid structure based on individual perspective and interpretation."

"Structure serves a purpose though," said Kurt, tilting his head a little and scratching his jaw. "Teachers and philosophers have spent their lives studying and developing the framework of each, for the benefit of others. And not without accountability. Because of them and because of these structures, people have guidance, clarification. Community too. We need that."

"You're right, we do. I don't mean to downplay the role of religious leaders or what they've passed on to us. But sometimes those same leaders, or others like them, end up creating all these hoops for people to jump through –hoops that determine whether or not someone is considered 'saved,' or devout, or moral, or whatever."

"But you're going against thousands of years of knowledge and experience."

"No, no! I'm not against them, not exactly. Those teachings and structures work for a lot of people, and that's great. My parents find a lot of comfort in their beliefs. It's just that those same structures exclude those on the 'outside,' and can lead to judgement and persecution. And I feel like they often obscure what's inside, at the heart of each. Which, in many cases, is often the same thing."

"Which is?"

"Love. And unity. I used to hate it when people would say religions are all variations of each other, as though they were all subjective and people could pick and choose the parts they liked and leave the rest. It felt like a cop-out to me. But now, I think it's rather remarkable that so many people from different times and places and backgrounds –be it Eastern or Western philosophy, American Indian spirituality, and even people meditating or eating or drinking psychedelics– so many describe the height of their enlightenment, or meditative state, or high as an experience of profound love and interconnection.

"A church I used to go to in Arizona once offered a presentation called something like, 'Jesus and Buddhism.' Something about the love they described at the heart of Buddhism felt so impersonal, especially compared to the God of Christianity, that I thought, why not just get a dog? When I was growing up, the idea of a personal god was so comforting to me. That he loved me, no matter what, made me feel so special and seen. Love that wasn't embodied in a personal god felt somehow less to me. But now, I think love is the center of everything. It's what's holding the universe together. There is chaos and suffering and atrocity. There is sickness and pain and hate. But there is love too. Not cold or distant. Not impersonal. But warm, rich, and deeply involved. It's everywhere. We feel it when we connect with someone; when we experience wonder, joy, and even heartbreak. This love heals, harmonizes, and makes us stronger. It's the salve on our wounded world. Moving toward this love may not change the world, but it can change us. It can bring us peace and hope and connection. Maybe one day, what I refer to as 'I' will merge with this love –that's the goal of Hinduism and Buddhism, right? But for now, I am happy with the experience of being alive –with all the pain and joy and heartache and sensation life brings."

"Most major religions focus on practicing love, so where's the conflict?" Kurt asked.

"They do, definitely," I said. "But they also create all these extra rituals, while arguing over whether the Bible meant this, or that. Or whether Buddha or Muhammad actually meant such and such when they said this thing or other. All these people debating over details reminds me of the blind men and the elephant. 'Oh, it's a wall!' 'No, it's a spear.' 'No, it's definitely a rope.' Each was so focused on the parts that they missed the whole. I feel like that's what happens with religion."

"And then," I blurted out as a new thought occurred to me, "when I think about it in view of the age of the universe, I feel even more baffled by our obsessions. Because the universe is how old? Do you know?"

"Thirteen billion, I think."

"And humanity has been around just a tiny fraction of that time. But we're so human-centric that we think it's all about us. I mean, even if time isn't linear, we're such a small part of this vast, incredible whole."

Kurt sat still and thoughtful, watching me. "And morality?" he asked, finally. "When we talked in Seattle, you said you felt as though you could 'do anything.' Do you still feel that way?"

"No, thank goodness," I said, smiling. Then I breathed in deeply and looked down at my hands before adding, "Derek was married. Did I ever tell you that?"

Kurt leaned back, regarded me, and shook his head.

Derek –the one who'd caused me so much pleasure and pain; the one with whom I'd explored my capacity for feeling and the depth of my weakness.

"I didn't know at first. But when I did find out, I ... I didn't leave as soon as I should have. I wish to God I had, but I didn't."

Other than a slight drawing together of his eyebrows, Kurt's manner remained unchanged.

"I knew it was wrong, of course. And I had no desire to hurt his wife or anyone. But I stayed. And the thing is, although I felt guilty, I didn't feel evil. Not like I thought I would. 'Evil' is just a label, of course. But what I mean is that when I was weak and selfish, I made excuses. I told myself, 'It's okay; I'm still me. I'll make things right.

340

Soon.' And meanwhile, I just kept doing what I wanted. I realize now that feelings are insufficient judges of whether actions are right or wrong. Our brains are masters at self-justification. At least, mine is."

I sighed and looked up at Kurt. He was leaning sideways now, one elbow on the table. With the knuckle of his forefinger, he was rubbing his chin, looking thoughtful.

"Maybe that's why the golden rule is so powerful," I said. "I might feel okay doing something, but would I want it done to me? Sometimes I think it all comes down to kindness and common decency.

"Do you remember that time I told you I felt I could do anything, and it wouldn't matter? My morality used to be so tied to God and Christianity that when I started questioning my faith, it felt as though nothing I did or didn't do would make any difference. As though, without the threat of hell or the promise of heaven, I lost all motivation for doing anything. Then later, I thought that maybe my actions should be determined by consequences –what effect would they have on those around me, and what kind of consequences would they lead to for myself? But that felt too cold and utilitarian."

"And now?" Kurt asked.

"I still think about the impact my actions will have on those around me, but I care more deeply now –about the people around me, my environment, my friends and family. I want them to be happy. To thrive. For their own sake, and for mine too. I am living in this body, on this planet, with these people, plants, and animals, and it only makes sense to me to do what I can to care for each. To nurture and respect each. Will I get the same in return? Not always. But that doesn't matter so much as living in a way that fosters growth.

"We are all going to be stronger, healthier, and more capable of doing greater things if we nurture the whole. We live in a world of our making —no matter what outside influences come at us. If I've got to sleep in this bed, I may as well make it up as nice as I can."

At the jangling of keys in the door, Kurt and I looked up to see a waitress locking the doors. I was surprised to see the room was empty, save for the three of us and the bartender, who was wiping down the counter. Through the front windows, I could see the streetlights creating halos over the cars beneath.

"I'm so sorry," I said to Kurt. "I had no idea it was so late."

He reassured me with a smile. "It's not every day I get to catch up with an old friend."

The waitress waved at Kurt, smiling warmly, before heading back toward the bar, where the bartender was waiting for her. Together they headed out through the back.

As I watched them go, I felt a growing dread at the thought of saying goodbye.

"I can't tell you how good it's been to see you," I said, beginning to gather my things while thinking how much I missed him already.

"What? That's it?" he asked.

My heart gave a little leap, and I looked up at him.

"You know I'd stay and talk with you all night," I said.

"In that case, tell me one more thing. Supposing it's as you say —why? What's the point?"

"To live —*truly* live! You know? To not just go through the motions, but to own our experiences —the good, the bad, all of it."

"Okay, then," he said, laughing.

I smiled and took a breath. "What I mean is, I believe the point is to engage life and experience existence. All of it. And connection is what allows us to do that. Connection with each other, with God, with the present moment, with the world around us. It's not always easy given how busy and distracted we —I— can be. But it's how we truly *live*. It's what gives meaning and purpose to life. And when things are at their worst, we can know we're not alone. That we're part of something. Life isn't all suffering. Or all pleasure. It's–" I broke off, feeling suddenly overwhelmed by everything I wanted to express. Life is laughing with friends and crying at funerals. It's the sun sparkling on a snowflake and the screaming in the night. It's color and symmetry and chaos and decay. It's the birth of a baby and the crushing weight of a headstone.

"Life is joy and anguish, beauty and destruction," I said finally. "Suffering isn't the end, and death isn't the final word. There's so much more. And if we can find our connection with those around us, then there's fullness and meaning too.

"I am so thankful for this life," I continued. "I'm so happy just to be alive. And really, isn't that what Voltaire's *Candide* and even *Ecclesiastes* are all about? *Siddhartha* too. Each of them –Candide, Solomon, and Siddhartha– went out and experienced pleasure and pain and triumph and meaninglessness, and they all concluded pretty much the same thing: that contentment can be found in the simple act of 'tending one's garden,' so to speak. Solomon said the best we can do is to 'be happy and do good,' and Siddhartha found joy sitting next to the river, listening to the music of life. That's what I want to do: I want to nurture my environment and those around me. I want to tend my garden and do good and be happy. I want to find connection. It's like that quote by William Blake. How does it go? Something like, 'I sought my soul, but my soul I could not see. I sought my God, but my God eluded me. I sought my brother, and I found all three.'"

I sighed and smiled, but then looked down, feeling suddenly self-conscious. "Others have reached different conclusions, of course, and this may not be where I end up. But I'm glad for the journey –to know that it's okay to ask questions and seek answers. That's what you told me, right? 'Keep going.' We all have our own journey, but no matter where we end up, we're still in this together. And because of that, because of all of it, I feel peace again. And purpose. For me it's enough to embrace life –the joys and the struggle. I want to cherish those around me. To nurture them and my environment. This makes me happy. I can honestly say I'm happy again."

"It shows," he said.

We stared at each other for a few moments. Then he leaned back and smiled broadly. "I'm glad I got to see you again, Ani."

"Me too. It's been so good!"

As we stood, I thought of all the things I still wanted to say to him. Goodbye wasn't one of them. How could I leave when I wasn't sure when or if I'd see him again?

"We'll keep in touch," he said, as he gave me a hug. His shirt was soft against my cheek. I inhaled the musky scent of him, and it was all I could do to let go.

"Thanks so much for talking with me."

"It was my pleasure. Honestly, Ani, anytime."

My eyes stung, making it difficult to look at him. I took a deep breath.

"Hey, we'll keep in touch," he said again.

We didn't though. A year later, the bar burned down. There was an article about it in the local paper. Kurt had been stoic, if nostalgic. Shortly after that he joined the military and became an intelligence officer. His ability to listen and connect soon earned him the trust of several tribal leaders in Afghanistan. Even so, in his emails home he described the abundance of improvised explosive devices and referred to his fate as an inevitability. Not long after, an IED detonated as his vehicle passed, killing him and two Marines.

Kurt impacted everyone, everywhere he went. I often wonder if he ever fully understood the difference he made to others, to me. I can still see him –his smile, the stubble along his jaw, the way he would recline, head on his palm, while listening. I can hear his laugh and the sound of his voice, the clunk of his boots and the way he would call out to someone. I hold these close. The memory of him is precious.

In the years since then, my path has been a winding one. I met my husband in a library. Soon after we married, we welcomed our first daughter. Looking into her eyes as she lay against my chest, so new to the world, I felt such overwhelming love and terror, I thought my heart would burst. Through her, I learned that love is stronger than the terror of losing those I hold so dear. Because of her, I pray more, hope more, laugh more. She taught me how to enjoy stillness; how to cultivate peace.

When she was five and nightmares came and shook her awake, I lay beside her in the forgotten hours of the morning, soothing away her tears, rubbing her back, and whispering into her hair that my love is always with her. Always. The love within us may be uniquely housed, uniquely marked, but the source is the same. As though we were once a single star that exploded outward, becoming the universe so that we might gain understanding through exploration, conflict, and experience. Together we are living out every story ever written. We are you and me, all who were, and all who will be. Abiding in separate bodies, we are nevertheless connected, and the more we reach out and embrace life in all its multifarious manifestations, the greater our understanding. The greater our love.

I have hoped. I have doubted. I have prayed. And I am here still: still learning, still growing, still figuring it out. I am a moment in time, thrumming with thoughts, feelings, and memories. This body I inhabit is finite and flawed, but also dear to me with its bright red hair; strong, not-so-pretty hands; and the deepening lines left by the passage of time. I am grateful for both the pleasure and the pain, the soaring and the sinking. Grateful also for the ability to reach out and touch other living beings. Pushing ever outward, we are still connected. No matter our faith, no matter our face, we are the Creosote Bush.

# Acknowledgements

I would like to thank Embry, Andrew, and Amy for reading the long and winding first draft of this story so long ago. Their feedback both encouraged me and helped me tighten the focus on what I wanted to convey. Professor Leroy Johnson was there for me when I desperately needed a guiding light. His wisdom and willingness to listen was a beacon that led me through a dark time. Mike was a rock and a refuge to me when I felt most weak. He remains one of the most brilliant and beautiful people I ever met. I am also immensely grateful to Carla and everyone at WKED for their interest, stimulation, laughter, and comradery.

A special hug and thanks to Rowena and Margarita, whose friendship and invaluable advice buoyed me and led to many constructive changes. Thank you, Rowena, for celebrating the weird and understanding the spiral. Thank you for listening without judgement and for sharing without reservation. Margarita, your ability to convey your sharp insight and clear perspective with such compassion is a gift.

Lisa, dear friend, you understand the journey, along with everything that entails. I love and admire you and am so grateful for all our discussions. Amanda, thank you for embodying the beauty of belief.

Eric, Ryan, and Sean, thank you for every chess game and animated debate (although I could have done without the forced bellyflops in the pool). As sounding board and devil's advocate, you challenged and stretched me. I could always count on your direct and honest opinions and your varied perspectives. Ryan, thank you for pushing me to go farther, try harder, dig deeper. Sean, thank you for your unwavering confidence in everything you believe in.

Carlos, my heart, thank you. You never shied away from my questions, discussions, or my obsessions. Sharing the journey with you is one of the greatest joys of my life. Without you, this book would not have been possible.

# About the Author

C A Legorreta was born in Colorado. She spent her nomadic childhood exploring the natural world and the many worlds found within books. Her three brothers taught her how to be tough and that praying for something (namely, a sister) doesn't always mean you'll get what you ask for. After taking ten years to earn a BA in History (during which time she travelled and tutored and found her way in and out of her head), she spent the next decade promoting books and access to information in the King County Library System in Washington State. She currently resides in South Carolina, where she balances writing with the mysteries and mayhem of motherhood.

Made in the USA
Middletown, DE
20 March 2025

72996684R00197